DreamEden

Other books by Linda Ty-Casper

The Transparent Sun, 1963

The Peninsulars, 1964

The Secret Runner, 1974

The Three-Cornered Sun, 1979

Dread Empire, 1980

Hazards of Distance, 1981

Fortess in the Plaza, 1985

Awaiting Trespass, 1985

Wings of Stone, 1986

Ten Thousand Seeds, 1987

A Small Party in a Garden, 1988

Common Continent, 1991

Kulasyon: Uninterrupted Vigils, 1995

Dream Eden

LINDA TY-CASPER

UNIVERSITY OF WASHINGTON PRESS
Seattle and London

Printed in the United States of America

Library of Congress Cataloging-in-Publication Data
ISBN 0–295–97586–5

The text paper used in this publication meets the minimum requirements of American National Standard for Information Sciences—Permanence of Paper for Printed Library Materials, ANSI Z39–48–1984. ∞

Cover painting: "Jack en Poy" (Sticks and Stones) by Lazaro (Aro) Soriano, 1987, 156 x 156 cm., oil on canvas, courtesy of Ateneo Art Gallery, Ateneo de Manila University

For Salvador and Freida Ramiro

and their sons

Romuel, Raniel, Renald

Contents

Vitaliano Family

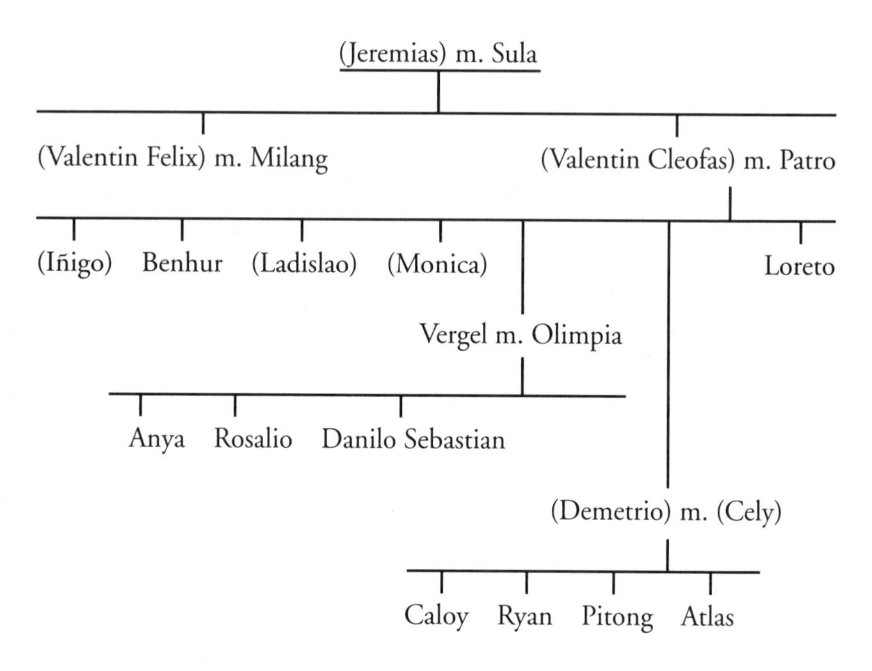

Moscoso Family

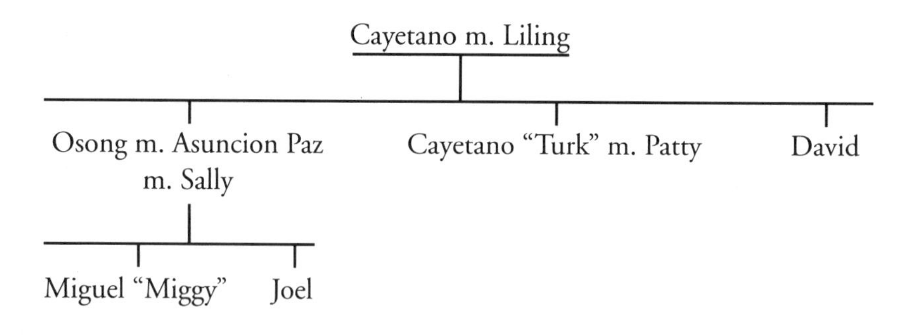

( ) = deceased

Prologue

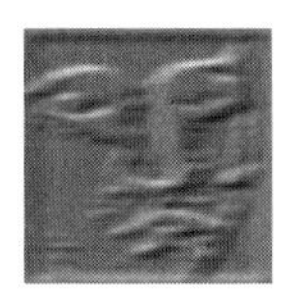

It just happens that Gulod

—designated Barangay No. 78 under Ferdinand E. Marcos—has spread like a field sown by a blind hand. Huts angle off on their own, facing all points of the compass. Yards lie uneven, pushed back into the earth by trees trying to escape the summer's heat, and lifted above the floods by roots choked with rain.

Once, the barrio streets had names that only long-time residents now recall. These have become trails overrun by grass and intersected by basketball courts. Not formally laid-out spaces allowing full scramble but simply measured ground every few houses, the courts enable children to aim at hoops nailed to trees or posts, and to dream—when their future comes—of playing for Great Taste Coffee, the team that won the first conference of 1986, and that might just win the Philippine Basketball Association's grand slam award for the year.

Gulod's trails are torn, the *caminos herraduras* of countrysides. Full of turns as tight as ropes because they occupy only what space is left between kitchens and bedrooms—as if the barrio were a single roominghouse—the trails require those passing through to hum or talk aloud, or else to call out: *Makikiraan po,* an old form of courtesy which alerts households to the possibility of being overheard. Feuds have broken out in Gulod from failure to observe this practice.

When the mailman is not laid off or sick, he comes with news—letters recounting crippling illness and death, every manner of indebtedness and misfortune; or with envelopes containing salary remittances from Saudi, Hong Kong, London, Hamburg, Rome—wherever in the world the Filipino has exiled himself from family and profession to earn what will feed his family at home.

He comes trailed by small children who bring the neighbors' news back to their own houses. He also carries messages from one household to another—there are no telephones in Gulod—delivering these out of *pakikisama* and to deserve the drinks and bits of food he is offered when he comes upon their infrequent celebrations.

Since house numbers have long ago been defaced, it is up to the mailman, Estong Calero, to know where people live, closer to the river as their fortunes decline. Their houses form a map in his mind. Every makeshift addition, every tree branching out of line, forces him to make detours that shift the coordinates.

With time, Estong's movements have taken on the aspect of light prowling, searching for Paradise where—many in Gulod think—it cannot much please God, or man, to look.

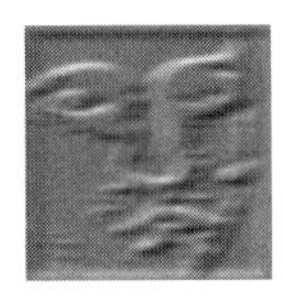

As if he were carrying fire,
something exhaustible and dying, Estong Calero hurries down to bring the mail to Gulod. Though it is in Metro Manila, he thinks of it as a coastal barrio because all sorts of people seem to have been washed ashore here. Their continual coming gives him new names to track down: names whose owners disappear or move out as soon as he remembers their location.

Waiting to recover from sickness, or hiding from those intent on taking revenge upon them, the new ones stay with relatives and friends no better situated in life, who have themselves accrued all manner of debts through gambling and loans (the kind written on water), through crimes against property and against person, crimes against honor—women wronged, friends betrayed or cheated, confidences broken out of malice or for trifles.

These misfortunes and transgressions, Estong imagines, give those who have drifted into Gulod the look of failure and defeat. It is as if they are the dead of other places. Meeting them on the trail, Estong occasionally hears about their lives, told each time in the same words, as if they are trying to come to an understanding of what has happened to them. The stories bring tears to their eyes, and his.

A few people of consequence, as they are called, remain in Gulod, occupying vacation houses they built before the war in 1941. Some glass panes are still upright in their frames, some *narra* doors are still on original hinges above the floodlines; but squatters encroach upon them. Suddenly at daybreak, lean-tos crowd their fences. Most simply pull up the posts to bring the fences closer to their houses rather than risk trouble for evicting the squatters, whose rooms multiply like oysters building on one another's shells. The older residents tell Estong of their dream to be able to live somewhere else, somewhere far away and as peaceful as Gulod once was in their memories.

Monday, after the snap elections of Friday, the dream is burnished by the possibility of Cory and Doy winning against Marcos and Tolentino. People intercept Estong, wishing to exchange hopes, and it is with much difficulty that he breaks away, leaning forward to his left to offset the weight on his right shoulder. Through the years he no longer stands erect even without the load. He makes love to his wife only by setting his body sideways off hers. Even then, he slides down on his sweat, she giggles, and nothing happens. Nothing has been happening for some time. Unable to sleep afterward, he turns and she gets up to iron, using a candle to save on electricity.

Instead of counting the days to inaugurating a new president, Estong counts the years to his retirement, knowing he might not make it. Still, he manages to be grateful. Though the February sun, at ten, is as hot as midday; in March and up until June it is already steaming by eight. Estong further consoles himself that, since he works during the day, he is not likely to run into drunks or drug addicts on the trails. Under martial law only the cronies and their bodyguards have firearms. The rest have to kill one another with ice picks, and he would prefer dying in his sleep, unaware.

"No letter," Estong shakes his head at Marcelo Andres, who stands outside his wife's store. Vilma's Store: her name is painted white on the red background of the Coca-Cola sign above the window. Peppercorns or garlic cloves, so few you could count them at a glance, hang in plastic packets against the wooden bars in front of the store, hiding Vilma, who is stacking cookies into large plastic jars.

Marcelo raises the picture of the Challenger in the *Bulletin* and asks, "Can you think of a worse way to die, Estong? It burned and then exploded. It must have felt like strangling."

Eager to get going with his mailbag, Estong does not try to imagine the explosion. "All kinds of people in the world, all kinds of ways to die, Elo." He smiles to himself because Marcelo looks silly standing beside the male papaya plant with stunted fruit no bigger than green worms.

Marcelo changes strategy. "I voted for Cory and Doy, though I accepted fifty pesos from the KBL to vote Marcos-Tolentino. But when Cory asks me to boycott San Miguel, how can I? I don't drink beer. It gives me hives. Did I tell you . . ?"

Estong moves on before Marcelo can talk about the railroad. Thursday, Marcelo already explained why he will sign a petition to Cory to oust the general manager if she is inaugurated president. Marcelo was among the 720 dismissed the past year and replaced with casuals, employees with no benefits accruing. The Merit System Board and Civil Service Commission ordered them reinstated in December, but to date no assignments have been given to them, and no salaries.

Everyone in Gulod has heard about rolling stock being sold as junk through relatives of relatives of officials. Marcelo himself has brought home barbed wire for a fence, saying that if he did not take it, someone else would have a wire fence. Official requisitions are unloaded at the gates of officials, according to Marcelo, who knows only two, possibly three, officials who have retired with just their pension and the same house they had before all the looting started.

That is no exaggeration, Estong knows, because when he went on the Express to Bicol, to bury his wife's sister, they sat on boards from which the upholstery had been ripped. No bars protected the windows. A young girl who had worked a year in Manila was hit by a stone thrown by troublemakers just before Lucena. Thinking she was dying, the girl sobbed into the bundle of clothes and food she had bought from her earnings as a waitress. The wound bled through the wad of tissue the girl was bringing home as a souvenir in its pretty floral box.

Such is life. Estong refuses to allow himself to hurt for another, because his own turn will come. Towards the end of an already long life—he's pushing fifty—Estong has learned that pain, to the point of wetting one's pants, is the one certain sign one's still alive. It's a further sign that God is testing a person to see if he's still a man or has turned into a dog, like many in the government, whose hunger is bottomless. Once they taste power, politicians become rabid, just like dogs.

With a child on his arm, Siso Feleo meets Estong on the trail. "I wish I could watch the counting of ballots," he says. "We might get a president who wears a skirt. What do you think?"

Siso has been saying that ever since Marcos's effigy was burned along with Reagan's in December. "It might look like that," Estong agrees. "But the man in Malacañang is full of surprises. He has that *anting-anting* buried in his back. How can he lose, with that amulet?"

"Duvalier fled Haiti on a U.S. military jet Friday, while we were voting." Siso lets the child down, holding it by the hand. "Here comes Pidiong. Let's see what he says." Siso faces the policeman. "Pidiong. You're just coming home while others are going to work."

"I was at my mother's in Baclaran. Did you hear that the computer programmers at the government's Quick Count Center walked out with the diskettes and hid in the church there? We watched them enter, followed by international observers and reporters. Then people came to protect them, because the diskettes prove Marcos cheated in the elections and is cheating in the counting. The programmers are wives of the military, so it must be true."

"Yes, I heard on Radio Veritas," Estong says. "The morning newspapers also reported the American senators are praising Filipinos for creating a new structure for democracy."

Siso Feleo digs into his pocket for change to buy Juicy Fruit for his child, but all he brings out is a folded copy of the psalm distributed during the election campaign. The peddler has already handed a stick of gum to the child, who clutches it. "Let's go home," Siso says. "Nani has coins in the house."

Estong Calero walks ahead, letting Pidiong pay for the gum if he wants to. With the bribes the policeman gets, he can support another wife in Baclaran. Everyone in Gulod knows it's a woman, not his mother, he visits there. Maybe Cory will stop all the foolishness. He himself has never been tempted. All women have two of one and one of the other . . . why go looking for headaches?

Like men burning trees down into charcoal, the two fall silent, staring at the ground between their feet while Estong goes hurrying past the window of Eliadora Guzman; the long story about whose letter worried Estong all last night. He almost walks into a shrub covered with drying clothes unfit to wear outside Gulod. Across from Eliadora is the room rented by the Silverios, who are both Metro Aides. On his way to Gulod, Estong had passed Metro Manila streetsweepers who were scraping off all the campaign posters on the sides of buildings and the posts of the Light Rail Transportation stations.

The Silverios never get mail. But Eliadora is remembered on her birthday by a sister in the States who sends a card with money inside. Just five dollars, according to his co-worker Perico, who also opens packages, picking out what he wants without bothering to reseal them carefully. *Kalag sa viaje . . .* he tells those who complain that twine slips off packages during transport. Above the ceiling of the post office are boxes emptied of their contents, and envelopes opened too carelessly to be resealed. Rats running through the boxes make them rattle like dry leaves. Each time a plan to renovate the post office is announced, Perico and those new employees, who need to hold letters to the light to see if there are enclosures, turn as white as turnips.

Narcisa Sotero, wife of the labor leader, stands up from leaning over to sweep her yard of the leaves of *ylang-ylang,* which bears yellow-green flowers with long tapered petals. Through the front window Estong sees the red and white Bayan flag carried to demonstrations by Bien Sotero who, unlike many leaders, does not declare strikes in order to be bribed into calling them off.

"None today." Estong looks into his bag before shaking his head. "Maybe tomorrow. Like a winning Sweepstake ticket, it will come one day."

"Bad luck and corruption is all that comes. And more of it everyday, as Bien says." Narcisa starts pushing her broom made from ribs of coconut fronds. "Like garbage collecting on Abad Santos. That's why Bien says 'Boycott the U.S.-backed Marcos dictatorship.' Boycott elections. Boycott the Cardinal who should not take sides. Even NAMFREL volunteers are openly for Cory when they are supposed to be nonpartisan." She does not tell Estong that she goes to Quiapo on Fridays, not for Mass but to pray to the Sacred Heart. Since Cardinal Sin backed Cory from the pulpit, she has not heard Mass.

The words "corruption" and "garbage" start Estong's mind going about stench that not even perfume by the drumful can overpower. Out of *delicadeza,* he does not tell Narcisa what he's thinking—something about women, that they can become virgins again and again; the way, after a night with the prostitutes, a man can become faithful once more. This has to do with his opening a letter once, when he needed cash right away because his mother had been rushed to North General, bleeding. Clots as large as fists. There was no money for the deposit required for admission. The letter he opened contained a five-dollar bill.

Estong recalls the signs on the blackboards when he was a schoolboy: *Honesty is the best policy;* he recalls his mother teaching him that if he died with a mortal sin, he would go to hell straightaway and burn. So he has always been intrigued by the gravity of crimes. Is murder less than corruption in the scale? If it's true that Marcos and Imelda bought buildings in New York from money stolen from the government, they would need a hotter hell than Perico. And where does rape come in? Or the *sexploitation* of children, as columnists call it, by tourists, some posing as ministers?

Like a caged rat trying to gnaw its way out of a trap, Estong's heart starts racing wildly. It usually happens only after he has passed the house of Dante Filemon up ahead. Estong walks slowly past. None of the children are outside. They are deaf, almost blind, from being dropped off boats to drive fish into nets. Without safety gear. Just homemade spectacles contrived with rubber bands and pieces of glass. It is the abrupt change in water pressure that causes eardrums to split, Estong read in the magazine he borrowed from a neighbor. Children are hired to maximize the boat's space. Even if they understand the dangers, what choice do they have? Some die instantly when air bubbles form and explode in their veins; but there are always new children willing to dive for the day's meals; always children being born who will be made to come up too quickly, so their blood runs *amok.*

Women coming back from the market are carrying plastic bags with shrimps no bigger than particles of sand. How can it be otherwise? His wife says that a thin slice of pork costs five pesos. *Galunggong,* the fish no one bothered with before, is fifteen a kilo. Many believe Cory will be able to turn prices around. He does not know. He did not vote because he could not find his name in the voter registration list, which had been scrambled. Out of habit he was going to vote for Marcos anyway.

Estong passes another fence on which hang rags that remind him of the Filemon children with their senses warped, their skin wrinkled. In Gulod, children suddenly appear, taking shelter near the river. Neighbors chase them—*Alis! Alis!*—as if they are puppies with fleas. He has seen dead children waked in rags inside a paper box. Children no bigger than infants. One time he felt so bad he brought wrapping paper to decorate the box, and a dress, old but mended. In the city itself he has seen the dead being waked alongside fences.

A group of young girls stir the air with their giggling. Estong feels young, thinking they smile at him, feels himself leap between his legs. So he places his free hand there to restrain himself. Even that, now, can overburden his heart.

Up ahead a dog is lifting its leg over everything higher than a stone. Nothing spills from it. He waits till the animal gains distance because fur has come off in clumps from its side. Dogeaters will not bother with this one. He himself has not tasted roasted dog, *azucena,* but some swear by its flavor. The dog disappears into a yard with a homemade sign: *Garage Sale—See Imelda at the Palace.*

Another dog comes running past him, its tail between its legs. He does not trust dogs. Some are just like people, attacking from behind. Some lift meat from the table as lightly as some people lift the print off ballots, off certificates of elections, off tally sheets. Just like politicians with their hocus pocus.

Without missing a step Estong slips a government insurance letter under a door, then goes on codifying crimes to keep his mind off food. Crime he equates with sin, his theology nurtured by holy cards he collected as a child. At least, Estong thinks, the devil does not claim to be good. He doesn't pose kneeling in prayer. Estong's mind starts circling when he's hungry. Sin is a worm writhing inside bodies, intestinal parasites massing in rotting flesh, like the stinking glob that came out of his sister's arm where cancer had eaten its way into her bone. Flesh balled like old fabric. Threadbare. *Durogdurog.*

Curtains stiff with dust hang motionless at windows barred with slats of wood to keep a hand from slipping through. Between the curtains he sees Cory calendars beside crucifixes, Marcos/Tolentino posters adorning small altars. The crosses are sometimes burned into wood, embedded like claws.

Small children overtake him on the trail. Two he recognizes to be Siso Feleo's. Wearing only T-shirts, barefoot, they chase a boy with comic books distributed during the election campaign, though none of them looks old enough to read. As they run, they pull out everything their hands happen to catch. They run, stomachs large and stiff. As long as their children's backs are covered, mothers believe them to be protected from sickness, as if it is only bad air that causes illness. But dying is not too bad really, Estong muses. It means the end of hardships, of poverty.

"Estong! Come a moment!" Bastian Canonigo seems to have been waiting for him. Bastian used to drive for the governor of a bank, but he lost his license during the investigation of an accident in which he was not even involved. Buried in the police files and requiring a bribe to retrieve.

By the time Bastian had P500 saved, the cost of fake licenses skyrocketed. P700! Bitter because the bank governor did not intercede on his behalf, Bastian resigned. He had even worked for free in the governor's garden, accompanying the wife to plant-nurseries in Los Baños, digging each specimen into the ground. Now he earns a few pesos, testifying to accidents he has not witnessed and raising game cocks for a rich Chinese from Binondo.

Used to having Bastian share only his misery, Estong asks, "What's this?" when Bastian hands him a steaming cup.

"Taste it and tell me."

"Coffee?" Estong slides the mailbag off his shoulder, lays it beside a tangle of vines on the ground. It's not gingerroot tea, good to clarify singers' voices but not prescribed for ulcers. "What is it good for? It's delicious."

"Sit." Bastian points to a bench made from pieces of wood that do not match in thickness or in color. "Sit for a while. Tell me what's new out there. I hear the American senators are leaving already, before the ballots are counted. And the radio reports a caucus in the Palace. Marcos must be planning to declare martial law if he does not get proclaimed by the Batasan today or tomorrow. What do you think?"

"I don't know." Estong takes another sip. His answer is good; about the cup and about politics, which is just a form of vaudeville as far as he is concerned: just singing and dancing. Same steps, different dancers. Same music, different party.

"Then tell me what you do not know, Estong. It might be different from what I do not know." Bastian watches the cup in Estong's hand.

"I heard Malacañang is burning papers."

"So you like it."

Estong looks from Bastian to the cup. "I do. It's good. Tastes Stateside. Must be expensive coffee."

"So you say it's coffee?" Laughter breaks apart Bastian's mouth. He is laughing so hard he has to get up, turn his chair around before sitting down again.

"Another joke?" Meding Canonigo looks out from the window. "Are you dreaming again, Bastian?"

"Dreaming? Perhaps. That's the best part of life. Dreams come from God, my grandfather said. Like smiles and good luck and happiness. The rest come from the devil." Bastian runs both hands up and down his thighs, does not look up at the window.

Estong himself remains silent, not wishing to tangle with Meding, who is a medium. He has heard her speaking in a childish voice when, she says, the Infant Jesus is speaking through her, and in a low voice when it is the Nazareno. She made Bastian build her a room in the yard where she keeps her images of the Infant Jesus, some of which, she claims, dance. People go to pray there, leaving donations along with their petitions. Meding crushes gingerroot to squeeze into the eyes of sinners. Mail comes to her from as far away as California.

As soon as his wife moves away from the window, Bastian points to the vines behind Estong. "Look. See the pods?" He lifts a length of vine. "I was about to pull them out when I saw the pods. 'Might as well see what the wind has blown here, beside squatters,' I told Meding, who can't grow anything with roots. Those are her dead plants in the rusty cans over which my vines grow. I had nothing to do one day, so I started popping the pods. Out came large red seeds. This big. I didn't want to waste the growing the vines had done, so I roasted a handful of the seeds and then pounded them in the *almires* Meding's mother used for her betel nuts. You remember the old woman who used to live with us before? And then she died? Well, I tasted the powder. A little bitter, but a familiar taste. I steeped a little in water. I could not believe it, Estong. I called Meding. She was afraid it was poisonous. 'Then drink, so we can die together,' I told her. I've been drinking it three days now. Since Friday. I was so excited I almost forgot to vote."

"You're lucky." Estong looks away to the fighting cocks tied to T-posts with enough rope to allow them to strut but not to peck at each other. His wife wants hens, to lay eggs. "Cocks don't eat much," Estong says, "and they keep away burglars. I always wanted cocks."

They sip in silence for some time.

"You're lucky," Estong repeats.

"Yes. Whoever gets elected president, I have my own coffee."

"Grow it on a trellis, Bastian."

"A trellis? Then people will notice and steal my coffee." Bastian lifts another end of the vine. Curved like new moons, the pods separate from the leaves, each unripe seed bulging like the eggs forming inside the bellies of house lizards.

Imagining himself seated under his own vines, with bumblebees fertilizing the flowers, Estong asks, "You have any seeds left?"

"The next time, Estong, I'll save you some, but don't tell anyone. Maybe I can sell the beans. Maybe you'll retire and be my sales agent. What do you think I should call my coffee?"

"Canonigo. Cafe Canonigo. It has appeal. Like Antonio Pueo Chocolate." Estong drains his cup. "You remember a street in Intramuros, where Spaniards used to live, called Canonigo? And one called Hormiga in Plaza Cervantes. The shortest and tightest street in Manila."

"Named after ants!" Bastian's brain is heating up with the prospect of going into business. "Just maybe, Estong, with the price of land going down because everyone is trying to emigrate, when profits come in, maybe I should invest in a lot somewhere else. Not to move out of Gulod. I'm not saying I will become too good for this place. But just instead of putting the money in the bank and then having the government close it."

"I read that a round trip to the States is down to P27,494. You can travel, Bastian. But you should have saved seeds from the first harvest, as farmers do."

"Pass by on your way back and let's talk some more about my coffee."

Estong goes quickly past *Aling* Maxima's store to avoid arguing with the men about the rumors and news of the day. Out-of-work men used to stay indoors, away from the windows. Now they mother their children out in the trails, gathering at the stores or at the hut where the *zona* meet before going out to patrol at night.

"Did you win in the Sweepstakes, Estong?" *Aling* Maxima mocks him. "Why don't you stop as usual?"

"I'm late already. On the way back." Wild thoughts of profit from Bastian's coffee are distracting Estong also from his habit of passing by the Vitalianos around noontime, so *Aling* Patro can ask him to sit with them. The food is always good, though it might only be fishheads from supper steamed in squash flowers; specially when tomatoes are not counted out like gold in the market. One of *Aling* Patro's sons, Benhur, is a lawyer; another, a doctor. The youngest son died during the time the military were dying so fast in Mindanao that the funeral chapels could not wake civilians. There was a charge that the soldiers of his platoon were shooting civilians and claiming they were NPAs. His name was never cleared, though investigations uncovered that some killings by the NPAs had been attributed to the military. The only daughter, with her long hair, looks like a movie star. Even the name stuns: Loreto.

A *ratiles* with children swinging from its low branches catches Estong's attention. Refracting the sunlight, the leaves appear to be yellow confetti dropping from the buildings in Ayala during the opposition rallies. "Go home," he shouts at the children. "If you fall, you'll break your necks. And those berries are good only for birds and appendicitis."

In the children's hurry to climb down, the hats distributed during the election campaigns are knocked off their heads as they scamper away with handfuls of berries containing seeds so small, ten thousand cannot fill a spoon. It is growing difficult to differentiate the children in Gulod. When mothers ask if he has seen their children, Estong can no longer say. It's easier to identify the goats by their forelocks and fur.

Hernan Sipalay is waiting to tell Estong about another sleepless night. "Since election Friday, I have not slept. So hot. No air. I can't taste the food and the doctor at the clinic prescribes medicine as if there is money to buy that, and food as well." He is living with a brother and sister-in-law while recovering from TB. As he sits by the door a dog licks his foot. "Better than antibiotics," he says. "But since it will make no doctor or pharmacist rich, no one prescribes a dog's saliva, Estong."

"That's the way life is," Estong answers, eager to go off and think about Bastian Canonigo's coffee, which has filled his mind with thoughts of buying real leather shoes, not just leatherlike, for his wake. He already has white socks saved in the pockets of white *maong* pants wrapped in plastic in the bottom of his part of the *aparador.* His wife will know what they're for one day when she finds them while looking for clothes in which to wake him. But if he retires to become Bastian's partner, he will not have to worry about his wake. His wife could then afford to buy him new clothes. Canonigo Calero Coffee sounds better than just Canonigo Coffee.

After his list of infirmities, Hernan Sipalay starts talking about Paradise. "The problem is how to find it, Estong. The world, I believe, was once a garden. All of it was Paradise. We might be on top of it now, but how do we find out? Will our leaders find it for us, and will they only keep us from getting our share of it?"

"Just be careful. You might meet the devil who might himself be looking for Paradise, Hernan." Estong hands over the letter without curiosity. Will Bastian agree to Canonigo Calero?

"The devil will take it to a Swiss bank immediately." Hernan studies the handwriting on the envelope, grinning. "That's my name all right. Gulod. How many Gulods do you think there are in the country?"

"As many as there are hilltops," Estong says as he walks on. Even if he and Bastian make money from the coffee, he has decided not to emigrate. Suppose he dies abroad? If he is not to be buried among strangers, he will have to be shipped back. That means the cargo section of an airplane, where he will be tossing about among the mail and fruits. And what happens to his pension?

Lost in his thoughts, Estong misses delivering the letter in his hand. He is confused as to how this happened. Without house numbers or streets he has to keep track of the residents through his peculiar system of association which, as if drawn on water, constantly changes. People arrive and move out, add and take down rooms. Trees grow into his paths. Some residents even block passageways, claiming ownership to sections of the trails. It is like tracking the flight of kites that must constantly be jerked back into air currents. The map in his mind keeps erasing itself as he heads for the Vitalianos.

Just like a mind circling, the children come upon Estong again. On seeing him, they begin pushing each other, crying: "He's coming! He's coming!"

From a distance, as if they are cross-eyed children who neither see nor think straight, Estong scolds them. *"Walang gawang magaling!"* Pulling out his handkerchief, he covers his nostrils from the dust rising like vapors on the trail where the children drag branches full of leaves, lifting their feet above the hot ground. Off the tangle of branches and roots, leaves are dropping on the road. Drying pods stick out of the still-reaching ends of tendrils.

Estong looks quickly up into the *macopa* tree bearing red bell-shaped fruits without taste. Full-crowned, it throbs in the sun like calves' brains inside pails at the slaughterhouse beside the river where, years ago when Gulod was just a slope of lonely trees under which General Aguinaldo might have stopped to rest in his retreat, American volunteers once crossed and recrossed, beheading the trees with gunfire.

Without another glance at the children Estong turns into a side trail leading away from the Vitalianos, afraid to find out that the long branches the children had pulled out of the earth are, were, Bastian Canonigo's vines.

Part One

Chased by his own
uncomfortable thoughts, Benhur Vitaliano runs up the slope leading away from Gulod. Louder than a peddler's, his mother's voice overtakes him. "Sally will see you and know her message got to you before you left. Why not stop and see what she wants?"

Annoyed by Patro Vitaliano's fear of offending the neighbors, Benhur brushes past vendors of *taho* on their way down to Gulod with metal baskets balanced across their shoulders on bamboo poles. If he can have his way, no one at their house will buy the soybean pudding, because plaster of paris is mixed with it to make it coagulate. Patro, however, insists that it makes up for the meat that appears only rarely at their table. She even adds, "I've eaten it all my life and I'm almost seventy."

Well, he's almost forty-six, Benhur thinks. Older than the Beatles and their psychedelic shock, he owns nothing that requires documentary stamps and civil registration. Besides, he'll probably die well before old age.

Following this thought to its foregone conclusion, Benhur steps in the way of nuns coming down to Gulod to lead prayers for an honest count of the ballots. Threats of fines and imprisonment only seem to energize the religious, who have been going to the chapel across from the Vitalianos, calling on the residents to pray until all the ballots are counted: "The international observers are leaving. It's up to us now to watch and to pray so Cory will be declared winner."

Benhur begrudges the dogmatic enthusiasm of those claiming to restore democracy but failing to honor the separation between church and state. No Marcos apologist, he still insists on the fine though not invisible line between declaring what is wrong or right from the pulpit, and declaring for a candidate. Cardinal Sin's chanting of Cory's name while wearing his apostolic robes cuts through that line.

Declining the nuns' request, Benhur wonders how his mother will handle it. After his father died, Patro yielded finally to her mother-in-law Sula's solicitation to convert to Iglesia ni Cristo. His *Lola* Sula explains her own conversion: Catholics pray over and over as if their God is deaf. Benhur wonders if the litanies and beads that are going to be recited in the chapel will tempt his mother back into praying on her knees. Patro has not given up the crucifix with the gold corpus encrusted with pearls which belonged to her mother's mother, who was from Paracale, the source of the gold. He does not recall witnessing her being baptized into her new faith, immersed bodily into it.

While talking with his brother Vergel, who came home before elections bringing his new family, he occasionally saw his mother look up as though hearing something besides words passing back and forth among those praying in the chapel, as though bells were bringing down angels from heaven, bringing back Ladislao, Iñigo, Demetrio, and Monica, their father Valentin; all their dead on whose gravestones, in extreme moments of sadness, he feels like writing his own name.

Did she, when she renounced her faith, ever feel blessings were taken from her?

Patro had such big dreams for all of them. Calluses have formed on her knees from years of praying for him and Vergel so they could keep their scholarships throughout college; for Demetrio when he enlisted against her wishes; for Loreto so she will find a good husband; for her grandchildren through Demetrio's wife, Cely, who died five years before, so they will amount to something and they can move out of Gulod.

He wonders if she prays for herself. Somehow, it comforts him to think of her pushing imaginary beads between her fingers, striking bargains secretly with the saints. When all are asleep, does she walk over to the chapel to approach the altar on her knees?

"Such a hurry, Benhur! Where's the fire?" Siso Feleo's lighthearted banter comes from their having gone to the same school up to the secondary level, when Siso dropped out to apprentice as electrician. He wires the houses in Gulod, mostly *gratis et amore.* Benhur helped him with documents to get a work permit for Saudi Arabia. Unfortunately, the labor recruiter ran off with the deposit for airfare for which Siso had sold his treasured World War II bicycle on which his father rode to work as train dispatcher in Tutuban.

Several of Siso's children stand around, eating hard pieces of bread. Siso takes care of the children while his wife, Nani, buys small items in Divisoria for resale in Gulod.

"The vote count starts today at the Batasan." Benhur stops to explain, so Siso will not think he's avoiding old friends. He has not intended to watch at the Assembly but does not wish to explain he is merely heading for his one-room office in Ermita, where he also sleeps to save on apartment rent. He waits there for classmates to phone in another of the odd jobs from which he makes his living: *Quick, Benhur, how do I move gold bullion?* Something of that nature. He is no longer particular, though he's still adamant about not enriching corporations or interest groups at the expense of the country; about not exploiting friends or becoming part of a chain of influence peddling. No outright graft, no bare-faced corruption—yet.

"We already know who'll be proclaimed, so I might as well stay with the children," Siso says, as if he has a choice. He tells the children to kiss Benhur's hand, wipes the chin of the youngest with the edge of his hand. "*Men, hijo.* He's an uncle. One of these days he'll be president."

To avoid having his hand kissed, Benhur used to slip peso bills into the children's hands; but he no longer can. Demetrio's children, his mother, his sister Loreto, his *Lola* Sula, all live off his writing: briefs for classmates, position papers to be read at conferences or submitted for promotions or to enhance a reputation for scholarship. He has to answer for the daily needs of twelve, including an aunt-in-law who sleeps all day to rest from playing mahjong all night. There are, besides, school expenses for the children: tuition, jeepney fare, clothes and uniforms, countless projects and contributions. There are the cups of coffee to sweeten with sugar, to color with milk.

Before Siso can begin reciting details of life important only to himself or disclosing ambitions he still harbors, although his children look as if they have already lost their father, Benhur proceeds on his way, for old times' sake leaving a folded twenty-peso bill with the small child in Siso's arms. "It's for ice cream." To deny his need and assert his independence, before finally placing the bill deep in his shirt pocket, Siso Feleo protests Benhur's generosity and, taking the money from the child's hand, hurries after Benhur half-heartedly. "He's always like that," he tells the neighbor who is shaking the beddings from the window and who calls after Benhur: "Time for freedom again, Attorney. We Filipinos are brave again, and Rizal will be smiling in the plazas. Coming will be the end of graft and corruption and greed. Then good times. Malacañang is up for rent, I hear."

Hopefulness and humor. They release indignation and, allowing people to survive day-by-day, enable dictators to hang on. On the trail, people Benhur does not recognize discuss the news with the confidence of news commentators. If only they would turn their energies into earning their living—planting vegetables if they cannot get employment—there would not be so much of the malnutrition his brother Vergel noticed in Gulod. Malnutrition aborts minds, Vergel said. The holocaust of poverty and illness had convinced Vergel to practice in the barrio some 270 kilometers away.

Another of Sally Moscoso's maids is coming down with a message for him. "Attorney . . ."

"I already sent the *barangay* captain over," Benhur snaps. So Sally will not wonder why he does not notarize the document himself, he has sent the official instead of the affidavit. Benhur hopes the man will declare not only that, to his knowledge, no acts of fraud or intimidation took place in Gulod but that he turned down a bribe to look the other way when "flying voters" with smudged fingers—indicating they had voted elsewhere—came by busloads, imprinting their votes on carbon to show they had voted KBL, Marcos's party.

Marcos, of course, is not the only culprit. Benhur considers as public enemies all those candidates who use the country to fight for their own political lives; who put themselves forward, artfully packaged through media hype, as the sole hope of the people; who treat government employ as a nine-to-five job, not worth their loyalty or time. And those like himself ...

The maid's slippers scrape the trail, littering Benhur's mind with harsh sounds. Benhur walks around her, furious that he must zigzag like someone dodging bullets and will still only run headlong into Sally. It's not even the affidavit she wants—it's him. She might already have sent Marcos her quota of fake affidavits to wave before Reagan's emissaries in order to prove the snap election was clean. Besides, Sally will not know what to do with the *barangay* captain. She needs statements instead from the inspectors and poll clerk, for, by law, the *barangay* captains must stay fifty meters away from polling places. But that's her worry.

Once, he was amused by Sally's attention, by her ruses to get him into the house and then into her bedroom, past the snickering servants. Now her name leaves a foul taste in his mouth, a poisonous milky juice that impairs courage.

Unused to climbing that fast and that hard, Benhur feels muscles tighten in his legs. He has felt that ripping pain before, when he was young and foolish enough to swim to the breakwaters in Manila Bay, risking sharks for applause as if that were all there is to life.

Benhur brings his thoughts away from himself into the safer territory of politics. At the bars and coffeehouses in Ermita, hints have been dropped that Washington has seeded the opposition with some three million. Dollars! If he were a NAMFREL volunteer, risking his life for free elections by chaining himself to ballot boxes that goons come to steal, how should he then think of himself? As being subsidized by the American CIA? If true, that converts him into a mercenary. If true, his effort to recover democracy from the administrators of martial law has been co-opted, the way the 1896 revolution against Spain was converted by American volunteers into a war of annexation—the benevolent assimilation of three million Filipinos against their will. Spain was paid what she owed the British war merchants who financed wars.

From time to time Benhur forgets how dangerous it is to think. He discovers more things to rectify than the scrambled voter registration lists, the crony capitalism that drains the economy until workers get only the equivalent of one and a half hours' pay for the day's work. He discovers his own complicity—his silence, his own selfish priorities. He could have volunteered to watch the election count but did not.

If he were young, his anger might turn him into another Rodrigo Ponce, Jr. What kind of life? What kind of death should he aim for? The first casualty of the Friday elections can no longer be rewarded with a government appointment if Cory is declared winner. Yet, since Ponce did not stay safely in the background, he could not have had that in his mind.

As Benhur analyzes the situation, there are two kinds of Filipinos. One is still keeping vigil, three days after elections, in some out-of-the way precinct unsecured by the presence of foreign observers and media, or has already been dragged into the fields, maimed and shot, again out of camera range. The other Filipino, who claims to vote his conscience but disappears when danger approaches, well, he is part of the fun crowd that includes socialites of both genders who scour hotel lobbies for the media wolfpack who can flash them in newsreels beamed via satellites across the world's screens. Prime-time coverage, giving an adrenalin high to those in search of thrills not found in a bottle or a needle: *And in Manila, another six headless bodies . . .*

It should be an international crime to traffic in the misery of another country. And, punishable by living, the offense of feeling sorry for oneself in the midst of national suffering, bleeding for the victims of salvagings and liberations—those summary executions by government or NPA, the military arm of the Communist party—while partaking of buffets in five-star hotels or watching ramp models peel off. It should be encoded as treason of the highest order to be safe and alive when so many are dying from poverty, from the politics of cronies and of relatives.

The long surge of Benhur's wish and dream comes over him each time he visits Gulod. It mocks his anger and despair to have to leave; to be sad that at forty-six he has not saddled the world, when children are dying before they are born. He fights the world for giving him personal goals, and himself for resisting and acting against himself when others are riding history as far and as fast as it will take them. Sometimes he can bury this sadness, but it comes up again with all the loneliness it creates. Sometimes he swears never to return to Gulod. It is like gathering at a family graveyard.

"Attorney!" He is greeted from the house he is passing. "Stop awhile."

Anger and sorrow hang over Benhur, and he feels mocked by the word *attorney.* Behind the empty stare that he fixes on the people coming down the trail is one Tuesday morning in Constitutional Law, almost a full generation ago.

Vitaliano: Professor Alcantara called him out of turn that morning. Standing up, he stammered an excuse: *There's only one book for all four sections, Sir. I could not read the assignment, Sir.* Like a blind, lidded eye, the Adam's apple bulged Alcantara's throat: *You're expected to be resourceful, Vitaliano. The only acceptable excuse is death, and I don't mean death in the family.* Thinking the professor would get on with the class list, he sat down. *Remain standing, Vitaliano.* He shot up from his seat, the smile still playing on his face, willing to be roughed up for a change, to end the teasing that he was Alcantara's pet. *Now, sir. Vitaliano! You! Turn left. Now take nine steps.* With the class list, Alcantara was hitting the table while standing between his chair and the blackboard. Nine steps brought Benhur to the ledge of the open porch that connected the classrooms. Three floors below stretched the field between the Law and Education buildings—Malcolm and Panlasigui—between which the ROTC marched on Saturdays, practising for their gala parade with cadet sponsors. *Now jump, Vitaliano.* Silence; then laughter trying to test that silence; then back again to solemn hush. *Jump.*

He might as well have jumped. Nothing was right in his life afterward. It could have been a death worthy of any man of honor.

Today, years later, he is increasingly powerless against the memory of an impulse that decided his life forever at age twenty-three, an impulse that reduced all questions to what kind of life/what kind of death? 1965.

Classmates claimed that he walked back across the room to within an inch of Alcantara's hands, forcing the professor to stagger against the blackboard. Osong Moscoso recalled Benhur swearing, under his breath but audibly: *To hell with you, Sir. Jump if you like.* Then, as if they had each one been mocked that Tuesday morning, no one mentioned it again. Some classmates even suggested he demand the newspapers correct the error in the bar results which listed him as *Benjamin* Vitaliano.

Luckily for him, the other Vitaliano passed the bar close enough to the top—where *he* was expected to finish—because Benhur never returned to his classes. His father took all that year and the next three to die. Distracted, his mother never wondered about his diploma, though there were all the others, starting with high school: Demetrio's, Vergel's, Loreto's—badges of honor that made up for the early deaths and marginal existence.

Short-fused, his blowing up in class could be understood—but not his failure to go to night school, to some other college. Twenty years later, when Imee Marcos was allowed to graduate without complete residence, Benhur wondered bitterly why the privilege had not been granted before precedence was made on behalf of a president's daughter. For him, there was just a semester left. Why didn't he think of graduation? Why didn't he think?

Now, many mornings he wakes up to that Tuesday. Again and again, and unexpectedly, he is against that porch ledge being mocked into jumping. The rage, that this is all there is to his life, travels still in his bloodstream.

Enough times he wonders: was it mere pride? Or was it primarily, and instinctively, a matter of that dignity which law is intended to protect and uphold, so that when he risked it, he was actually defending the reason legal systems evolved? Law for the sake of virtue, Aquinas said. And virtue has to do with perfectibility, with individual and human dignity. Impossibilities.

But the ideal against which to measure oneself. Law for the sake of souls. And art for drawing out and preserving what is fine and humane in human sensibility. Of what avail the declaration of universal human rights?

Benhur could have gone on—distracting himself from feelings by following his thoughts into images that pass on into the visions that leaders need if they are to be lifted up from the details of politics, so that thinking becomes purely a function of the body and amenable to indifference, no longer for the sake alone of aspirations—except that the trail is filling up with people going to work that Monday, February 10. He checks the date on the Rolex watch Osong gave him, one of three acquired from Imelda.

A child about to throw the night's wastes wrapped in newspaper waits at the window for Benhur to pass before hurling it across the trail.

Nietszche comes briefly to Benhur's mind. In the long run there results something that is worth the trouble of living—virtue, art, reason, the mind against which to contend when trying to defend the will. Something that transfigures. Today, this morning, those words add up to hell for Benhur. St. Jerome, who brought his books into the cave where he retreated from his desires, said that not even God can restore lost virginities. Opportunities. Vitaliano's law reduces all that to two words: *No parole.* No remedy for life, not after Tuesday morning in Constitutional Law. No escape from the world where he can no longer love.

Their hands the only contents of their pockets, with not enough flesh to fight an illness and wearing the clothes in which they slept, some men are lounging in front of *Aling* Maxima's variety store.

"Good morning, Attorney Vitaliano," *Aling* Maxima calls out. "Can't I sue these men for blocking my store? They frighten away customers? Did I say men? There are not enough good parts from all of them to assemble into a decent body. All fake, like Marcos's medals."

"Look who's talking," Marcelo Andres winks at Benhur. "Fake medals! Wasn't it she last Wednesday who attended Marcos's *miting de avance* in Luneta when the clouds, seeded to drop rain on Cory and Doy's rally the day before, soaked the World War II bandanna of our *dalagang bukid?*"

Another of the men, whom Benhur does not know, starts shaking his hips to describe how Maxima walked to the KBL rally supporting Marcos.

"Out of here! *Puñeta! Puñeteros!*" Maxima waves her broom. "It would not be too bad if they bought something once in a while. Even on credit." She whacks the notebook hanging by a string alongside the bunch of bananas, knocking out the pencil stuck into the spiral. "My mistake, Attorney. Last week they bought a stick of Marlboro. They passed it around and used an entire box of matches. They're like women afraid to leave the house. Go and assault some strikers. See how accurately you can throw molotovs." She's angry because her son may be among those who were hurt when police and military units allowed strikebreakers to set fire to the strikers' makeshift shelter in Tenejeros. She sent her husband to check the bottling plant, but he has not returned.

"Maybe she only went to Marcos's rally to hear Nora Aunor and Vilma, not Imelda, sing *Dahil Sa Iyo,*" says the man Benhur does not know.

Broom in hand, Maxima runs out of her store. "Cory is the only one who can force Marcos to concede, the only one with balls besides the nuns." Her face is flushed. "And if you must know, I voted Cory and Doy. I am no *balimbing* like those turncoat politicians. I don't need your buying one teabag, one Band-Aid at a time."

"Oyes! Oyes!" the men run out of Maxima's reach, ahead of Benhur on the trail.

Marcelo is laughing so hard, he falls against the others when he stumbles. Seeing they have run out of Maxima's reach, he stops to throw out both arms and whine, "FM is a real man. *Barako. Si Cory didipa na lang. O heto. Iiyak pa.*" Then he demonstrates how Cory will break into tears in the scenario he imagines, knowing Maxima cannot chase them up the slope.

Benhur does not take sides. He understands that there is no money to be had in Gulod, or elsewhere; that the residents have to borrow what they need from the storekeepers like Maxima. Borrow and borrow until they die. Then their children will borrow some more for their coffin and wake. Some wakes last beyond the three ordinary days so the families can make a little money from the gaming tables set in the yards, and also to give everyone a chance to make a small donation. Maxima herself borrows, sells things on commission, even the cookies. If she had to pay taxes, too; if her husband's cousin were not a BIR examiner who fixes her accounts, Maxima would have lost her store years ago. Who ultimately pays? Perhaps God.

But is he any better off? Benhur turns against himself. He's a fake, like FM. A fake attorney, *siga-siga.* Not *siga,* a real big shot, as he lets people in Gulod think he is.

Within sight of the highway now—he can hear the buses sweeping along—Benhur takes a quick look back at Gulod. Floodwaters from the road gush through the huts toward the river, carrying pots and some chairs; short-circuiting television sets that barely work anyway, being jumbles of lines and shadows; junking reconditioned refrigerators that make more noise than ice. The river cuts and slices down Gulod to add to the other bank, where squatters multiply faster than mushrooms around stalks of bananas after a rain. Old-timers claim its sand used to yield white-shelled clams for *sinubukan,* to grow peanuts and watermelons that ripened on the vines—there being no squatters, once upon a time, to pick the still-green fruits. One or two also claim to have seen General Luna and his aides, refusing the protection of trenches, waiting on the banks to take the Americans' advance at a halt in 1899. Gone now is the tree under which Bonifacio camped during the revolution of 1896 while the Spaniards and their *guardia civiles* scoured the *cogonal.* That tree was hacked down for firewood during the Japanese Occupation, after it had been used by the Japanese to hang those who refused to bow to their sentries. Even the roots were pulled out of the ground.

Benhur has to stop, almost doubling up from the wild beating of his heart. Rooted deep in his lungs, the pain almost crushes him, and he straightens out only slowly, like an old man with a breakable body. As soon as he can stand upright again, he gives in to bitterness, his mind circling.

He should have brought Terence Hugg to Gulod when the photojournalist asked to be shown a barrio. An urban hell is probably the truth that escapes projections and analyses by political pundits. The whole of truth. Hugg might have been able to answer the earth-shattering questions being asked in Gulod: *Who's the best of the anchormen? Koppel, Brokaw, Jennings, or Rather?* Away from the noise of Manila Hotel's Taproom, Hugg might have been able to explain why the millions spent on TV coverage by the networks—just the CBS transmitter in Mindanao reportedly cost $5 million—might have been better spent on the poor.

But starvation is not a matter of life and death for the West, where the growth industry is diet clinics and health spas—woodchips for fiber, nothing to do with nutrients, but everything with thinness. And Gulod, in the estimation of its residents, is not poor. The poor are those who sell a child to feed the rest of their children, or allow them to make a living following the white and Japanese tourists on sex tours in Pagsanjan and coastal resorts; or who give them up for adoption to smooth-talking perverts, or who leave them with Mother Teresa's orphanages in Tayuman and San Nicolas until they gain weight, then redeem them until they fall sick again. An actor told him that when *Apocalypse Now* was filmed in the country, the child whose body took the bullets was still alive, sold by his parents because he was dying anyway. Each life more desperate.

But what of himself? Isn't he, too, just a half-step from begging, since, after he divides what he earns among several households, he has not enough for what he wants? Having learned his procedure and codes better than the *colegialas* learn their catechism, Benhur is a lawyer's lawyer. He gets anywhere from 2,000 to 4,000 or even 7,000 pesos, for briefs that are exhaustive and incisive, well grounded in arguments, with impeccable citations. He might scribble speeches on the spot, but they contain memorable phrases, flashes of insight that startle those used to platitudes. Draft legislation, reform programs, incorporation papers, contracts—nothing that bears his own name—every manner of document or policy comes out of Benhur's brain as if a permanent ache, a metal crab, has not burrowed there as well. Were that ache a bullet, he muses often, its downward trajectory would exit through his mouth.

Another hole in the head he does not need.

Why didn't he just laugh along with the class that Tuesday morning in Constitutional Law? One can survive humiliation, but not starvation. How many in the opposition have qualified for government largesse and appointments by carrying Imelda's perfume sprays, dousing her just before the plane touches down so the crowd will be overwhelmed by her fragrance?

It will be interesting to see, if Marcos is toppled, how many in the new administration will subordinate the country's survival to their own.

Water is collecting in the grass, carrying the suds down the trail from the large basins where women wash clothes beside their doorways. Ears burned by the sun, young boys carry cans of water across their shoulders on poles; young girls balance jugs of water on their heads, dancing as they walk down hill.

Children figure in Benhur's fear of an explosion more deadly than that set off by weapons. Every year in the Philippines there are a million and a half more children. That's a 2.4 population growth, an equation for disaster, requiring millions of non-existing pesos for schools, health care, food, and jobs. It is a nightmare from which leaders avert their eyes, thinking that if God created the children, He will provide for them. In parts of Metro Manila, people already live on top of garbage dumps, alongside canals that carry out to Manila Bay the refuse of those who are better off, in shelters so cramped they cannot stand up to their height and must take turns sleeping, must cook and wash and hold their wakes alongside the streets. Families have been seen sleeping under the shrubs in the Luneta. What do the minds of those children contain when their every waking hour is occupied with survival? Is the soul long healthy in a starved body? What keeps together that part of a person which dreams, has longings beyond food and sex?

A few more steps and Benhur ceases climbing. He is officially out of Gulod. Space appears between the fences. Here whole chickens are barbecued whereas, deep in Gulod, the intestines and the feet are roasted on bamboo sticks: IUDS and Adidas, they are called. That Filipino humor again, that safety valve of anger. Not light years away from there, five-star hotels cater to those with jaded palates, to locals who leave their plates filled to indicate they are not a bit hungry. At the cost of tens of thousands of dollars, the Philippine House in New York is redecorated for an Imelda reception or a night of disco; dollars taken out of the future of thousands of children whose faces, in his sleep, come to him as lost children with nothing in their lives but the shirts on their backs; dead children. The misery is caught truer on film than in the tourists' eyes.

Shielded from the trail by a thin row of evergreen *aguhos* within the adobe wall, Sally Moscoso's house abuts the highway. To its left, across the trail that leads down to Gulod, is the drugstore from which the barrio people buy aspirin, one tablet at a time. To purchase magic against dying they sell their last good shirt, pawn family earrings, heirlooms from a time that will never exist for their children; or go into debt to keep alive children who will die anyway, children bloated not from fat but from worms.

Benhur can think of no good news that poverty announces. If only, in all simplicity, one could believe that men die and become suns, that children die and become angels—not that they can't die before their last breath. It is impossible, in these terms, to think of man as sacred.

As each step reduces the distance to Sally Moscoso's pink stucco house, Benhur's thoughts gain in disorder. He tries to catch up with people walking past the house, to use them as cover. She used to wait for him. In the evenings. At all hours. *There's beer in the fridge. Such a hot day, Benhur. Shall I have some coconuts cut down for buko?*

Part of Saturday's *Daily Inquirer* flaps against a scrub lantana. Something about the violence, terrorizing during the snap election. With the dollars invested in the American bases, will Reagan allow Marcos to lose? *Politics is for the good of the leaders, not of the country they purport to serve:* Vitaliano's law of political reality. It's pure sentiment to declare that the obligation to vote comes from God.

And how she waited, Benhur recalls—sitting in the porch off her bedroom in a pastel gown of polyester, large hoop earrings, dark face the size of a carabao platter. He imagines the insides of her mouth as wrinkled as the satin linings of coffins. *Such a hot night, Benhur.* But he does not come with clean hands required in order to accuse; he knows that mole between her legs. *Barako,* she called him. *Come quickly.* Not a few times he did. And Osong Moscoso is his friend and classmate, his fraternity brod.

Trapped in a childlike, impetuous innocence, in an irrationality at odds with his fixed obsession about discipline and his belief that governments themselves need acts of purification, such as will enable citizens to develop the soul and thereby sustain and enrich the country, Benhur has decided to remain politically neutral. He did not vote in the Friday election because he was not sure people's lives would be made better. Even though his brother Vergel had persuaded him to take a risk, to believe that people can be upgraded from subjects to citizens, his name could not be found in the registration list.

It was just as well. It's the same martyrology always: government and dissidents get their martyrs from the poor and oppressed, not from among their ranks, as if the country could be saved without saving the poor.

The impractical wanderings of Benhur's mind—avoidance certainly, though occasionally highminded, detached, the key to his political independence—fail to save him from Sally.

His last step brings him to the wedding-cake house with the sign at the gate: Villa Salud. There is Sally Moscoso's blue grotto built out of smooth river pebbles. Lilies float in the miniature pool that now breeds golden snails, after the goldfish lost their scales to old age and disease and looked poached in *salza blanca* as they swam between the umbrella reeds. Like fur, grass grows up to the front steps. And there, inside the green 8-cylinder Buick aimed at the road leading to Quirino Highway, there is Sally Moscoso herself, waiting to give him a ride.

Huli!

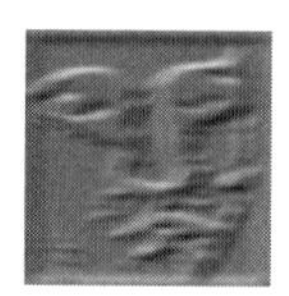

Hurting, because he is grateful

with no wish to be so—by seven in the morning jeepneys and buses no longer stop for passengers who line both sides of the highway like devotees struggling for a view of a procession—Benhur slams the car door after getting in beside Sally's driver. His throat is drier than if he had swallowed a fistful of stale bread.

"*Tito* Benhur!" Joel and Miggy lean forward in greeting, calling him uncle from his long friendship with their father.

"Long time . . .," Benhur catches himself saying, cutting out the rest of the greeting that dates him a generation back.

Sally leans forward to within a whisper of Benhur's ear. "The inauguration is on the twenty-fifth. Tuesday. You will come, won't you? The Commissioner has several invitations, all front seats with the generals."

Benhur mumbles his reply. The only Marcos inauguration he attended was when fellow-students threw a papier mache crocodile at the president-elect, who was on his way to Congress to deliver a speech. Demonstrations were gentler in the late sixties. Throwing that crocodile now rates a zero on a scale of ten for protest.

"Mamá. Better wait until he's proclaimed. The vote count has barely started." Joel and Miggy exchange glances around their mother in the back seat. Joel taps his shirt pocket to remind Miggy of the letter to the editor they had worked on all night. "Now," he mouths silently. "Let *Tito* read it."

Miggy says, instead, "*Tito* Benhur, why was no date set in the Omnibus Election Code for the taking of office, only for the proclamation and inauguration?"

"Because Marcos didn't resign when he ran again."

"Meaning he did not intend to lose," Joel says.

To end the discussion, Sally holds down Joel's hand. "On the 22nd, Benhur, is the Commissioner's birthday. A surprise, so don't tell Osong. I'm inviting classmates and those in the commission. Maybe a few ministers. And Madame! What do you say to a real barrio fiesta with everyone in *saya* and *baro?*"

The idea has just occurred to Sally and she is sailing right into fantasy. Madame attend! The toast of *Life* and the *Washington Post,* of Reagan and Johnson and Nixon, attend a barrio fiesta in a real barrio? Fat chance, when she spends millions on her own receptions where dancing goes on all night and favors run into girls for the evening, not just Cartier watches! For Jerry Falwell's reception, close to a million in dollars was spent. Sally's barrio fiesta would be slumming for Madame. What minor European royalty could she meet in Gulod? What B-movie Hollywood actors? Does she even know that Sally Moscoso is one of her Blue Ladies, or that Fructuoso Moscoso is a commissioner in their conjugal dictatorship? What is it to her if Sally does not get to dance with Benhur Vitaliano? Vitaliano who? Is that not a common name?

A season behind Manila's fashion of loose and trendy cottons straight from Paris fashion magazines and the "Vive la Femme" motif for 1986—hourglass figures, backless and bare-ribbed, blinding satins and silk if not rough cottons—Sally wears polyester belted at the hip. A white leather handbag completes her outfit. Also made in Marikina, where many goods marked *Made in Italy* actually originate, her shoes in peach fabric match her dress.

"And invite your friends," she turns to her sons. "How about the Kundirana group so we can have an ensemble?"

Joel and Miggy grimace. Their mother has been after them to join the performing groups at La Salle, when music is farthest from their minds.

Though their hairstyle and clothes might suggest café performers, that Monday they are heading for the NAMFREL Quick Count Center in the La Salle Dome. So as not to alert Sally, they have asked to be dropped off at a friend's house, from there supposedly to go on to an Opus Dei meeting. Since Opus Dei bothers only with the best students, Sally is pleased.

"Why don't we take you directly to the meeting and save time?" Sally suggests.

"We can't change plans now," Joel says. "Others are involved. They'll bring us back, so don't worry."

"Early?" Sally insists. "Remember the time I thought you were in La Salle when actually you were attending the hearings at SSS into the Aquino assassination? If I did not know anyone from NISA who saw you . . ."

"It was an assignment, Mamá. For a paper," Miggy says. "*Tito* Benhur, we were there before the start, but when Magsaysay Hall was opened at eight, all the seats had been taken by government employees."

"All the generals were wearing *barongs*. They coached Ver earlier in a big room made to look like Magsaysay Hall, down to the spotlights and mikes," Joel adds.

"Is that so?" Benhur smiles, pleased by the boys' commitment when their father will not even acknowledge that the situation has become increasingly grave: *Don't mention the poor, Benhur. They're like boils that disappear by themselves. Apply remedies and they'll only pop up elsewhere. Leave them alone. They're part of reality.*

"Is not Fairview where Radio Veritas operates its transmitters?" Sally asks.

"It's also where the Anselmos live," Joel says.

"If anything goes wrong, your father will blame me." Everything is left to her, she thinks ruefully. She gets all the aggravation. Osong merely answers her phone calls with messages signed, F. Miguel Moscoso, Commissioner, as if everything between them has become official, beyond question and appeal, now that he does not come home any more. Fructuoso! As in old script, the *F* is labored over, teased into tendrils.

"Don't worry, Mamá." Miggy places a hand over Sally's arm. "Nothing can happen. It's three days after the elections."

"Nothing! The news about armed men picking up marchers on Capitol Road during the fortieth anniversary of the Universal Declaration of Human Rights is nothing? And how about the pillbox thrown among those marching in Baguio's *Luksang Bayan* Rally?" Sally becomes agitated, recalling the pictures of relatives around a makeshift coffin, signing the names of those who have disappeared. Mourning for the country!

Sally is even more distressed to catch sight, on Benhur's side of the highway, of a bananacue vendor who reminds her of Catherine Deneuve, except for the dark hair and the honey skin. How can anyone look naturally stunning while *she* turns gray under foundations that are supposed to narrow her jaws, lift up her cheekbones, deepen her eyes, and shape her lips thin and pouty? Peeling with chemicals and ultraviolet has left her face looking sun-scoured, as coarse as sand from which the waves have receded. Only after she had eyebrows permanently tattooed, to save herself wrinkles from squinting to get the brows even, did she learn that, with age, the eyebrows can slide over her nose.

On her arm, Sally centers her fake Cartier wristwatch from Hong Kong, slides the 24-carat gold bracelets up her other arm. She has meant to ask Benhur about Ting Dolor, who, friends tell her, was given a real Cartier by Imelda. Ting Dolor has also been seen often with Osong. She tries to say the name, but she can't bring herself to name any of the other women. So she keeps having those terrible dreams of waking up and finding herself sewn to the mattress, of the maids refusing to approach, saying *Ma'm has AIDS.*

That dreaming started after she read about the new disease, said to have escaped from the American bases. It supposedly destroys a person's immunities. The telltale marks were not described.

Sally takes Joel's hand, then Miggy's; slaps each playfully.

"Telling fortunes, Mamá?" Joel teases.

"No. I was thinking." But she does not tell them she wishes they would take singing lessons. Gary Valenciano is giving solo concerts in Los Angeles. Something like that for the boys would be terrific, even without the commercials and hot-selling records. Her sons never want what she wants. They made fun of her offer to give them body-building lessons so they could try becoming ramp models. The son of a family friend models ready-to-wear and has been offered movie parts. They started but didn't stay with their tennis lessons, which she had thought would enable them, eventually, to take part in the National Open at the Polo Club. She also urged Osong to take memberships at the exclusive clubs, and he *may* have taken out shares at the Club Filipino, Wack Wack, Polo Club, even the Philippine Columbian; only she's not the one he takes there.

"What, Mamá?" Joel waits.

"Nothing. I try to be a good mother so you won't waste yourselves on ordinary ambitions, and I end up being the witch. That's all right. I'm used to it." Instead of listening to her sons protest their gratitude for her concern, Sally reads her horoscope for the day: *Romance starred. Someone you have not seen for a long time will contact you.* Benhur?

The problem is that she is not satisfied with emotional love, passion in the mind. She can husk the floor upstairs and down, which her sister has done ever since she became widowed—*It's only once a month the urge comes, and mind over body works.* She can recite three rosaries but her desires still flare up. She needs to fill her arms as well as her heart. Just thinking of Benhur now, within reach but distant, hurts like a mass of papercuts, like waking up from giving birth. She hides her thoughts in the ad for *Aling* Asiang's Valentine Day Menu: Lovers in a Blanket; Lady Chatterley's Berries; Laguna Seduction . . .

Can she ask Benhur to lunch, just like that? Long ago she and Benhur took the boys to Baguio for the Holy Week. Joel got sick from the sharp turns on the Zigzag, and Benhur took the car off the narrow road so Joel could throw up on the grass everything he had eaten. Osong would have shrunk from the sour breath, would have ignored Joel until they reached the city where there was someone else to attend to him. Osong never takes them even just to the Seven Sisters in Cavite. It's always *Next time*—which never comes.

"We'll take the bus from here, Mamá," Joel and Miggy simultaneously kiss Sally on the cheek and are out of the car before she can hang on to them.

"Only last year they were *totoys,*" she says to Benhur, who is watching them dash for the red MD bus that has cut in front. "Look at that." The two catch on to the arms of passengers hanging on at the door. "Suppose they slip under the wheels." She touches her hair, stiff from spray to hold it in place. Hot oil treatment fails to soften the strands that stick out like nails. Young women looking for older and successful men manage to have shiny, soft hair.

Darting, across three lines of traffic, a cigarette vendor runs to their car at the driver's signal for two sticks of Marlboro. The traffic starts up again, and the driver tosses out the peso fifty, forcing the boy to run between the buses after the coins. "Attorney?" Benhur accepts the other stick of cigarette so the driver will not think he refuses because it's not imported.

"If we hit oil in Palawan, prices should drop," the driver lures Benhur into a conversation.

"Could be."

Sally is trying to follow the red MD up ahead, critical of Joel's smudged sneakers and his *Bantay-ng-Bayan* shirt—election giveaways—whereas Miggy has a dress shirt. No blue jeans for Miguel Alfonso Moscoso. "Doesn't Joel look like a strike breaker?"

"At least he's not wearing all those Cory paraphernalia." Benhur refers to the yellow bands and hats, of which Sally has been complaining.

The driver points to his hip pocket to indicate where Joel keeps those until he's out of his mother's sight.

The red MD, which the boys boarded as if it were a merry-go-round in a carnival, is being pushed ahead by cars, jeepneys, and blue-and-white Metro Manila buses, past bakeries, past funeral parlors with caskets displayed on wooden trestles on the sidewalk, past vendors selling fruits and vegetables already cut up and bagged in plastic, past drugstores, barbershops, hardware stores, medical and dental clinics, hairdressers, tailors, and camera shops with films on display in cases facing the sun. On the right stands the Iglesia church, white and green like a fairy castle.

"Why can't they go to movies instead? In our day we went every time it changed. *Silver Bullet* is showing. Dino de Laurenti's blockbuster. And in a bus. Suppose they're held up?" Sally doubts that the inmates of penitentiaries reported to have been released to make trouble will recognize the boys as the Commissioner's sons. She recalls the time a maid took Miggy to town in a jeepney: *Ma'm, he cried and cried. He wanted the other passengers to get off.*

"Where to, Ma'm?"

Sally can't decide. Usually it's to Malacañang, to wait on Imelda's pleasure. Dancing during receptions now outlasts Sally's legs; she feels giddy, as if the chandeliers are swinging. In the beginning, she and Osong had the first dance at least. She enjoyed the secrets being whispered over soup, the flowers being brought up from the airport, the salute of white-gloved palace guards. But the last time, in the courtyard, there were crates the size of coffins being nailed together where the fountain flowed with colored lights.

A thought occurs to Sally, but it is quickly gone. Was it important? she wonders. About whom? About what?

Sally's remark about her sons being mere boys just the past year pulls Benhur from his own thoughts, but not directly into hers. He wishes it were not beneath his dignity to jump aboard a bus, too; to hang on the *estribo* as the two boys did, waiting for space to open up inside.

Even this he blames on Osong, as he also blames Tuesday morning in Constitutional Law on his classmate, *compadre,* patron: Commissioner F. Miguel Moscoso. Had Osong simply pulled him down, he would not have walked over to the window like a robot. *Sit down, Brod* would not have been difficult to whisper out of the professor's hearing. It could have brought him to his senses. After he had stared down at the ground between the Law and Education Buildings, it was a *fait accompli.* All he could do was walk out, if he had any pride, sideswiping Alcantara, who by then had lost control of the situation. It had become second nature to Alcantara to bully students ever since he missed being named Chief Justice by one *querida* too many. In a lifetime of turpitudes, one is kicked up; but not in his case. No other chief justice had been credited with mistresses then.

The way floods carry debris, eddying their way to the sea, Benhur's mind bears him forward and back to that Tuesday morning when, as if *in extremis,* he let go of three years and five months of law school to be able to boast that he had made the Second Cry at Balintawak. A bid for freedom, like Bonifacio's.

An incipient wound, that memory is his illness from which no remission occurs except briefly, the way madmen have a few moments of sanity.

There is a life behind every cry, however silent; a life before, but not necessarily after.

Friday before the Bar exam, Osong picked him up at Gulod. Convinced he would fail without Benhur, Osong did not even want to try. Afterward, no matter how he reviewed the situation, Benhur realized it was crazy to agree to drive Osong to the exams, then to allow himself to be talked into going up, finally into taking the first test for Osong. How? when the test questions were numbered, the seats counted! Unless everyone, including the monitors, were in a dead stupor! Dead from trying to keep all the law they had crammed into their heads the past summer alive and ready to leap at the test questions. Leaks kept coming, up to the last moment, confusing them. No one wondered why Benhur was there. It was assumed everything was made right. Tuesday morning in Constitutional Law remained in no one's mind but his!

In any case, because of him, the test in Constitutional Law raised Osong's grade-point average to a few fingers off the bottom of the list of successful barristers. Good enough for jubilation so that the Colonel and Mrs. Moscoso threw a party.

Osong's dependence on him escalated from that time, compounded by superstition and real need, so that now Benhur has to sit in on conferences in order to feed Osong background data, instant analysis, bold proposals. *Quick, Benhur, what will I say?* Not a week passes but Osong calls from whichever house he has slept in. *The driver is coming for you, Benhur,* forgetting he has assigned Benhur an official car complete with gas ration, which Benhur tries not to use for his personal purposes. Any time, Osong's secretary could be calling: *Is your passport still current, Sir?* And a red government issue arrives for him, with appropriate visas.

It matters increasingly to Benhur that he cannot cut himself off, though there are other ways of paying his rent and supporting the family in Gulod beside the consultancies Osong throws at him. *Here, Boy; another bite!* The accumulation of favors is not all on his part, but it has produced a mouthful of bile which embitters his thoughts, twists his heart.

Never sure of how the sheet is balanced between them, this uncertainty remains the preoccupation that starts and ends Benhur's days. Conference-hopping together, they have seen most of the capitals of the world; but Benhur still dreams of getting to sign his own name to the papers he writes, to deliver the arguments himself, to receive the applause, the appointment, the promotion.

As for Osong, Benhur's dream has to be his nightmare—what if Benhur breaks free?—but he knows Benhur is too scrupulous, too conservative in his ambitions and self-esteem: which traits keep Benhur loyal. Benhur has not let anyone know about the wedding in Esguerra, when Osong was assigned there to the Commission on Elections.

Responding to Osong's telegram—*Come immediately. Urgent. Secret*—Benhur found out that Osong simply wanted his opinion of Asuncion Paz, whose mother allowed her visitors only after the lengthy evening prayers and three mysteries recited with the rosary passing back and forth between the two women. *Would you, if you were me, marry her?*

By way of reply, he asked Osong if he were ready to bury himself in Esguerra, watching the salt drying on the fishnets spread over the boats. It is not clear whose idea it was to wait for Asuncion outside the church that Sunday; or to see the priest afterward. Whatever the intention, on whomever's part, the two ended up registered in the parish books as man and wife. Asuncion never took off the veil she wore to church which reached to her waist. Benhur assumed the marriage was consummated that forenoon when he drove them to the beachhouse, staying behind the wheel while they walked out to the water on the sea-encrusted sand. The clouds, he still remembers, were white, unlikely crows. If Osong returned to Esguerra without him after he was reassigned to Manila, it could not have been more than once. Sometimes Benhur thinks of Asuncion and wonders if he is to blame for not dissuading his friend. It was the first chance to separate them. He thought of Asuncion when he stood as candle sponsor for Sally and Osong, at their wedding with the complete Toledo rites. He thinks of her now.

Sally points out *Aling* Asiang's restaurant, but Benhur is not paying attention. She begins to feel that the people standing on the curb, waiting for their ride, are right up against her face. No look of desire crosses the faces of the men who see her inside the car. In all truth, she asks herself—reminded of the peddler who resembled Catherine Deneuve, for whose autograph she waited in line in New York once—have you ever really changed a man's feelings? Asking Benhur once if she must leave Osong to the younger women, who think it is to their credit to be seen in public with married men, Benhur had shouted: *If you want. It's between you and him. I have nothing to do with it. It's your integrity. It's your. . . .* She had expected comforting.

She is beginning to see that Osong and Benhur cannot be permanent parts of her life; she must concentrate her efforts on her sons.

To test her will, she decides not to say another word to Benhur. It feels as if her own life is over, especially since he's already with her and there are all those intriguing Valentine's Day entrees at *Aling* Asiang's.

But she tries. Only when she thinks Benhur is about to get out does she give him the tale: "We might have a doctor in the family, Benhur. Did you know? Miggy has such a fascination with cutting up cats that it's impossible to keep one in the house . . ."

Among the crowd waiting
on the grounds of the National Assembly for the official counting of the ballots on Tuesday, Olimpia Vitaliano sees herself strangely as a face in a locket. She tries to stand apart from Vergel so people will not notice she is older than he. Seven years and one month. She assumes people know what everyone in Kapalaran knows. And a *viuda,* too, people say, widow of the pastor Celso Icasiano, whose bullet-riddled body was found in the chapel he was building with bamboo from their farm. Cause of death in the police report: undetermined.

Why she will marry again puzzles people back in Kapalaran. Does she need another child? The deeper riddle for people is what Vergel Vitaliano, doctor in the regional hospital, sees in her. She herself does not know any answer.

Mostly young and still staked, the trees and the already blooming shrubs make the grounds of the Batasan resemble a garden into which she has strayed. Her thoughts about herself wind and twist about what people must think. How can she explain that she refused Vergel Vitaliano; that each refusal only made him more insistent. A young doctor who could be making a fortune back in Manila or abroad would choose to practice in Kapalaran and to marry a widow? She worried that his family might wonder about that, too, and might blame her. But if she did not feel welcome right away, she does not feel unwelcome now.

There is simply no explanation on earth why Vergel would choose to walk through the fields, in the sun and rain, to reach those who cannot afford the trip to the hospital in town, to bring sample medicines to those who are ashamed to bring their children in rags to the town clinic.

Nothing makes sense. Celso was shot three times in the head for refusing to give God's money to those who did not believe in God. Who are they? Where are they? In Kapalaran she stood trembling at the window, looking toward the hills and wondering if the men were watching her through binoculars, planning to make her a widow again. Unrecognized, are they there today on the grounds of the Batasan while, inside the National Assembly building, assemblymen battle over the counting procedure and the opposition's demand that the matter of electoral cheating be taken up first?

Celso was not the first one they killed in Kapalaran. Manuela, who sold carabao milk and *kesong puti,* was shot on her way back from the market for not paying tax to the dissidents—those with livelihood or property are forced to give twenty pesos a month. For not giving information about the military, the minister who helped Celso with the successful conference where twelve were converted and baptized was shot. He was preaching. Suddenly men burst through with automatic rifles. The gunfire woke up his sleeping children, who began at once to cry. Not until the next morning, after the body had been washed and the wounds covered, while the coffin was being nailed together from pieces of wood being saved for the chapel, did the police come.

Three weeks later, it was Celso.

Everything she remembers is an image buried in her body, which remembers the crying.

She looks about in the Batasan grounds and what she sees is the wooden cross on which Celso's name was burned while those neighbors who were not afraid to come stood there in the yard before walking in long lines to the cemetery. While Vergel is talking there to friends, her memories come with the force of blows being struck.

From time to time Vergel looks at her where she stands under the shade of a young tree with leaves she does not recognize. She wishes she had not come, wishes Vergel did not meet friends who must think her dreadful and old. While she cannot feel like herself as she stands there quietly, Vergel appears at ease, confident in his scuffed sneakers and the clothes he also wore in Kapalaran.

Any money Vergel makes, beyond what they need and what he gives away, goes toward a book he's writing about herbal medicine. He hopes to break people's reliance on expensive prescriptions that cost their life savings and are too strong for their narrow bodies, so that they suffer debilitating side effects. After he finishes the book, will Vergel then leave Kapalaran?

In Gulod, Vergel talks mostly to Benhur. The brothers look so comfortable together, as if they're twins. Their mother Patro brought out pictures of them growing up. Benhur is so funny, making Vergel laugh as she has not seen before. Each time he comes, Benhur brings ham and pies and pan Americano on which they spread real butter from Australia. He sends for food from *Aling* Maxima and won't let Vergel spend. Benhur even said that perhaps Rosalio and Anya could stay behind when they return. Celso always wanted Anya to become a nurse. She's already fifteen, beginning to have suitors.

Benhur understands why Vergel must return to Kapalaran. *I can't see you in an office with ads outside: VD, Circumcision/Pregnancy Test—2 minutes/Lab result—5 minutes!* And Vergel laughed. *How about: Instant Beauty/Noselift, Bustlift/Expert Cosmetic Surgeon?*

In all her life Olimpia has not seen a crowd as large as this one waiting for the ballots to be tallied. Linking arms, youths are chanting freedom slogans. Every arrival of election returns, escorted by the same volunteers who chained themselves to the ballot boxes to keep them from being stolen, sends up a surge of hymns and applause. Seminarians try to moderate the cheering so as to give the anti-riot policemen no excuse to ram into the opposition. Helmeted and wielding Plexiglas shields, the police stand between the larger Cory/Doy crowd and those wearing *Marcos Pa Rin* shirts, youths organized by Imee Marcos.

Olimpia is reminded of her mother by the women wearing white and blue sashes to honor Our Lady of Lourdes, whose feast day is the 11th of February. Facing the winding driveway of the Batasan, Olimpia understands why her parents never stopped talking about the first Independence Day. From her mother's description she imagined as a child how the Philippine flag furled and unfurled, whipped about by the breeze from Manila Bay which made it ripple with the sound of rushing waves. Her father remembered best the pigeons shot out of cannons into the air. It worried him that their wings would be torn until he saw them flying, from where he stood, as if pulling the flag upward.

It cost her parents the price of six sacks of milled rice to come, plus the traditional gifts of chicken, eggs, and *chicos de primera* for relatives with whom they stayed. What has it cost *her* to come?

Olimpia struggles under Vergel's arm, wishing he would not pull her to himself while his friends watch. It was to show Danilo Sebastian to his grandmother Patro and *Lola* Sula that they came two weeks before the snap election. It is two years since Vergel saw his family. People in Kapalaran said they were trying to escape the political unrest during the campaign, not to get blessings for Danilo and for their marriage.

If Rosalio were there, he'd be writing what he sees into his notebook. It is Rosalio who kept the newspaper report of Celso's death, a brief paragraph in the weekly occurrence in the provinces: *A pastor, Celso Icasiano of the Methodist church, was shot inside his thatch-roofed chapel, allegedly by the NPA for refusing to contribute and give information. The week previous the pastor attended a liaison meeting with the regional command, the Ecumenical Movement for Peace and Justice, and other social action groups with a view to helping stabilize the situation.*

People are arriving with new placards: *No freedom in cheating. Return stolen wealth to the country.* TV cameras zero in on the placards and the seminarians, whose white cassocks remind Olimpia of the butterflies her pupils brought to class, wings pinned to boards, bodies still squirming.

A man walking by makes Olimpia think of the Pentecostal minister who officiated at Celso's funeral. Others remind her of the neighbors who nailed the coffin in the yard; of the priest who brought coffee and a small donation and gave a brief invocation: *The bodies of the dead are still temples of the Holy Spirit, so we protect and respect them. God Himself protects what He created, and renews in His love those who destroy.* She was a Catholic before she married Celso, who was a Catholic, too, before he came to Kapalaran. Until she saw his wounds, she thought he had just fallen asleep in the chapel. Remembering how he looked, Olimpia feels she, too, is decaying in front of the crowd.

"Tuta! Tuta!" The Marcos crowd, who have been given food in boxes, are mocked. *"Hakot!"* Paid to rally. Lapdogs. More placards converge on the grounds. *Tyrant, step down!* proclaims Laurel's UNIDO party. "We're just making a living," someone on the Marcos side explains; "We're really with you. We just need the rice even if Marcos's name is on the sack." Others look out from the improvised tent of Marcos streamers; like their shirts, red and blue.

Wearing expensive clothes, the kind that wrinkle fashionably, some more of Vergel's friends come by with their wives.

After she is introduced, Olimpia looks at the trees again, hiding her eyes. The Batasan roof is so long and massive it seems to support the sky. The red tiles . . . she looks down at the grass, trying not to think of the stains on the chapel floor. Celso had his genitals blown off. When they laid him down under the *ylang-ylang* until the police could come . . . that's the way the light appears to her, the same light beating . . .

The memory flattens the roof against the sky.

One day she will tell Rosalio and Anya the words Celso said, speaking for the Lord: *The nations shall know that I am the Lord when in their sight I prove my holiness through you. The prophet Ezekiel promised that God will take away our hearts of stone and give us the ability to feel, to be compassionate, to respond.*

With the wedding towel she never used, she washed Celso's body before calling the children, and while she was washing him, her own body felt full of stones. Celso and she were young together.

"Are you all right?" Vergel moves closer to shade her with his body. "Would you like anything?"

Vergel's friends are telling him about their children. "I thought that since they grew up under martial law they would not care about democracy. But they are helping to collect for the *Pakikiramay* Fund." Another says, "They voted against Marcos, actually for Laurel because he agreed to be second to Cory so as not to split the opposition. It takes guts. I never liked him before."

"It's a rare politician who will come down from his ambition for the sake of the country," Vergel agrees, passing on to Olimpia the page of the *Times* which lists the Fund at P6,450 as of February 11.

"How many children do you have?" one of the wives asks.

Olimpia thinks. Does she mean the children she has borne, or those she and Vergel have? The staked trees make her think of toddlers learning to walk inside *andadors.* Rosalio walked at nine months; Anya talked before she was one and a half, speaking in complete sentences, which delighted Celso.

"One. Danilo Sebastian, going on two," Vergel answers for her.

"What a name!" the friends remark. "Named obviously for success. He's bound to discover something like penicillin and make millions or become a movie star. And make millions."

"Why didn't you bring him so we could see him?" the wives exclaim. "Who does he look like?"

"A little of both of us," Vergel says. Wearing jeans, he looks not much older than the young demonstrators in sneakers and T-shirts with names of their candidates, so that Olimpia wonders when men start to look old. Her father was old from the beginning, from working in the fields as a tenant. And Celso . . .

"Where are you staying?" the wives try to draw Olimpia out.

Olimpia smiles, forgetting completely where Vergel's mother lives. She wants to go home and see the children. She would have preferred to have brought them along. Ryan, Vergel's nephew, who is as lively as a top, hangs out with seventeen-year-olds, though he is only Rosalio's age. What could the older boys want from him? There are teenagers lounging along the trails night and day, smoking and drinking, taunting passersby and waiting for trouble; if not making it. Four-year-olds who have not tasted school look as if they have tasted drugs or smelled glue or polish remover.

"Gulod," she answers, recalling the name. Loreto, on seeing her, said to her mother, "Without make-up, Vergel's wife looks beautiful. Imagine how beautiful *with.*" The remark softened the fears she had of being introduced.

"Gulod?"

In Kapalaran the mangoes will have started to form. Large butterflies the size of her hand come out wet from cocoons, she wants to tell the women. The *ampalaya* and eggplants will be fingersize. And the *calamansi* and okra. In Gulod it is expensive. Pork is 52 pesos a kilo; chicken, 50; oxtail, 70. In Kapalaran the meat she buys is only for Vergel and Rosalio. The broth is for Danilo Sebastian. She and Anya prefer the vegetables.

Mystery shot kills man: the man standing beside the tree reads out the headline. "I was at Ugarte when it happened," he tells Vergel and his friends. "It is as the *Daily Inquirer* says. The man was carrying a *Marcos concede* sign."

"That's his fate," Vergel's friends agree among themselves. "When it's your time to go, it's good-bye."

Olimpia thinks of Celso. Once she dreamed of him hanging from the tree outside the chapel. In another dream she is running after men who are carrying away Danilo, who place him on a tall fence as if he's a piece of laundry. In her dreams she is neither crying nor singing; she is trying to speak sounds that hang across her body the way bandoliers of bullets crisscross the bodies of the military and rebels; sounds like that of the guitar Celso strummed.

"Just before the shots, a friend called to me, and that saved my life," the man continues. "I was standing next to the man. Imagine, in that crowd, a provincemate sees and recognizes me when I have not been back to Zamboanga in years."

"So he was a six-footer," Vergel says, reading the newspaper. "Another Larry Bird." When Benhur went to Boston, he brought back Celtics shirts for Vergel and Rosalio which waited until they came to Gulod.

"The Mass of Thanksgiving had just ended," the man continues, speaking to a larger audience now. "I can almost see him. If I stretched my arm, I could have touched him. He was wearing a white T-shirt with a yellow button this big. A Cory button. His jacket sleeves were tied about his waist. I was this close to him when the trucks came to bring people there to the Batasan and when from the front, up in the buildings across, shots were fired."

"The Trust building," Vergel says. "The *Paris Match* correspondent quoted three witnesses."

A huge plastic container, as big as those on the carts of juice vendors in Manila, is being passed around. *Piso for Cory* is printed across it. Vergel drops a twenty. His friend peels off a hundred, while the other puts in two fifty-peso bills. In Kapalaran, collectors for Cory ask only for coins. Some cannot give even that.

"We already gave," one of the wives says, standing like a cover girl on a magazine, with legs apart. "We gave to Radio Veritas as well." Her face looks like a painted vase.

"Did you go to the turn-of-the-century carnival at the PICC? Do you like fashion shows?" the wives ask Olimpia. "There was a *Flores de Mayo* last December. The one crowned *La Bella Filipina,* what do you think of her?"

Olimpia can't guess at their opinions from their shrugs. Her feet hurt in the black step-ins she wore to Celso's funeral. She feels like throwing up, so she tries swallowing. The sky and the hills seem to be coming toward her in waves that will sweep her away. All she wants to do is lie down, clutch a pillow to her body as she does in Kapalaran when she feels this faint.

"Let's go see *The Delta Force* at the Ever," Vergel's friends are urging. "It's Chuck Norris and Lee Marvin. Come on. They won't finish the counting today."

"They'll take their time arguing and then they will count it any way they want. It's always that way when politicians work." An old man who has just arrived gives them his opinion. "They're mostly Marcos's men in there, greased with money; but if we stay here, there's a chance something different will happen this time. A chance for democracy. That's why I'm standing here when my knees tell me to go home."

"How does it hurt?" Vergel asks.

"The same. I have lived with it for longer than since you were born, *hijo.* Democracy is more important than my knees. My father saw President Aguinaldo and the delegates to the Malolos Constitution, many in dark suits, *de lana,* pass between the raised swords of soldiers to and from the sessions in 1898. The Convention met in the Church of Barasoain. To prove we were not ready to govern ourselves, my father said, the Americans took to Washington some Filipinos from the mountains wearing G-strings. Why not also those who framed the Malolos Constitution?"

Vergel and his friends look at one another.

"When I was young, long ago, and we were asked what we wanted to become, we answered: Rizal. Or some: Bonifacio. We wanted to save the country, too. Now, you ask the young and see what they'll say. They'll answer what they want to *have,* what they want to *do.* Abroad to tour Europe. A car. Credit cards. Instant money. They want a salary which will allow all that, preferably a salary which will not require them to work. That is the general run. But there are still those who want to become, maybe, Magsaysay or Quezon."

"*Lolo,* you should be inside to tell the assemblymen what duty demands of them," Vergel says.

"Not me. You young people do it. Tell the politicians to stop taking with one hand while the other makes a pledge to the flag, grabbing faster and faster, taking more and more. Let's see if the opposition will be better. I see politicians lining up for Communion, taking the Host, kneeling. Receive the Body of Christ and what do they join to that Body but the body of a prostitute, a political prostitute. Reconciliation means to them the toleration of one another's graft."

Vergel stands closer to him in case, in the intensity of his feelings, the old man breaks down and collapses. He seems to be by himself, wearing newly pressed clothes still smelling of the strong soap in which they have been laundered. Vergel guesses the old one's wife made sure he will not be embarrassed if he has to be brought to the hospital because of an accident or emergency. People in Kapalaran and Gulod are careful, the poorer they are, in such matters. Clean and mended, if not new, *calzoncillos.*

"Come later to the house then," Vergel's friends invite him. "We have a tape of the Hagler-Hearns fight. Three rounds is all it took the Marvelous One to batter his opponent into submission." One of the women says, "We're parked by the Asian Institute of Tourism. *Pakwan* and *galantina,* for the occasion. I serve capons only for fiestas."

"Maybe," Vergel says. "We'll see."

"Hagler fights Mugabi in Las Vegas. Let's fly there for the fight. Ten knockouts since 1980! Is it a deal? It's going to be Cory, Vergel. We'll celebrate in Las Vegas."

Vergel laughs. After they leave, he turns to Olimpia, holds her by the hand. "You are cold. Do you feel faint?"

"Just tired."

"Something refreshing to drink? Coke?" Vergel looks for the vendor carrying a basket of soft drinks.

"No." A sip is all she wants, and the children would enjoy the Coke more. The twenty Vergel dropped into the *Piso for Cory* could have bought four family-size Cokes. Or an apple. Or a Sunkist. Benhur said he'll buy them apples and oranges to take back to Kapalaran. *What else?* Benhur wanted to know. The children will not miss having food they have not tasted.

New ones arrive, squeezing into space. Reporters look for likely interviews.

A woman wearing slippers too small for her feet intercepts the reporter heading for Vergel. Before she can be shoved aside, she says, "I came because I want people to see what a poor woman looks like. I have nine children and we have nothing to eat. I want them to go to school, but we have no money. Since Saturday I have been here because I don't have money to keep coming here and going home. My life is hard."

Somewhat embarrassed the reporter looks about for someone with loftier reasons for being there.

The woman hangs on to the reporter's hand, repeats herself without crying. The heels of her feet are cracked. "I've tried everything. I sold *calamansi.* The police drove us from the sidewalk and confiscated my basket. I ended up poorer than I started. I . . ."

Vergel's hand tightens on Olimpia's shoulder.

"Every life is hard," says a woman whose children are eating sandwiches and drinking from matching plastic cups which a maid keeps refilled. "You take the children to Shoemart and they want everything they see. On a salary, that is hard."

"Too bad we can't eat grass," a man who is listening starts joking.

"That will drive up the price of *sacate* for the horses," another replies in the same vein.

"Why are you here?" the reporter has managed to break free of the woman and is asking the old man.

"To remind the assemblymen inside that they are responsible if Marcos, after the cheating witnessed by the whole world, wins. Marcos needs collaborators. He can't be a dictator all by himself. The Speaker who is presiding over the counting is the one who managed Marcos's campaign."

"Marcos is history. Eleven more computer programmers quit yesterday," a man presses close to the reporter. "And who is to be believed? The Government's Commission on Elections which has Marcos ahead 3,056,236 to Aquino's 2,903,348; or the NAMFREL, where Aquino has 6,499,817 and Marcos, only 5,785,348? That's why tanks are reported to have been moving into the Palace. Marcos knows he lost."

Short of collision, the Cory and the Marcos groups are rushing each other on the Batasan driveway. Someone comes out, complaining that the galleries are packed with government men. Only KBL is inside where the ballot boxes and regional tabulations are kept in the Speaker's office.

On a transistor radio *Onward Christian Soldiers* can be heard, merging with the *Our Father* prayed on the grounds in English and Pilipino.

A man who says he's employed at the University of Life in Pasig—founded by Imelda when the University of the Philippines refused her an honorary degree; in revenge she tried to entice faculty from the state university with salaries difficult to refuse—tries to get the reporter's attention by saying fake ballots were printed in the university basement. "Including the Ballot Protection Stickers, which were given to the opposition crowds who might not know that affixing one to a ballot invalidates it."

"Ingenious!" The old man shakes his head. "The Filipino can't be beat at the game of politics. Dirty politics."

Children collecting newspapers to sell are making paper balls from torn pages the way Olimpia remembers making them for her children. Anya's best friend Vangie could make paper birds. She joined the dissidents after vigilantes killed her father and brothers. One day the vigilantes serving the military began pulling down houses to force people to move into the towns. The huts of those who hesitated were set on fire with the embers on which they were cooking rice. Gasoline was poured into the huts, and Olimpia felt they were pouring it into the mouths of corpses. A woman who complained had her lips cut out, and it turned out that the radio reporter was reporting the death of his brother without realizing it.

Vergel had helped Celso bring the wounded to the regional hospital. When he first came to Kapalaran, Vergel wore Lacoste shirts and Calvin Klein pants, had a Rolex. In less than a year he was wearing local jeans and scuffed sneakers. Celso admired him because he did not, like some doctors, stay in Manila and let the barangay captain collect his salary in exchange for certifying that he was serving in the barrio. "Vergel is making a point," Celso said. Was that what Vergel was doing when he proposed to her after Celso was killed? Proving something with his decision?

Olimpia has not nursed Danilo Sebastian since early morning, and her breasts feel hard and heavy. She slumps inside her dress—it is beginning to stain in front—and brings her arms across her chest. She wonders how Patro is keeping Danilo from crying. He is not used to being away from her. She wonders if Anya should stay behind when they return to Kapalaran. Vangie has been asking Anya to visit her in their camp in the hills.

Another contingent with a certified list of their precinct voters brings the crowd to their feet, cheering: *Cry of the People—Protect Our Ballots.*

The police watch with their shields on the ground.

Nothing more happens until a limousine approaches. Instead of Senator Lugar or some international observers, it brings just another assemblyman who missed the night session.

People return to their newspapers and conversations. At the top corner of a page, Olimpia sees a picture of Lech Walesa. Olimpia looks up at the sky. Her mother said that when she saw the pigeons flying on the first Independence Day and the flag on a pole taller than a *molave,* she felt one soul was in all of them at Luneta.

Olimpia wonders how that feels; if she is the only one on the Batasan grounds unaware. All she hopes for is a sign that terrible things will not happen again; but how, when the air is bouncing like a paper ball?

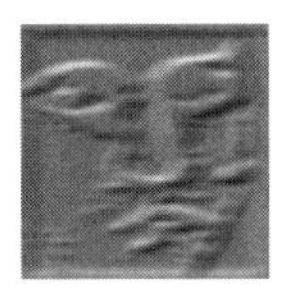

From the media assistance center,
where TV and radio news is monitored around the clock at the La Salle Dome in Greenhills, Miggy Moscoso snaps a picture of his brother Joel, yellow cloth binding his head, pieces of paper thrust into every pocket of his NAMFREL vest so it looks as if he's coming apart. The camaraderie inside the college gym—the executive and professional rank no higher as volunteers than the student, typist, or messenger—gives the impression of a barangay where people come together to celebrate or to mourn. Miggy captions the pictures he is snapping *Giant barangay in the sky,* because, in the light deflected by the sections of glass above the bleachers, the Dome appears to float.

Nuns in habits, former senators including Lorenzo Tañada, executive council members, volunteers in the message center calling out problems to the strike force, which in turn rushes to the site of the trouble, telephones ringing, the computers processing the returns from the 86,000 precincts—acts that make Miggy feel something is being purified by the simple tallying of votes on the tote boards for all to see; acts that are almost sacred.

The excitement of forcing incumbent President Ferdinand E. Marcos to concede on the strength of the NAMFREL count—the first certified reports began on election day Friday—causes outbursts of energy on the gym floor, where signs are directing the flow of activities, of lifeholding rituals. If they blow it, Miggy knows, it's back to Marcos and crony democracy. Back to heroes of the government.

In many ways, Miggy wishes his *Tito* Benhur were there. His father's friend never is one to look out for himself, so that seeing Benhur even briefly charges Miggy with a sense that everything good is possible, even for him. Miggy has a hard time being with himself, especially with others. He wants to be like Benhur, who will be with others only when he chooses. His father and Joel try to captivate everyone. The smallest issue excites them, as if it's the excitement itself that matters. While *he* is scared people will laugh at him, will become disenchanted and think him coarse if not timid, someone, in any case, whom they would not care to know. He thinks of himself as an unknown place.

There is Joel now, with delegates from the Center for Democracy Study Group. Miggy supposes they have also interviewed those in the Commission on Elections headquarters in Intramuros and the convention site. It just seems as if everything is up in the air. If Cory does not win, he might as well give up. Only fifteen in 1984, when NAMFREL monitored the election results for the assemblymen, Miggy already knew that social and political conscience does not equal good grades or a meaningful job. Taking sides has to be crucial to oneself and to the life of the country; like staying, instead of emigrating. A friend of his is collecting unemployment in Los Angeles, where he went on graduation from high school. The friend's father gave each son $60,000 to qualify for a trader's visa, no questions asked. The father has not talked to him and Joel beyond a greeting. *So what are you up to?* Their answer never merits a reply.

Emilio Luna is the other person Miggy respects, though Luna, who lives in Gulod, is so unpredictable he has walked past Miggy without looking at him. Mostly, Emilio Luna stays in the family home, which used to be merely a vacation cottage, though he has a degree from La Salle and a pilot's license. Miggy would love to know the reasons and causes, but there is no way of asking without showing undue interest. To rely on what neighbors and the maids say is to be captive to their imaginations.

Encounters with Emilio Luna are even briefer than with his *Tito* Benhur. Once, Emilio came to the house. He had just arrived from Iloilo, he said, pulling out a box of long, tapered cigarettes. *By boat to Guimaras.*

When or why was not explained. Emilio looked as if he had just come up from somewhere deep, had not had time to unbend. They sat under the trellis in the side yard, communicating in what might pass for a code but which, then, Miggy thought he understood. *Seven times a day they pray and sing. Four hours they work. The ground is hard.* Miggy looked at Emilio's hands, callused and red. Then Emilio ended the visit. *Is Brother Exequiel still there?* After that visit, occasionally he would see Emilio and his mother walking up the trail to the city.

Whenever Miggy starts to wonder about the whole range of desire, he thinks of Emilio Luna. Sometimes he would like to be someone who cannot be made to want anything, not even what he has, not even praise for humility or abstinence. Brother Quiel says: *Holy is to be out in the world where it suffers: to see things from where God stands. Though very few are holy, everyone God created is sacred.* Sometimes he understands why Emilio Luna would go to Guimaras. He himself has thought of going to a place where he can waste himself praying. It is radical and tempting. But does he go because he is needed? or because he needs? Sometimes he wants a life that is the equivalent of using the earth for the altar, nothing coming between; then, like a reflex, he frees himself from wanting to be broken for God, the way a drowning man perhaps attempts to rise for air.

Waiting for spectacles, the media hover about the gym, moving from those praying, to those in front of an assortment of personal computers on loan to NAMFREL. Electric fans add to the restlessness, radiating air from the command post.

Like a seismograph registering pressures, as though the terminals marked by provinces are lighting up inside him, Joel is everywhere; dodging chairs, tables, other volunteers, observers. Seeing Miggy, he signals: *Come.*

It is easy in the maddening crowd—800 foreign observers have been accredited and are taking leads from the message center of trouble spots where the power has been cut, or armed men have arrived to steal the elections—to slip out of Joel's sight. Miggy returns to the media assistance center to glean the news from TV and radio.

From there he can see the power-huddles on the gym floor. Joel appears always to be doing the whole work by himself. If any volunteer knows, Joel would know if there really are back-up systems to the Operation Quick Count, and if so, where they are. Two generators free the Dome from relying on the Meralco for electricity.

During the campaign and elections, it was Joel who got interviewed with his picture in the papers, though they were both mauled. Shirt torn, face bruised, Joel vowed on camera not to change his shirt until Cory and Doy were declared winners. Certainly not an original idea, since a professor of theirs vowed earlier not to have his beard cut until the killers of Climaco were caught and brought to justice. People say: *You can't be brothers.* He'd like to answer: *Ya. He's full of clenched fists in his veins. All I have is blood.*

He doesn't envy his brother, resents only the inequity in people's responses. Quick to learn, Joel has even been taken in by the group processing computer data in order to anticipate the government. He himself does not have the patience to learn the grids; would rather be in the strike force.

It was Joel who managed to get them out of the house while their mother watched Marcos being interviewed by Bryant Gumbel, claiming victory by 13 million votes; and Imelda thanking the people for their big win though hundreds of thousands of ballots had not yet been received from outlying precincts.

There is Joel, probably telling people about the Gumbel interview on tape or getting incensed again over the Saturday program on the government Maharlika station where J. V. Cruz mauled the NAMFREL executive council members with insults. Joel's walk is a dance as he helps anchor a camera, lifts wires out of the way of two men lugging a desk. His speaking is a kind of declaration. When he sings the national anthem or *Bayan Ko,* when he recites the *Ama Namin,* tears come naturally to Joel. Without stopping to think, Joel would donate his heart for a transplant. It's not arrogance, though Miggy would like to think so at times; nor indifference, nor even hostility to the self being sacrificed.

It's just that Joel attracts attention the way some trees in the forest are lightning rods while some are meant for railroad ties or conference tables. People love Joel to death.

It was Miggy who retrieved the voter list and tried to save the film when the goons tore the camera out of the volunteer's hand; but it was Joel who was asked to recount how it felt risking his life in order to record the cheating. And there is the girl in shorts hugging Joel. The one who is tall, as thin as a beam of light, with almost straight legs and pale narrow eyes that disappear even when she's not smiling, so that she looks like an abstraction, someone without fingerprints, who would burn without ashes. Blossom Guerrero is always checking to see who's looking at her.

He's coming! Cardinal Sin has just left his residence! The announcement mobilizes volunteers whose cheering bounces against the rafters, opening space. Smiles circle about like streamers. No one is indifferent to the Cardinal.

From time to time, people look toward the entrance while they run about on their chores. The nuns—dubbed by the media as *SWAT team against election fraud*—give the gym a strongly prophetic atmosphere, something biblical and ancestral, so that Miggy is reminded of Macling Dulag's protest against flooding the Kalinga tribal hills in order to electrify Clark and the multinational factories, the exclusive villages of Metro Manila. When asked to prove title to the land, Macling said: *Such arrogance—to speak of owning the land which will outlive us. Only the race owns the land, because it is the race which lives forever.*

A rush to kiss the Cardinal's ring sweeps Miggy from his thoughts, but keeps him where he stands. It is as if none of them has seen the Cardinal before; has never attended his Masses during the campaign. Pieces of paper, hats, are being thrust forward for autograph. The impact of the Cardinal's presence catches up with Miggy's feelings as the cheering mounts, almost drowning out the benediction.

Miggy thinks the Cardinal is looking straight at him, saying, "In you lies the Spirit. Many have died for our country. I ask you now to live for it. This is our Good Friday but Easter Sunday is coming. Stay and see the Resurrection . . ."

He is being asked to share in the work of truth, to become an instrument of justice, not of revenge but of reconciliation; to become that altar on the bare earth. During the other liturgies, the Thanksgiving Mass at Ugarte, at Luneta, his thoughts remained on the symbols. Now his mind picks up the blind beggars on P. Tuazon, the car windows being raised as they approach; the children carrying children with soiled lungs to beg at intersections where the passengers are likely to look away, determined not to be taken in by pity. Is he being asked to waste himself for these as his first love? How about Joel?

The Cardinal's blessings make Miggy feel he is part of the mystery which does not begin only to end; that all there is worth seeking is the mystery. He thinks of the nine young men of Cauayan who went off to vote in the 1984 elections and whose bodies were brought back lifeless to their town, which, unable to protest their deaths, hung swatches of black cloth at their windows, recalling how, when they heard the distant sound of gunfire in the afternoon, they already knew the men had been killed by the military. Miggy thinks of the bodies found hogtied with barbed wire in the river back in Gulod, the deaths justifying Marcos's secret marshals empowered to shoot at will and on sight. He understands Macling to mean the people, not their leaders, when he uses the word "sovereign." The people nourish the future with their sacrifices.

While Miggy's thoughts replay what the Cardinal has said, is saying, someone comes to bend over the Cardinal, who turns to those gathered in the gym for the citizens' count of the ballots. "An hour before noon in Antique, masked gunmen in two jeeps cut off Evelio Javier, opposition leader and former governor as he was coming out of the capitol in San Jose de Buenavista, forced him into the square, firing M-16s . . ."

So quickly coming upon the Cardinal's benediction, the message sharpens the silence that meets it; that gives way to cries. The former governor is only forty-three.

Trying not to think perversely out of anger, or to disown himself out of fear, Miggy holds on to what, moments ago, he had almost perfectly understood even as he recoils from the anguish spreading in the gymnasium; even as he thinks of his own anguish one morning years ago, when he came upon the maid in the kitchen plucking a circle of feathers from a chicken's neck, then tapping it with the flat of a knife to make it throb and pulse. Her feet on its struggling wings, she neatly made her cut, guiding the blood to fill the white plate underneath.

"Evelio is safe now," the Cardinal is saying, hands raised in blessing. "Trust. God is with us and with Evelio."

A short while back, Miggy felt something timeless had begun; but now, as though the earth has swallowed itself, the words bring him shattered illusions and disconnected realities which hold time savagely upon that white plate.

Whether wearing a tuxedo
—of which he has two—or a monogrammed shirt, or a *barong* embroidered in front and at the cuffs, Osong Moscoso still looks like someone whose highest ambition is to trip on some peanuts or watermelon left unharvested in the fields. It's the feverish look, the pitch in the voice that betrays his anxiety—the worry of vendors trying to sell out before all the fish turn limp—that makes Osong look negligible, no matter how he swaggers or poses.

He is posing again as he leads Benhur to his office, on the way demanding that the secretaries all look for the tickets he has misplaced. "To Morris Cerullo at the Araneta Coliseum. Right away." Not until everyone has gone into the motions of searching does Osong enter his office and close the door. "Time to get new secretaries. Or else get a change of uniforms for them. Pink and maroon is positively deadening, like attending a wake. What do you think of pink and green? Preppie!"

It doesn't excite Benhur.

"Sit down somewhere. It will be some time before they find anything out there. The tickets can be right in front, against their face . . . I might have them in the car. But let them look so they'll have something to do. They're Ting Dolor's. She might have them, too. It was her idea to go because it's Lent. Did you get your ashes?"

"What?"

"Ash Wednesday, Brod." Osong points to the smudge on his forehead.

"You went to church?"

"Ting went to church. She's very pious, you know, *Manang,* but you would not guess it."

"And how did you get the ashes?"

"She rubbed against me. Sweet, ha? And she wants to see this American prophet, this man of God, Morris. Do me a favor and take her."

"You're going somewhere else?"

"She asked for you to escort her."

"Actually asked? By name?"

"She said for me to ask a friend if I could not go. You're the only friend I have, as far as that goes. Real friend. We've known each other half our lives and more." Osong settles in the swivel chair. "There's a poster somewhere. Maybe in the car. She really wants to go and I can't."

"What besides ashes is she after?"

"Just healing, Brod. Evangelical stuff, which Catholics don't do as well. Charisma, not just religious faith. It's religion with pizzaz. Try it."

"What kind of healing?" Benhur asks but does not press for an answer. He watches Osong toying with a new lighter as if conducting a stress test for the manufacturer. Why doesn't he insist on knowing? It's an attitude that concedes to charlatans the whole field, allows appearance to be separated from being.

"Look." Osong raises the lighter. As he flicks it, the fully unclothed body of a woman glows inside the glass case. "Try it?"

"I've given up smoking." Marcos started encouraging the fundamentalists and evangelicals after a 1969 Rockefeller Report suggested that conservative Protestant sects were more trustworthy allies of the United States in the Philippines because the Catholic Church had begun to withdraw its support of Marcos.

"Did I show you the other lighter I had at the Rotary meeting in January? You were there at Manila Hotel."

He heard the 2,000 Rotarians cheering Cory. And at the Makati Chamber of Commerce meeting, when Cory pledged herself *to flush out the putrid stables of bureaucratic corruption and cronyism and to retrieve the money stashed abroad by thievery.* "So your Boss accepted your explanation you were attending to see what the opposition is up to?"

"Next question." Osong flicks the lighter a last time.

"I'm going."

"Good. Ting Dolor will be pleased. I'll call her."

"Going as in leaving, right now; not taking Ting Dolor to attend a healing." Benhur, however, continues to sit down. "Why not take her yourself?"

"I've explained it to you." A trace of annoyance slurs Osong's words. His face swells into a sulk as color spreads across his cheeks, having realized he has placed himself between the limits of Benhur's friendship and that of Ting Dolor. Benhur is capable of cutting his own lifeline, but not yet. Someday he will be brought to his knees. Osong would give next to his life to witness that. *Gumapang lang si Benhur.*

Benhur recognizes Osong's ungovernable-child act. If he leaves, there will be long recriminations on the phone followed by *mea culpas* and offers to make amends, and then a return to the original demand. Waiting to see how soon this will happen, Benhur faces the Renoir nude, framed back-to-back with the print he suggested Osong get from Harvard Coop: an Ernst print of a yellow bird across a red sky stratified like a hill. It turned out that the nude offended no one, so it has faced out since being hung, drawing out guarded libidos into unbelievable confessions that Osong forgets to tape. So the Ernst faces the wall.

"Well, she can hire an escort," Osong says, laying the tickets on the desk within Benhur's reach. "Look what I found!"

"Good." Benhur gets up, not wishing to go into the escort business. Osong has told him that Ting Dolor's mother has a permanent escort, a young man who earns more than lawyers by partnering widows to dances, theaters, overnights. This particular young man used to be a dance instructor. Ballroom dancing. Ting's brother challenged the escort to a duel, shot him in the foot; so the mother took the escort to Europe, to a specialist.

"Brod. Sally is related to Cory through Ninoy. So, no matter who wins, we can still attend those conferences. Do you remember the cylinders and tubes that were guaranteed not to leak? I wonder where the catalogue is."

Benhur walks to the door, recognizing Osong's attempt to get him interested enough to stay. Yes, he remembers Osong planned to send sample penis implants to the classmates. *Pasalubong.* In plain brown paper. The plan dwindled to just a Xerox copy of the page from the catalogue, to go inside the Christmas card. Even that didn't materialize. The old *ningas cogon* mentality. Short-lived enthusiasm.

"You must have the catalogue, Brod." Osong plays with the lighter. "Prosthetic penises. That was the platinum edition we read about while having won ton soup at Young Yee on Church Street."

"Good-bye."

"Wait, Brod. I'll sign these papers later. Let me see. Car keys. What's that?"

"Keys to the red car. I just turned them in."

"Take it back. It's for you. I'm asking at Customs about one of those impounded Mercedes that arrived last week. I don't need the red car." He drops the keys into Benhur's willing hand. Then he glances at the tickets to Morris Cerullo. *Share God with 200,000.* He decides not to pressure Benhur directly.

On their way out, Benhur pulls at the newspaper on the secretary's desk. "By the way, Evelio Javier was shot. You must have heard."

"I did. I meant to tell you. Wasn't he in Cambridge, too, when we had those long lunches at the Faculty Club with Ninoy? I wasn't very clear what Evelio was really angry about."

"We called him Evi. He was angry about institutional poverty, institutional corruption. Same faultline for both. I wrote that in a speech for you. Greed is the common faultline for poverty and corruption. Another's greed; one's own."

"You did?"

"We talked about Ninoy mobilizing grassroots support, remember? The young no longer knew who Ninoy Aquino was. That was three years ago." He looks about while Osong signs a pile of papers.

"Those lunches. Curried chicken salad in a croissant. I got the leather globe in the luggage shop. And we discussed Bailey's against Brigham's chocolates. It seems just yesterday. I wonder if Sally got the chocolates for the boys."

Benhur does not mention having seen the box of chocolates among the crystals in Sally's house. Nor the old Pinoy whose photograph was captioned: *Killed 500 Germans single-handed.* That was on another trip. Eighty-year-old veteran, Philippine Scout, sitting at an angle in the picture; as if he had been slid into the chair, his shoes pointed out in perfect parallel. War decorations on his formal suit, vested, outer coat folded over an arm. A cane. Side-by-side, a picture of his landlord. 350 bulging pounds, who claimed the old Pinoy had threatened to kill him. Arrested for having an arsenal of World War II weapons in his apartment, the old Pinoy looked even punier in the picture shot from a height. A relic photograph, the kind one sent home after years of silence, signed in fine handwriting on the back: *Recuerdo. The Original.*

At the trial it was brought out that the guns all had welded barrels.

"We were two hotshots in Cambridge!" Osong tells his secretary. "We gave some Cliffies some truly memorable Third World Experience, didn't we, Brod? And I'll never forget those implants. What a choice! Plastic or bone, rigid or semi. Activate on demand. Erector sets. There, all signed. I hope I didn't sign my name to something illegal. But Benhur will take care of that."

"The papers in the IN basket signed too, Sir?"

"Find out." Osong pockets his pen with his name inscribed in gold. "Come, Benhur, before I get ambushed with more work. Wasn't the problem that the implantation required a urologist?"

Benhur is walking ahead by three desks.

Osong pulls Benhur's arm. "I'll go over and ask her a question. Tell me what you think. The clerk with red-rimmed glasses. She and I had a long lunch and afterwards. Afterwards!"

Benhur quickens his steps. He knows those businessmen's lunches where young girls, who start out unable to look the clientele in the eye, learn to toss their heads while they model different states of nudity. Some graduation. One explained the money is for the removal of a mole in the path of her tears. *A bad omen, Sir. If I don't have the operation, I'll become a dolorosa.*

"What do you say?" Osong overtakes Benhur through the outer door, his whisper getting loud. "She called me *sir* throughout. *It hurts, sir.* Clinging to the covers. Lovely skin, thin as onion, as if the light is coming from within. She'll turn heads at Harvard Square, Brod. And so tight. Unbelievably tight!"

Benhur says nothing. Without looking, he knows a blush stains her face, the imprint of another kind of ashes. Wishing he did not need, wishing he could give up the consultancies from Osong, Benhur knows he and she both crawl. He does it standing up.

By the time they get to the curb, the righteousness is gone. Were it not for that Tuesday morning in Constitutional Law and the failures it dictated, Osong's conquests, beside his, would be nothing but a pitiful heap; playing with paper dolls. But is that life, or death? He lets Osong into the passenger side of the red car. "Where to?"

Waiting for the PAL flight to Bacolod, Benhur and Vergel stand together in the Domestic Airport, looking in separate directions. They have run out of conversation long before the flight is ready for boarding and are just repeating themselves. At two o'clock the heat stifles.

Off to the side, Danilo Sebastian sits on Olimpia's lap clenching and unclenching a fist with such seriousness, his face has become as tight as the hand. Patro taught him the handplay. Male and female, every infant in the country is probably taught that motion to the chant of *arimundin-mundin:* words whose meanings have escaped but the sounds still work their spell.

The rhyme brings back to Benhur the story their *Lola* Sula used to tell about a very young girl who begged to be taught how to pray the rosary, until, to silence her, and knowing it impossible to teach her the long prayers, her grandmother told her to say *kwintas, kwintas, magkabila'y butas* for each bead; and the girl prayed so intently that God listened to her heart.

"How did you find *Lola* Sula?" Benhur stares down the runway, thinking of subjects that can be explained.

"I did not want to frighten *Nanay* and Loreto, since nothing can really be done; but *Lola* Sula suffers tiny strokes while she sits in her doorway. She wakes from each with less memory than before, less strength, though not enough loss to be noticed. She will go quietly, I think; each day a little less of herself. See her as often as you can, and encourage Loreto. Though she will not always act happy to see you, she is happy to be visited."

Benhur resents the suggestion, as if it's a slur on his concern for the family. He almost asks: *When will you take over?* At close to thirty-nine, Vergel wastes his opportunities in an out-of-the-way town, when he might instead charge the limit for his surgical skills in Metro Manila. Early in his pre-med days, Vergel used to say he would become a plastic surgeon to soak the rich and vain. *There are plastic surgeons in heaven,* Benhur wants to say. Benhur recalls giving Vergel his favorite shirts which, he found out during this visit, Vergel gave away in Kapalaran. Osong might be crazy, but Osong always brought him something; Vergel, not even something without any value.

"Proust describes this preparation for dying," Vergel continues. "In *Remembrance of Things Past,* which I read, do you remember the volumes I asked you to get me the first time you went abroad? *There is something about the renunciation forced upon us by the gradual, steady diminution of strength when every effort is tiring if not painful.* Not exact quote. *It gives to inaction, isolation and silence the blessed strengthening and refreshing charm of repose.* I would prefer a more vivid word than *charm,* but that is how it is exactly; unless we die suddenly, violently. I left her some medicines, but I know she will only hide them."

"With her Japanese Mickey Mouse money! In case they are redeemed in the future." Benhur is impressed with the sensitivity of Vergel's diagnosis, like a gentle anointing; and he is sorry about his earlier sentiments against his brother. It's envy he blames, envy and helplessness about having to take Ting Dolor to Morris Cerullo. The bright side is that Osong must have another life interest, as he calls it; another lady playing commissioner to the Commissioner: demanding commissions for her intercessions. Ting Dolor will not miss that part of the relationship. She is connected with so many charities that she can't keep track of the checks sent directly to her, payable to her order, by friends and mostly acquaintances who want to impress her with their trust. "What can I send?"

"I'll let you know," Vergel replies. "Maybe you can send the sample medicines that some of my classmates promised. And those from the medical missionaries, the Sons of Mary in Leveriza. Simple relief like aspirin is beyond the means of many. Imagine, aspirin!"

Benhur wishes they had more time to talk about these things. During the visit in Gulod there was always somebody else to entertain, morning to midnight, and no chance to talk about themselves—what they wished for themselves and each other, for *Lola* Sula, their mother and Loreto. But the flight is being called. Benhur puts an arm about Rosalio who does not want to be left behind; takes the handcarry from Vergel.

Awkward with affection, the brothers give each other a full *abrazo*. Benhur kisses Danilo Sebastian on the cheek, presses his face against Olimpia's, avoiding eye contact.

"Come back soon." Already Benhur misses Vergel.

"Come visit us. Any time."

Benhur waves, his hand as clenched as the fist Danilo Sebastian holds to his face as they walk to the plane.

As the Philippine Airline heads for the runway like a water bird on land, a Beechcraft is landing. Benhur watches it taxi toward the terminal after the Bacolod flight lifts off.

The wingtips make Benhur think of the *gurions* their father made for them, large kites from rice paper and bamboo strips flying across the river in Gulod, sailing above the trees and just below the clouds. From all around, spectators hurried to watch. He wonders if Vergel remembers.

With this thought, Benhur turns to leave, and he catches sight of a white hearse heading toward the Beechcraft. Red letters on the white streamer across the vehicle announce: *Evelio Javier.* A small crowd surges forward after the light plane comes to a stop.

The coincidence of being at the Domestic Airport when Evelio Javier's body arrives takes Benhur back to the afternoon he and Evi walked by the Old Burial Ground on Church and Garden in Cambridge, Massachusetts. Evi was saying that the kind of life he wanted for his sons and himself he also wanted for the people of Antique. He was not thinking of them as constituents, voters on whose cheers he could ego-trip. Evi is the only authentic hero he can call to mind. Even the opposition leaders who are beginning to come home are thinking now of Mercedes Benzes, of residing in the exclusive villages or new subdivisions south of Manila, where houses worth several millions are being built on 500 square meters. Evi did not have such possible dreams, which eventually pervert democracy.

With no intention to follow the hearse, Benhur gives right of way to a truck bearing more mourners. Another streamer, also white, announces: *Evelio, We Are Proud Of You.* In the surveyor's office next to his, Benhur had seen the film clip from Clark Air Base of the Mass and the funeral cortege to the Antique airport. When he can, he falls in line. Out of the driveway the hearse plays Evi's theme song, the song he had hummed in Cambridge days: *The Impossible Dream.*

Benhur wishes for stronger feelings to accompany the occasion, without working himself into despair or hate. That would be most unlike the Evi he met in Cambridge, and knew.

Along the way to the wake at the Redemptorist Church in Baclaran, men take off their hats. A loudspeaker on a jeep declares continuously: *This is the body of the former Governor Evelio Javier, killed without mercy under the rule of President Marcos.* As in a film clip people are weeping. Bystanders flash the Laban sign, forming an L with thumb and forefinger.

Benhur recalls a news report: *Once the killers cross the river, the crime will be forgotten. Nothing will be done. There have been many dead bodies around here.* Rodrigo Ponce, a farmer from Capiz with three children, was killed because he recognized those who snatched the ballots. Evelio Javier campaigned for Cory and Doy. A woman and three armed men appeared in the Mambusao elementary school, where Ponce was assigned, to "borrow" the ballots, which they wrapped in a Philippine flag they had taken from another school. Hooded men gunned down Evelio Javier with high-powered rifles . . .

On foot and by car, mourners join the lines of the 500 who started from the airport accompanied by foreign correspondents. Evelio's coffin is draped with the flag, flanked by calla lilies and white daisies. Benhur keeps right behind the truck as the mourners swell to four lines on the road to Baclaran. When it turns, Benhur sees on the passenger side of the cab, in white letters on black, the word: *Utopia.* Below it is a white square lined in black, and inside is a bird, wings boxed into the upper corners. Painted struggling. Benhur wonders if the logo will be rendered true. For whom?

Coincidence or predetermined? Logo and the words of a song written for the revolution against Spain prefiguring each other.

Benhur slows down to allow people to fall in line with the cortege. Preceded by the sun in its long descent, they arrive chanting in Baclaran: *Ibon mang may layang lumipad.* He restrains himself from weeping.

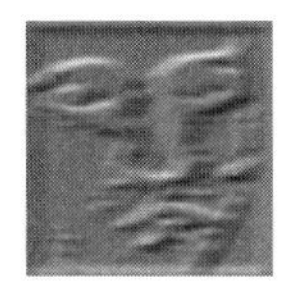

Anger that can usurp the radiant dance of stars brings Benhur to the soccer field of Ateneo de Manila, the first Friday in Lent, for the funeral Mass of Evelio Javier. The anger is from falling asleep during the wake in the Redemptorist church at Baclaran and, now, for bringing a small wreath in the shape of a cross; the same kind he brought for his father years ago when all he had in his wallet was bus fare.

Stopped by traffic in front of the shops selling wreaths on Magdalena Street where his parents used to live, on impulse he called over the shopkeeper to ask about the cross of white calla lilies. Though he did not haggle, the owner came out to blame the price on politics. *Kasama sa pulitika yan, Boss.*

His mind on the skimpy offering, Benhur takes the first chance to divest himself of the wreath. The crowd gathering for the evening Mass does not pay him attention. Their interest is on whoever of importance is coming. Freed to concentrate on Evelio Javier's death, Benhur soon enough begins wondering what else, besides still another dead body, a sacrificial altar needs. Surely God has a glut of corpses.

Not wishing to be provoked into more questions that only tease the mind without guaranteeing survival; nonetheless, with sustained clarity, he wants to know the answers. The question moves through his thoughts the way, in the chapel without walls in Gulod, birds fly in and out singing. He came there once while a little girl was being waked. Children were standing around the box in which she lay while sunlight played on the tip of the candle being saved for the day of her funeral.

He superimposes other images upon that memory: the glass flowers in the Agassiz; the medieval chapels moved, stone by stone, from churches in Europe and set up again in the museums at Worcester and in the Isabella Stewart Gardner. But Bacon's engorged bodies hanging on hooks intercept his thoughts, refuse to give way to the Henry Moore reclining in Harvard Yard, where he and Evi once stood, intrigued by the way emptiness took shape within the statues, entering and leaving through the same buried interior space as the sunlight. That was when Evi said he had decided to return, to run for assemblyman in the 1984 elections. Evi's protest of that election is now moot, Benhur thinks. How is he to be declared winner, now that he has joined the seven who were killed on the bridge at Sibalom for campaigning for him, as he in turn has been killed for campaigning for Cory?

People are pushing at the line. Benhur decides to step out. If he could not give Evi a good answer in the Yard, what can he do now for his blood-soaked body by paying respects twice? He's not a politician who keeps on recycling promises, recycling hopes in order to multiply photo opportunities. He writes position papers, reorganizes corporations, pens briefs and resolutions: words that have never stopped bullets. Or fired them. Words that only release anger, might even falsify, betray, lull. What else can anyone do in the presence of a power machine capable of grinding down mountains?

But politics goes on. At the funeral Mass it is the politics of mourning. Around the widow, Precious, are some whose motives are entirely unconnected with grief. Dabbing her eyes, there is Ting Dolor with a pin of rubies shaped in a heart upon her white dress, working the mourners in the pews she passes. That skull of a face sickens Benhur. The lively sadness repels him. She tried to liven up a party once by saying *vivace* that her doctor had informed her the size of a woman's mouth is the exact size of her vagina. He looks away from the lipstick bleeding on her lips, and leaves before the Catholic Bishops' Conference message for that Valentine's

Day: *Massive fraud has destroyed the legitimacy of the Marcos government.* It has taken Evelio's death to nail that.

Only on Friday past were the snap elections held.

Inside the red car, Benhur pushes back into a pile the newspapers on the passenger's seat, jumbling pictures of Joan Collins of *Dynasty,* which Osong follows avidly, having them taped in L.A. and flown in by PAL, Philippine Airlines; of Duvalier, Liberia has joined Spain and Switzerland in refusing him asylum; of Lech Walesa, on trial in Poland. There is an announcement of the Marlboro Mabuhay International Alcohol Motor Rally; of the Body Building Championship in Iloilo. And the *Pakikiramay* Fund of the *Manila Times* now totals P33,791.

It occurs to Benhur as he backs up that he could be nurturing his soul with all his anguish over the situation, only to end up bartering it for a condo or a gold credit card. If the gates of heaven are everywhere, there could be a mall of shops by the entrance. One day, vaguely thinking, he could head for one instead of the other. There is something to commend value-free living: one pays no attention to such as Aristotle's saying politics is for the good of man and his city; of his soul.

Entering the side gate of the Ateneo campus, he slows down for students entering on foot with banners. Nothing they can do with their lives can cancel the significance of their feelings now; while nothing he can do with his can condone his having done nothing to stop martial law. But any country can use only a handful of heroes. Planned scarcity makes gold and diamonds valuable.

Whistling himself into cheerfulness—the guards' snappy salute fires his confidence—Benhur decides to drive through the University of the Philippines campus. He even looks up at the Malcolm building, humming the Alma Mater song.

It connects him to the Oblation in front of the Administration. Between this statue and the lagoon, now overgrown with what appear to be scrub trees, graduation and Cadena de Amor ceremonies take place: the country symbolically held together by a chain of love.

Tolentino's sculpture of Filipino youth offering itself to the country looks disinterred. It cannot have happened that, one long-ago evening, Osong climbed up that statue and, throwing down the camera for him to catch, commanded: *Quick, shoot before I fall down.* Benhur stands there awhile, like someone awaiting betrayal, thinking of deaths: and of heroes known only to God.

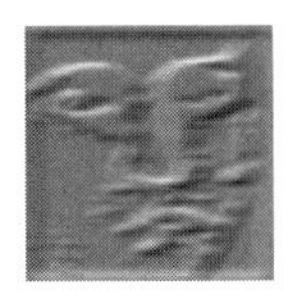

Unable even in parody
to climb the Oblation, Benhur nevertheless gets a message from the outstretched body, at once corpse and newly born: he will emigrate to get his degree in Boston, to handle immigration and naturalization cases in New York or California; or in Manila, gag on his pride and take courses side by side with . . . the children of classmates, compete with them in the Bar. Either way he faces tough, life-consuming forces.

The difference between himself and Evelio Javier, Benhur considers as he leaves the campus, is that he has no clear sense of who he is. At least he's not a mercenary. When he writes speeches and proposals, it's not strictly for the money but for a sense of rightness. Not exactly on the level of those artists who, through the ages, have created masterpieces to adorn churches: unsigned pieces mostly, fine gifts in praise and gratitude for giftedness.

He must have missed out when giftedness was being distributed. He can think of no particular talent that distinguishes him. His life the gift? the message? He should not have torn up that picture showing himself at age one with a pacifier in his mouth. It could have been his passport picture. Bit in his mouth. Part of the rein Osong grips in his hand.

His mother's simple wish deceives him into thinking himself wonderful. All she wants is for him to get married and have sons. So gentle a wish. His own? His name on the door: Attorney, Assemblyman,

Minister—steps on a ladder he could have climbed to the top by now, except for Tuesday morning in Constitutional Law.

Like reflecting mirrors, Benhur's recriminations run on as he approaches Taft on United Nations, formerly Isaac Peral.

"*Mamà.* Six for five pesos. So I can go home." A small boy thrusts five *sampaguita* garlands through the open window. *"Sigue na, Mamà. Makauwi lang ako."*

Benhur does not believe that's all that's left. The boy's friend is probably hanging on to the rest of the flowers, or the boy himself might have hidden the rest in the gutter somewhere to freshen the buds. But he thrusts out five pesos, the same way he buys the newspapers that hawkers bring to his car window, choosing the most ragged children who disrupt his dreams. He buys gum, too; small oranges in plastic bags, *suman,* every manner of wares as he also gives alms: though the government says there are no beggars. When he has an assortment, he goes home to Gulod and unloads.

Hanging from the rearview mirror, the *sampaguita* with its *ylang-ylang* pendants partially obstructs the windshield. The flowers catch the headlights and street lights, distracting Benhur from the headlines of newspapers being held up to the passing cars by very young vendors. *Extra precincts discovered in Ilocos.* It fails to compete with the ongoing news in Benhur's brain: Tuesday morning in Constitutional Law, around which his hours orbit. Like bile it poisons his memory until failure has become part of his genetic component, something to pass on along with his name.

Seeing the Court of Appeals up ahead, another irony of his life occurs to Benhur. He works and lives down the street from institutions in which he cannot practise. An old term for lawyers was *practicante.* He should be able to slip that information into a speech. Slim part of history, but worth preserving.

Benhur parks where the security guard of his building sees the car, brings out the newspapers. *Philip Habib is being sent by Reagan to assess the totality of the Philippine situation.* Another photo opportunity.

At the corner are some tribal people from the Cordillera region resting in a circle where they might have earlier danced to the beat of cooking pans. He looks away. If he emigrates, he will probably continue to interrogate his soul. Interrogating and hanging himself with pity. It does no one any good. The whole country is to be pitied. *Habib: Japanese aid.* Now it's Tokyo calling. It used to be Washington. The response from the Filipino is what Juan de la Cruz gave to the Spaniards: *Pag-utusan po ninyo.* Command me. The unsovereign self.

"Attorney." The security guard greets Benhur, rifle strap over his right shoulder, name tag over a pocket: S. Enriquez. "An American was looking for you."

"Shoeshine, Sir?" The bootblack leans away from the wall.

With the newsprint rubbing off onto his shirt sleeve, Benhur takes the stairs running. No one is outside his door or sitting in the highbacked chair below the painting of a house and garden separated by a wall of trees. He has never liked that painting. Sadness pours out from the sun; the green is faded; the flowers are averted from the light. But the son of the building's owner painted it with all his nightmares in place.

The American is not in front of Rafols's door. Maybe he is inside the surveyor's office. But suppose the American is an interviewer? a correspondent? Terence Hugg, with whom he has split a case of beer, who likes asking questions immune to facts at the end of the day: *What's it worth to you to keep on breathing? to look for daylight in the morning?*

That won't bring brilliant colors to the painting on the wall, Benhur thinks, fitting the key to the lock.

"What office hours you keep, Vitaliano!" It *is* Terence Hugg sitting at the desk. "Thought you're never coming. No secretary. No answering machine. You must specialize in secret transactions."

Displeased with Hugg's offhand usurpation, Benhur throws the newspapers at a chair. "I personally screen all appointments. What can I do for you?"

"Sorry about the old credit card trick. I unlock only friends' doors to avoid lawsuits. I came to ask you to dinner and drinks. On the house."

"There's a bottle somewhere here. No need to treat me."

"I want to. Down the street, then dinner. A glass each is all that's left in your bottle. I found it, looking for a pad." Hugg reaches for the phone as soon as it rings. "Sorry. It's for me. I gave your number. About something I need checked out . . . Hello. Yes. Hugg here. Yah. Yah. I suspected. Terrific. What a scoop, God Almighty. Anything else? This will do for now. Thanks, *amigo*. . . . Where were we?"

Benhur glances at the newspapers. The *Manila Times* headline: *Cory sees Marcos-U.S. Conspiracy.* Thursday's guiding rate for the peso is 20 to 1. Dinner should not cost Hugg that much. But steak has become too rich for his stomach. It makes him ill just watching patrons enjoying it.

"Here's your desk back, Vitaliano. Nothing touched but the phone, and all the overseas calls were collect. What do you say we go now?" Hugg continues to sit in the swivel chair. "If I get time off as I requested, I'd like to write about holy politics here. Might even be able to retire sooner than I expect or end up with a desk bureau, but that's not my style. Here's my card. U.S. address." Hugg tidies up, replaces objects he has moved on the desk, gets up, pushes the chair close to the desk. "Let's go."

"Don't forget that envelope."

"That's yours, Vitaliano. No strings."

"I don't sell information." Benhur stiffens.

"Information? Nothing! It's a going-away present. Just some loose cash. Let's say it's for the lift you gave me when the taxi stalled on Pedro Gil, Herran. Since you keep giving the former names of streets, I recall what they're no longer called. Good thing it's not street-to-street fighting I'm covering."

"That's bullshit."

"Actually, you might run into a couple of confirmations I can't seem to get. They're noted inside. If you don't, no sweat. Besides being free and clear, it's not all that much, Vitaliano."

"I'll take a raincheck."

"News is all played out in Manila so I won't be around much longer. I'll be at the usual. When I move out, I'll call." Hugg frees his hand from his side pocket, extends a handshake. "For old times' sake, Vitaliano. A few laughs and a drink. How about the Hilton, the other direction? Or Max Fried Chicken next block? No. Let's check out the Hilton."

From the window, Benhur watches Hugg cross, flag down a taxi. Why didn't he think fast enough, throw the envelope into Hugg's hand with the repartee: *Is this my seven dollars at the present rate of exchange?* At the turn of the century, Uncle Sam paid the Queen of Spain $20 million for the Philippines. Population: 3 million. Birds, cattle, and fish thrown in free.

He was too tired to bring this up from history. Too tired even to go for the rum and coke in the mini-refrigerator.

Where Hugg took the taxi, a man is now standing, a home-made bed unsold on his back. Who in that fleshpot of the city will buy a bed with the splinters still in the wood? Better to peddle a basket of broken dishes at Plaza Ferguson in front of the United States Embassy, because demonstrators are always running out of stones.

He goes for the rum and coke, stops at his desk. How much can such an envelope hold? Depends of course on the denomination. And whether in pesos or dollars. Just curious, not interested. Is Terence Hugg actually CIA? Or one of those the United States Embassy fields whenever a crisis develops? The possibilities play in Benhur's brain like light passing through a prism.

He spins the envelope about, tips it over on end. Nothing written on either side. Maybe Hugg also dusted off his fingerprints. What if he had brought Hugg to Gulod, introduced him to Loreto who collects shells and small glass animals for the light to pass through on her window sill? Loreto will not even meet his classmates. They're too educated for her, she insists.

Shocked at how quickly he has been tempted by the envelope, Benhur pulls out the PAL playing cards from the side drawer. Time to play pretend: Hugg did not leave that envelope.

He deals a solitaire across the blotting paper marked Harvard, another purchase from the Coop. Did Hugg notice it? Should he have put a sign at his door: *Not for sale. CIA, KGB need not try?* Why not? There can't be many immune to greed. There are all those ideologues who have green cards, or who preach revolution then go off to Canada or Europe to collect contributions. Part-time activists; full-time self-promoters.

Maybe Hugg thinks he's with those for dismantling the bases—he admitted he did not vote, and the Communists boycotted the elections. It seems a month ago at least, but just the other week really. *Time gallops for the old,* his *Lola* Sula says, *death hurries me.* Time and dying.

Benhur Vitaliano, card-carrying Communist! Ideologies have never attracted him. Right-wing, left-wing. They're part of the truth, not the whole truth. The crux is whether one uses ideology to further one's self-interest. The Soviets have privileged classes. America has its homeless—bag people wearing all their clothes, possessions in bags and sleeping in the streets over the grates in the winter, in the parks in the summer.

Self-interest. His ground of orientation. His lack of it is the only thing that saves him. He's uncomfortable with anyone looking for his own advantage. *Panay kabig na lang.* Patriotic slogans and piety can disguise self-seeking, self-anointing.

A radio down on Orosa is playing "Bayan Ko," first sung when American sharpshooters of the 1899 war aimed their bullets exactly where the *revolucionarios* would run into them. He pushes the envelope to make way for the aces. Now America is aiming dollars. Money is extremely hazardous to morals.

Benhur scoops up the cards into a pile, sorts them, shuffles. The most solitaires he has had were five in a row. Once he starts, he plays until the numbers start popping up at him, until his brain snaps like the burned-out filament inside incandescent bulbs. After dark he plays by the street lamp outside the window so no one will suspect he sleeps in his office. He plays until an idea too significant not to write down flashes through his brain cells. Less and less now that happens. All that the playing gives him now are fused fingers, a wracked back, and nausea.

Why didn't he tell Hugg to stop meddling? It was Hugg who said the United States Embassy had recommended the press relations firm that handles Cory's image in the U.S. *The nominal fee was waived, about a quarter of a million. You're not just whistling Dixie when it comes to press relations.* And, almost as if the Philippine elections were being held in the States, a conservative Republican firm handles Marcos. Are those firms pledged to tell the truth and nothing but?

Maybe he should open the envelope just to see if a short-wave radio goes with the assignment, with which to report directly to the political counselor in the Embassy. Maybe he'll find out he's only being instructed to watch for Halley's comet, to count its tails. Talk about eternity and infinity! That same comet was seen by Isaac Newton and by Julius Caesar, no less. The hand about to dip into the national treasury might stop to think about that.

He scans the envelope from a distance of arm's length, turning up the cards and dealing them out abstractedly. Maybe what Hugg wants confirmed is the rumor Marcos is dying, that a kidney specialist *balikbayan* from the States was killed to keep him silent about the secret operation performed either aboard the presidential yacht or in the Palace itself. Or if there is going to be another impeachment try against Marcos. Or who divided up the multi-million-dollar rescue package. Even the monopoly on matches can finance a presidential ambition.

Maybe the contents of the envelope, Hugg's loose change, can help him abscond from his obligations in Gulod. Bit players in his life, he is *numero uno* in theirs, though his concern for them is dwindling into a mechanical exercise of charity that reduces love to an emotion.

Just three cards remaining and he can't pull that three of clubs from under the King of Spades that's under the Queen of Diamonds. Why does he take the cards all that seriously? The really free man should be able to decide what will be irrelevant. Should he live up, then, to what people expect? Siso tells him that people in Gulod speculate that he has a lot of chicks, perhaps many of them movie stars. What a life they imagine for him.

He looks for the sheet of paper where he lists the combinations of three cards that have frustrated him.

It's amusing how the Americans are worrying about anti-American feelings, when at no time in history, except just after liberation from the Japanese, is there such an outpouring of affection for Americans. Just as it's not necessary to pass around an already-filled basket to make it appear that crowds are supporting Cory and Doy. Gimmicks only cloud the issues, destroying the distinctions between candidates.

He used to think it made all the difference. In '69 he got excited into joining the demonstrations in Mendiola after he happened upon government trucks hauling away moneybags for Marcos from the Central Bank, which was supposedly closed for the elections. He was in the First Quarter Storm, saw first hand the battles inside the University of the Philippines, which the students had renamed Stalin University. He attended the sessions of the Constitutional Convention of '73, remembered word for word the invocation by Fr. Pacifico Ortiz, S.J.

Now, he has not joined a single rally, though human rights violations appall him and he supports the lawyers' cry for integrity and nationalism. It is as if he is vigilant so that goodness will not get a foothold in his life.

He might as well look for Hugg, for old times' sake. He returns the cards to the drawer. Having given himself a choice of reasons against taking the envelope, Benhur picks it up, takes it to the window. The man with the bed on his back is standing at the corner directly across from the restaurant Bulwagang Filipino, waiting for the traffic to allow him to cross. The light has darkened and dropped, so the rough wood appears to be nailed to his back.

In Benhur Vitaliano's hand
the small silver box he draws out from his desk drawer appears to reflect the sky outside his office window. Inside is a key chain, one of several he bought in Boston in 1983, the year Ninoy was assassinated. Three years later, another assassination: Evi Javier. Both men were at Harvard when he and Osong spent the summer in and out of Cambridge.

Sister Madeleine, Carmel, 4 Gilmore, is printed on the box in his handwriting. About time she got the key chain. About time he decides how to react to the massive cheating in the 1986 snap election that Marcos called to prove he had the mandate. How much should he risk himself in open opposition, in civil disobedience? How much weight to the consideration that passivity, but not deliberate silence, is a form of selfishness?

The space of time enjoined by the souvenir creates an urgency for Benhur. He decides right away to deliver the box.

When he arrives at the Carmel of St. Therese of the Child Jesus, reasons not to enter the closed gate rush to his mind. He reverses gears. But two Sister Externs show up in his rear-vision mirror. One walks past the car to throw open the metal gate while the other stands aside, smiling, carrying a bag in each hand.

Benhur does the logical thing and drives into the compound to park headlong into the bougainvilleas. It might be interesting; he encourages himself towards the monastery into which the two Sisters have disappeared. His next thought alarms him. What will she say? Will Sister Madeleine recall that they were classmates, that she took the Bar but then, before results were posted on the walls of the Supreme Court, dropped out of sight? Only years later did anyone learn that Elen Rodrigo had entered the Monastery of Carmel in San Pablo. Not Elen, who placed in the Bar and who, after lessons on statutory rape, erased the genitalia Espe had drawn in the upper corner of the blackboard, which everyone had pretended not to see! Not Elen, who wasted all those years of study by burying herself in the Carmel of the Incarnate Word! What could be more illogical, irrational, and out of character!

What will we talk about? Benhur asks himself, pushing open the iron door that is part of the grille wrapped around the front of a building that sits like a box under the trees. Does Sister Madeleine know anything about the February 7 elections? Do cloistered nuns vote? Other nuns Benhur has seen leading demonstrations right up to the barbed wires. If she knows, if she asks what he's doing for the country, he does not have to explain anything to someone who has escaped into prayers. That must be first-class passivity. Selfishness or selflessness?

A different Sister Extern is standing behind a glass display case that holds religious inscriptions, vestments woven and rosaries beaded by the nuns, booklets about contemplation—Asian spirituality in two volumes by a Susana Jose—some other thick and heavy books. He would not be surprised to discover Sister Madeleine had authored them. The legality of prayer, perhaps.

"Whom have you come to see?" the Sister asks, after she has allowed him to look over the display.

"Sister Madeleine."

"Which? Of the Holy Face of Jesus, or of the Agony of Christ?"

"Holy Face," he guesses, writing his name on the piece of paper the nun has slipped toward him. If it's the wrong Sister, does he get another chance to guess? His courage fails. He restrains himself from asking, distracts himself by thinking that the Sister's habit is the color of dark chocolates from Brigham's on the Square, chocolates that would melt in the heat almost upon landing in Manila.

"Please wait in the Small Parlor. Down the hall, through that door. There is a sign above the door." Sister carefully steps down to deliver the slip of paper, walks noiselessly in her brown socks and black slippers, parts the curtains covering a door.

Do all nuns smile without showing their teeth? Benhur hesitates before the iron grille that divides the entry and the long corridor like the arms of a cross. The open sky is on his left. On his right are closed doors and windows.

Another short hall starts from the door marked Small Parlor, ending the length of its wall, at a double wooden door, barred like another gate. It makes Benhur think of abandoned altars.

Holy Face of Jesus. What a name! Standing just outside the Small Parlor, his back to the door, Benhur faces pink and orange bougainvilleas that scatter the colors of the sun on the gravel of the walk; they make him think of partial embryos, so mired is he in the dread of waiting.

That summer in Cambridge he ducked a rainstorm on Massachusetts Avenue by slipping into the Thomas More Bookshop. With Osong grumbling, he leafed through the first book within his reach. He opened to a paragraph on pitch: *Highly pitched human beings, for whom God has prevenient grace, have a distinctiveness which separates them from human nature. They are idiosyncratic, unusual, particularized. Pitch is simple positiveness which pushes such beings toward the infinite.*

Word for word, the quote returns to him. *Prevenient!*

Benhur is elated. That's a word with which to answer Sister Madeleine. She will ask him questions, he is certain; and insist on answers. A quirky sense of justice prevented her from accepting judgments that took rights from one party to invest in another. She was always thinking *people,* not the *law.* Laws are for people, she said. Law is the minimum we have to rise from. Obligations do not end with observance of the law.

Was that the clue to what she would do with her life?

Benhur turns to look through the partly opened door, which even then looks sealed. He has been there ten minutes by his watch. Suppose she knows *prevenient,* could she be expected to have familiarity with *ecdysiast?* How about *caoutchouc?*

If *yes/no* was difficult for her then—it was *yes/but, no/but* for Elen Rodrigo; her precise mind saw imprecisions, the second heart of the matter; no one was better than she at doubts—what is she doing now in a monastery, engaged in silence? With whom does she argue now? Locked in contemplation, what irrelevancies does she object to, and who is her court of last resort? One after another his questions betray his own spoiled hopes.

Thinking he hears an inner door opening, Benhur enters the Small Parlor. A loosely woven curtain hangs against the wooden grille that divides the room. In his half sits an electric fan above a chromo of a child being led by an angel from a precipice. Unmatched chairs surround a table by a window that opens to the corridor. The concrete floor is waxed. There is no clutter.

He realizes she will not enter through the same door he entered.

Five more minutes.

Having to wait never fails to irritate Benhur. Can she refuse to see him? Anyone? He can, of course, simply leave, scribble a message on his way out: *Sorry. You took so long.* Twenty odd years ago he would have done exactly that. Except that the office—is it a position or just a vocation, no other, and what difference to anyone?—of a nun requires formalities. Nothing flippant. *Ecdysiast* won't do.

Maybe Sister Madeleine of the Holy Face of Jesus is in prayer. *In prayer.* That phrase amuses him. It parallels *in labor.* He looks up at the chromo. The angel is stepping on a thin, unthreatening snake.

Maybe she does not wear a watch, has no idea of time's passing. Time is, just is; neither past nor present nor still coming.

Fifty seconds pass. Enough provocation to leave.

A minute, thirteen seconds.

Sixteen minutes going on seventeen. Time to go.

But simply by coming, he has implied a contract to be there—validated by acceptance: the selection of the Small Parlor—when she comes out. Elen Rodrigo will think so and will insist upon fulfillment. Satisfaction is the word she might use. She was a tall girl with straight hair. As closely as he is able to recall, she was always in a hurry, always talking and out of breath, her mind racing in several directions at once. Her answers were right with regards to where she had reached but were no longer so for the question originally posed. Never totally wrong; never absolutely right. No small talk with her.

This improvisation of Elen Rodrigo from his memory makes Benhur wonder why he never asked her to the dances the Dean of Women monitored through her thick *doble vista* glasses. The Dean was sweet in an innocent and yet suspicious way. He can still see the hairnet pinned behind her ears. Dean Ursula what? Her name comes to Benhur along with the fact that he never saw Elen dance. She must have danced. She wore shoes with straps and always flowers or bows on the straps. Her fingernails were painted with designs of contrasting polish. Such random memories make him feel foolish, as if he's making her up completely. But he'll never forget that in their junior year she changed her handwriting to make it legible for the Bar examiners; broadened her letters, changed the slant to upright. An act of pure will anticipating her coming vow of renunciation which puzzles and irritates him, as if she has challenged him.

What does Elen Rodrigo recall of him?

The curtain is pulled. "Benhur Vitaliano. Is it really?"

He did not hear a door open, then close; but she is there. He knows she is there though he does not look in her direction, as if he might be blinded or struck.

"Hello, Sister." That was not hard, not hard expelling the greeting as deeply as a breath. Now he sees the light behind her is on his face.

"I'm refectorian for the day so I had to finish cleaning up in the dining room, but we have time to talk before *None.* Prayers, you know. Let me see you. You look different, but that's a compliment, Benhur. Unless we grow, we cease. Life is alive in growth. We exist in the world; we live in ourselves. Inside is where we are most alive." She answers questions he does not ask. "Sit. Take that chair."

Obediently he sits, and lies that he does not need the electric fan when she asks him to turn it on, though sweat is running down his chest like soft fingers, as if he should make an act of self-renunciation in acknowledgment of hers. Unsure of whether staring is permitted in a cloister, he looks around her to the sky. Through the window behind her, he sees part of some trees, the top growth of shrubs, a low roof, perhaps a hermitage. He becomes guarded when she pulls closer to the grille and leans back on his chair, as if to avoid her scrutiny.

The openings in the wooden grille force him to see her face as in a stained glass window. Without seeming to, he attempts to see the parts together. He can't tell if she's looking at him. Her hands appear to be inside pockets he can't detect.

"Well, Sister?" Cocksure Vitaliano acting as if he's standing on red-hot coals. Impossible to imagine.

"Well, Benhur!" She presses her hands together, resumes the breathlessness he remembers so well, which makes him relax, as if he has survived an initial testing. "People come with petitions which, of course, they can make directly, but it comforts people to see a face when they seek something beyond their power. They bring offerings. The first *upo* from the vine. *Espasol* made at home. Once when it was my turn to make *merienda* and the *polvoron* kept crumbling when I released them from the mold, in dread of having nothing to serve, I prayed in quiet, out of myself, *sa kaibuturan,* as we say: *Holy Spirit, help me.* In sheer panic, but not desperation. And a good friend came with a box of special *polvoron.* And if the Holy Spirit will respond to such a simple matter, how much more when our country is *in extremis.* All we need to do is acknowledge our helplessness."

Benhur wonders if she's trying to urge him to state his reason for coming, to hold on to his side of the conversation, his tongue and thought tied in knots; but he cannot think of a word with which to ask or to state. Besides, what kind of information does someone who prays all day need, or possess?

"Before Vatican II this would not be possible, your being here. The curtain could not be pulled aside then, except for the strictest of reasons. I would ask you to lunch, which would require Mother Prioress's permission, and I can't think of an excuse, though Mother Prioress, who is a niece of José Rizal himself, is kind. Of course you would not like the food. No meats, only vegetables and rice. Eggs if one is sick. Fish. When I entered, finally courage came to me and certainty, and I had to leave everything at the door, entire pocket's contents, handbag, shoes, so I could take on the brown habit of a postulant, worn, wrong size; and when I was brought to my cell, my bed just a mat and a thin cover, I felt I was in heaven. All I wanted. Still want. To be unencumbered, simply myself before Him. But you must tell me about yourself."

Benhur swallows hard, clears his throat, but nothing comes for him to say. His hand finds his shirt pocket where, instead of a handkerchief, there is the box. A way of presenting it does not come to him. Before he goes, perhaps.

"I ramble. On and on. Forgive. It's not because of the silence we observe, except for two hours after meals. A total of two hours to spend on personal prayer, as opposed to liturgical. And when we're summoned to the Small Parlor. I always rambled. My fault. I can recall faces and names. Tell me about Belen. Ortigas? No, Melencio. And Osong? The one from Naga. I would prefer, of course, hours of silent veneration before the Eucharist. We are a word in the Word; that is the Eucharist of which we are a part. Body of Christ. Our body and our soul, through which God works His will. Praise Be. His impulses of grace. Go live my life. Despite ourselves the whole creation spirals upward through a kind of recollectedness His mercy makes possible."

Benhur sits as still as he can, afraid to break into her thoughts, wary of being overpowered.

"Purely selfish of me not to ask about you. How are you?"

"Good." Too late he wonders if she is referring to his spiritual rather than his physical state. "Good," he repeats to answer both questions at once.

"Benhur, I was recently in Naga to give forty-four lectures to the community there; fifty-four to the novices. Beautiful souls all. Formation of souls is the basis of their illumination. Enlightenment tends to be taken as secular, ideological; dealing with the humanly possible. But radical solitude, self-emptying is what enables the soul and God to become One in Him. The Christian's vocation is a vocation of love which demands fidelity to unspoken vows, to strangers."

Benhur clenches his jaws. *I'm not one of your postulants. Save the formation lecture,* he wants to say.

"Did you know the Carmel at Naga is so beautiful that people who see it say it has to have been built by God Himself. Impossible to be made by human hand. Somehow that reminds me of you and Osong. Always together like twins. You have come across the theory of opposing twins? Hostile twins? A proposed theogonic structure in comparative mythology. Greek, Roman, German, Egyptian, Iranian. Very biblical as well. Myths predating the Old Testament attest to the theory. You know this as well as I, Benhur."

He is enjoying this rush of words, loaded with implications as usual. Twins fighting in the womb for kingship. The soul as the throne; interesting, if untrue. How is the soul seen? its struggles imaged? Spiraling upward! Too poetic to be true. Possible to confirm only if feeling and thinking take place outside the body as well as inside.

"Sophie?" she asks in the middle of mentioning Esau and Jacob fighting for primogeniture. "And also in our Civil Code. And Paula Bermudez, how is she? She and Marcela Bascon were very good friends I remember."

He notices her heavy clothes, woolen it appears. She must be burning inside, and she the one who needs the electric fan. "Elen . . ."

She repeats her name. "I've not heard it for years and years, Benhur. Mother no longer calls me Elen. She has released me finally. It took ages. I was her Mary-Magdalen, her cross. *How can God be enough for you?* she asked. *You are capable of the highest ambition.* I thought, I discovered, that *that* is to be exalted in God. Words. Mamá was as stubborn as I. Father thought I'd be the first woman appointed to the Supreme Court? By the way, Mamá has had a stroke . . ." Sister Madeleine's voice softens. Her hands are now inside sleeves that meet across her waist.

"How come you're here? Why?"

"Why?" She looks first at the turn, a wooden drum set to her right, at the end of the grille so visitors can place there an object they wish to give to a nun, thus avoiding hands touching. Then, her reply comes, carefully and without agitation. "As clear as I can remember, Benhur, I just flew to His call. I had tried other solicitations. But it's not only I. All of us. The Triune God draws all of us to the crucified and risen Savior. Only for this have we been created, and in His mercy, in His inexhaustible love which keeps us noble, He who is crucified and risen in each of us, in our sufferings . . ." The words are flowing out of her directly, it seems, from the very heart of her God.

"Are you happy?" He asks, full of doubt.

"In His love? Yes. Yes. He intends us all to be. When we know our nothingness, we are happy, because he exalts our souls, making us like Him. He wants to clothe us in His beauty. Purely through His mercy I heard His call, Benhur. I wish you could feel the very delicate and most unique intimacy of His love, given to all who lovingly accept total loving abandonment in Him. I only have to leave Him totally free to work His will in me. He makes me know happiness just by being where He wants me to be, at every single moment."

It does not sound to Benhur like the confession of a difficult love, but something whimsical. Almost defensively, afraid to be drawn into the throb of her reality, her feelings so powerful they do not need to enrage or to terrify into submission, Benhur makes an inward recitation of his own.

Obiter dicta: That only is deemed to have been adjudged in a former judgment which appears upon its face to have been so adjudged, or which was actually and necessarily included therein or necessary thereto. Continuing to resist, he thinks up other legal formulae—*res judicata,* estoppel by judgment, bar by former judgment, conclusion of judgment: all terms of effect from which appeals may nevertheless be made. The words rattle on inside him, make way for her.

"God who is our own sweet, gentle reward, our consuming reward, knows you're here, Benhur; for your coming must be for a reason which can lead only to His glory. And thanksgiving and praises to Him. In the whole cycle of day and night, happiness is for souls to be able to reflect Him more clearly. He is visible through us, to us, while we are seriously trying to be holy, which is when the evil one works relentlessly to win us over, to make us faithless, vulgar of heart and of mind. God works through His gifts to us, and I know how much He has gifted you."

Benhur looks down at his hands grasping his knees, trying to understand these words he did not come to hear. Happiness? She could have practised brilliantly. Instead she chooses to be trapped in prayer. If God is as great as she is telling him, how can it be that Benhur Vitaliano is worthy of His time, His thoughts? Let alone His love? He of all people, in God's hands? Does God intend Sister Madeleine of His Holy face to be with him, Benhur Vitaliano, at that very moment? Why?

"We are the very utterance of God Himself, Benhur. Every life. All history is His life. The original and radical solitude of God is His all in all. Everything, everyone He has made is good. Everyone. He sent His son to save, not to condemn. He knows our hearts, the secrets we hide there, yet He continues to love us, to offer us everlasting life, which is what heaven is. Just be. Be. That's what He asks, Benhur. When you're ready, love Him back by caring, by loving others. Our vocation is to love everyone. He who is in all things, in all places, in all events; He loves us. It's a mystery. The mystery is all. In faithfulness if not in love, even in bitterness if faithful . . ."

"I don't believe," Benhur counters with an admission of his wild heart. "I don't need to. How can God love me when I don't want Him to? When I don't love Him?"

"Of course, you love God, Benhur. So very unmistakably. You are not uncaring. But you resist, trying to understand, to be convinced. Or, afraid of becoming lost in Him, you doubt His love. You will not succeed, Benhur. Not if He wants you. His inexhaustible love will overpower you. I doubted, too. I tried not to believe. All U.P. students are heretics by reputation. Atheists, pagans, are some of the names we were called. Barbarians, like those who did not belong to fraternities. Outsiders. I was proud to disbelieve. I insisted upon it. Purely through His mercy I am here, believing in the heavenly Jerusalem which is coming to all. Praise be. Don't wrestle with your angel, Benhur. You have the power to be in Paradise now, if you want to be."

At that Benhur looks up at the chromo. Horizons appear to meet in the layers of paint on the wall, in the light falling into the room.

"Of course God loves you. That's unconditional. Impossible to believe that we don't have to do Him any favors in order to have eternal life. Inexhaustible love, love that goes beyond obligations and duties, beyond the law, beyond what is humanly imposed. God aches for us, Benhur."

She is giving him in one outburst what has taken her years to understand, expecting him to leap at her words, say Yes/Amen, as if he can see them coming directly from God, unmediated. She's still impatient, still using reason along with faith and hope, perhaps because she does not expect to see him again there. Or maybe, he thinks, she has a quota of souls to save. He is immediately sorry for this thought.

"Forgive. Remember I always crammed? Now, I'm trying to pour into you the mystery and the splendor of His glory, of longing too deep for words. No wonder you look confused and angry. Do I remember your temper? And it's purely selfish of me. Next time you must tell me about yourself and the classmates. I promise not to talk. Now I have to join the community prayers. For the country. At U.P. I thought I'd save her by becoming a lawyer. Here, I need Mother Prioress's permission to read last week's newspaper in which fish and vegetables come wrapped to the kitchen. That's the experience of indigence, of nothingness. Helplessness and failure and defeat. All for His glory. I resisted with all my strength and only slowly learned to accept, to trust fully in Him. The evil one stalks monasteries and convents, homes where people are trying to be holy."

It is painful to hear this from her.

"But grace came to me. The discipline of emptiness I received purely as a gift. Through prolonged and faithful prayer I am keeping His gift. I am prepared to desire only Him, in a sacrifice of love. I pray for all who will not go to him out of ignorance or anger. I pray that as a people, spent as we are by poverty, oppression, repressions, we might be able to act with magnitude and in love. But only when and if He wills. I told the Cardinal that martial law is our Good Friday, but that Easter Sunday is coming. I'm praying extra hours of adoration for a peaceful transfer of leadership, knowing that sovereignty is permanently in the people as a nation. Correct, Benhur? I've forgotten more than I ever learned. I'd flunk the Bar if I took it now. Benhur, pray that we can rise from our woundedness without violating one another, without violence. But leave God free to say NO . . ."

Benhur stands in his half of the Small Parlor while the door opens and closes behind the curtain that Sister Madeleine has drawn across the wooden grille.

On stepping out into the corridor, Benhur remembers the small box that had been the reason for his coming. No way to turn around and call Sister Madeleine back. Anyway, does she have something to lock and unlock of her own?

Quickly through the outer door he passes without a word to the Sister Extern.

The sun has risen from the roofs, from the pine trees that, on entering the compound, he thought looked very much like mourners standing over a mound.

He can smell flowers from a garden he cannot see. Her words are still tumbling over him: is he his own twin, the object of his own hostilities, and also the one from whom God, of which she spoke, expects something marvelous? Or God's own hostile twin: a heretic's thought? The one imperiled from birth and fighting the will she called adorable!

Pink and white and yellow flowers have fallen over the car from the branches of the bougainvillea, making the light itself pale. Benhur wonders, as he turns the ignition, if God, moving through Sister Madeleine's thoughts while she's lost in exaltations and adorations, is ever tempted to linger; and also if it's true that Teresa of Avila's breasts when she died, overwhelmed by ill-health and old age, were those of a young virgin.

The covering of trees in the Moscoso compound in San Juan allows Benhur to emerge gently from the monastery's stillness which he has been hoarding since Saturday. As if caught in an undertow, at the mercy of dark waves, he had not gone out for breakfast that Sunday when Colonel Moscoso called.

It is that way after coming from Gulod. A different urgency but an equivalent intensity. In such a state he can be taken advantage of, to make promises, to accept compromises.

Though Osong's father did not ask him to come, merely asked if he knew where Osong could be reached, he offered to come right away. Unable to look at the world, at himself in the mirror with his Vitaliano ears spread like sails in the wind, eyes like burls buried in the wood, he felt summoned.

At the Moscoso gate, an hour and a half's drive, he wonders why he did not wait to be asked; why he did not impersonate a secretary: *Attorney Vitaliano is not in/not expected/is in Europe/Davao. Please call back or leave a message.* Of all people, he has done that to Osong, who believed every word: *He shouldn't leave without letting me know. What should I do now?*

Mang Genio, the driver, comes to the gate. "Benhur! You just missed Cayetano."

"Is the Colonel home?"

"He's always home now, so I have been promoted or demoted to gardener. Come in, Benhur. I'll bring you a cup of coffee in the living room."

"Cafe *barako?*" Benhur asks, recalling the strong Batangas coffee the Colonel preferred. He used to stay in that house on weekends, sharing the family's meals and some of their secrets, and he has a sense now of coming home.

"The same. I brewed it for Cayetano but he left before it was ready. The Colonel drinks instant now, and only for breakfast; but who wants to live as long as Methuselah? Wait here."

Standing in the driveway Benhur notices birds of paradise along the fence. Colonel Moscoso used to have them pulled out, never cared for wild growths, profusions, or for flowers with scents, so the *camias* and *sampaguitas* had to be planted in back of the garage, threaded there for the family altar. Sometimes *Mang* Genio's wife would send garlands of the flowers for his mother.

"How is Mrs. Moscoso? How's your wife, *Mang* Genio?" Benhur asks, stepping into the house. He does not tell the driver that he has turned off the water hose, which had been left nozzling the ground near the doorsteps and digging a hole such as an animal might make. Tendrils of bridal bouquet hang over the doorway.

"Good," *Mang* Genio answers. "And is your sister married yet? I used to bring messages for you in Gulod. Is that where your family still lives? I remember the river and fruit trees."

"So Cayetano was here."

"Cayetano is in and out. Osong, though, comes now like a visitor. Not since Christmas, and only then for an hour to bring gifts and take his gifts with him. You must see more of him. Osong could take his father out, for example, though the Colonel stays home now. Japanese tourists upset the Colonel. Me, too. I was a Scout during the War. Bataan and Corregidor. People don't think about it anymore. Everyone drives Japanese cars. Watches, TVs, tractors. As if we were not tortured during the Occupation. No one mentions the Death March. Here is where a Japanese soldier shot me. In the face."

Benhur takes the effort to look, though he remembers the scar when it was fresher and Osong saying *Mang* Genio's grin was that of a corpse.

"The last time I took the Colonel out was to Fort Santiago. At the cell where the Japanese killed 600 prisoners of war, Japanese girls were posing as for a magazine cover, with hats on and displaying bare legs. Such disrespect. It's another invasion all right. Another occupation. They're all over. Don't mention them to the Colonel. Sit down. I'll call him."

Benhur remains at a side window from which he can see the red *cutsaritas* lining the walk. The tiny cupped leaves remind him of little girls who play house, serving those leaves on tiny plates. The *mabolo* is still in the yard, but for lack of a male tree it has not borne fruit. Is there no male *mabolo* in San Juan? From Osong's bedroom they used to watch the moon, as it came up, bending the branches of the tree. One night, and never again, in reply to a question no one asked, the Colonel said, "I owe my life to an American. How he knew I was still alive, I don't know. He pulled me out of a trench where I had been tossed among other bodies for burial. I don't even know if he survived the Death March, but I think of him often."

At another window a parrot is swinging on its perch, beak parted as if it might start to talk. Its feathers filter the light coming into the house. First with one eye, then the other it fixes Benhur with its attention.

"That's a bright one." *Mang* Genio is back. "Cayetano brought it from General Santos City. It can talk. It repeats what it hears. 'Genio, have you had breakfast?' No secret is safe with that bird."

Benhur steps up to the bird, whistling.

The parrot walks to the far end of its perch, lifting and lowering its head as if after a scent.

"It can whistle all right. This morning I was watering the plants and I heard it screaming *Coup! Coup! Time to go!* Luckily the traffic is loud, or it would get us in trouble. It must have heard the Colonel and Cayetano." *Mang* Genio turns his back to the bird. "Cayetano must be on a mission. To go so quickly after arriving. Reformists! I think he's with them. I'm all in favor. Marcos's overstaying and absentee generals raking in everything. Low morale in the ranks and among junior officers. I hope Cayetano becomes a general. You know that the Colonel was cheated out of a promotion, or there would have been a General Moscoso. I hear things. But I don't jump up and down, screaming like that bird there."

Benhur laughs. If *Mang* Genio were not so old, he would have said: You start doing that and you'll get chained to that piece of bamboo perch!

"If there's a coup, Benhur, we can all go to the farm I have on the slope of Mount Halcon. Your family, too."

Benhur places an arm about *Mang* Genio. "Thank you. I hope we don't have to." Ever since he can remember, *Mang* Genio has been looking forward to retiring there; while serving the Colonel, planting his future in the mountain.

"Time to go. Time. Time." The parrot stares at Benhur, bobbing up and down on its perch.

"Be quiet or you'll end with the stuffed lemur and pheasant on the wall. I have not brought your coffee, Benhur. I'll do that now."

Benhur walks to the piano where Cayetano's graduation picture from the Philippine Military Academy nudges that of Osong with the tassel over the wrong edge of the mortarboard. He has a graduation picture, too, taken during the first semester, before that Tuesday morning in Constitutional Law. Inside the glass bookcase beside the piano is the unopened box of Battle Games: MacArthur's Major Campaigns, including Bataan and Corregidor. He brought it back for the Colonel from his first trip to the States. Through the plastic wrap he reads: *Lead the dogged resistance of American and Filipino troops which upset the Jap timetable of Pacific Conquest. Giant Game board. Authentic historical commentary. 5 offensive and 5 defensive Battle Dice. 24 Troop Movement Cards.*

"Colonel, *Kumain ka na?*" The parrot screeches, head cocked like a loose doorknob.

"Benhur!" the Colonel calls out from the stairs, running his hand down the bannister and on the tops of the chairs he passes on the way to Benhur.

"Belated happy birthday, Colonel." Benhur grasps the hand extended to him without shaking it. "I didn't forget, Sir, but I could not come last Sunday. Vergel and his family were home."

"You're better than Osong. My son remembers the President's birthday but not mine. Sit down. So Vergel is married. To another doctor? He should bring his family over. And how is your mother? Your sister? She has the same name as my mother, you know." The Colonel sits down in the pose of his framed wedding picture on the piano. "I named the parrot after Cayetano. Tano. You remember how noisy and never still Cayetano used to be."

The bar on which the parrot is swinging casts its shadow on the January issues of *Panorama* arranged on the coffee table. The parrot cross-steps its way from one end to the other, its neck moving like a fat snake.

"My wife was just saying we have not seen you: and here you are. But she's out with Cayetano's wife, visiting. With the children, too. Patty insisted she come."

The urgency to which Benhur thought he was responding by coming has been replaced by solicitations proper to social visits. "How was your birthday?"

"There are some who came. Cayetano ordered a *lechon de leche,* so tiny there was no delight in eating it, but only Marcos's cronies can afford *lechon.* It used to be P80. Now at least P1,000. Things get worse instead of better, but, as *Mang* Genio says, we can't change things any more than we can plow the sea."

This can't be all the Colonel has to tell me, Benhur thinks, but he goes along. "It's the same with Max Fried Chicken," he says, genially. "I told the waiter it used to be just seven pesos instead of thirty-six. His answer was, 'It was P3.50 when I started here.'"

"Is it still good?"

"It is as good as I remember. The roll is smaller."

"The *lechon de leche,* too, was just like a centerpiece. We could have done without it. Mrs. Moscoso thought it would be unlucky not to serve it. Very few remembered. Osong did not. Just as well. Cayetano's family stayed. The two children."

Mang Genio appears with cups of coffee on a tray. Behind him, a woman Benhur assumes is his daughter, with a small platter of *ensaymada.*

"You remember my sister. You visited her with us in San Fernando. She sent those."

Benhur wonders what other trivia they will talk about. "I remember." She was a small, thin woman who preserved limes, *santols, calamansi,* filling them with *pastillas* after cutting lacy designs on the rinds. When Cayetano was a plebe in the Philippine Military Academy, they passed by her house to pick up food for Cayetano and his classmates.

"Do you remember going to Baguio to visit Cayetano? One night the brakes went just as we passed the last checkpoint in heavy rain. *Mang* Genio ..."

"Coasted all the way to Dagupan in the dark." He lets the Colonel serve him coffee.

"That was Huk country then."

"We brought ice cream in dry ice, barbecue to grill over balled-up newspaper; and Cayetano was ordered to guard duty every time we brought up a celebration feast."

"You know, Benhur, just this morning Cayetano told me he's with the Reform Movement. If necessary, they will carry out a preemptive raid on the Palace. That's all I know. What their fallback positions are he didn't tell me. I would not have asked. They're idealists. Patriots who want to restore integrity to the military so they can protect the Constitution and the country. About politics you know more than I. What justifies military intervention, Benhur? Is RAM justified?"

"It's a matter of legitimacy, Sir. Did election frauds destroy the presidential mandate; vitiate his authority? Is the military the right agent of change?"

"Cayetano just joined. He was not with RAM when they broke ranks at last year's graduation ceremony. This past election he threatened to fire on colleagues who engaged in electoral fraud and coercion. He just reached the point where he could not stand by while corruption escalated. I asked only one question—were they going to assassinate the president? He said no. I'm worried because there is no room for failure."

Benhur thinks of the envelope Hugg left him. Is it about RAM that Hugg is concerned? Is RAM secretly funded by the CIA, as NAMFREL purportedly is? and how is the fight for freedom thereby compromised? Crafty as usual, is Marcos using RAM for dissimulation?

"I haven't told Mrs. Moscoso. I don't want to have to tell her. Osong probably does not know or care." Colonel Moscoso explains the situation.

How far can he indict military usurpation of political power without condemning Cayetano and his ideals? Does it depend on whether they intend to seize power or aid in its transfer? There is that fine line between legitimate overthrow and rebellion. Motives do not justify an assault on legal processes. Until it came under a cloud over its operations against dissidents, over the protection by some military officials of the business interests of landlords and multinationals, the military was the noblest of professions. Osong almost talked him into taking the entrance tests for the Philippine Military Academy. Soldiers are as much victims of official greed. But RAM, the Reform the Armed Forces Movement, could become subverted by that greed.

The coffee has become cold but Benhur drinks it. Across from him, on the wall, life-size figures of the Last Supper come very close to looking like guests seated at the dining table, which is polished to a shine. The representation is new. It reminds Benhur of the Capas memorial to the Death March.

"I did not die for my country. You know the story, Benhur. I fell during retreat. I survived. That's not paying the full price. Maybe it will be exacted from Cayetano."

This statement rearranges even the room where the parrot has fallen asleep, head tucked under a wing, standing on one leg on the bamboo perch that barely moves. Lining up authority on the legitimacy of military rule, on its role as a regime changer, on the desirability or necessity of a military junta or a coalition government will not justify not serving the country! The parrot might as well have jumped up to ask: *Benhur have you served the country? Have you served?* But it makes it easier for Benhur to fit his emotions to these new bearings with the discovery that the Colonel, because he survived the Death March, is as obsessed with failure as is he himself because of that Tuesday morning in Constitutional Law.

"When you come to think of it, Benhur, the country is all of us, and also all we have."

Mang Genio's daughter comes in, but, seeing the pastries untouched on their plates, the sugar glistening on the buttered crust, she leaves as silently as she entered.

The silence, the quiet, the stillness recall to Benhur the intensity with which Sister Madeleine tried to tell him of her experience of God, her words radiant with her own personal hurt and longing. *Tissues of one flesh* occurs to him, though he is not certain she spoke them. *Co-redeeming.* Words that heal and tear apart. Is the country served the way God is served? Why should she invade his thoughts, sit on his reasons the way angels are supposed to be buried in the woodwork of churches, interred in the walls of stone, so they can listen to the prayers of the faithful? Why entice him with bread reserved for angels?

But Sister Madeleine's words rain and thunder in Benhur's thoughts while the Colonel looks up at the sky through the iron grilles that cover the window, as if his own thoughts might fly in like birds approaching the *mabolo* outside. "Cayetano is no coward. I have no intention of disowning him or even stopping him, Benhur. He has his own conscience. And I hope I do not give the impression I am shifting the burden to you. I just want you to know, in place of Osong."

"No, Sir. I'm sure Cayetano knows the risks and will not be used for advancing the political ambitions of selfish men. I mean those jockeying for position around Cory, in case she becomes president."

"That's a long shot, Benhur."

"Still, she will need a mind and vision of her own, a will to risk everything including herself for the sake of the country, because democracy can't be saved without saving the people first." It is what he'll write if anyone now asks him for a speech. Only Sister Madeleine believes that political obligations come from God, and leaders take their pledge on the beatitudes.

"You did not taste the *ensaymada* Choleng made. I'll have it toasted again because it tastes better warm."

Mang Genio has come into the house. Without specifying Benhur, he asks the colonel, "Two sacks, Colonel?" referring to the fragrant rice from Mrs. Moscoso's farm which they give special visitors.

The Colonel nods.

Benhur is grateful for the delicacy with which the matter is brought up and decided; for the Colonel's assumption that he will keep their conversation confidential without being asked.

On the way to Gulod he feels it was right for him to go to the Colonel, who bid him good-bye, saying, "Don't space your visits like leap year, *hijo.* I'll tell Cayetano you came."

He recalls the words that passed back and forth in the house, no less powerful for having disappeared into sounds, echoes of the bodies that spoke them. The curve of this feeling heightens as he looks up at the sky through the windshield that *Mang* Genio cleaned on his own initiative.

In the brightness of his feelings, Benhur imagines the parrot shrieking to the trees: *Reformist! Reformist! Disinformation. Death and existence. Co-redeeming!* Then tail and beak and feathers flashing like semaphore: *Benhur. Benhur. Have you eaten?*

Full of longing
that takes her nowhere, Patro Vitaliano sits at her doorway watching her grandchildren play basketball in the space between her house and the chapel. The light moving across the front yard goes through her like a sound swelling and dropping, intensifying memories of Benhur; of Vergel and his son Danilo Sebastian; even of Olimpia's children, Anya who stayed behind, and Rosalio who refused to be separated from his mother.

So happy was she when all were with her that she bought everything good in the market, spending the week's allowance in one day so that Benhur had to give her more. If only Benhur had his own family.

Her knees together stiffly as if a child is asleep on her lap, Patro looks up when the shouting swells. Pitong always shouts on making a basket, thrusting his arms up as players do on television. From his trips, Benhur has brought the boys some Boston Celtics shirts, the envy of Gulod.

"You're too noisy," Patro raises a finger across her lips. "Neighbors are asleep. It's early in the afternoon. Rest a while," she tells them as she used to tell their father Demetrio.

Briefly they mind her, then they lapse back into their excitement. To save his clothes for school, which sadly enough is not the most important part of their life, Pitong wears sleeveless *sando.* When he gets warm, he pulls off the undershirt, wipes his body with it, then puts it back on. But instead of the rubber slippers the others wear and then toss into the pile under the post and metal hoop, which is all that is left of the basket, Pitong wears sneakers. He insists on it, refusing to save his pair for Atlas to wear the next school year, because he says he wants to be a basketball player for Crispa and needs to get used to shoes. Atlas wants to play for Tanduay Rhum. Ryan, thirteen, wants to become a movie star; has started to part his hair at the side. He asked his *Tito* Benhur to buy him a wristwatch and a Pierre Cardin belt. It is all he talks about, the way Demetrio talked about birthstones.

Pitong's ball dances on the rim of the hoop. From the sideline, Atlas laughs. "You're no Larry Bird." Two years younger than Pitong, who is eleven, Atlas is already as tall. He is lighter of skin, almost like Benhur except for the high forehead, which makes Benhur look as dignified as a senator. It is a Vitaliano feature. Her husband, Valentin Cleofas, had that. Even Danilo Sebastian. Caloy, who is fifteen but looks eighteen, looks like their father Demetrio. Caloy waits on tables in the Kamayan. All his earnings go to concert tickets. Home briefly after the funeral of Governor Javier, he said the Valentine Day Concert at the Intercon was poorly attended; that during the final rehearsal, Governor Javier's casket passed by on its way to the Ateneo Chapel and everyone became disconsolate. He wants to be an air steward so he can travel. But how, when he has stopped going to school?

Such low aspirations disappoint Patro. How will they ever get out of Gulod if they all rely on Benhur? She aches for them to fulfill her dreams, to discover their finer selves. It is two weeks since the snap elections, and democracy has not happened.

If Valentin Cleofas were alive. . . . She can't understand why she continues to mourn him when they have three, four children already dead. Iñigo died at seventeen, of severe reaction to penicillin; Demetrio, in combat. His company, the newspapers said, fired indiscriminately into a village. Benhur is trying to clear his name. It is now five years, perhaps too long to be able still to reinstate the truth. Ladislao died at thirteen, and, soon after, Monica. It is Monica's picture on the dresser. Two years old. Her face is that of Patro's own mother.

She and Valentin used to walk along the river, planning the trees they would plant; some for shade, in front of the house; some for fruit, in the backyard. Then, as if time collapsed, the next thing, Valentin was dying. All those past years that seemed to be hard on them are actually the best years; they keep entering her present thoughts, while she stares in the distance, as if watching herself coming from a long wavering point, approaching on a trail like someone coming in her dream.

When Valentin was dying, he would wake up to say he had just come from a place that was bright without the sun. *If you had been with me, I would not have come back.* After the radiation treatment failed, Valentin warned her, *I might just stay. Come after me if I don't return. We'll be happy there. I felt no pain. There are no sounds of quarrel. I did not feel afraid.*

Patro looks at her hands as if they hold a photograph. Vergel most resembled Valentin. Such a happy face, even when he's not smiling. Vergel never studied as hard as Benhur but he did not lose his scholarship at the U.P. His *Lola* Sula sold off her jewels, piece by piece, to give to Vergel. Even then, Vergel asked only for what he needed, not what he wanted, and gladly wore Benhur's cast-offs. Vergel liked to talk to people. I should have named him Clarence, Valentin often said, after Darrow, because he certainly makes a good lawyer. During the visit, Vergel walked rounds with the *zona* at night. During the two weeks, the front yard was a clinic, mothers dragged in their children for Dr. Vergel to diagnose and treat.

The boys look as if they are Vergel's children. Newcomers mistake them for Vergel's.

A fistfight is breaking up the game. "Neighbors will hear you." Patro shushes the boys.

"Dilát! Dilát!" Atlas, who was named Amado, and only the year before decided to be called Atlas, is teasing Pitong, who tends to stare, especially when concentrating. "You're no Jaworski or Brown."

"Ryan, make them stop." Patro raises a hand. "Enough, all of you. If you can't get along, separate."

Ryan is the mischievous one, but it is also he who surprises Patro with his questions. *Does the devil suffer, too? Suppose we meet him in Paradise?* She does not know where his questions come from, or where they go. Such a strange thought. The devil prowling in Paradise.

Patro is certain that Paradise is where Valentin Cleofas is headed, after purgatory, because he was so good he would not do anything that might lead the children astray by his example. He would rather eat salt and rice than steal or lie. No one can escape God's holy knowledge, hand, or judgment. *Kung hindi tao, Dios ang sisingil sa atin.* Sister Gertrudis, who, with three other nuns, is sharing the misery, the rats, and the smells of sickness and garbage in that part of Gulod where the poorest live, says: *We can't escape God's love. Before we are struck, the blow has hit Him. He is crucified and risen in each of us.* It is her reply when asked why they live in Gulod instead of returning to their convent.

Until Sister Gertrudis came, Patro used to be afraid of her memories. If she were reminded of the white salt crackers in the blue and white tin which Valentin asked for in the hospital, she would cry for days. She still avoids the street where they first lived, in an *accessoria* with half a month's rent left because an aunt was returning to Camarines Sur. A chair and a table were all the furniture they had. Valentin Cleofas rolled out a mat at night. Inside a circle of pink and red roses, he had her name entwined with his. She was a *colegiala.* All she knew how to cook was rice. Their first night, they opened a can of sardines.

Her parents had used their savings to send her to a school run by the nuns, hoping she might meet a good marriage prospect in a classmate's brother. Her sister married a widower with a piggery; has been writing to ask her to visit them in Mindoro. Valentin was a law student. When they were expecting their first child, Iñigo, he gave up studying to work in the *Times* office on Florentino Torres. His mother never forgave her.

They even moved to Gulod, near his mother's vacation house that became her permanent home. Patro would see his mother watching while Valentin taught her how to swim. Along the shallow parts he carried her on his back until she learned to float. The sun glistened off their bodies. Now she will not walk to the river and be reminded of the days when the sky seemed to begin at their feet. She will not plant in the red sticky soil that holds the roots of rice seedlings but makes the banks slippery.

The pale droning of light provokes Patro's memories. She has stopped shrinking into them, so painful have they become.

The memories bleed into one another. In the aunt's apartment, the two weeks they lived there, Valentin would shut the windows so passersby could not look in, and they would dance without music; their bodies stuck the way during the summer one's clothes sucked one's skin. They would have a party in the moonlight as soon as the trees he planted grew above their heads. The memories take her across many lives until she feels she has lost everyone; feels like the river smothered by the debris it picks up as it floats past the factories, past the fields on its way down to Manila Bay between towns where, during typhoons, floods rage and pull down huts and carry away trees. One November, when it howled and rained for nine days and nights, some iron roofing from far away cut down the papayas in the backyard, landing flat against the house. Fridays, Valentin Cleofas took them all to Luneta, where he bought the children popsicles and *balut,* boiled peanuts in paper cornucopias. They planned to buy Rogers silverplate from Heacock in Dasmariñas. A few more years and Valentin said they would be going by car instead of *calesa* to Pasay, to walk on the seawall and watch the freighters anchored in the Bay. They would eat at the Manila Hotel.

The good things never came, the better things.

So hard of heart, Valentin's mother Sula would not come while he was dying. When they walked past her house, the old one never asked her in, only Valentin; so she had to stand in the garden while Valentin went inside her house to look at something.

It hurts as much to live as to die. Patro thinks back. She never left Valentin's side when he was ill. While he slept, she sat on the bed. In case he did not wake up anymore, she stayed awake to close his mouth and his eyes. *Don't let them see my body,* he asked her, but he did not answer when she asked, *Who?* In the backyard every morning, she buried the pieces of cloth into which he had bled during the night. She held his hands, trying to absorb his pain.

People have said she has hands for healing. Very ill people have recovered after she has laid hands upon them. Good energy has flowed from her. Even after the nuns moved to Gulod, many still asked her to sit with them during childbirth. It is hard to watch children unable to breathe, mouths sucking at the air, their bodies clenching in the effort. Burning with fever they toss until it is all over. She hears their moaning in her sleep.

In Gulod it often feels to her that someone has just died. Old men are found on the trail, slapped by the wind. Patro wonders if the dead still love. And how do they love?

The boys break up the game. Atlas and Pitong run to Patro asking for two pesos each for ice cream. They go over the arguments against the dirty ice cream sold from carts. "*Tito* Benhur eats them when he comes. He buys it for us."

"Go turn on television. Playing just makes you hungry."

"It's broken, *Nay.*" They call her Mother, too.

She remembers now; that's the reason she cut the curtains for Sally instead of watching *Heredero* after lunch. For three days she has missed her soap operas. *Victoria Hills; Andrea Amor. Mansyon* is her favorite. The brother and sister are always fighting about money, but that's life. In *Heredero,* the heirs are always about to be reunited. To catch *Maynila,* she has to miss half of the other programs, so Benhur has promised her a Betamax that will record programs. If it will record Charito Solis's movies, she will not have to go to town in the heat. Loreto tells her just to write the script herself. It's just tears and more tears. She knows the formula for keeping the viewers' hearts pumping: let the characters strain toward each other; good always against evil, with evil slightly ahead. However, she just wants happy endings. She will not watch, no matter how hard Loreto begs, the imported serials about killers. She's too old to be interested in sins.

"Instead of ice cream, rent comics," Patro gives each grandson two pesos, watches them run off toward *Aling* Maxima.

A lizard drops from the ceiling. Briefly stunned, it crosses Patro's path on the way to the kitchen, then runs up the wall. Its pale flesh unnerves Patro. She is always afraid to walk in the dark at night, to step on the lizards.

The wash is blowing in the wind. Loreto and Anya are hosing the ground till it is wet with suds. Since she came, Anya has been washing the clothes while Loreto rinses and hangs up the laundry. The soap is too strong for Loreto's hands, her fingers get very red and swollen. After the wash, both of them always polish their nails.

On seeing Patro, Loreto says: "*Nay,* we'll polish your nails."

"I'm too old to be frivolous." Patro looks up at the coconut tree. It is too close to the door and its roots are growing into the foundation. She could have had it cut while Vergel was there, to use the heart of the palm for *lumpia.* But then they would not be able to have the green nut, which is good cold. "Are the drums filled?"

"Yes, *Nay,*" Loreto answers. "Maybe Benhur will get us our own connection to the main pipes, so we won't have to buy our water. People are always trying to get ahead of us at the Adeas, and Mrs. Adea is raising the price of connecting again. She said she'll talk with you."

"We'll see," Patro does not argue. "Benhur can't do everything for us." She has refrained from asking for a ceiling in her bedroom. The tin roof burns over the bed in the summer, and when it's cold, as in February, she has to place a blanket over the mosquito net to keep warm at night. "Come in. Just leave the door open so we can watch the clothes."

"I thought you don't like the door left open." Loreto leaves her wooden shoes outside.

"We're all here anyway. It will be safe." Patro wishes she could hire someone to do the laundry; then the girls would not have to hide their hands when people come to visit. Instead of staying home all day, they could go to Manila as she and her sisters did. Her sisters talked about suitors and clothes, not about movie stars. A *costurera* sewed them new clothes every week. All they had to do was choose the fabric from the textile stall they owned in Divisoria. Twice a day they changed clothes because they had a *lavandera* who lived only to go to the movies in the afternoon, so that she would fold still-damp clothes in order to catch the first showing after lunch.

"Remember when I saw my half-slip on the washline next door."

"I'll be here. Go to your bedroom and rest." Patro has heard *Aling* Maxima shouting at her son to encourage him to call on Loreto. If Robles comes, just to be civil, they'll ask him in, of course, but it will be a dull afternoon. Maxima should know better. Robles is not good enough for Loreto. She has a teacher's diploma, while he went to Saudi as a contract laborer. However, some people have skins as thick as a turtle's and have to be told plainly; then they get insulted.

Every year the prospects dwindle for Loreto. There is only Emilio Luna in Gulod. The father, who used to be under-secretary for President Quirino, has been dead almost ten years. His death has made a difference to the family. Patro has seen Mrs. Luna coming from the market, by herself since the last maid left, with her basket only a third filled, usually the tiny shrimps held in a fold of banana leaf, some greens. They used to have parties, and before the road became overgrown with grass, cars came all the way to their gate.

Anya comes out to show Patro her fingernails and to ask if she'll have her nails done in the same color.

"No, *hija.*"

"Loreto says to tell you that you look as young as Charito Solis. *Peks man, Nay.* Cross my heart and hope to die."

"It won't look good on me. Go ahead."

"But Loreto said . . ."

"Never mind. It will be a waste on me." Patro walks past the bedroom on her way to the front door, where she sits to wait for the boys. Her thoughts begin rising vividly before her like a landscape. Emilio Luna used to be so handsome, so tall and pale it hurt to look at him. A driver used to take him to La Salle. Then he went to FEATI to take lessons in flying. But something happened. He stopped going out. Now, when she sees him with his mother once or twice a month, the impression he gives is of great sadness. It is as if his face has been erased. He no longer stops to greet her, and Mrs. Luna herself does not look up. It is as if a line of trees or a mountain stands in the way.

Maxima has stories about the Lunas. She has seen furniture, she says, including the piano, being carried out of the house, and not for repair. It is Maxima's way of praising her son Robles, who has worked in Angola. According to Maxima, were it not for Robles, the Filipinos working the Kafunfo diamond mines might have all been shot. She dramatizes the rescue, the march to the coast, and the release just after New Year two years ago. It can't be Robles's account, for the son can't speak three sentences without gagging. Besides, even if he were paid $2,000 a month, he's still just a laborer while Loreto is a teacher.

The next time Maxima brags, she'll stop her immediately by asking her to pay her loan to the community project so her share can be given to *Aling* Dionisia, who appeared in Gulod four years ago with two grandchildren who have since disappeared. If Maxima says Robles's money is being saved for a grand wedding, she'll say no one in Gulod is good enough for Robles. That takes Loreto out of the picture.

Several children come running into the yard, dragging one another by the hand. Some are carrying leaves shaped like the *isis* that her mother had growing near the kitchen window, so the maid just had to reach out for leaves with which to scour the pots. Her mother used ash to clean their good plates, which otherwise crack, like nail polish on those who work with their hands. But nowadays even fish vendors have manicures. When Loreto thought of working at the parlor, she asked her: "So you're willing to touch the hands and feet of people you don't know?"

Patro watches them looking for the snake among her plants. One of these days, they'll get bitten. They have been head-butted by goats being raised for Saudi; fallen out of trees. After a while, Patro chases them off and they disappear down the trail, running like arrows to a target.

Loreto and Anya are asking for her permission to go to Sally for pink thread. Sally pays Anya twenty centavos for each pink rose she crochets. Loreto does not have the patience; but Anya, since she came, has finished a hundred ten. Anya thinks she'll send herself to school this way, and Patro does not want to discourage her. Sally thinks up new schemes every week, in addition to buying and selling dollars.

They walk out, singing along to the transistor radio. Anya is dark, but her pointed chin makes her look delicate. Loreto never darkens in the sun, just like Valentin Cleofas's mother, who could sit in the sun all day and still be as pale as a turnip. Patro slips the wedding band around her finger. Underneath the ring is the only pale part of her body. Even the wind darkens her. Loreto has a thin face that always looks the same; like all the Vitalianos, her features are fixed. Anya has a soft face that changes expression. Patro can't decide which she prefers.

Eventually, she knows, Benhur will go abroad. When that happens she hopes he takes Loreto with him, if she has not yet married. She hopes, by then, that the boys will have started college. It's her biggest dream.

Suddenly the words of the song Anya and Loreto play, from the tape Benhur brought, run through Patro's thoughts. Loud music banging on her ears makes her ill with the repetitions. She looks out to see if the girls have returned. Loreto has not talked about her father for some time now. She used to dream of him night after night. On waking up, Loreto would describe what he wore.

If Cory is president, will things be better? Patro worries until everyone is home. She worries when Benhur comes, afraid he will run into a feud or a death squad. Secret marshals have come into Gulod. Bodies have been found in the river, caught in the weeds. Some have had stab wounds; some, bullet holes. *Aling* Dionisia, who walks about Gulod day and night looking for her grandchildren, has found some of the bodies. People greet her: "Another dead body?" Dionisia, who takes everything seriously, answers, "None today. The other day, however, by the slope . . ." As if she is the mad woman of Gulod, Dionisia can go anywhere without arousing suspicion or alarm.

Every time she thinks of Dionisia, the woman comes around. This time she is carrying Siso Feleo's youngest child, over whose head she is holding a large leaf. *Dionisiang Hilo,* some call her because she always looks stunned out of her wits, as if the wind is blowing her about. Benhur has given her bus fare to enable her to look for her grandchildren in Manila, by the Ermita area, where the rich used to live, but now where tourists come looking for children and young girls.

"Come in, Dionisia. How old is that child now?"

Dionisia appears to be counting in her head. "It was born in August. I remember because there was that mock trial to impeach Marcos for graft and corruption. The thirteenth anniversary of martial law. It's teething. See how sore its gums are."

"Thirteen years already," Patro leans over to hold the child's foot. "There was the time hand grenades were tossed into movie houses and cockfights. How did we survive all the bombings? Thirteen years. As old as Ryan. Human rights lawyers and journalists have been found killed, and we are still here. Why are you taking care of the child?"

"Siso is grating coconut. Nani decided to cook *guinatan* to sell for *merienda*. She was cutting up sweet potatoes and bananas, so I offered to take care of this one."

"Just two ingredients?" Patro cannot decide if she will send the boys to buy some of the *guinatan.* It is a way of helping Nani pay her monthly on the Livelihood Financing Program loan of P500. To keep the program going, Patro sometimes pays the share of those behind in their payments. Tempting the child to smile, Patro tickles its foot. "It has a dimple. Too bad it's a boy. Is it a boy?"

Dionisia's shoulder blades, deepset in her body, look like plows left to rust in the field. She is wearing one of Patro's dresses, a size too large for her, so that when she dances the child to sleep, the dress slips off of one shoulder, then the other. Patro is trying to get her into the livelihood program. Meding Canonigo makes *tocino* and *longaniza* which Dionisia helps to peddle in Gulod. Selling vinegar from clay *tapayans,* the Filemons make ten to twenty pesos a day; and Eliadora Guzman, when her fingers are not stiff, weaves macramé bags for export. Sally Moscoso provides the twine.

"Look at it smile in its sleep," Patro kisses the child's hand. "Angels must be playing with it. Let me hold it."

On being transferred into Patro's arms, the child wakes up and cries. Dionisia takes it back, starts dancing even harder to quiet the child.

"You're spoiling it. Let it cry. It's good for the lungs, Dionisia."

Dionisia avoids the charge by talking about Patro's sister-in-law, who lives with Sula. "Milang says her sister is sending her tickets to Los Angeles. I asked who would live with the old woman. Your mother-in-law has only good words about Milang, who must spit on the old one's food to make her so tame."

"Milang has been saying that for years." Patro does not allow herself to say the rest of what is on her mind.

Still trying to distract Patro, Dionisia says, "Nani is asking Siso to help so he won't go out as a strike breaker. It's a hard way to earn a living."

"Strikes are illegal, especially against Marcos's cronies." Patro succeeds in taking the sleeping child. She now makes small dance steps to deepen its sleep while Dionisia sits down on the ledge on which flowering pots are set beside the door.

"When I was a child, during Christmas and Three Kings my mother took me to the big house on Heroes del '96. I was shy. I stayed in the kitchen peeling garlic while my mother stirred and mixed the sauces. Sweetmeats were her specialty. The owners of the big house gave as gifts the *tocino del cielos, plantanillas, brazos de la reina, turrons* my mother made. Their friends tried to take my mother away to their kitchens. Her *croquettas* melted like butter on the tongue. She threaded *mechado* with suet, made *relleno.* I used to remember all the names of the food."

Patro is surprised by Dionisia's memory, because the woman she knows has only a lean-to roof pitched from the side of the Bermudez's house. With only one wall, people help themselves to things only Dionisia has use for, even the coffee jars she uses as drinking glasses. The little that Dionisia owns can fit in a carton box under Patro's bed.

"One day," Dionisia continues, "the owner came out to the kitchen. When he saw me, he took me by the hand and brought me to the guests. 'Go. Choose a gift,' he told me. There were boxes with pretty ribbons, fruits, nuts, apples. I was barefoot. I didn't have time to look under the table for my slippers."

"What did you pick out?" Patro stops dancing. The child's fists are clenched against her.

"I took a nut, and everyone laughed at me, so the owner pulled out a doll, as tall as I; but his wife took it away. 'What will she do with a doll? She needs a dress, slippers.' The wife gave me a piece of cloth with butterflies printed on it."

"What I remember is my mother insisting that certain foods go together. *Pochero* is served with a sauce of boiled eggplants and squash in vinegar; fried fish with *buro; mongo* with *escabeche.* I liked the chicken's *tumbong.* Bishop's mitre, my father called it."

"My mother never brought food home, but while she cooked she would put bits of food in my mouth. I can still taste the morsels."

"I, too, remember the food my mother cooked. Few people recall nowadays how food should be prepared," Patro says. "Hot and cold food have to be balanced for health. Seafoods are cold; meats are hot. In a month's time, my mother never served the same food. What was served for lunch did not appear on the table for supper."

"I can just drink water and swallow, and I taste my mother's cooking again. If one can remember having eaten well, how can one be poor? We had democracy then, didn't we; when we were growing up?"

"Here, Dionisia. Take it. Something hot is dripping between my legs. It always happens." Patro tucks the wet part of her skirt, folded between her knees as she sits down.

Taking the child, Dionisia walks a short distance to the gate, then faces Patro. "I have not told anyone."

"About?"

"Yesterday. I saw the sun. It was moving fast, dancing for about thirty minutes, and all kinds of colors were coming out of it, whirling."

For the sake of friendship, Patro does not question Dionisia, though she cannot herself imagine the sun acting like a bird that can sing and fly.

"It was about three in the afternoon. I wonder what it means."

"I have seen the moon passing across the sun at noon. In 1954 it grew as dark as night and the roosters crowed. We all watched from here. Benhur and Vergel were up in the star apple tree, which used to stand beside the gate until someone told us to have it cut down because if the roots reached the front steps, someone would die. It happened anyway." Patro looks up at the sun, then quickly away.

Up the trail, Dionisia is walking with her strange gait. With eleven children, none of which have stayed home, Dionisia needs repairing. But it is too delicate a matter to bring up. It has to be the reason Dionisia is always tired, bleeds when she lifts weights. She should not even be carrying the Feleo child. Ashamed, Dionisia would not allow Vergel to examine her.

Hernan Sipalay stops to talk with Dionisia before heading down past the Vitalianos' house.

He has seen Dionisia come out of her gate, has seen her at the doorway. So Patro waits to be greeted by him. She will not offer him coffee as Benhur would do because he has TB. Valentin's mother never served strangers from her own set of dishes; invited only relatives. Dionisia has a cup from which she drinks. Sometimes one of the boys will make a mistake and use it.

Hernan Sipalay stops long enough to ask about Benhur, Vergel and his family. Then he tells Patro again how easy it is to grow orchids. When he gets well, he'll ask for a loan from the credit group Patro administers for Gulod. "Cattleyas are fifty pesos a flower, *Aling* Patro. When I grow orchids I will separate some for you. Just tie them around a piece of charcoal and attach them to the bark of trees. In no time at all you will have flowers falling down from these branches. You don't have to be rich to have beautiful things, *Aling* Patro."

Patro smiles, looks up the trail and down to see if the boys are anywhere. "I'm afraid they crossed the highway and got a ride to town."

Hernan Sipalay has said everything he usually says and walks on. He is always walking around Gulod, but never away from the main trail, for exercise. Always trying to get well, he looks the picture of death, belching his way up and down. People avoid him. Only the mailman talks to him for any length of time; and Benhur. Some say they can't understand Sipalay's accent.

Estong the mailman tells Patro that Hernan's sons were shot by ranchers who took their small plot in the hills—so far into the hills, they thought no one would want to take it—and Hernan keeps dreaming of them: One night, one comes to tell his father that his brother had died; the next night, the other comes with the same story. Estong also tells Patro that Dionisia's daughter, the mother of the two children Dionisia brought to Gulod, is a teacher. One day she did not return to the apartment.

So many to take care of in Gulod. It is to help them that Patro watches the homemakers' health care program on television. It is from that program she learned about rehydration salts for diarrhea; *camote* leaves for indigestion, instead of Lomotil; toothpaste for emergency healing of burns. One time one of Siso Feleo's sons placed his hand on the flatiron. She helps with difficult childbirths, but never with abortions. It is the younger wives who resort to that means of birth control, and they go outside Gulod for it. Some never come back. Patro cannot imagine any woman allowing her womb to absorb the child she's carrying, allowing it to be killed with synthetic chemicals when the breath of the unborn came from God. She is sure aborted children are in heaven. Others she has persuaded to watch the program, but they do not remember a thing. In her sleep she can list the seven leaves that are boiled for asthma.

Younger children have taken over the basketball court. There will be a fight when the others return. The shortest one, one of Hernan Sipalay's children, has just made a basket, prompting Patro to applaud. *Bulilit,* the others call him.

A while longer Patro watches, thinking that Anya and Loreto are long gone. She hopes they do not pass by Maxima's store. She never liked the son Robles, who, when he was little, lifted the skirts of any woman walking by. Maxima bragged that her son only wanted to see what's between their legs, as if that curiosity is a sign of early brilliance.

She could have asked Dionisia to have Nani Feleo send a bowl of *guinatan* for *merienda.* Nani barely covers the cost of what she cooks, after she has sent bowls to neighbors to whom she owes favors, after she feeds her children. It's just as well. Nani will not accept payment, and Loreto can make *champorado* from the cocoa Benhur brought. There are enough *tuyo* for each child to have one dried fish apiece.

Suddenly, unexpected and sharp as the onslaught of pain that stops the breath, Patro feels someone move inside the house—she remembers the wash on the line, the open kitchen door. Trying to calm herself, she guesses it's only a dog that has wandered in, brushing past a chair, around the table where they crowd one another during meals, elbows and drinking glasses in one another's way.

The shadow of a man crossing the kitchen, a shadow of someone, coming like a sound before it is made, stops Patro in the dining room. As if the house is burning, she wants to run out; but she stands where she stopped. A figure she does not recognize heads for the fence, leaps over.

Only after a wait of what seem to her to be hours does Patro enter the kitchen. Right away she sees the jar of coffee, where she keeps the money, gone from the shelf. Untouched are the tiny glass figurines Loreto collects, buying them for a peso each and taking her time choosing from the cloth spread on the ground at the market.

The tins of corned beef are gone, too. What else?

Luckily she keeps the rest of what Benhur gave in the pouch inside her blouse, tied in the handkerchief Valentin gave her, in which she keeps the crucifix she should have given up when she converted to Iglesia.

How did the man know which jar contains money?

When Patro is able to go through the kitchen, she stands at the back door. The wash is hanging from the line. None was taken. The sheet hangs like a bleached tombstone. The whiteness threatens her. Unwilling to think of the dead, she walks away toward the river, away from the house as if it now contains the dark of the moon.

Grass reaches to Patro's knees. To discourage the children from playing near the river, she has allowed the weeds to grow tall, and seed.

Some distance from the bank, Patro stops again. Why did Dionisia say the sun was bursting like a lantern? Full upon her, the sun is buzzing louder than bees enraged by flowers.

As from a dream she cannot make sense of, Patro looks up. The sun is going through its savage dance; and the earth is screaming through her dead children.

Almost two months in Gulod,
Anya still gets sticky glances from the men, bursts of whistling, and, reversing the usual flirtation, serenades from behind windows and doors she passes. From the women she might get curious looks. It is as if they pull their hopes out of the air and refuse to draw her in. Anya, however, delights some older women who claim she reminds them of Dina Bonnevie. They suggest that she become a film star so they can go to see her in the movies.

This attention, which has gotten Atlas, Pitong, and Ryan into fights, has made Loreto jealous. She treats Anya like a younger sister, to be petted or commanded as her mood directs. Noticing this, Patro reminds Loreto that Anya is a guest, and one so young she cries for her mother at night. The advice only makes Loreto meaner, which escalates her mother's remarks about her acting like an old maid who'll certainly scare away suitors with her sour face.

"Don't look!" Loreto tells Anya, hurrying her away from Maxima's store.

Whistles are coming from the men playing checkers on the table where the game has been burned into the wood, and from the spectators around the pool table. The whistles set the dogs barking. The men roughhouse and encourage Robles to ask Anya and Loreto to stop by. Tending store for his mother, Robles is held back by the wooden grille protecting the store. Much is made of his apparent timidity: *Tatanda kang lelong. Ang hina mo pala.*

Distracted from trying to unnerve the pool players, some sit on the benches that are borrowed by neighbors for their wakes.

Loreto cannot understand why she feels so unhappy. It used to be fun walking through Gulod, visiting with neighbors and having a taste of what they were cooking. Why couldn't Vergel have found someone other than a widow with grown children? What makes Anya so attractive, anyway? She is so dark the lipstick does not show on her mouth and it would be useless to apply eyeshadow. Powder only makes her skin glisten, gray.

While *she,* on the other hand. If she let her hair down to her shoulders, Loreto could give the bold starlets heavy competition, even if they pout insolently for the cameras and bare everything. This morning she has pulled her hair severely back. Narcisa Sotero, the labor leader's wife, calls out to her, "Loreto. You are prettier than Luningning." Why does she remind anyone of the pre-War actress, when it is Anya who is so dark she disappears in photographs?

Soon enough Loreto feels ashamed of her harsh thoughts and gives Anya the handkerchief in her pocket. "It's new, Anya. One of the four Benhur gave me." When she graduated with a teacher's certificate, she asked Benhur for the white handkerchief embroidered all over with no space left in between the stitches. It cost thirty pesos then. Now, none can be found any more. She went through all of Santa Cruz.

"Thank you, *Ate* Loreto."

"It's nothing. Don't thank me." Loreto is perplexed. She feels she is all separate and different parts that don't fit together even after she has taken back her angry thoughts by giving Anya the handkerchief. She both likes and dislikes Anya; wants her to leave and also to stay. She pities Anya for the things she does not know and envies her for the tenderness and gentle desires she herself no longer has. Full of unarmed discontent, Loreto walks ahead by herself.

Perhaps if she worked she would feel better. If Marcos concedes, it will be safe for her to work in the city; she can afford an apartment and maybe her mother will live with her. And Anya? Since Anya came she has not seen a tree full of flowers or large butterflies hanging from the leaves of the mango, drying their wings.

Anya catches up. She has washed her hair and rinsed it with *dayap* crushed into the water. A waste of lime, Loreto complained.

In her hurry Anya has stepped onto small stones, almost stumbles. "The dust is hot, *Ate* Loreto."

"Can't you walk without falling?" Loreto shrinks away. Anya has such long fine fingers. It feels like needles on her arm.

Whistles come from a hut. Everyday there are more strangers in Gulod. *Coming for a place to die,* her *Lola* Sula says, with much disdain. They set up cardboard walls against already standing fences; take their baths along the trails.

"Are we going to Mrs. Moscoso's party Saturday?"

"She always invites us and the Lunas," Loreto answers. "She hires a cook because Benhur does not like *Nay* to help." She does not want to go if people keep admiring Anya.

"I'm invited, too?"

"You can wear my blue shoes. You can tell from the way the heels click that they are imported. Benhur brought them."

"Do you think Sally Moscoso is beautiful?" Anya asks. She has seen Sally standing, arms akimbo on her porch, in a hot pink gown that echoes all the sounds from the highway.

"It depends," Loreto says, stepping off to one side of the trail, away from where a woman is scooping the thick waters in the ditch, using the water to wet down the dust. "You'd think she'd be careful," Loreto mutters, snapping her eyes.

Anya is not able to avoid the slime spreading on the trail. She stops to clean her slippers on the grass.

A child runs across from one of the newly raised huts, one room deep, which force the trail to narrow. Some women who do not recognize them throw soapy water down the trail, making it slippery with suds.

Loreto picks her way angrily, steps away from a small child who slips and falls against Anya, still holding a dragonfly. "Put him down," she tells Anya, who picks up the child, wipes its knees with her hand.

"If that pretty girl did not catch you, you would have fallen on your nose. Say thank you." A woman runs after the child, waiting for Loreto to smile back.

"Why didn't you stop?" Anya asks Loreto.

"Why stop? Didn't you see no two of her children look alike? And they're all mestizos?"

"So?"

"She must work in the bars. Probably does not know the children's fathers. Her son is also *puta,* lives off the foreigners. And you held the child against you!"

They walk in silence toward their *Lola* Sula's. Bits of songs and news come over the radio and television in the houses they pass. The sun is at their back. They walk into the wind coming from the river.

"Loreto, listen!" A neighbor comes out. "Suppose you are bathing in the river and someone steals your clothes, leaving you only a face towel. Which part of your body will you cover?"

"Bastos," Loreto says, walking on. "Come, Anya."

"I'd cover my face and run," Anya says to Loreto.

"Don't waste your mind on problems that will never come up."

They walk past a stretch of sunflowers, then a woman cooking *suman* in a clay stove by the trail. A plate of grated coconut and sugar is drawing flies around the banana leaf covering.

"It will be ready soon," the woman invites them to return.

"They're communists. NPAs." Loreto pulls Anya away. She has seen the woman talking with Narcisa Sotero, who used to ask Patro to keep boxes of papers and a typewriter for her husband, usually just before demonstrations—and then, after their house had been searched, would take them back.

"My friend Vangie is NPA."

"What?"

"She left school to join her brothers in the hills. I miss her." Anya remembers the amulet of grass seeds Vangie wore.

"I don't want to talk about communists or politics. There's *Lola* Sula's house. I'll wait for you outside. Go get the plates. Don't tell her I'm with you, and if she asks you to pull her white hair, say you'll do it later."

"What white hair?"

"She likes the new growth pulled, she says, so that heat will escape from her head. Don't give her a chance to tell stories, or we'll be here until the crow turns white."

"How old is she?" Anya hesitates, delays having to go in by herself.

"Ninety-four. She'll live to be 100 because she's waiting for her curses to come true. Now go."

With much fear, Anya walks into the yard. Taking a deep breath she brings the old woman's hand to her forehead. It feels very light, unattached; and pale as if part of a portrait fading in the sunlight. "I come for the plates, *Lola* Sula. So we can bring you supper."

"Loreto?"

"Anya, *po.*"

"Anya? What plates?" The old one hangs on to Anya's hand. "What food do you mean? The food the cat won't eat? Patro never learned to cook. It might be good enough for the market crowd, but not for me. When I went to market, I bought only *lomo* and first-class fruits from Dulong Bayan or San Andres. My *recados* cost several times the meats because I was not afraid to pay the price. Patro will put the money away first. Her *pochero* is so watery. The one time I went to their house, I was hungry, so I sat down. Patro brought out a plate of *dinuguan* that I pulled to my place. Then she brought out a plate of rice and four plates, one with three bananas. It turned out the *dinuguan* was for all three of us. No wonder Valentin never put on weight. Tell her, I fed whatever she sent to the cats and threw away the plates."

Anya looks for Loreto outside the fence. "I have to go, *Lola.* I'll get the plates now." She walks past the old one sitting in a wide chair in the doorway. There is a child's hammock in the living room. She finds the plates inside a pail in the sink. A dipper floats on top of the water. Anya looks for Sula's other daughter-in-law, Milang, and for her children, who, Loreto says, are just waiting for the old one to die so they can inherit everything—jewels and furniture and house. She has seen them passing in front of the house, wearing fancy shoes and carrying handbags.

The plates in hand, Anya returns between the same chairs in the living and dining rooms. This time she takes a peek into the big room. Empty boxes of tissue paper, matches, jars of Vicks Vaporub are on the round table, as if trophies. Things for the light to cling to; to fill space.

There is an old radio the size of a chair. On it, a framed wedding picture rests. The background and pose are the same as in the framed picture in Loreto's house, but the brides are different. In another old photograph, two women pose with their ears pressed to each other so they seem to wear the same earring. In the other room the mosquito net is piled over the bed like a sheer hammock. A large *aparador* mirror catches her looking in.

Once more Anya brings the old woman's hand to her forehead, taking her leave.

"Sit down. I have something to tell you." A heavy locket swings forward from the necklace as the old one indicates that Anya sit on the ledge. Long gold earrings loop the old woman's earlobes with stones of particular brilliance. Now, Anya understands what Loreto means, that her grandmother is tempting a hold-upper at her doorway. On the old woman's fingers are several rings. In one, smaller stones are set in a line like the seeds of tamarind. Through the light blouse with a wide neckline, the straps of the chemise are visible.

"But *Lola.*" She looks quickly for Loreto, to give her a signal.

"What's your hurry? It's not tomorrow already, is it? I will tell you how to tell real diamonds from glass. Look for pinpricks of carbon. Moles, we always called them. If you don't know, you'll be sold a piece of drinking glass."

Anya sits under jasmine vines hanging from the trellis over the doorway. Their shadow on the ground is that of worn curtains. Anya wonders if it's the flowers or French perfume she smells. Loreto says Benhur always brings French perfume to his *Lola* Sula. The white flowers are repeated in the design of the old woman's *camisa.* The soft white hair makes her look like someone whose life is getting better.

"Did you see the statues of saints in my room? My mother set aside the best rice fields for the support of those statues. Well-watered hectares with the highest yield paid for velvet robes with gold threaded through. I used to pull those threads out to wind round and round my ring finger. Those with faces of ivory, how pale and clear. Now everyone looks sallow because electricity thickens skin, makes the face tougher than the hands of laundrywomen. Wicks in oil dishes or candles make the best light."

Anya goes to the radio beside the old woman. Set between two stations, it is playing two songs at once; two newscasters are reporting.

"Leave it alone."

Surprised, Anya looks back to the trail. Loreto might have gone back and left her. "What do you do sitting there, *Lola?*"

"Why, I'm talking to the saints. They feel slighted if you miss them. *Masamang magtampo sa iyo.*"

Anya has been told that *Lola* Sula has converted, so why is she talking to saints?

"Here. Your fingers are stronger. Open the locket. I am fifteen in the picture. The other picture is of Valentin Cleofas, who was three months in my womb when his father died. That's his First Communion picture. Already he looked like Rudolfo Valentino. I named both my sons Valentin. Felix and Cleofas. You know Patro enticed him. She put something in his food or had him bewitched. Such things can happen."

Anya hears her name being called from the trail. "I have to go, *Lola.*" She can see *Aling* Dionisia's lean-to, the table where a clay stove is being tended. All kinds of plants grow in cans. Thicker than walls, so dense that animals cannot push through, the plants give *Aling* Dionisia some privacy and protection.

"My husband was a surveyor. Valentin Cleofas was going to be a lawyer until that Patro got him and he had to give up his studies to give her children . . ." Her mouth hangs open, as if she's waiting for words to enter her. Her molars, Anya notices, have moved forward to the front of her gums, giving a crude shape to her mouth. "Valentin Felix died on the night of his birthday. Milang passed out on waking up. She keeps asking her mother in California for a ticket, to apply for her, but the old one is wise and wants to make sure Milang and her children inherit this house first. Are you also waiting for me to die?"

Taken aback by the question, Anya blushes.

"Good. I'm not about to die. I will outlive everyone, because God wants me to defend Him, to avenge Him."

"Why don't you just forgive people, Lola?"

"The Bible says evil doers have to be punished."

A puppy has wandered into the front yard, goes sniffing around the chair.

"*Alis! Alis!* Chase it away."

Anya makes a motion to scare away the puppy, which proceeds to roll on the ground, exposing its soft underside.

"You know, I sold my jewels for Vergel and he brings me sample medicine. *Que ingrato!* Lightning strike me if that's not the truth." She sounds like an old tree weeping and singing in the wind.

Anya thinks of her grandmother in Kapalaran, hair still thick and down past her waist, who sits by the window waiting. Sometimes she weaves a trap of grass for Rosalio to catch birds; but only if Rosalio promises to release them afterward. She wishes she had gone back with her mother, wishes she had sent something back for her grandmother. Feeling the handkerchief in her pocket, Anya decides to save it for her.

"Who is that woman looking over here?" Sula asks. "I've seen her before, bringing men to the room she rents in that direction. I tell you, it's sinful. All these women whose children will meet their fathers in the city and not recognize them. Look away. It's an insult to God's eye."

Anya is surprised to see it is Loreto, trying to catch her attention between the hibiscus shrubs. She does not know how to reply.

"All our troubles began when the Japanese came. People began to look out for themselves, then to become greedy. We never locked our doors before the War. Now, even with ten locks robbers break in. Ignore that woman. Pretend she's not there."

"I have to go, *Lola*."

"Go to my room first and bring out that picture of me in a *saya*. That was sewn by the same woman who sewed the coronation gowns of the Miss Philippines. I used to know people of quality. Before everyone got greedy. That's a merciless disease; the same as *cadangcadang* that brings down coconut trees. Like leprosy that eats the flesh, greed eats the heart and the soul. I'm glad my husband never saw what I saw after the war."

Anya gets up, plates in hand. Loreto is now walking back and forth, looking in.

"Do you remember in Intramuros there was a church in every block. You couldn't walk far without meeting friars in every color of habit, and you had to genuflect and kiss their hand for a blessing. I'm glad I'm free of that now. The paschal candles were like fat pears from China. My husband used to say my legs were shaped like tapers on the altar. I wish he had been converted with me. Only Iglesias go to heaven, you know. During the Japanese Occupation, they did not touch Iglesias. Only Catholics. But the steamer sank. Do you know how to pray?"

"Yes, *Lola*."

"Pray then that my husband's body will be found so he can be buried in holy ground and his soul can rest. And when you pray, kneel down with your knees close together. Then if you should die while you're praying you'll go straight to heaven. There's that woman again, trying to be friendly. Maybe she thinks I will invite her in."

Anya darts out through the gate, not pulling it after her. The vines of jasmine cover the ground with their shade.

"I told you to come out right away," Loreto scolds. "You talked to her all morning and I wanted to go to the movies. Now, *Nay* will not let us."

"Can you use this?" *Aling* Dionisia is standing in front of a poster of a concert at the Cultural Center, one of the things she found when she went to Manila to look for her grandchildren. She brings out from her pocket a handful of used rubber bands. On her table, the only furniture she has beside a bench, are piles of newspapers which she cuts up and makes into paper bags, a dish of vinegar in which tiny red peppers float, a pot of rice on which she has placed two small eggplants as thin as one's finger and a piece of dried sardine. She offers these.

They thank her and move on.

It is almost noon. Anya holds the plates over her head.

"Don't look!" Loreto almost hears the whistles before they are made. "They're watching to see if we'll react." Someone says, intending to be heard, that she is prettier than Anya. Pleased, she offers to take Anya to the simultaneous opening of *Sensual* starring Chanda Romero and Lito Gruet. "Unless there's another bus strike and *Nay* does not let us. But if we go, we'll pass by Rustan and ride the escalator to the bridal shop. All imported gifts."

As soft as air, the whistles follow them.

They pass the *vaciador* with his grinding machine on the handlebars of his old bicycle. "Don't turn and look at him or he'll drop his pants as if his possession is worth seeing."

Anya looks down on the trail until the *vaciador* has passed.

"All men want are our bodies," Loreto says. Even to herself she sounds like her mother, but she enjoys Anya's full attention. "All I want is to leave this place. Anywhere will be better." Hips that might have been Chanda Romero's move in restless orbit to "I Wanna Have Fun," a tape Benhur brought. It is as if the earth is turning inside her body. "I could have married. Long ago, if I wanted." She does not want Anya to think it is out of necessity she's still a virgin.

The rest of the way home the wind is at their back, stroking the tops of trees and the napes of their necks.

Like someone ill

refusing to die, the *vaciador* comes to Gulod hoping to sharpen a few knives, although he knows knives are necessary only to cut meat, and the staple in the barrio has become vegetables that can be snapped into pieces; chicken necks to boil in coconut milk and peanuts; fingersize fish that can be roasted or thrown into the pot without gutting. Good times, like relatives who have gone overseas to live, have passed out of the barrio's memories, and his.

Anyway, he comes; because suddenly he gets the feeling that death is about to wrestle him to the ground. After nights of sleeping out in Ugarte Field, surrounded by the high-rises of the financial district—where, during the day, those with homes applaud opposition speeches and attend Mass, thereafter leaving it to the homeless to keep Marcos men from taking over the field in the middle of Makati—for no reason explainable, the *vaciador* starts feeling trapped. It begins with being unaccustomed to the new camaraderie with the better class—a speaker said that's what they had at the tent city in Ugarte—to the smiles of the matrons whose blood-red lips make the *vaciador* think of raw meat hanging from hooks in the market.

A sense of something sacred going on has kept him in the open field hedged in by buildings. When he closes his eyes, he can sometimes see the Host being broken into smaller and smaller pieces so that some mornings, what people receive is not much bigger than crumbs, but it still is Christ, all of Him. He has summoned up the courage to stand in line and has had to step aside, crying . . .

"Knives, scissors, nippers!"

To stop his thoughts from going back to Ugarte—useless thoughts that will buy him no cigarettes; observations that will not hold a place for him to sleep—the *vaciador* fastens his attention on the trail so he can guide his bicycle between the stones. The water splashes inside the plastic container tied to the handlebar.

It used to be that people asked him in for some talk and coffee. Now, it seems people are holding their breath inside their rooms, waiting for him to pass; as if he's the avenging angel against whom they must disguise their doors. Angel of Satan.

That morning, it's either Gulod for him or getting in the way of demonstrators flooding Manila with their bodies, their streamers, and their demands that Marcos resign. An impossible dream, with the military in the president's hand. Day Three of the boycott of crony banks by the opposition, he was caught in the rally of factory workers and students at the United States Embassy on Roxas. *Out with the bases.* The *vaciador* understands that's a cry for freedom, which is about not having to agree with what disturbs your conscience. He had been marched out of his corner when the Task Force Civil Disobedience Group picketed Magnolia near the Monastery of the Carmelites, occupying the seats inside to keep customers from buying crony ice cream. At Mendiola, he barely escaped being pushed against the barbed wire barricades when the Presidential Guards charged the Anti-Fraud and Terrorism Group heading for Malacañang Palace. *Marcos cheated: should be evicted.*

Power deadlocked against power; that's how he sees it. Power that is not, say, a building that can be torn down and permanently destroyed: power existing not just between government and people, but between any two persons. It's a kind of power when you can make another happy or afraid. And the struggle goes on inside, too. Take him for an example. He's forever trying to make himself behave, as if he's his own child for which he must answer.

"Gunting kayo diyan. Gunting."

His words echo back to him. Some day he would like to walk into Gulod whistling, the way they used to go to the province on Sundays; before secret marshals and dissidents began reducing the population, which, he read, is greater in numbers than that of either Spain or France.

"*Gunting . . .*"

Before the war, you could go to visit relatives, talk and eat, talk some more before returning to the city, hauling back eggs and fruits in the same baskets in which you brought bread and canned meat.

He steadies the two whetstones between the handlebars. The sun is burning his ear, making it ring.

Now, people are lucky to have a place to sleep, let alone to visit. He saw someone going into a crack in the seawall where it caved in, then pulling a piece of sackcloth across the opening. People are sleeping with the crabs now? He has seen cooking fires for whatever can be caught from Manila Bay. He has even heard singing, not just the radio playing. Not again, but *once* he watched a woman combing her hair on the seawall, long strokes disentangling the strands as far as her arm could reach, while the sun scattered the colors of the rainbow across the upper sky, over the ships and equipment salvaging wrecks from the different wars. Singing! Those seadrift people are luckier than those who sleep openly on the sidewalks, clinging tightly to themselves; foetuses expelled too soon into the world.

Who is responsible for the homeless? for himself? What must God think when he sees Arturo Sanchez, *vaciador,* asleep between crates in the market, on a bench narrower than his body? Like the stall owners, will He call: *Alis, Alis?* Out of there!

Gulod is Paradise. The possible dream. People have roofs, tables on which to set their plates. Their children's pictures have walls on which to hang. So what if the houses face in all directions, as though a typhoon uprooted them in its fury, then dropped them on top of each other? So what if the streets, according to the mailman, are torn trails running between kitchens and bedrooms, as if Gulod were one single roominghouse, with walls and secrets and enmities shared? To trick oneself into going on living is to believe in Paradise, to believe it occupies ground you will stumble upon, if not the next day, then the day after. Hernan Sipalay can't be too crazy because he believes in Paradise. Eden. "Knives. *Balisong.* Scissors." He tells himself to practise patience. Eventually fish bite the hook. Impatient ones never get to heaven, though what a waste of time it is waiting. He has been squandering his life thinking of things he will never see or have. It's picking on a scab, keeping the wound bleeding to prove you still breathe.

He bends down to pull out the leaf caught between the spokes. At night he cleans his bicycle before he washes his feet.

A toddler comes running into the trail, wearing a shirt below which his bird hangs like a dark root. A beak. Surprised at seeing the *vaciador,* the child turns around on legs as thin as an insect's. The distended stomach makes the *vaciador* think of the Japanese Occupation, when food was shipped to Japan. People were reduced to eating coconuts. Their extremities swelled. They dropped dead in the street. The memory makes him shiver. If only he could choose which part of his memory to recall, could select which parts to call true.

He has always eaten anything—Adidas: roasted chicken claws, stiff as roots but tasty—IUDs: intestines skewered on bamboo sticks—helmets: heads. . . . In Bangued, he remembers seeing Japanese soldiers entering houses and biting off sausages drying over the clay stoves, their trucks carrying away the harvests. His mother and her sisters smeared their faces with charcoal and left their hair uncombed during the day when the soldiers marched through the streets, taking what they wanted. He wishes he had pictures to show people how beautiful his mother was. There was a life-size portrait of her with her sisters. She was so beautiful, no one else could play the Virgin in the passion plays. There were diplomas on the walls of their houses. When he tells this to the people in the market, they smile, thinking he is full of air. But it's all true. Only, he would be ashamed to show his face back in Bangued. Who would recognize him as Arsenia's son?

He has tried other ways to make a living. He drove a *calesa* in Binondo, scooped the horse's droppings into the sack as municipal ordinance required. He could even eat from the same pail as his horse, because horses are clean. No fermented garbage or sewage for horses, unlike pigs. During the war, the meat of imported racehorses was sold in the markets. He has tasted everything.

What he would like, though he doesn't pray for it, because he's reserving prayers for serious illness, is to win the Sweepstakes and buy a small house in Gulod, close to the river so he can watch it flowing. If he happens to be that lucky, he will not keep everything for himself, but walk about the city, dropping small bills into unsuspecting hands. The beggars on P. Tuazon he can't help, because they beg from cars stopped at the lights on EDSA. Epifanio de los Santos. Epiphany of the Saints. What a name to give a son!

Maybe he'll just invite the beggars to a meal, beggars like those who sleep in the carts used to haul loads by the day. It's ten pesos a load, fifty American cents, except foreign coins are not negotiable. Those in Santa Cruz who sit in the churchyard offering to buy dollars do not accept coins. One thing he has not done is carry loads. It takes all morning for dockworkers to make deliveries, all afternoon to try to collect. *Comerciantes* do not let go easily of money; not the first and last thing during the day, according to the custom. Those who do not die of curable diseases make him mad. They're as stingy as hell. They and those who do not attend the same Mass as their servants; who sit in the front pews as if God Himself reserves those seats for them; who never fold the money they drop into the collection baskets, so others can see how much they give, which is never as much as they should; who judge everyone, playing God.

The *vaciador* suspects that the poor will always be poor because the rich are too busy getting richer to care. It ends up with only the poor sharing with one another. After the tent city in Makati folds up, it will be back to hardship and hunger for those who have been given sandwiches at noon.

He himself is always hungry. Whoever can invent food that stays permanently in the stomach will become a millionaire. Far-fetched as that is, it will come to nothing in the end because worms eat you, rich and poor, all the same. So actually, the most powerful are worms; which makes democracy possible. To them a president is the same as a *vaciador,* who is the same as a beggar: someone who has not tasted the food and women of happy-happy places. Leaning his bicycle against a fence, he fans himself with his cloth hat. It looks as ragged as the piece of cloth with which he tests a blade's sharpness. The sun is burning holes in the sky, even the trees appear to be fighting for breath.

Several young men pass him, transistor radios held to their ears. By the stations they listen to, he can tell if they're Marcos or opposition. Radio Veritas has become popular.

He eases the bicycle back on the trail. That morning he has not encountered anyone he recognizes, just as in the market there are more and more strangers. Every day, almost, he discovers another one has died. Veins get too weak to hold blood. Crazed from hunger, the body starts growing lumps. It's either disease or vigilantes: germs that walk on two legs and shoot pistols.

"Knives, scissors, *patalim.*" If it's ice cream he's selling, he might get children running. Only one or two will have money, but the rest will wait to be offered a lick. Tired of talking to himself, which is what thinking is, the *vaciador* looks for anyone at the window. If he sold *balut,* would people open their doors? *"Balut, penoy, baluuuut,"* he sings the call. None open their doors. If he had three pesos himself, he would buy a *balut.* Some people eat the embryo feather by feather, pulling a wing here, a leg there. He always swallows the whole duck egg. His stomach is sensitive. He read that the English roast unborn lamb foetuses. Same pure protein, so why do the tourists curl their lips at *balut?* If people could afford *balut,* tuberculosis would not be on the rise. His wife died of it.

He tricks himself into not getting sad by asking himself whether he would prefer to be blind or deaf? Lame or with stubs for fingers? What is more important, food or drink? None of the questions he thinks of can be permanently answered.

The stone he kicks rolls only a few feet away on the trail. Maybe if he repaired umbrellas he'd get a customer. He has met the umbrella man in

Gulod, carrying old umbrellas to cannibalize for parts; and the vinegar man whose pants fall off when he sneezes.

It's also possible to die from overeating. A rice-cake vendor gave half a *bilao* of *bibingca* to a soldier who had escaped the Death March. According to someone who saw this, the soldier died before he could finish the last piece. Impossible to believe. He supposes anything can kill. All that's necessary is that it's your time to die.

Two cigarettes are left in his shirt pocket. If he does not earn enough for lunch, one cigarette can fool his stomach into thinking he has eaten. He knows a few such tricks. When he runs out of cigarettes, he stands near the curb to inhale exhaust from passing cars. Trucks are the best. They belch the thickest, richest smoke.

A man returning to his hut greets him with a nod. No word is exchanged. It's the man from Mindoro, whose sons became deaf and blind from diving without equipment to drive fish into trawlers' nets. Though it's none of his fault, he feels guilty about it. It's beginning to seem that Gulod is all hard luck, too.

Where is Paradise then? It's not in the scale of payments, Attorney Vitaliano told him, explaining compensation for injuries suffered. The loss of a life is not at the top of the list, as he recalls, the winning combination being the loss of an eye and a limb. The blind beggars on P. Tuazon are losers in any case because a syndicate controls them. Getting rich off the blind should be rewarded with hell fire. Maybe they're lucky after all, since they can't see the misery about. Though it's certainly possible to hear suffering.

Hurrying home from the market, women rush past him on the trail. Spit is fermenting inside his mouth from having no one to talk to. Attorney Vitaliano always stopped to talk to him, to offer him a cigarette. He wanted his son to become a lawyer, someone good with words. The *vaciador* lays his bicycle against a tree in order to take out his wallet. Its sole content now is his son's picture. He holds it at some distance. Just above his hand he imagines his son playing on the trail catching a dragonfly while his wife says, *Catch it by the wings.* He once tried to catch a big red dragonfly that pulled away, leaving him with its tail. The sun bears down on the picture. He does not have one of his wife, has this only because the photographer agreed to wait until the coffin was taken to the cemetery. His son was three years, two months then. In June his son would have been twenty-three. He can't imagine how Junior would look now.

No time to waste, he takes his bicycle by the seat and handlebar and sets it on the trail. When he passes a church, he remembers to pray for his son. How will they recognize each other in heaven, if heaven is now and here? The world can't be ending anytime soon because there's so much to correct in human nature. Maybe the old man who sold *galapong* in the market is right: living is our punishment, the hell and purgatory after which heaven had to be next, for how can God bear to see people in hell fire after this kind of life? Death can't be the only way to escape poverty. The harder one tries, the more hardships.

"I thought you're the vinegar man." A woman stops in her doorway, the pink curlers in her hair like deformed flowers.

"Vinegar man!" he mimics. "If I showed up with jars instead of a whetstone, you'd be coming out saying you thought I was the *vaciador.*"

"Tse!" the woman says, her nose up in the air. The door she slams looks puny beside her pique.

The *vaciador* shrugs her away. Another one of those. Women are either scented or unscented. This one is neither. Scents he breaks down into imported and local. Outside all categories is the woman whose natural odor is that of petals bruised gently by the wind. This is what his father told him. Fragrance pouring itself out of a woman's lips—and poisonous odors, too.

"How much for a small knife?"

Not expecting a customer so soon after the contentious woman, the *vaciador* quotes the old price, but, grateful to have a *buena mano* for the day, he does not amend it. Five pesos. While the woman disappears inside to get her knife, the *vaciador* kicks out the bicycle stand, steadies the wheels on the ground. Then, to get a laugh from the children who have appeared at the door, he goes into the motions of the exercises the Chinese perform early morning in Ongpin and Luneta.

Trapping their laughter with their hands, the children watch the *vaciador* slip a rubber ring over the pedals so he can turn the whetstones.

The children make him think of his son, of the last time, just as he was going out—with a heavier whetstone that threw out sparks like Roman candles—that time. His mind attempts to evade the memory of himself angry, the reason having long since escaped him, though it was fierce on his mind that day or he would not have taken the broom to whip the boy . . .

"Here," the woman extends the knife, her skirt catching on the hands of the children starting to dance in the doorway. Tightly held, a banana oozes between the youngest's fingers.

It is to make himself laugh that he turns the knife in his hand saying: "It's as dull as my head." Had he ever made his son laugh as the children are laughing?

"If you had passed by yesterday, I could have sliced the ham as thin as parchment for breakfast. To go with eggs *estrellado,* don't you know?" The woman smiles broadly, to indicate she's exaggerating for a bit of fun.

Compelled to pick up her jesting, the *vaciador* replies, "Never mind. After I'm through with this knife, you can debone the chicken for supper and your husband will wonder how you pulled the wings out without breaking the skin."

"Relleno? Why we just had stuffed boned chicken yesterday! Tonight it will be *escabeche.* Sea bass. Hurry so I can slice the peppers and onions. The carrots I cut into petals. Maybe I'll cook the fish in white sauce. *Salza blanca* is a good change."

"Of course. My wife uses imported corn starch."

"So do I." The woman carries the joke further. "I never go to the wet market. *Talipapas!* Only supermarkets and then only first-class fish and prawns. Tenderloin from Australia, don't you know? None but the best. See how big and fat my children are. Grapes from California. Chestnuts from China."

"You're another Imelda, I see." Tired of the banter, the *vaciador* hurries to be on his way.

"How do you know?" challenges a boy old enough to wear pants under his shirt.

Glad to be relieved of the woman's tiresome talk, the *vaciador* tests the blade before turning to the boy. In slow and measured tone, as if expounding on the state of the economy, he says, "I'm the knife sharpener at the Palace. I also cut Imelda's diamonds to change their shape when she gets tired of them. When the president saw my work, he asked me to sharpen every knife in the country . . ."

"Macoy is on his way to join Duvalier," someone calls out from across the trail. "Cory will evict them from the Palace, and we'll live happily ever after."

"For free?" the boy asks. "I don't believe you."

"Insolent!" The *vaciador* spits the word out into the dust. "And I was just thinking you are one of the *angelitos.*"

Everyone understands he is referring to the hundreds of schoolchildren in public schools who, early in December, received First Holy Communion at the Cathedral, with Jaime Cardinal Sin himself officiating. In identical white with large blue bow ties, they also marched in the Marian procession from San Agustin to Luneta, part of the Marian Year; the pride of the Cofradia de Damas y Caballeros, and of everyone who watched.

The boy presses his lips together, refusing to back down.

Looking across the way to the woman who said the president was joining Duvalier in exile, the *vaciador* acknowledges her, "Any knife, Mrs.?"

The woman giggles. "Mine was borrowed."

"Borrowed!" The *vaciador* gives her an incredulous stare which he then passes around to his audience. "So you never heard what my father said on his deathbed! Never heard it from your own father or mother! Tsk. Tsk. Tsk."

"What did he say?" The woman leans forward, propping her elbows on the sill. Her tone is partly serious.

Pressing the knife to the whetstone, the *vaciador* starts pedalling even more furiously to turn it. When sparks fly, he sprinkles water from the plastic container. Splashed, the children jump back, wipe their faces, while the *vaciador* concentrates, making the woman wait for his answer. To be able by himself to make people wait is to be like the president on whose word people hang. That's what power is all about; when the mere sight of you makes another falter. It's the reverse of feeling guilty about someone else, of taking pity on another person; because that way you are in the power of another, your thoughts never become free of them.

"What did your father say?" Curiosity blanks the faces of the others.

The *vaciador* takes his time, tests the knife on the piece of cloth he pulls out slowly from his back pocket, pulls out a handkerchief to press to his lips. To be able to make them wait is to be able to take what he wants from them; is power and Paradise.

"He forgot," the boy says, smirking.

"Forgot!" The word comes out of the *vaciador* with the force of a curse. "Boy, you are looking at a man who went to school with Ferdinand . . ."

"Bolero!" The woman across the way laughs. "You?"

"Hurry up," the woman who owns the knife has her payment in hand, and resents the other woman's intrusion.

The *vaciador* starts coughing, and cannot give any of several answers he could possibly give: "Is the president the only Ferdinand?" Or, "Doesn't attending the same school, years apart, make you classmates?" He might tell the woman at the window, "My father said, your spouse maybe; but your knife! Never let it be borrowed." But he's coughing so hard his body feels like a shirt coming off, inside out. He can tell by their eyes that they're afraid he might spit out blood. In his anger other answers hurtle through him like train wrecks, but not past his coughing.

"For free?" the boy insists.

The woman at the doorway has pushed her children behind her. Windows open out. People passing by stop.

He comes out of the coughing like a plane coming out of a tailspin. "Yes, for free!" he faces them. And just to show them that they are yo-yos on a string that he can walk on the ground, he adds, "I'll even pay anyone who gives me a knife to sharpen."

"It's a trick," the boy says.

"Look at me, boy." The *vaciador* spins the boy about. "You see me? I'm a man of honor. You know what that means? You don't doubt a man of honor. He's not like a politician who can lift the print off documents just by passing his hand over them. He's not a lawmaker who breaks the law. With a man of honor you need not lock your doors. Now, bring out your knives. And those who want to watch, stand over here."

"Why?" Several ask.

Like a sailor paying out rope from a coil, the *vaciador* takes his time. "Because."

"Because what?"

"Because I'm charging everyone for watching! That's what!" And he mounts his bicycle, turning and twisting with the trail, leaving them laughing and confused. He feels justified. Will they remember that morning! He has cut through their lives with his wit, unlike those politicians who put their own campaign managers to sleep by recycling their promises, year after year, town after town.

The boy with the insolent face actually fed him lines. They should do a vaudeville together.

Confidence recovered, the *vaciador* stops to light one of the two cigarettes in his pocket. After all the years of thinking he has mislaid himself, he discovers he has a face after all. A name and an occupation! A man of honor! He can make others pay attention. That is power and freedom and Paradise.

A hand on the handlebar to steady the whetstones, the *vaciador* negotiates the holes on the trail. Movement inside the Vitalianos' front room catches his eye. He dismounts, cigarette between his lips.

Inside the room open to the trail is a girl about thirteen, fifteen; young, trying to put a baby to sleep against her shoulder. It appears she's alone. The long shiny hair bouncing off her chest attracts him. It reminds him of the 90-foot-high Christmas tree around which the Holiday on Ice skaters performed at the Araneta Coliseum. Unable to afford a ticket, he studied the posters.

"Where's your mother?" he asks.

Anya looks at the *vaciador,* then quickly away. Pressing her face to the cheeks of Siso Feleo's child making sleepy sounds, she brushes the *vaciador* off as if he's a pesky little insect and turns her back to him.

The *vaciador* leans his bicycle on the gate, continuing to look in. There is no other sound in the house. The trail is empty. Ten minutes is enough time, he thinks; watching her dance on the concrete floor, the softly rounded heels pinkish; making him think of *macopas* hanging out of reach on a branch, growing spicy in the sun between new leaves, thoughts starting to overpower him as his eyes move up on her legs, up to where they join; strong thoughts colliding inside his head, grinding him up inside.

In the same motion of stepping into Paradise and desire, intercepting himself, the *vaciador* pulls away from the doorway. Still filled with longing, he steps back into his shadow on the trail. Guiding his bicycle with one hand on the handlebar the other lightly steadying the whetstones, he follows the trail where it lengthens between the houses, like a river held within its banks.

Waiting for Osong's call

about her Saturday evening party, Sally Moscoso walks the corners of her bedroom, stopping at the window to the porch but avoiding Gulod outside the curtains. To her it is a damaged fresco of nature, the slope pulled bare of grass around each house to force snakes into visibility. Once, she took the boys to the river, to picnic under the *alugbati* which no longer grows there. On passing the Vitalianos she invited Benhur, his mother, and Loreto, who was then the age of her sons. Benhur improvised shade from banana leaves and some sticks. They sat on a sandbar, at an old table that the current slowly pulled away so by the time they were through it was floating down with the banana leaves on which they had eaten with their fingers.

Except for the Vitalianos—because of Benhur—and the Lunas, Sally cares to know no one in Gulod. Gulod nevertheless manages to enter her dreams. The steel factory upstream dumps its shavings in the river, so the women who wash their clothes there tear their hands on the metal. Just thinking about Gulod and its open sores makes her dizzy; her body starts making demands that she go out for a drive, phone someone, check on the boys, sleep. Going away is like falling out of hell.

But unless they move away, she can no more avoid Gulod than she can avoid the dead eyes of fish in the market, especially of the squids. The mere thought of it sends a tremor through her body.

If she could go back to sleep, she would forget about the party that evening. Phone calls to Osong went unanswered. Do his secretaries make paper balls of the messages? After many demands and promises on her part, Miggy and Joel tried to see their father. No success. She herself went, but when she saw Ting Dolor's car, courage failed her. She recognized it from the descriptions given by friends: they keep track for one another of their husbands' infidelities. Benhur was never in his office. As usual, the two were on some escapade. For such a small city as Manila, people manage to disappear.

An American was knocking outside Benhur's door. He talked to her for thirty minutes, maybe ten, on the elections, politics, and New York while she sat beneath the painting in the hall. She invited him to the party. He had heard of Gulod, he said. Imagine! Another *bolero!* Terence Hugg. A made-up name for a CIA agent. Why was he trying to see Benhur?

"Is Loreto there?" She calls down and one of the maids asks if she should summon Loreto.

Other calls have to be made to make sure people will come as they promised.

If Osong does not come, whose birthday will they celebrate?

If he finds out, her brother will say, *I told you so.* It's her brother who bought her the house. It is in his name. He built a house for their mother, too; from his many business deals: buying and selling dollars, a cattle ranch, a restaurant, real estate. He is generous to them. Once, after asking her to count the hundred-dollar bills into batches of ten thousand—he's too cheap to invest in a machine—he gave her all the loose bills. He has memberships in Wack Wack, Columbian Club, Manila Polo Club, buying them like he buys condos: for investment, not for his use. Pleasure comes from young boys. He buys orphans from around the American bases and spends for young mestizos who go to exclusive schools. One is even in the same class as Miggy and Joel.

Mababaw ang ligaya.

Sally goes into the boys' room. Shoes shined. *Barongs* ironed. Black pants hanging so the creases remain sharp. Should they not wear farmers' attire? Too late. She should have thought of it a day before.

Once more she calls downstairs to see if Loreto has arrived. She is very close to giving up, to having her brother adopt the boys and going off; to putting an end to everything. She wants Osong back, so she can leave him—take the boys and go—or have her brother take the boys, but it would be gruesome for them in his household. One day he's rolling in dollars and the next, he tallies only losses.

The phone rings but no one is answering.

"Will someone answer!" Sally shouts, tying her robe tighter about her as if to choke herself. "Someone!"

"Wrong number, Mamá," Joel calls up to her. "We're waiting for you. Come have breakfast."

Waiting for her? Weren't they in their beds when she checked their clothes for the party?

Pushing her hair up from the sides, Sally goes downstairs and directly to the dining table, where she insists they have all their meals instead of in the kitchen. "You're not drinking your Milo."

"Is the party still on, Mamá?" Miggy asks, reaching for the glass of Milo.

"You're in for heavy competition. There's a wedding at Villamor Air Base. General Piccio and primary sponsors are . . . you guess!" Joel stirs his glass.

"No games. Who?" Sally pushes away the plate at the head of the table. She wants just coffee, and a banana. Cigarette afterward, for dessert as Miggy says.

"It's in the papers, Mamá. The First Lady and General Ver! Reception at Manila Hotel. I'm sure Papá will not miss that." Joel is now turning his plate counterclockwise, slowly.

"Or the ordination. Same time." Miggy says. "Two new priests for Cory. Papá might attend that."

"Papá?" Joel laughs.

Sally calls for coffee. If Osong were invited to the wedding, he did not ask her. Perhaps he's taking Ting Dolor and Sunday's papers will have a picture of them, captioned: Commissioner and Mrs. Moscoso. If he comes after the wedding, he might bring her. "Are you all deaf in the kitchen. I asked for coffee." If that happens, she'll pretend Ting Dolor is just another guest. The First Lady has Dovie Beams and rivals, some of whom are picked up by helicopter and brought to Malacañang Palace. Who does Imelda have besides George Hamilton?

"Sorry, Ma'm." The new maid comes in singing: "San Miguel/Red Horse/Gold Eagle/Miguelito . . ."

"What?" Sally pinches the maid's arm. "Stop that."

"The beers we are boycotting, Mamá." Joel starts singing. "Come on, Miggy. Together now. We better keep in practice."

Sally places a hand over Joel's mouth, getting up from her chair. "Stop it. And take that thing off." She means the NAMFREL vest made of rice sack. "Wear your blue striped shirt like Miggy's."

"I'll wear it tonight, Mamá. This is just for this morning. We'll be back . . ."

"Be back? What do you mean? You're not going any place. It's your father's birthday. He can come any minute."

"We told you yesterday," Miggy drinks his Milo, making a point of letting his mother see. "We'll be back at three."

"Noon," Sally says, realizing she has just been tricked into giving permission. "It's over two weeks since the snap election. Don't you think if something will happen, it should have by now? You're wasting your time with your boycotts."

"Boycott Day Watch 5, Mamá. You should come. Some mothers join and they have fun, too. President Marcos is still stoppable. Very." Joel says each word with exaggerated stress.

"You have invited your friends?"

"Everyone we ran into, Mamá. Everyone."

"We better go, Joel. We still have no gift."

"Three sharp, then. Pass by your father in the office. Check our . . ."

"Four, Mamá." Together, both kiss her on the cheeks.

Sally watches them leave. Joel always slides his way to the door, leaving parallel tracks on the waxed tiles. Miggy takes the time to brush his teeth. It's just so impossible, Sally thinks. She can't get obedience any more.

It's all a charade. The opposition thinks they can cry *Poof,* and the President and Imelda will disappear like the Shah of Iran or Duvalier. So naive.

Imelda took her in the entourage she brought to celebrate Iran's 2,000 years. Sally knows she will not see anything as grand, a modern fairy tale. Air-conditioning in the desert. Such opulence. It made her believe Salome, Cleopatra existed. And the Queen of Sheba, too.

Lost in those memories, Sally goes to the door too late to wave to the boys, to remind them to check the mileage so they'll know if the driver, instead of waiting, rents out the car in Santa Cruz. Will they learn to stay away from photographers! She expected Osong to blame her when their picture appeared under the Youth Coalition vs. Crony Corps banner. They should know NISA is monitoring those activities. At least they should tie a handkerchief across their faces so when they're up for a job later on, no one can bring up the photos. How can you reclaim your children? Just a year ago, she could tell them anything.

How innocent they really are. For a small certificate of appreciation from NAMFREL, they risk everything. She can't imagine 500,000 being deceived into thinking it is their civic duty to monitor the elections and the counting, and to force the president to concede.

About to lock the door, Sally stands there to wait for Loreto, who has appeared at the gate, and stops to check the goldfish in the miniature pond. "Hurry. You're late. There are all those calls to make. Have you had breakfast, or shall I have the ham reheated?"

Loreto takes her time entering, annoyed by Sally always giving her a chance to refuse instead of just having food served. Should she admit all she had was coffee and a *pan de limon* because the boys polish off everything within a minute of their sitting down and she does not dare ask if that is all, because her mother is already wondering what to serve for the next meal, afraid the money will not last until Benhur comes or sends the week's expenses?

As usual, Joel and Miggy left their plates almost untouched. The food is returned so often to the refrigerator—Sally will not waste it on the servants, who cook their meals in separate pots over sawdust in the backyard at the same time they cook the dogs' food, that it dries up or molds inside containers.

"Are you sure? Then we can start making the calls." She pushes together on the glass *frutera* the fingersize bananas she could not get the boys to eat. "Try these? They're very sweet."

"I'm not hungry." Loreto goes to the television in the living room.

"Nothing but old movies, Loreto. Try the bananas. If . . . I weren't fat, I'd eat them."

Loreto knows she's expected to protest; but she's past the stage in their relationship when she will flatter Sally, who is fat everywhere: hips and face and ears—brain, too. Not for all the clothes in the world would she live in Sally's body, though many think Sally pretty.

From the kitchen comes the maid's singing of the boycott jingle: Miguelito/Coca Cola/TruOrange/Sprite/Cheezie/Cream cheese/Sour cream/Chocolait/Buttercup Premium/Magnolia . . .

"*Puñeta!* Stop it. *Ang sarap kurutin sa singit.*" Sally gets angry.

"Shall we make the calls upstairs or here?"

"The phone in the room is not working. I dropped it. The one in the boys' room you can receive calls from but not call out. Do you like the color?" Sally shows Loreto her nail polish.

"Depends on what you'll wear."

"I can't decide."

"I can't tell you, then."

"Why don't you get married, Loreto? Anya will take all your suitors from you. How about Emilio Luna? I hear Maxima's son is calling on you."

"You hear wrong, Sally. I don't even look at him."

"That's good. I hear the Lunas spent everything on Mr. Luna's tomb. Living room, kitchen, bathroom, dining room around it, so on All Saints' even if it rains, they will have shelter. Have you seen it? P37,000 I heard. Nothing left for a wedding."

"I don't know."

"When is your mother coming to make the pastel? No use turning up our oven when the bakery where I order all our bread can just add them to the *pan de sal.* But then Patro should finish them in time. Did she say when she's coming? I ordered three *lechons,* good-sized ones. Then there's *relleno, pancit, bibingca.* All barrio fiesta food. *Dinuguan* and *puto.* For the boys' friends there will be lasagna; pizza, which I'll send for from Shakey's at the last minute. Will you make the fresh *lumpia?* Check if there is enough *balat.*"

"There's a bamboo sliver every twenty-five wrappers. What is there to count?"

"Do you think the Commissioner will bring her?"

"Who?"

"Never mind. Go make the calls here. I'm so tired. I didn't sleep. I kept hearing trucks and planes. I kept dreaming of caves. I wonder what that means. Doesn't *Aling* Dionisia interpret dreams?"

Instead of sympathy, Loreto scolds Sally. "That's what you get for inviting socialites who'll check your plates for cracks, turn over your silver to check the brand. I hope you don't make me take charge of the silver and have me count it afterwards. Use plastic."

"Loreto, you're so funny," Sally yawns. "When else will I use the Havilands I got from the De Guzmans when they emigrated? I'll just take a nap and I'll be down." Partway up the stairs she looks down. "How did that stray cat get in? Throw it out. *Dali.*"

Sally watches Loreto push the cat along with her foot. She can't bear to touch it herself, with its eyes shut. It must be Dionisia's cat, which followed her when she came to wash. Dionisia is so undependable. When she's needed, she's off to the city; at her age, still looking for a man.

Not until she hears Loreto on the phone does Sally lie down between the pillows, in the same position she woke up from the dream of herself saying, *I always wanted to see the Opera House,* while the walls of what looked like the Metropolitan throbbed like the membrane on plucked wings. She had tried to escape but was sucked into a cave where shops, churches, parks, cafés all formed parts of demolished walls. Women praying without emotions carried pictures of their own faces, all teeth; clear images of war and masks leering. She remembers being chased to be thrown into a bonfire, to be burned for an effigy. The sea rained down. Space opened and closed like a child's fist. She remembers thinking, *This must be a dream. Only a dream.* There were hats on neon trees. A procession with everyone wearing feathers. An ambassador who turned out to be Osong sitting in the presidential chair when the canopy of lace turned into smoke. Flags burning in vigil holders. A statue raised an arm to touch her face and she ran into a mirror and when she crossed her arms over her breasts, the glass stuck into her like needles . . . She tosses and turns. Clouds seem to be passing through her. Someone is tying colored cloths about her, knotting the ends in her mouth. *Twelve sharp. Four sharp. Day Thirteen Boycott Watch. Dismantle the American Bases. Down with the Marcos–U.S. dictatorship.* All the words turn into bricks people begin throwing at her. *Stop! Stop!* she calls out. *I'm your mother . . .*

"Sally! Sally!"

Sally sits up. Loreto is at the door. "What is it?"

"You were shouting."

"I was dreaming. The perfume bottle dropped from my hand." She swings her legs off the edge of her circular bed.

"I thought something was wrong. That's the share of the angels."

"What?

"*Nay* says. She tells me to leave the lid off pots so angels can smell the *kare* cooking. Whenever we have something good cooking."

"Have you finished the calls?"

"I couldn't get anyone. Either I get a recording . . . *The number you are calling is not yet in service.* The same numbers I called yesterday and the other day and got answers. I think your maids use the phone when you're not home. There were male voices calling. One asked me to be his phone pal. I told him to go hang himself if he has nothing better to do. The nerve!"

"I'm so tired. Keep calling. I'll be down there."

Loreto sits on the bed, rubbing her leg where she skinned it rushing upstairs. Something in her responds gently to Sally's exhaustion, but not to Sally's ragings. This time, Sally is not bored with happiness.

On her way out Loreto looks about the bedroom, which resembles a warehouse. Under the bed are bags and boxes filled with projects that failed: clothes copied from the department stores after the fashion had passed, macrame wall hangings, slippers, pencil cases, bandannas. On top of the three sewing machines are more boxes of fabrics and threads. Laminated newspaper pictures alternate with photographs on the walls.

Loreto decides to check in on the maids before calling to remind the guests. The kitchen is immaculate. All actual cooking is done in the shed, the dirty kitchen where fish are gutted and poultry dressed. She has never seen the oven in use. For all anyone knows, mice are nesting in the coils. The side-by-side refrigerator, in avocado green to match the oven, is locked. The old one, vintage late fifties, is in the shed. New maids have to be watched so they don't store chickens, feathers and claws, in the freezer.

Lotus and umbrella plants shade the goldfish in the pool. Birds of paradise with blue throats rise against the hollow block fence on the side of the trail down to Gulod. To bring good luck, coin-shaped leaves of the money plant are used to cover the ground between the shrubs.

Smoke curls up from the wood stove, which slow-cooks the tough cuts of meat in pitted aluminum pots. Beyond the shed, on sawdust, the maids' and dogs' food are cooked.

The maid tending the wood stove keeps wiping her eyes on her sleeves. Her fingers are as black as the clay pots. Another maid is still shelling shrimps, throwing heads and tails into the mortar to be pounded, then strained for their juice. Banana leaves have been cut to size for roasting fish over charcoal.

Loreto shakes her slippers clear of chicken feathers that lie underfoot, the way hair mounds in beauty parlors under the chairs of customers, until one of the attendants sweeps them into a dustpan out of the way of the electric fans. As she steps back into the kitchen, she sees a child's head duck from the fence. Attracted by the smell of food cooking, children stand in front of the barbecue pits in the highway, close to those roasting corn over charcoal even if the embers occasionally land on their bare feet.

She doesn't feel like making any calls, but she can't go home until Sally wakes up; so Loreto sits in front of the television without turning it on. On the coffee table is a copy of the *Inquirer* reporting that Imelda is selling her gems in New York, and the P8 million kill-contract for the governor of Antique. Anything over a thousand pesos, she can't visualize, so the impact of the news is lost on her.

There is a picture of workmen rushing to complete the inaugural stage in Malacañang Palace for the Tuesday ceremony. It seems that daughters of former presidents are contacting foreign embassies to get them to boycott the inauguration, but the Russian ambassador has already congratulated President Marcos on his election.

Sally's horoscope is underlined. Loreto looks for her sign. She is cautioned to postpone making an important decision. What important decision? She never thought seriously of going to work for Sally's cousin who has a nursing home in Los Angeles. Marry an old-timer for his green card and his dollars? Not her. She'll go abroad only if her mother comes, too, or if Benhur takes her; or Vergel. She does not have a very clear picture of the future. If it does not come, she might join Sister Laura . . . if the nun stays in Gulod. That way she won't have children. She asked her mother how painful childbirth is. *Painful but bearable. That's what we're for. Men can't bear children.*

Sally said, *You'll find out when you get married. It's like crystals passing through you. It's what makes you a woman.* She already feels like a woman. Crystals? Why not like fire? Either way one becomes pieces. Loreto thinks of the string of hurt pearls Sally owns.

She has reached an impasse in her thoughts and decides to get through with the calls. To save her nail polish she dials with the eraser end of the pencil. While the line rings, she studies the metal peacocks above the television.

No telling if the other party will answer, hang up, or be a colorum line who will refuse to yield. It's a cross line: "I'm calling Australia, can't you tell? Put your phone down. This is long distance. Overseas call. Don't you know?"

To a softer tone, Loreto would have yielded to reason, but she will not be intimidated. Responding to belligerence, in anger she replies: "This is a single-party line. *You* put down your phone."

"Yield."

Loreto bangs the receiver, immediately dials again before the other line can connect.

The woman is still on, angrier. Loreto can almost see the veins crawling up the woman's neck, her voice sticking like barbed wire to the air. *Totoong makapapatay ka ng tao.*

Letting the woman curse all she wants, Loreto holds the receiver away from herself, only faintly hearing, "*Maleducadas.* Just now you're learning to use the phone. All right. I'll tell you, you Marcos people. My brother in Australia heard over television that there's an order to arrest Enrile. A coup. A revolution and we'll die . . ."

"What is it?" Sally is coming down, feet bare like someone coming in from working in the field. "Is it the Commissioner?"

Loreto extends the receiver to her. "Listen."

Sally holds the receiver with both hands. "It can't be true. The minister of National Defense and the president are like *that.*" She frees one hand to hook her middle finger over the index. "I'll call my cousin in California. Call the Commissioner first. Say that we heard cross lines. Ask if it's true."

"The woman is still on the line."

"Turn on Radio Veritas. Do the boys know? Where do you suppose they are? Maybe Colonel Moscoso knows. Osong's brother works with the Minister."

"It's just music, Sally."

Sally sits on the stairs, pulls her skirt over her knees, what she is thinking not yet able to come across her face as she stares at Loreto. Suppose Osong knew, suppose he and Ting Dolor are on their way abroad? Who will come to the party? The questions are carrying her back to her dream. "Try."

"I'm trying." Loreto feels as if she's standing on her head, unable to scream. As if the windows are boarded up. "I better go home." Does Benhur know? What about Vergel? Why does he have to be so far away?

Sally gets up, to sit at the dining table. Staring at the wall as if she's watching images forming, she reaches for a black grape which stains her nail, all around, the way blackness rims condolence cards and announcements of death. Repelled, she drops it on the plate where it rolls, eyeball-like.

The phone rings.

Loreto gets it. The phone pal again. She slams down the receiver. "Let's go up, Sally. I'll give you a manicure." Released from anger, her breath returns.

Sally stares at her hands. "What color?" she asks, as if she has forgotten she is a woman.

Loreto reaches for Sally's hands. They are cold. Are there clouds passing through her body? "Up, Sally. I'll stay until the boys return. Come upstairs. *Lola* Sula always says that there is time enough tomorrow to undo whatever happens today. So! Up."

Part Two
February 1986

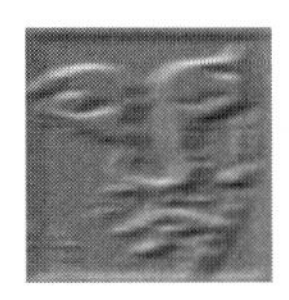

Not since he began sleeping
in his office, giving up the top-floor apartment with its view of Manila Bay, has Benhur seen the sun either rise or set. The sky, blocked by taller buildings, has become as narrow as a city lot. Benhur can no longer rely on the light to wake him.

Whatever the time, though, as soon as he wakes up he heads for Za's, where the waiter always greets him: "Hot last night!" Hot hot? Hot spicy with the heat of another body? Hot with friction of losing ground? All that: but none in particular.

"Coffee," he orders Saturday, arriving at three. His phone has been *caput* since Wednesday, so he slept through noon.

Stepping in from the sidewalk, the newspaper boy gives Benhur the clean bottom paper. He does not need it. Za's is one of those cafés where you meet the people who make the news, or you see them and overhear them if they're not acquaintances. At Za's, the news breaks as it hits the headlines, remains as rumors kept alive by opposing loyalties.

"Ensaymada?" the waiter asks.

Reminded of Colonel Moscoso and his sister's *ensaymada,* Benhur orders the pastry. The Colonel said not to space his visits like leap year. The exact phrase.

"That's all, Boss?"

"No. Give me fried eggs and *longaniza* with *sinangag.*" He decides to start with breakfast and work his way to supper. He is so hungry; not just in his stomach but in his bones, a wracking he knows food will not satisfy. He should go dump his garbage on Sister Madeleine and see what she can do with it. He didn't sleep last night until it was almost daylight because earlier he thought he had seen Ryan with some young men walking toward the Park. He followed them but lost them in the crowd after the PhilAm corner. He tried to call Sally Moscoso, to ask if a maid could go to his mother's place and check if Ryan were home. Unable to get through to Sally, he sat first at Bulwagang Filipino, then at Barrio Fiesta, finally at the pastry shop to be near a pay phone. Home after midnight, he could not stay in bed.

Of course, he has not had a good night's sleep since he gave up the apartment. He has thought of stringing a hammock across the room and humming himself to sleep with *Sa Ugoy ng Duyan,* a plaintive song about a child remembering being rocked to sleep. Some nights he pulls the blanket down to the floor, on top of the cigarette butts that missed the ashtray. People in Gulod think he has rental properties in the rich villages along EDSA, fat bank accounts, land titles, connections that explain his frequent trips abroad. What people think no longer worries him. It's what goes through his head, what he thinks in his sleep, that he's afraid of. He has not had a dream lately, though the country itself is going through a dream: Marcos concedes and Cory/Doy governs. A willfulness. If it becomes true, Benhur will get a lot of requests for letters of resignation good enough to be read on the air and run on the front page.

Since it is difficult to relinquish power and privilege, it will merely be a transfer of allegiance. Poverty itself can't be relinquished. It was some dream of his mother that because the stars are in them, as she tells the grandchildren, they should make something of themselves. Benhur is sure that Patro never read about the Big Bang theory of creation, so how does she intuit that starry debris and celestial atoms are recycled through generations? Nothing in the cells but litter—possibly divine, certainly human.

Benhur recognizes none of the afternoon clientele.

In the street two Metro Aides in yellow and red outfits are resting from sweeping cigarette wrappers and butts, fruit peels along the sidewalk. Hat brims touching, they make him think of *bandera españolas,* their riotous petals flowering along the river in Gulod. A watch-your-car boy is making small passing sweeps at the chrome of a car. At her post the girl who hands receipts for street parking for the Metro Manila Commission is trying to ignore the attention of drivers waiting for their bosses. Almost the same things can be seen from the Hilton down Orosa. Just different angle, height.

At the table to his right a man studying the racing tips does not look up when a woman joins him. Her veil, as sheer as curtains, falls unevenly on her shoulders. She has either come from a wake or is going to church at Ermita that evening, or is in some sort of costume for a party.

"Give her TruOrange," the man calls to a waiter.

She changes that to coffee. "Very hot. And a plate of *pancit.* Do you have *lumpiang ubod?*"

"Only on Friday, Ma'm."

"Okay. Just that, then. And a glass of water with lots of ice." A birthmark centered on her forehead has the shape of ashes smeared on devotees during Ash Wednesday. Running just under her jaw, across her upper throat, is a red mark. Almost brown.

It does not spoil her appearance, Benhur decides. Why is she satisfied to be seen with a large man who occupies his chair like a mass of gelatin?

His coffee comes with the jar of sugar and can of evaporated milk. He does not like the powdered cream. He uses three drops, does not stir the cup.

"Circle your choices neatly." The man slides the newspaper across to the woman. "If you want the necklace, choose well."

So that's her role. Benhur imagines her riding a horse bare, covered with veil instead of long hair. Lady Godiva. Too bad there are no more carnivals. He could come as Lord Godiva. For hair . . .

The *ensaymada* comes toasted, with a pat of butter. Hadn't he canceled it? Anyway, Benhur cuts into it, pushes it aside when the breakfast plate of rice, sausage, and eggs comes. Wiping the fork and knife with his napkin, Benhur catches the woman's eyes. So she can't take her eyes off him!

Did she think of moving to his table, having sized him up as having the future all measured? It would be interesting to see how they can communicate without speaking. In a Bogart movie—he and Osong sat through several afternoons of a Bogart film fest at the old University Theatre on Brattle Street—the man would be sending his message through a waiter.

Benhur smiles toward but not at the woman, who immediately pulls her veil across her left arm as if he has touched her. The man continues to study the horses she circled.

"More coffee, Sir?"

It's not what he wants, with his imagination racing and her glance getting sticky. *Ermita Church? Third pew from where? How about him? Suppose the horses win?*

Two men sit in back of Benhur, continuing their conversation without lowering their voices. "The president is good at dissimulation. He always has several scripts on hand. Whichever works, he'll use," the fatter voice says.

"But there are always mitigating and aggravating circumstances. And, of course, there is fact."

"And rational and irrational virtues, as you always say fondly," the fatter voice says. "Look, Marcos has people shot down, then holds a procession for them. A Mass, inviting participation for the victims of the elections. Did you notice the first reading on the day of elections was David and Goliath? I thought it a splendid coincidence. *Hustong husto.*"

"So you doubt the existence of a plot against the president who, along with General Ver, knows who the plotters are?"

"From the time of Ninoy's assassination everyone has been predicting that something will be happening very soon. What something? Anybody's guess. Bring in the Minister of National Defense! Isn't he administrator of Marcos's martial law?"

Benhur looks toward Arquiza to see who are sitting behind him; sees students with black armbands collecting for Radio Veritas outside the cafe.

All he sees, without turning around, is a hand pouring San Miguel into a glass; an elbow on the table. He can't recognize the voices.

The waiter comes with his chit. "Anything else, Sir?"

Benhur drops a hundred peso bill on the table. It just covers a moderate tip, too. Pushing his chair in, a habit from childhood, he walks past the woman with the veil that has again fallen off her arms. He stands a while on J. Bocobo searching for coins to give the watch-your-car boy and wondering if Cayetano and the Reformists have anything to do with whatever the two men were discussing.

It doesn't make sense. General Ver has a quarter-million army and an arsenal from the Pentagon. Why should a couple of hundred Reformists rattle the government? He looks through the door. The two men are still talking, eyeball to eyeball, like fish sucking air in a fishbowl. Twelve million has been spent on the inauguration planned for Tuesday which, if spent on the homeless, could make some difference. Marcos can simply write out that amount. So, what's the target? The equation will be tipped by Uncle Sam, no doubt. Marcos is number one *tuta.* Lapdog. No disagreement there. Status quo assured. There are no troops massing on J. Bocobo or Arquiza, a stone's throw from the United States Embassy over the roofs. He might as well go on to Gulod with the week's allowance.

Some facts are true but incomplete, not to be seriously considered. That's what the exchange was. Opinions, not necessarily expert. But suppose? He should have turned around to ask his questions. No faux pas. It's accepted protocol to pull out a third chair and take sides. Too late to claim the two men's attention. And the woman! He forgot to smile at her when he passed. Did she look up? The waiter is bringing her another TruOrange. What did she think of him? He can watch her through the door.

Did she see through, that he is the kind who fulfills promises he never made? Like bringing the money himself to Gulod when he drew up the incorporation papers for a classmate's messengerial service agency and so received a lifetime membership, gratis. Like feeling obligated to bring the news he overheard at Za's to Colonel Moscoso in case it ties in with

Cayetano and the Reformists. It's on his way to Gulod. Afterwards, maybe go to the ordinations Sister Madeleine mentioned; because she wishes she could attend and he feels he must fulfill the wish for her.

It's too bad he can't, like Terence Hugg, depart at the end of an assignment. He, Benhur Vitaliano, is in the Philippines for good; to stand proxy for Osong at weddings and baptisms. . . . Benhur turns back into Orosa to head through to the Park wondering if there is enough in the envelope Hugg left in the office, enough to buy him out of his obligations. His mind is like a typhoon at sea, changing course with each blow. If there is a coup, after all, it will be Hugg's bad luck to have left.

Someone very much like *Aling* Dionisia's grandson darts across España with a bagful of Stork cough drops, popular with jeepney drivers and riders whose lungs are corroded by the black exhausts from ill-maintained public vehicles. Impossible to stop in that traffic in order to check.

He passes Santo Tomas, an internment camp during the Japanese Occupation, and recalls the pride with which he told the student guide in the Harvard Yard that Santo Tomas is older than Harvard.

It's glare to glare, crossing Governor Forbes. It has to be the heat that stuns people's minds into violence; forces the heart to pound, to drum. A helicopter is crossing the lower sky. Benhur supposes that from the air the stalled vehicles might appear as unmarked graves.

Thoughts like this enable him to bear traffic, loneliness, and feelings of failure. Magsaysay High School. North General.

He scans the traffic lines for someone hawking *sampaguita* garlands to bring to his mother and his *Lola* Sula.

Suddenly space opens just ahead. Benhur guns his engine to claim it before the car on his right can swerve into line. The idea is to graze the other car without lifting off its paint. No evidence of assault. Taxi drivers do it with impunity. Sporting for a fight, the other driver closes in. Benhur's excitement comes partly from knowing that everything is personal, that casual remarks or glances can end up in a shooting or stabbing. The driver sees a different space to claim and rams his way into it. Young driver with no finesse—yet.

It must be the heat that brings on such foulness of mood and temper; all disasters are equally unforgiving; all announcements of death are met with the heart jabbing the ribs, trying to pitch itself out.

Benhur sees the other driver swing close to the curb where two likely passengers stand, waiting for their ride. The jeepney up ahead swings into the space; slams its brakes on seeing the other driver. Around them a traffic jam forms. Benhur inches past. Tight maneuvers make a rotary out of the pile-up. He must learn to discriminate among encounters or he'll end up with his day lost to feuding. Not everything is meaningless encounter, though.

See the threat positively, for example? Moving into space along España is very much the way women pray the rosary: claiming each bead at a time, moving on. Possession, release. He can't stay long in Gulod. He has to make that contract airtight for a client who was burned dealing with a Japanese, who kept wheedling information about the business and then, after acquiring enough to go on his own, disappeared. And he has to repair the damage worked by loose tongues and minds . . .

Now he has become reluctant to stop by at Colonel Moscoso's; but feeling committed, he wants the Colonel to laugh it off, say Cayetano would have come if the two men at Za's were right.

He could save gas by not idling the engine, or by going via Legarda and Santa Mesa, up from Ayala and the Nagtahan bridge. But if the rumor is true—*if*—that area will be secured with barbed wires.

Approaching the Quezon City rotunda with its monolith like a hard-on, Benhur catches the news from headlines of newspapers being offered by small boys. Philip Habib is arriving with another message from Ronald Reagan. Habib seems to be as adept as the local politicians, up to a point. Political *rigodon* must go by different names around the world. In the end the people lose, everywhere, because the choices between politicians, intent on their own survival, is the same as the choice between hardcore and soft pornography. The victims are always left out because they are the means to hang on to power. Hanging on to power? The people are dying. Long live the people.

He wonders where Miggy and Joel are. Does Vergel get the news quickly? He must remind Vergelito about applying to a foundation abroad for funds to build a hospital. An orchard could pay for some of the operating expenses. Cashew could be sold for the nuts; the pulp could make wine. Maybe his mother and Loreto would be better off in the province. Demetrio's children would be safer there. And fruit trees are beautiful as well.

Leaving the rotunda Benhur realizes that the things he wants for himself—marriage, children, a house with a formal garden—have been drained out of him. Right then all he wants is to drop in on the Colonel, go on to Gulod, and get back to bed. Male menopause, their class historian/philosopher/sociologist observed at the last reunion, occurs earlier and earlier, is not just hormonal. When did he stop wanting for himself? Joel once said he did not want to go abroad because he would be tempted to stay: *I don't want to scatter.* "Scatter" brings to Benhur the image of a body being hit slow-motion by a bullet; the bullet's trajectory on high-speed film slowed down to the sequence of entry/exit, splatter . . .

No sign of agitation on the way to Colonel Moscoso, if he does not count the traffic snarls. Ricebirds are flying in and out of the trees inside the yard. Coming in late at night, Osong and he used to climb into the upstairs bedroom through the mango tree, brushing against the butterflies just coming out of their cocoons. What a surprise to learn, in a homily at St. Paul's, that butterflies are an image of resurrection.

Mang Genio peeks out before throwing open the gate. "I thought it was Cayetano returning. I'll let the Colonel tell you. He was trying to reach you, but your phone was out of order."

"My alarm clock, too. I just got up." Benhur notes that Cayetano has been there, making the conversation at Za's credible. "How did Cayetano look to you?"

"Ask the Colonel." *Mang* Genio accompanies him to the door. "They've been discovered. They might be under interrogation by now. Mrs. Moscoso and Cayetano's family are in the resthouse. On their way. In

Angat. You remember the farm. They were supposed to go to a wedding at Villamor Air Base but that's out. I heard Johnny Enrile's name."

Like a leaf hanging low and heavy from a branch, the parrot swings from its perch with its head down. "Reformist! Reformist! Have you eaten?" The parrot swings upright, drops to hang by one claw, head cocked toward Benhur.

"Pesky bird," the Colonel comes to Benhur. "It will make trouble for us. Did you notice anything on the way here, Benhur? Some troops? Tanks? Roadblocks?"

"None of those," Benhur replies. "Not where I passed."

Against the far wall, the television blinks light and dark, imprinting Benhur's eyes with unintelligible signals.

"The government might have ordered a media blackout, Benhur. Cayetano came. Brought his family, then left. If they come for Cayetano, they can arrest me in his place."

Benhur composes his questions so as not to intrude. The Colonel's matter-of-fact statement suggests that he is willing to discuss the possibilities. "What's the worst scenario?"

"The Americans intervene."

Benhur agrees. The Americans will be thinking of their bases, all five of them; will recall Marcos supported them in Vietnam.

"It might be a long siege. Anything can happen. Or nothing. We'll have to wait, Benhur. That's the hardest part. Sit where you want. Beer? Or coffee?"

"Anong oras na? Anong oras?" The parrot must have heard someone asking for the time. It walks with clumsy gait on the perch, rocking. Like electric wires running through the trees, light flows through its feathers, ruffling it. *"Anong oras?"*

Benhur looks over the coffee table. Sunday's *Panorama* has a college student on the cover. The *Times,* neatly beside it, has a girl playing the guitar. He picks up the closest to him, flips the pages. There's an article on Helen Taft: "The First Malacañang First Lady in This Century." No time to read it. Or "Why the Philippine Revolution Failed." The art section features Anastacio Caedo: "Purity of Spirit Is the Essence of True Art."

Separate realities, he thinks, dropping the magazine on the table and startling the parrot into standing still, its body cocked.

The coffee is brought out on a tray by *Mang* Genio's daughter. Benhur nods to her, stirs the sugar, his movements deliberate, taking the place of serious conversation, while the Colonel tries to get news on the radio.

Like mice playing, music comes in at each station; fades. Benhur thinks of the time he and Osong, during a rainstorm, played 45 rpm records at 75 rpm speed, forcing Cayetano to sleep under his pillow. Is music abnormal programming for the stations? He never has time to listen to the radio, or to watch television. The minute he sits down, mind unoccupied, he falls asleep.

The parrot is now standing on one leg, head tucked under a wing so it looks beheaded. A spot of red on its body looks like a misplaced eye. Bloodshot. If there were nothing else, Benhur thinks, he could write pages on that observation.

Priscila is back. "Colonel. Mrs. Sally Moscoso on the phone. She's asking for the commissioner."

He didn't hear the phone, Benhur thinks, glancing at the Colonel, who throws out a hand in answer.

"He has his office. He doesn't live here; doesn't she know?"

Benhur watches Priscila as if she might not appear again, as during his last visit. On her way back to the kitchen she smiles, but not directly at him. The quick parting of her lips might simply be a reflex, if not a response to his curiosity.

"That is Genio's daughter. Did you recognize her?" The Colonel checks his watch. "There is beer, Benhur. Ask Priscila, if you want one."

Is that an introduction of sorts? or a reminder? Priscila is "family." Object of respect. No touch. Amused, Benhur feels almost flattered. Apparently it's not so evident that what is unrestrained in him has been tamed. Unsure of what response is expected, Benhur pays his attention evenly to objects in the room. Large, dark furniture with the shine of permanence makes his mother's furniture look like matchsticks. Patro's chairs have all been purchased on impulse from door-to-door vendors or brought to the house on the backs of neighbors repaying or expecting favors. They are spindly contrivances and soon enough shrink around the nails. Insects embedded in the wood bore their way out and into the clothes. *Kalsos* of wood or paper have to be set under the legs so they will rest evenly on the floor.

Priscila comes out again to serve an early supper. Under one arm is a flyswatter of newspaper fringes pasted to a ring at the end of a stick.

"Come, Benhur," the Colonel invites. "At least I won't be eating by myself. I remember you liked the specialties of *Mang* Genio's wife. It's too much of food cooked in coconut milk, but they are good. Osong likes this. It's his birthday, you know. It's too late now, if he's coming. My wife thought he would."

Though he has just had breakfast and lunch at Za's, Benhur serves himself some of the shrimps in *gabi* leaves boiled in coconut cream. Priscila is bringing out the *leche flan.* Thicker and richer than the *creme reversu au caramel* at the Peacock in Cambridge, the pudding sits in its sauce like a miniature sun.

"Go on, Benhur. Start. This could be our last good meal for a while. It is lunch and supper. Enjoy it for Osong."

Benhur wants to stare at Priscila, whose red blouse colors her cheeks without giving a blunt expression to her face. But he does not. On the chilled bottle of beer she places by his spoon, her fingers have left their shape in the frost. Benhur likens it to pressure indenting flesh without bruising.

They eat silently, each in his own thoughts; then the Colonel's observation lifts the almost suffocating air in the house. "It's time to take risks, don't you think? All the way. I'm old. Much less courage is required from me than from you who still have the future. And we can't compare ourselves to those who will come out ahead without lifting a finger. I don't know if they're lucky or we are."

Benhur is tempted to observe that he doesn't much care whose side wins. If a third force is involved, is that Cayetano and the Reformists? Recovering tact, he only says, "It's the powerless and poor who never land on anyone's priority list." For some time now he has included himself in this out-group. If it's not reality, it could be the result of atrophy of glands, of brain cells.

"It's possible a move has not been made." Colonel Moscoso serves the chicken. "They must concentrate their force; win over other companies. They're only a couple of hundred." He gives Benhur a second helping of everything, though he himself has not touched his plate, on which the food is mounded separately as if in illustration of a maneuver. "If the Reformists succeed, everyone should be eating this kind of rice. Rice equals dignity, equality, all those innate rights. Filipinos used to be virtuous. Rascals were the exception."

Besides the positive values the Colonel is enumerating, Benhur considers the deaths from an outbreak of fighting. He can accept his own death, but should he seek it? And who is to benefit? The options shift as he adds and subtracts factors, not yet ready to state his position. There will be treachery. "I believe in human dignity, Colonel. Justice is a means to that. It's not an isolated end in itself. I have met vulgar and depraved people in all walks of life: academe, business, politics. And some spiritually empty churchmen, as well—churchgoers running down pedestrians in their hurry to get to church." In the midst of this declaration Benhur is reminded of the provisions his mother will need if there is a coup, a revolution. The rice he brought from the Colonel must be gone by now.

"Rice and dignity, Benhur. That's the way to put it. Justice and dignity. The right people and the right motives. I wish we could find out what's happening right now."

Priscila comes in with freshly broiled fish.

"You must taste that, Benhur. It's from the fishponds of Cayetano's in-laws." The Colonel lifts a whole side to Benhur's plate, on top of the rice which is so white the grains resemble fine coral built up from shells of microscopic organisms. Fragrance comes from the leaves of *pandan* which line the pot.

His mind on what could be happening elsewhere, Benhur almost thanks the Colonel for the gift of rice until he realizes an expression of gratitude could be taken as a request, a reminder.

"The next time the door opens it could be Cayetano; or Ver's men. Ver is a desk officer. ROTC, not PMA. That's a point in our favor."

"Does that offset the arms and men the government has?" Benhur defers in matters of military strategy, eating after he's no longer hungry, as though finishing what the Colonel has put on his plate is a test of loyalty. The foam on the beer has burst, leaving a flat layer of liquid inside the glass. Drawing his eyes across the room, past windows sheltered from the outside by trees and vines with white and yellow flowers, Benhur notes that the Colonel himself is not eating. Are similar thoughts passing through their minds? His thoughts go to Jose Rizal being executed in Luneta by the Spaniards, turning around so the bullets hit him full front instead of in the back. Will Cayetano and Reformists also refuse a blindfold? How does one side with the people?

"Listen!"

The word "Emergency!" has cut into the music with the impatience of doorbells. Emergency! Minister of National Defense, Juan Ponce Enrile is calling a press conference at Camp Aguinaldo for four o'clock that afternoon.

It is past four. Benhur checks his watch. What now? Is it over? or never held?

The Colonel pushes away from the table. "What will he announce later that he cannot declare now?"

Lacking information to explain the announcement, Benhur says nothing. Part of his distrust lies in Enrile's ambition to become president. Is he going to speak for himself, or for President Marcos? Why not Marcos for himself?

"Where are Laurel and Cory on this?" the Colonel asks. "Camp Aguinaldo is vulnerable to artillery from Pasig. The University of Life is there, Imelda's university. What about the camp personnel? The Logistic Command is there. The Military Intelligence . . ."

Benhur can't think of alternatives. Military matters and revolution are not within his field of expertise. It's like asking Sister Madeleine's opinions on birth control. Though she might very well have ideas on that subject. Until he saw her, née Elen Rodrigo, he did not think she had a body that could laugh. Even now, he feels impure and deformed, thinking of her commonly. What did she think that Tuesday morning in Constitutional Law? She must have given the answer after he left. He better stop referring to her. She could become an obsession worse than any of Osong's fixations.

"I wonder who's in control. Shouldn't General Ver be making an announcement? The transmission isn't being jammed, so the airwaves are not compromised. Isn't that so, Benhur?"

Priscila comes to check, begins clearing the table in order to bring the dessert forward.

"Dessert?" asks the Colonel.

"Just coffee," Benhur says, looking down at the white rosettes on Priscila's *abaca* slippers. His desires might have become restrained, but not his preferences. The woman at Za's was noticeably older than he. The type for trysts, exciting because impermanent. Olimpia is the Maria Clara type, good for men like Vergel who avoids distraction. He can't recall his brother having a real girlfriend, though girls were always asking about him, inviting him to their parties and to dances. But even then in high school, Vergel wanted to be a barefoot doctor like Tom Dooley; to take care of the children in the Vietnam War. Priscila is for serenades, for folk dances. She is exquisite nostalgia, the one lost but still-animating memory. She would disappoint otherwise.

"Do you trust Laurel, Benhur?"

Interrupted, Benhur feels guilty about indulging himself with irrelevancies in the midst of an emergency. "Only after he agreed to become Cory's running mate, Sir, sacrificing his own ambition. Still, not all the way."

"I wish we knew what is really happening."

Benhur looks at Colonel Moscoso and at the iridescent shells laid side by side in the cabinet behind him. Is the Colonel wondering where Osong is at the moment? If there is going to be a coup, should he himself not be on the way to Gulod? If Aguinaldo is within range, so is the Moscoso house, which is behind Camp Crame, across Aguinaldo on EDSA. Epifanio de los Santos highway. But to leave now would be desertion.

Colonel Moscoso remains beside the radio while Benhur gets up to walk to the window. The light is dropping with the sky. He turns to the Colonel, as if to say something, but only faces the parrot. In the darkened room, he notices a smudge on the pane—wing feathers imprinted on the glass, where a bird, seeing the reflection of trees and sky, might have smashed itself against the window.

The thought imparts an urgency to which Benhur feels they should respond. If Ver's men come for Cayetano, would they not have to use fists against M-16s and Israeli Uzis?

Priscila is bringing the coffee. She sets the cups on the table, then for a moment so brief he almost misses it, she looks at him.

"Have some candles ready, in case the lights go out," Colonel Moscoso tells her. "And check the rooms upstairs. Close the doors. Remember the vigil candles before the altar in the bedroom."

"Would they have arrived in Angat?" Benhur asks, to show his concern.

"Before dark. There is no phone but if they need to, one of the soldiers will come with their message. It's all arranged. Nothing to do but wait. Cayetano might send a message himself, if he is able. Sit down. We will need our strength. It's way past the news conference hour."

Except that Colonel Moscoso might think it frivolous, since they are waiting, it seems, for betrayal, Benhur wants to say that people should be given blank time on the air: the people could make up their own lies to counter official propaganda. Or could just remain silent, saving electric power, so there would be no need to flood tribal lands up north in order to shoot electricity down to the American bases and the multinational corporations that compete for the local capital and ship home their profits. Hugg would think that witty. If he had stayed, they might have been waiting together. Hugg has a surefire way of getting his angle unobstructed: *"Get out of my way or I'll stick my ass in your lens when you aim your camera."* It worked for Hugg.

Long wait. Perhaps the conference is over.

The moon is rising, coming up paler and paler through the branches of the *camias.* Osong used to like sucking the sour, stubby fruits that grew out of the bark in clusters. Fruits as fat as slugs, which a classmate from Mindanao also liked. Jainal used to stay weekends at the Moscosos'. The first time, Osong told his mother that Jainal was from a royal house; was by right a *datu,* and that his grandfathers led their men against Blackjack Pershing early in the American Occupation, forcing Pershing to ask for a gun—the .45—to stop the Moro in his tracks. *Mang* Genio's wife served no pork on those weekends, but she used lard, forgetting that it, too, was pork.

"It's seven," Colonel Moscoso calls the time. "Too long for news to be blacked out."

Benhur feels something falling on his shoulders and arms. On looking up he sees ants swarming, dropping their wings, which bend the light as they fall. The soft bodies run on the table, the chairs, on Benhur's neck and into his hair. All over the room, white, dry wings flutter.

"Priscila!"

Priscila comes with a basin, which she holds under the light. Ants begin crawling on her lifted arms. Down inside her blouse unwinged bodies fall; run on her feet.

Benhur takes the basin from her and she goes to the kitchen for more water. He knows a broom will not be used at night because, as in his mother's house, that is supposed to bring bad luck. He is waiting for her to come back when the radio picks up the news conference, hours after it was announced.

"That's the minister," Colonel Moscoso says.

Enrile is saying that, as Minister of National Defense, he can no longer, in conscience, recognize the president as commander-in-chief.

"Genio. Come listen," Colonel Moscoso calls, turning up the volume so that the minister's voice begins to vibrate like the swarming of ants.

Admissions of guilt continue, in answer to press questions. "In my region, my own region, I know we cheated to the extent of 350,000 votes . . ." The assassination attempt on his life, just before martial law was declared, was faked. And the assassination of Ninoy Aquino could have been carried out only with "an order from above."

How far up? Benhur anticipates the question from the press. Imelda?

"No one other than FM or Ver."

The Colonel turns the dial to clear Radio Veritas of the other stations. "I knew it." Background noises still muffle the questions and answers.

Vice Chief of Staff Fidel Ramos has shocking revelations of his own: military officers of the top rank are "practically servants of powerful political figures," whose private troops are armed from military arsenals.

"Those overstaying generals." Colonel Moscoso says. "Now they wish to be absolved."

"I knew that," *Mang* Genio says. "When I would wait for Mrs. Moscoso, the other drivers told me about a dentist who demanded to be paid in Uzis and Galils by military patients of his. I told the Colonel."

"Shhhh." Colonel Moscoso leans toward the radio.

Enrile is saying that he has no desire for glory, wealth, or power; will not serve in the successor government; and, even if not supported by the people, he has taken a stand from which he will not waver.

Different voices, unidentified, provide a kind of stammer to the conference. Someone is calling on all concerned citizens to support those bracing for an attack by the government. "We'll meet in Cubao." The report is being filed from a phone near the conference room and picks up nearby sounds.

There is a plea for a peaceful dialogue, then Enrile again, asking the people to join, "if they want the experience of mortar fire," and saying he expects to die.

"Cayetano could be inside Camp Aguinaldo, Benhur." Colonel Moscoso goes to the window. The moon is climbing the trees, branch by branch. "I remember the moon was in the sky the night we marched to meet the Japanese in Bataan."

Music comes on, then a replay of the news conference, making even more unreal what is already difficult to believe.

It's possible this is a trap, Benhur muses. If he were to say it aloud, Colonel Moscoso might think he is indicting Cayetano. He wonders if his mother is listening to the radio; if all the boys are home. He'll go in the morning. This late it is no longer safe. He goes to the phone after asking if he might use it. Sally Moscoso's line is busy. He tries several times.

"That was Bishop Vidal asking for a peaceful dialogue," *Mang* Genio says. He takes Mrs. Moscoso to the Redemptorist church in Baclaran every Wednesday. His wife threads sampaguita garlands to drape over the picture of the Mother of Perpetual Help in the stairwell of their house.

A public resignation interrupts the replay on Radio Veritas. Then music. General Ramos is heard asking people to join the defenders in Camp Aguinaldo.

"In a firefight the civilians will be vulnerable," Colonel Moscoso says, still facing the window. "The camp itself can be easily knocked out. If I were Ramos, I'd move to Camp Crame. It would be easier to secure, though neither camp can stand a firebombing. All Marcos needs is to give Ver an order. You know, Benhur, that Cayetano was not asked even once to join the Palace Security Command? Imelda likes her aides tall and handsome. Mestizos."

Benhur turns on the other stations. "What I can't understand is the silence from the Palace. Is the president not listening to his minister and vice chief of staff?"

"Marcos is keeping them guessing, Benhur. Ver has the Marines, the combat troops from Mindanao. Unless the military defects, Enrile and Ramos and the Reformists have no chance. We should rest." Colonel Moscoso sits down. "If he can, Cayetano will try to call. How about your mother, Benhur? Is there a way for you to reach her?"

"I tried. The neighbor's line is busy. They will be safe. Gulod is far." Benhur keeps the rest of his thoughts to himself. If his mother knew he was with Colonel Moscoso, she would find a way to reach him. As long as they stay together in the house, he reassures himself, they will be all right. Schools will be closed. *Aling* Maxima's store will give them credit. His grandmother said that during the revolution against Spain they could not buy anything with their money. And during the Occupation, the Japanese Mickey Mouse money became so devalued that a sackful bought only one guava. Hoping the war currency will still be redeemed as part of reparations, his *Lola* Sula saves the Japanese money, gets mixed up and tries to spend it when vendors pass by.

Mang Genio comes in to tell the Colonel that the neighbor is inviting Mrs. Moscoso to pray with them so they can decide if they should go to protect Enrile and Ramos in Camp Aguinaldo. "I said we have started to pray, so I would not have to explain that she's not here. Anyway, it's after nine and too late to be out. Will Benhur be staying?"

"There's the answer for them," Colonel Moscoso points to the radio.

It is Cardinal Sin on the air asking people to pray and show support for Enrile and Ramos. "Take them food if you want. Protect the defectors." He is followed by a call for transportation for those ready to go to EDSA, the highway between the two military camps.

At the second ring, Colonel Moscoso gets to the phone, saying, "It's probably Osong making excuses for not coming. He doesn't even know where his mother is. Hello?" There is a hard pause, as if a fist is stuck in his throat. He gives Benhur a sign. "Other telephone, Benhur."

By intuition Benhur goes up the hall, taking the stairs two steps at a time. It is Cayetano telling his father a hundred men have landed inside Camp Aguinaldo. *Their* men. He wants to let his father know where he is.

"Speak louder," Colonel Moscoso is saying. "What about the president? General Ver? What is the situation?"

"He has asked to talk, but the minister refused. The minister told General Ver the die is cast."

"Any defections, *hijo?*"

"General Farolan of Customs. Two helicopters, both unarmed are here, but no air force, otherwise. No. Not General Tadiar. The Marines will be tough. Papá, correspondents are asking to use the phone so they can file their reports. Good-bye, Papá. I love you all."

Colonel Moscoso still has the receiver to his ear when Benhur gets down. *Mang* Genio's wife is making the sign of the cross on her forehead, her lips, over her heart. "They expect to die, don't they?" she asks Benhur.

Colonel Moscoso stands by the receiver, waits, then turns to Benhur. "We'll go to Camp Aguinaldo, Benhur. We'll go to Cayetano." Then he tells *Mang* Genio to bring out the food prepared for Osong's birthday. "We need candles and flashlights. Load blankets, and a thermos filled with coffee."

It is chilly outside. Benhur looks up on his way to the car. The moon has shrunk to a neat circle in the sky. He feels daring, about to break out from defeat by going where the rockets will certainly land. But half steps will not bring the country back to the time before martial law, before Marcos. And politics cannot be left to the monopoly of politicians.

Unlocking the trunk, Benhur goes into the house by way of the kitchen, where the third Moscoso son stays. David fell off the guava tree when he was nine, without a scratch, but he has had seizures since. Because it is difficult to bring him down for his meals, and to have someone always beside him to place the wood block in his mouth when he is about to have a seizure, so he will not bite his lips and swallow his tongue, he has been in the kitchen since, in an alcove. Benhur has seen *Mang* Genio and his wife take turns rubbing David's arms and neck until he comes out of his convulsions.

"Sir," Benhur looks up when the Colonel comes in.

"David is in Angat, too," the Colonel says. "Come."

For the first time that day, *Mang* Genio's wife approaches Benhur to give him a handful of *sampaguita,* mostly buds. "No time to make necklaces for the Virgin. Just give this to her." She speaks of the Virgin as of an intimate friend. How does she know if statues will be brought to Camp Aguinaldo?

Helping load the trunk with what might be useful, Benhur wonders if there is a theology to fit what they are doing. Politics as the place to test one's conscience, to seek salvation. Sister Madeleine will say: to sanctify, make holy what God created. The assemblage of words he puts in her mind strikes him deeply. Holy politics/political holiness. In what speech can he insert them? It is what he is doing, feeding and clothing and educating those in Gulod; keeping a roof over them when what he wants is to be liberated, not from sin but from them.

But intercession is what he does for others; is not his own recourse.

It takes almost as long to reach EDSA, once they leave Horseshoe Drive, as to head for Balintawak where the revolution of 1896 began with the tearing of personal *cedulas.* Benhur takes note of houses and walls, as if he might not pass there again: St. Sopher Finishing School, Diamond Motor Shop, drugstore, Batangueña Store, Xerox, Commercial Investment Agency, gas station. Camp Crame on their right.

People are heading to Camp Aguinaldo in numbers. Into possible cross fire, they are bringing candles and rosaries, food to last the night, and jackets, for the air is chilly in February. Children are asleep against shoulders.

Instead of cutting into one another's lanes, cars are yielding right of way, practising courtesy to an extreme.

"Will the military fire on civilians?"

"That's the big IF, Benhur. In my time I could tell, but these military I don't know. Who can we trust these days?"

"It is like *simbang gabi,*" Benhur says. He remembers waking up before the roosters crowed to be able to attend the nine Masses before Christmas. In houses along the road, the rosary is being prayed.

"When they come, we will see the rockets across the sky," Colonel Moscoso says. "Maybe the government will forget they have bombs. Mortars and shells. Didn't Cayetano say that General Ver asked the minister not to attack the Palace? With two unarmed helicopters?"

"It could be a feint. *Disimulado,*" Benhur suggests, returning the Laban sign of small children pressing thumbs and forefingers against the car windows. It's the opposition password: Give me an L.

"Think of what a single mortar shell can do to this crowd," Colonel Moscoso says. "Nowhere to run to but to itself. At the moment we might be centered in the hairline sights of Ver's guns. It won't be a quiet wounding, Benhur. Not something to be borne in silence like circumcision." He remembers his grandfather coming into the house to declare, "Another man in the house," after each circumcision. That's when they passed from short into long pants, and the right to say something in conversation. "What I am coming to conclude is that, in our relationship to the country, we must adopt the tribal view of ancestral land. Belonging to all and to the future. Held in trust as well are all vocations and professions. It's the country and the future which must be served. This is the only way I see, if we are to be restored to dignity and honor. This is what the Reformists must feel."

The observation surprises Benhur with its simplicity and yet its intensity. Sister Madeleine could not declare it more precisely, with her mind always ready for action. She would indeed posit God for country. To convince him, she might quote Descartes. God is the pure and simple intention. Benhur grants that. But he will not go so far as to agree to place his thoughts on God, so as to be absorbed by Him. In the Small Parlor, she implied that God desires through her. If so, what does He desire through *him?* through Cayetano? through those gathering at EDSA?

There is singing and praying along the road. A young boy holds up a poster with Cory's picture. Right behind him a man is carrying an image of Our Lady of Fatima. Is the same happening in Tuguegarao, Sorsogon, Abra? in Cebu and Zamboanga? in Kapalaran? Is the whole country wrestling with its devils? He tries to imagine Sister Madeleine praying, for how long? In his plea for people to come out and protect Camp Aguinaldo, the Cardinal announced he had asked the contemplative nuns, especially, to pray unceasingly. How are all these events and prayers connected to wings falling off of ants in flight, and whales playing off of the rocks in Cohasset, making the sea writhe? And to Colonel Moscoso reaching the conclusion that corruption is a sin against the country and its future?

Some cars are backing up. There is no way to enter EDSA or to park nearby. Still, people continue to come as if no one expects to be dead by morning.

Benhur is reminded of the wake for Evelio Javier, of standing in front of the Oblation. Is it only through the bodies of the dead that God, Sister Madeleine's God, can be praised?

"Look!" Colonel Moscoso draws Benhur's attention to the intersection of Santolan and Epifanio de los Santos which can't be seen for the crowd heading towards Camp Aguinaldo.

Benhur estimates the crowd coming from Cubao to number between ten and twenty thousand. Flashbulbs pop as correspondents aim their cameras over the heads of people. With their horns, cars pick up the rhythm of the singing. As they are carried past, towards Camp Aguinaldo, the banners bend the headlights on high beam. Is there a way for Marcos and Ver to see this?

When a break appears between the people marching from Cubao, Benhur starts the engine. Cheerfully, the crowd lets him through. A man even stops the marchers for Benhur, to allow him to enter Boni Serrano where it continues on from Santolan. Just as they cross, a car backs out of its space in the barricade.

"It is intended that we be here," Colonel Moscoso explains their good luck.

They struggle with their baskets of food and the thermoses to Gate One of Camp Aguinaldo, where a guard is telling nuns to go elsewhere. "We'll be shelled before four o'clock, Sister." While the guard's back is to her, a woman squeezes through the window of the guardhouse.

"We're Filipinos, too," the young nuns protest. "The Cardinal asked everyone to protect the defectors, so we come to pray with them. We come to protect the army."

"Come," Colonel Moscoso leads Benhur along the whitewashed fence. The mango trees inside the camp are darker than the sky.

Benhur follows Colonel Moscoso through the main gate as it opens to let in a truck. They walk briskly. No longer startling in its brightness, the moon falls lightly on the buildings, on the statue of General Aguinaldo on horseback where the parade grounds start.

They bear left, heading for the Ministry of National Defense, with the reviewing stand on their right and the headquarters of the Chief of Staff up ahead. The choir is practising in the Episcopal chapel. The first floor of the Ministry is in darkness. They grope their way in from the parking lot.

Colonel Moscoso recalls the processions inside the old walled city. Through the narrow streets, starting and ending in a church, carriages carried patron saints. Each block had its church, each church its devotees, before they were turned to rubble in the bombing during the Japanese Occupation. He remembers particularly the glass *viriña* protecting the flames of candles.

Candles have been set on the stairs, and the praying of nuns seems to come from the candles. Thin light is coming from the second floor, allowing them to see that all space has been staked out, the way squatters scramble over vacant lots.

Here the Colonel stops. "Benhur, call me Papá; not to disclaim your father, but because you're no longer just the friend of my son. We might die together here." He pulls Benhur to him, presses him close; then leads the way quietly.

They would have been separated anyway; Benhur justifies his failure to catch up after people push between him and Colonel Moscoso. Might as well go to Gulod, get canned meats and sardines to his mother, then return before he is missed. But suppose meanwhile that shelling hits the camp? Suppose infiltrators from the left and the right or the government are also there, attempting to subvert the crowd to their own hostile interests?

Suppose the Reformists are wiped out in an all-out fighting and the dead cover the ground as in the revolutions against Spain, the war against the Americans and the Japanese? He warns himself to let his mind handle the wild urgencies with calm reserve. He cannot bring the Colonel to a place of dying planets; and then escape.

The cool air in the parade grounds sharpens Benhur's thoughts. He walks against the sound of singing and praying, eyes on the ground. When he looks up, he sees a statue of the Virgin being raised at the gate, and, afraid to be held in her eye—as the Virgin of Guadalupe held the image of Juan Diego, whose tunic she imprinted with her own image as a reward for his faith—he looks away, past guards who are helpless to keep people from entering the civilian gate and Gate One.

Unsure of whether to stay or leave, Benhur watches the people surging to bring food into the camp. He wonders what message the lights of candles and the singing are sending out into space.

In matching yellow shirts and denim, the jeprox look of television personalities and entertainers, Ting Dolor and Osong Moscoso are standing side by side, being interviewed. Osong is doing the nodding while Ting Dolor creates a new and fake image of herself as opposition leader, when all this time she has been a Palace habitué, getting all she can out of the First Lady and excusing it—after all, if she doesn't take it, the foreign celebrities and minor royalties will. She stands very close to the interviewer who has a day's growth of beard down his neck.

People are pressing forward, thinking it is Cory. Then they stick around, mesmerized.

Not able to get a word in, Osong scans the crowd. On seeing Benhur he pulls away from Ting Dolor, who does not miss a beat of her repertory. "I've been trying to reach you. Quick, write me a resignation," he hisses. "Just a few stunning lines and the formal letter can be sent later. Where have you been?"

More triumphant than sarcastic, Benhur gloats, "With your father. We prepared for your birthday. Waited."

"I need it written. You don't have a pad? There's a store. Wait here." Osong runs off, after checking his own pockets for pen or paper.

Benhur tries to distract Ting Dolor, but she is intent on speaking clearly into the mike. Yes, she's ready to die there. "Why bother to come, otherwise." She catches sight of Benhur staring but does not waste a smile on him.

Wait until she has something she wants from me, then she'll turn silky or wet, Benhur thinks; with no intention of waiting. He's not on a retainer's fee.

"Here's a sheet of paper. I don't need it filled. Just something to knock people down. I lost my pen. The gold Cross one, too. Have you one?" Osong returns out of breath.

Benhur takes the sheet, walks to a parked car on which to write. It will be interesting to see what he can pull out of the air.

"I tried to call the house. It's my birthday, did you forget? Papá and Mamá always expect me, but this is a once-in-a-lifetime event. Ting called me the minute she heard. We were here at four, but General Ramos arrived only after six. I could have slipped down to Papá and Mamá, but no one knew there would be some delay. I'm sure they're asleep now. I'll call and explain tomorrow. I just hope Cayetano is not in on this."

Benhur does not attempt to straighten out his friend's thinking. Being there, he is in it too. What a Brod! Still, Benhur cannot resist saying, "Your Mamá is at the Angat resthouse. Your father is inside. He might even be with Cayetano."

"Cayetano! That sissy who dumps all his problems on Papá so he can act macho captain! And Papá lets him. Papá, the *pater familias* . . . That's enough, Benhur. Short with a punch."

"It's *your* resignation," Benhur shrugs.

Light from stores across the street plays on the sheet of paper Osong is reading: "Since fraud and deceit have vitiated President Ferdinand E. Marcos's mandate. . . . Benhur, that's somewhat strong. Can you tone it down? All this could come to nothing by morning."

"You're free to change it, Osong."

Avoiding confrontation, Osong folds the sheet. "I'll read it later. There are so many foreign correspondents, I can pick my time. By the way, is your friend Hugg around?"

"Not that I know of."

"Ting and I are going in. Ting wants to pose beside Minister Enrile and General Ramos."

"Already thinking of posterity!"

"She likes you, Benhur."

Benhur steps aside to let a family approach the gate with their Santo Niño. Made of plaster, its cape is red. Along Evangelista in Quiapo there is a wide choice of statues made of *escayola,* the same material supposedly in the *taho* his mother buys for the children to eat every day. A few more sidesteps and Benhur is free of Osong and statues. He decides to head down Serrano toward Libis.

Government troops have not moved in. But a firecracker can throw a crowd into panic; can draw return fire. Saboteurs throw pillboxes at demonstrators to destabilize rallies.

Benhur stops at one of the stores where, on the glass case displaying shirts and layettes, a black-and-white TV shows Ferdinand Marcos denouncing Enrile and Ramos as slay-plotters and exhibiting apprehended Reformists. A Captain Morales appears.

"He's Imelda's aide. This is a replay," the storeowner is telling newcomers.

Slight and hesitant, the captain confesses.

The replay is followed by a live program of the president announcing he has the situation under control. People on the sidewalk and street laugh. "That's not FM," someone says. "That's a fake, like his war medals."

An argument about whether this is also a replay fizzles into bantering. "This is the third. The first was at 11 p.m. and he looked sick; the second at 1 a.m. He looked sicker. He looks worse here, so this must be the third. It's already Sunday!"

The president's face is stressed, like fabric into which irregularities are woven to give it a one-of-a-kind look of originals.

"I can't bear to see the man. Just to get him out I will even vote for a dog." The man immediately behind Benhur leaves.

Those who stay hear Marcos saying: "Stop this stupidity and surrender." He bites off the words denouncing "the aborted conspiracy to liquidate me and the First Lady." Another supposed assassin is shown. Five combat teams are said to have crossed the Pasig in order to attack the Palace. As electricity surges on and fades, the president's face falters.

Benhur recognizes the study room in the Palace. When the scene is flashed again, he recognizes some of the generals seated behind the president in the first press conference. People start pushing to get a glimpse of the program, and Benhur moves on.

The road is along Camp Aguinaldo. On top of its fence, candles have been stuck in their own wax, the way lights are placed in windows during processions. Boni Serrano is like a fairground. In the middle of the street a man walks holding high a length of bamboo plugged at the top with a burning kerosene-soaked rag. A man with a guitar is accompanying the singing while younger folks are dancing to quick-stepping music. A mimic competes for attention, imitating vendors selling peanuts and corn, doughnuts, cigarettes, *balut* and *penoy,* gum, ice cream. A barbecue is being set up in a corner while tables have been placed where food can be donated. Nuns are asked to take charge of distributing boiled eggs, sandwiches, rice cakes. Someone drops off a pot of rice and a tray of *pancit.*

It is cool. He would settle for *bulalo,* the bits of meat clinging to bones boiled until they release their fat and marrow. It would not entice Ting Dolor, who's rabid about nouvelle cuisine, food separated by sauces, entrees sliding on the designs like the beaches of Rio de Janeiro; here and there a sliver of unrecognizable vegetable. His thoughts are about as heroic as daily conversation; Benhur turns against himself.

He steps around people who have stopped to exchange pleasantries with friends and relatives they never expected to meet in a revolution. The word is used loosely, Benhur thinks. One or two children, not young enough to be asleep, are wandering off.

A girl in a yellow shirt with Cory and Doy's pictures thrusts a poster of Enrile into Benhur's hand. Underneath: *I will not surrender.* Rolling it into a tube, Benhur walks on.

A man in a dark-blue shirt is buying cigarettes and Hall's cough drops from every vendor he meets. "For the soldiers. Who would think of me doing this when I used to curse each time I saw someone in uniform?" He waits for Benhur to reply.

Three men stop Benhur to ask where General Ramos is. They want to shake his hand and bring him a relic. "We know he's a Protestant, but everyone can use a miraculous relic. *Milagrosa ito.*"

"Must be at Camp Crame," the man buying cigarettes says. "I saw him come out of Crame around midnight to thank people for coming. Yes, give him the relic. He climbed on a jeep and waved."

Ramos must have moved to Crame after the conference. Benhur looks at his watch. It's really Sunday. Two o'clock; and quite cold. A moon the color of unfired pottery has crossed to where it will be when the sun rises.

If he had gone to Gulod, he might be back by now with as many neighbors as could fit in the car. Siso Feleo would want to come. For Siso, the question would be whether to feed the children or pay the fare to EDSA. He wonders, is Ryan home? He should bring the rest of the food in the trunk up to the Ministry and leave. But it's too late to go to Gulod. He might as well stay there as return to his office. It could be over soon.

"Cardinals Vidal and Sin," a young man with transistor radio pressed to his ear identifies those speaking. "Now a resignation is being read by the daughter of Justice Alampay."

Facing Benhur, the young man says, "Sir, you look like someone thinking of resigning, too. I'm a first timer. I never attended Cory's rallies until the Cardinal asked people to come protect the army. My mother came, too. She can't walk far so she's waiting in the car with the bag containing everything for emergencies. Ointments for cuts. Perfume in case anyone faints. How are we doing, Sir?"

"Giving it all we have. *Pinagbubuti natin.*" He is flattered with the attention given only, he supposes, to friends; or to someone recognized from the newspapers. Who does he look like? Not Osong!

Before reaching Libis, Benhur turns to head back to Crame, in case General Ramos is thanking the people again. Over a loudspeaker a priest is saying, "We are for peace. Let us be peaceful here on EDSA for the sake of the country and each other."

He sounds like the brother of a special friend. When he was a sophomore he loved someone who wrote poems, whom he saw everyday for weeks, either in their classes or on the steps of the Liberal Arts building. Then she died. According to those closer to her than he, by her own hand. A brother of hers, already a priest, also died. She wrote a poem to him, wrote "Benhur" at the top before giving it to him. He could make no sense of the lines, which filled him with desire every time he ran them through his mind.

We are here to fail/failure is love; and/death is rising; is/being buried in a flowering./Bleed/Don't heal.

The lines are hand-held candles on Epifanio de los Santos.

Laughing her head off at her companions' remark, a woman wearing an outfit that might have come out of *Elle* stumbles against Benhur; then, still laughing, tells him, "Ask for a *sorry* and I'll give it to you."

Just coming out of the lines dedicated to him, Benhur reacts after she's out of hearing. Fashion for the guillotine, he thinks. In the last century the *garrote* was used to execute by strangling Filipinos fighting against the Spaniards. Are all deaths a form of drowning? Americans invented the .45 for use against the Moros whom ordinary bullets failed to stop; the Gatling repeating gun, against the *revolucionarios* who refused to stand in trenches. So much for history. The same side always ends up defeated.

There's just so many ways to die. In the morning, firing squads might be standing where people now are awaiting the revolution. *Wait for death/ As for a lover. Wait/With cunning./Wait with hope.*

Meanwhile the atmosphere is that of Mardi Gras without the hysteria. The sky is almost purple. What if nothing happens? What if it turns out to be just another day? Or another night?

A hand on Benhur's shoulder makes him turn. It is the man who wanted him to research Florida resorts for ideas on developing Talim Island in the middle of Laguna de Bay. "I heard you opened an office in Beverly Hills; that you're getting rich from immigration cases. Still a bachelor?"

"Still. With a family of ten. Still scratching for chicken feed." Benhur scales up or down, according to people's expectations. "You're the one who looks prosperous."

"Not so. I ran out of money, so the project is on hold. Cement went sky high. My partner went to Australia. But I'm working on it. I go around buying pieces of houses. I got a lot of doorknobs from Pines Hotel when it burned down. I was there on my honeymoon. I've got doors and hinges, walls. All I need is foundation to attach them to. Meanwhile. Do you know of any homes being torn down? Old houses. There's that old one at the foot of the bridge in Bigaa, which the heirs might be willing to sell. My wife is here, too. There." He points to a group praying. "She thinks this would not have happened except for Marian Year last year. I can't join them because I can only pray in English. Even some seminarians have to be coached. Look at that one. There."

A man in a jogging suit runs between them. "What? No gas masks! For tear gas, you can use *calamansi,* wet cloths."

"Just this!" A man lifts up a sports bag. "My protection is in here. We're unused to bloodshed; a single Uzi will scatter a crowd like this. We can't win; but we can reduce the casualties, by disabling a few of the enemy. It's not too late to have a mini urban guerrilla teach-in. A few principles." He indicates other men placed strategically among the crowd, with similar sportsbags.

Benhur will have nothing to do with urban militia of any persuasion.

"To keep awake." A man is offering ice-cold water from two plastic containers strapped to his bicycle. "My wife is making *champorado* to serve for breakfast. Maybe someone with *tuyo* will bring some. Poor man's breakfast."

"That's okay," Benhur says, getting a drink. "The rich and poor meet here in friendship. It's just one revolution." He remembers the soldier saying bombing will start at four. Why four in the morning?

Wheeling his motorcycle carefully between people, a priest stops to take a drink. "Straight from the fridge! Can you come with me to Libis? Men are needed in case the Marines come up from the back."

"I will as soon as I return with the *champorado,*" the man on the bicycle says.

"Come down to Libis," the priest calls. Jeans and sandals are visible under his soutane. "Be rear guards."

"No one is guarding the area of the Mormon church," someone says. "I came in that way. Took the last parking space."

"I'll go." Benhur straddles the seat in back of the priest. Holding with both hands to the seat, he grips with both knees. Even then, when the motorcycle roars off, Benhur feels whiplashed; almost falls off. About twice the age of the priest, he should know better than to ride macho-style.

They make way for several on wheelchairs.

"The Poles have Solidarity; we have Peaceful Revolution. I think the military will listen to the Cardinal's appeal that they not use their weapons on the people. We're all Filipinos. By the way, I'm Case. Casiong to some; Sonny to others. Casimiro Valdez."

Benhur gives his name.

Case takes his hand off the handbar to flash back the Laban sign. "Beautiful the way the young are in this. When this is written about, it will be in the form of a love story. A people's love story."

"*Peaceful* is already stretching it," Benhur says. If Ting Dolor heard, she would think Case means revolution is sexy. She tells casual acquaintances that she gets a migraine if she does not get her daily *sexcitement.* "I can have it on the grass; isn't it shameful!" she told Terence Hugg, who repeated it to Benhur. "Is she for real, Vitaliano?" New battle cry for freedom.

A woman steps out from the curb with a child in her arms. "Father, tomorrow is her birthday. Will you bless her?"

Taking the opportunity to unflex his knees, Benhur gets off while Case steadies the motorcycle, both feet on EDSA. "What's her name? Irene! Beautiful. Beautiful to celebrate on the highway of the saints." He places a hand upon the child's head, intones the blessing, then kisses the child on both cheeks.

The lights of candles are centered in the dark irises of the child's eyes. The moon seems to have stopped overhead, while the man playing the guitar continues to hum along, eyes closed.

"She's part of the love story of this revolution. All about God's love, not power. Erotic love has to do with power. Do you mind? I'm thinking aloud the homily for tomorrow. But this revolution is the story of God's love in our lives. This is the walking theology of love. I have not had time to clear it with our resident theologian. Am I coming through to you?"

"I'm getting the semantics. But that's not a criticism. Just my mind-set, as they say. I like certainties."

A transistor radio being held to a loudspeaker announces that Minister Enrile has contacted Cory and Doy in Cebu. Cory asked him what she could do, and he asked for her prayers.

"I never thought I'd hear the Minister asking for prayers," Case says, walking his motorcycle through the space claimed by people on EDSA. Some have bedded their children in the waiting sheds. Some watch portable televisions, waiting for daylight. One holds out a bottle to them.

The needles of the *aguhos* are slight tracings on the ground.

"You look like a professor," Case says. "I was wondering. Does something of what is happening here vibrate everywhere there is a Filipino? Anywhere in the world. Fantastic possibility."

"Tonight I have heard that loss and possession, death and politics are power plays. Paradise might well be erotic. I met, in New Orleans, a librarian who said Filipinos have been in Louisiana since the eighteenth century, when Filipino sailors jumped ship to live in barrios they named after the places from which they came. Yes. I think Filipinos everywhere know something is happening." Up to his neck in darkness and chill, the sounds of EDSA beating inside him, why should he not think they also beat elsewhere? Benhur tries to justify matching points.

"You know, of course, Matthew 8, verses 28, etc? About unclean spirits entering the bodies of swine after they are driven from the men they possessed. This is about FM not being the only villain."

"Unclean spirits being driven *into,* not only *out* of, men?" Which one will run when the bombardment starts?

"Exactly. We should not feel superior to the cronies or be confident we cannot be tempted. I'll use the image then. It's not obscure. You saw it before I mentioned it. And the opposite of power is not helplessness, but love. Is that what puzzles you?"

Benhur is back where he was earlier that morning. There are the concrete water towers and the sign: *This way to Araneta Center.* Did Ting Dolor ever get to hear Morris Cerullo? To the left there is Imelda's mini-park. For all he knows, the same people are still in front of the bowling and billiard hall. This is where, earlier, he turned around, only to come back.

"Is that what puzzles you?"

"Me?"

"What frames the mystery for you?"

"I have not thought about it," Benhur admits. He can be open to Case in a way he cannot be to Elen Rodrigo. She is out to convert him to her way of life, while Case's concern comes from his feeling for everyone as a human being. To Elen, he is Benhur Vitaliano. "Is the mystery everything? All there is?"

A man kneeling in the middle of the road has *sampaguita* garlands in one hand and a rosary in the other. Like firecrackers, flashbulbs pop about him, but he continues to stare ahead.

Case waits for space to open around.

People are standing in front of the barbershops, bakeries, tire-supply stores, and general merchandise bazaar across from the fence of Aguinaldo, in the doorways of medical and dental clinics, boutiques and dress shops, copy centers, houses and apartments. Benhur recognizes the Little Star Tutorial Center, which makes him think of Loreto, of how she can open such a center in Gulod, become a secular evangelist teaching the alphabet and numbers.

Over the loudspeakers comes a message from a Captain Andrews, Air Force, urging his comrades-in-arms to help block the movement of hostile troops coming to retake Camps Aguinaldo and Crame from the people: *The time to die for our country has come.*

On the approach to Katipunan Road, which runs in back of Camp Aguinaldo, separating it from the subdivisions that overlook Marikina Valley, Case drops off Benhur. "This is it. Keep a group together here while I proceed down to Libis. I'll be back. Take this."

Benhur surveys the corners, three occupied by Caltex stations. To the right are the nurseries where Sally Moscoso buys her plants and driftwood. He checks his watch. Almost four a.m. Just in time for the bombardment.

Already a group has assembled. A young man is sharing his transistor radio by holding it to a microphone. It is Jaime Ongpin, calling on people to show their concern for the country by coming to the defenders at EDSA.

A nun goes over to Benhur. "See that man. He has been trying to get us to move out. He's either a government agent or an infiltrator from the Left."

Benhur looks at her. Whom does he trust? Suppose she's not really a nun but someone in a borrowed or stolen habit? To whom could he confide this suspicion if he felt it probable? "You're not on your knees, Sister?" She appears shrouded in her dark gray habit.

The nun tries to see his face clearly in the lights of candles and the brightening edge of the sky. "Our old and sick are praying in the convent. The children in the orphanages under the Cardinal's care are praying. The Poor Clares, the Pink Sisters, and the Carmelites. As long as our attention is on God, we are praying; we're living the mysteries we pray on the rosary."

He's sorry he asked. "Sister, I was just trying to . . ." The word escapes him. Does he use the word joking, teasing, with a religious whose crucifix is a pierced heart inflamed with fire?

"That's all right. I know you know we are sitting down to a meal with the Lord here. EDSA is our table. Do you want some coffee? Sandwiches? There's a lot of food. People give donations, wrapped lovingly, you know; and money. Look, here's another box."

Two taxis are dropping their fare. Refusing payment, the drivers say: "Donate to the revolution, Boss. Make it good."

Benhur is tempted to take a ride back to his office, instead of manning a barricade; except that people are starting to arrive, to stand with him, looking at his hand holding the rosary of green beads Case has given him. He does not recall a word of the prayer. He goes over to the nun who, with several others, is accepting food donations. "Sister, lead the prayers to get people to stay here." Somewhere from the dark ends of the intersection, the government's troops will be coming in tanks and armored personnel carriers, and the barricade here is made up of people sitting on the ground around candles, staring at the lights. Resting, some nuns are sitting up stiffly, like the candles, legs covered by their habits, arms across their chests. Are they part of the barricade, or only more of those to be protected with the children and old women in loose blouses and long skirts? Should not his *Lola* Sula be there to awe the enemy with her curses?

Soldiers without flag patches! The warning comes.

Those sitting stand up. The nun goes over to the soldiers, offering coffee and soft drinks. "We're all Filipinos," the nun says. *"Mga ka-puso."* Cameramen rush forward. A crowd gathers.

Hostile troops have been sighted coming from Blue Ridge. Another report comes. *Armed with Belgian Fals.*

How do you check information? To which should they react? Benhur asks some youth to check out what's coming from the White Plains end of Katipunan. They go off, their radios playing "Mambo Magsaysay," which Raul Manglapus composed for *the Guy's* election campaign almost thirty years before. He's now an opposition leader in the States. Benhur met Manglapus at a Movement for Free Philippines meeting in Cambridge.

"Something's wrong." A man shakes his radio. "Enrile was just saying he will die fighting, and he goes off."

It could be trouble at the Malolos transmitters of Radio Veritas, Benhur guesses; or in the station at Fairview where, the driver said, Joel and Miggy were headed the Monday after elections. Astonished by the size of the crowd arriving at the intersection, Benhur reminds the nun to start praying. The man with the radio has given up trying to get Radio Veritas back on the air. The radio is hanging from his neck like a gas mask.

When the prayers start, those who are dancing sit down. The man with the guitar plays softly. Not knowing the prayers, Benhur thrusts Case's rosary into his pocket and walks to the table from which to keep watch on Libis.

On the table piled with food, someone has left a paperback introduction to the thoughts of Teilhard de Chardin. A slip of paper marks page 46. Curious, Benhur opens the book to read by the candle. *To a perfectly clear-sighted observer, who watched it for a long time from a great height, our planet Earth would first appear blue from the oxygen in its atmosphere; then green from the vegetation that clothes it; then luminous . . .*

Benhur looks up from the word: *luminous.*

Flickering on the page, the candle dissolves and renders designs upon it: *and ever more luminous—from the intensification of thought on the surface: but it would also appear dark—and ever more dark—from the suffering that grows in quantity and acuteness in time with the rise of consciousness as the centuries pass by.* He lays the book down as he found it, but the words are winding inside his thoughts.

Something happening in the human mind registers in the universe? Sister Madeleine pierces the layers of the atmosphere with her thoughts?

Lost in the image of the words, Benhur stands there as if the ground is covered with tender ashes, though the words are hard thoughts demanding to become acts. It matters what one thinks, as well as what one does. One is not the equivalent of a stone but is the proper object of God's love. How can it be?

From long habits of protecting himself, out of fear of becoming absorbed, one of many, Benhur unspeaks the words by beginning to count the hours from the morning of the second day: Sunday. The sun has pushed itself up the sky, postponing mysteries. What if that is all there is? Mysteries in which one continues to be created?

He pulls the rosary from his pocket but there is no one to whom he can give it.

Bullhorns are directing people to Masses being celebrated at the gates of Camps Aguinaldo and Crame, and inside. Soldiers with flag patches stitched or taped to their sleeves—the stars and sun on the white triangle at the bottom—are recognized. "They're ours! They're ours!" the people exult, accompanying them to General Ramos, on the way genuflecting before the statues of the Virgin and of the Infant Jesus along EDSA.

Fighting emotion, Benhur stops at Gate One but thinks of the things left in the trunk. Should he bring them in to Colonel Moscoso; but how is he to explain his disappearing? He protects himself by trying to recall, word for word, what he read in the works of Teilhard de Chardin. What color emanates from partial truths?

A monk with a knapsack and umbrella walks by, smiling. Benhur thinks back to the Santo Niño church in Cebu, where he and Osong came to see the cross of Magellan, which is still growing, like a tree in the forest, according to people and an old priest in the courtyard who had chosen in the last century not to be repatriated back to Spain. What do such lives mean? What do they hold together on earth?

The sun is now where he had seen the moon, the night before, rising behind the *mabolo* in Colonel Moscoso's garden and ruffling the feathers of the parrot.

Suddenly in the middle of the road, stopping in Benhur's way, a family considers which Mass they will attend. "Go to Father Case," Benhur says.

"Where?"

"Somewhere down in Libis." Benhur imagines Case would be where he last saw the priest. A place like Gulod, a slope leading to rice fields instead of to a river, would be where Case would talk about revolution and love! Do souls make their way to God the way sperm fight upstream?

He can hear homilies over loudspeakers, and he blames his own indecision on weariness. How many hours' sleep has he had since noon Saturday? None in some seventeen hours, enough time to cross continents and oceans; against natural time. His internal clock must be all confused again.

"Attorney!" Elpidio Torres, the policeman from Gulod, is calling to him at a run. Out of breath, he explains, "I defected, Attorney. No more

Marcos graft and corruption for me. No more gambling after Cory closes the casinos. My wife voted for Cory because she promised to close casinos."

An old man, mistaking Elpidio Torres for a soldier, presses a pack of cigarettes and two pesos in coins in his hand. "A gift, not a bribe. Don't worry. We will protect you against Marcos."

"Who else is here?" Benhur proceeds to ask about Elpidio's family before asking about his mother and Loreto, the boys.

Used to soliciting bribes from sidewalk vendors and jeepney drivers, the policeman doesn't even notice the old man's disclaimer, but it bothers Benhur. Is honesty a matter of semantics? He attempts certainty. Or is it a virus that, introduced into bloodstreams, begins to leap into generations, becoming genetic? In a speech—Osong managed not to stumble over the words, as he read it in impeccable news-commentator accent, partly Ateneo—Benhur wrote that small-time, grassroots corruptions do not rate an entry into statistics with upper-echelon malfeasance; but they can become a country's genetic flaw. He thinks of a corollary: perhaps, ultimately, honesty will—also being genetic—fight as antibodies. Pre-colonial Filipinos picked from what traders left on the shores, leaving behind produce of equivalent value: dyes, shells, gold. Is that not encoded in the Filipino soul?

A call for volunteers to fill sandbags at the Ortigas end of EDSA sends Benhur and Elpidio Torres racing each other past the two military camps. Benhur wonders how sandbags can stop tanks. The best barricades are symbolic: the *aguho* felled across EDSA, its needles reflecting the moon and the candles.

Without losing her stride towards Ortigas, a young woman repairs her lipstick as she passes Benhur. Her short hair and the yellow trim of her eyeglasses make her look like another Cory clone. She winks, on catching Benhur's eye, and a cameraman snaps their picture.

"EDSA an altar?" she asks back, as the microphone is thrust between her and Benhur. "No! It's a dance floor. This is a celebration. Look at the celebrities. Their fans have followed their favorite stars, to sing and dance with them. I sang all night with Freddie Aguilar. Headlights. Trucking fans and singers. Everything impromptu. Fun. Did I sleep? No. The whole world is watching. My voice is always like this. Throaty. I have French blood . . ."

"I have no quarrel with what she says," Benhur says. "EDSA is different things to different people."

"What about the religious aspect?"

"No quarrel with that, either. It's part of being Filipino. Maybe cultural. Maybe something to get high on. But also a longing." He wishes he could recall what Sister Madeleine said, but the woman is trying to get the microphone so she can boom her voice to the world. *Religion is spectacle for some, but also purification.* He recalls, but does not know if he should mention them, flagellants on Good Friday, the tableaus of the passion of Christ during Lent, and children dressed in the habits of religious orders as thanksgiving for recovery from illness. And the rockets and shells will have their own truth and beauty when they streak across the sky. The long trajectory of their burst will be no small fire.

"Somebody has to go. It might as well be Imelda, huh?" the woman leans against Benhur. "We're all for democracy, so Filipinos will start returning home. So we better start dancing. Revolution is a marathon dance."

"Democracy is not song and dance," Benhur says, stepping away. "People have died. Nor is it a question of law. Nor mere exuberance. It is about being. Becoming. Significance, not greatness."

"Democracy is a yellow ribbon." The woman laughs. "Modern tribal artifact. Symbols are more trustworthy."

The reporter brings the microphone back to Benhur as if recording a debate. "Why a government of laws?"

Elpidio Torres makes the motion of cranking up an engine. "Attorney!"

"How do you exhibit freedom taken away from a country? By the wounds?" Benhur recalls victims of Hiroshima talking to high schools and peace groups in Massachusetts; but do the victims of the Death March, of the flamethrowers of retreating Japanese soldiers even have spokesmen or think of exhibiting themselves as victims?—As many died from those flamethrowers and bayonets as from the atom bomb—The walls of the Philippine General Hospital, against which retreating Japanese smashed the infants they found in the children's ward, were whitewashed immediately after liberation. What's wrong with the Filipino? Osong likes to tell a joke he heard in Los Angeles—An undertaker is auctioning off three unclaimed cadavers: What am I bid for the Japanese? *His* brain can compute yen without a calculator. (The bidding is stiff.) What about the German? Philosophy, music, technology springs from *his* brain cells. (The bidding is stiffer.) Now, what about the Filipino? *His* brain, unused, is as good as new—"A government of men would be unpredictable."

"Please! *Paki abot lamang."* A young boy sitting high up on the lamp post asks for the sandal he has dropped. There is a scramble to see who can throw it back. At the fifth try, he catches the sandal to much cheering and applause. The interviewer maneuvers the boom as high as it can go up the post.

A noisy sun, the helicopter's slow circling is picked up by the loudspeakers on EDSA, competing with a homily on transfiguration. Benhur thinks of the birds flying in and out of the chapel of the Holy Sacrifice at the University of the Philippines; of the funeral cortege for Evelio Javier where, on the passenger side of the flatbed truck, a trapped bird is painted flying. What is the message? As usual, only the bearable part of history will be faced; its meaning will thereby be lost, the response scattered.

He could have said, had he not been repelled by the woman's aggression, that the purpose of governing is to show the way and not be guided by what is popular, by what will ensure re-election. Politics is not a marketplace. Should not be.

Riding his father's shoulders, a little boy is waving his flag at the helicopter. Another tries to follow its flight with his pointing finger, and pinches it out of the sky.

Instruction on how to react peacefully when the government troops arrive is being broadcast on Radio Veritas, the words wavering and running together.

The terminals must not have been completely repaired, Benhur thinks. Elpidio Torres is nowhere around; must have gone on ahead; already bagging sand for the barricade at Ortigas while *he,* loaded with private anguish as usual, has lost his direction. He can't imagine now why he reacted so strongly to a woman he does not know and will never see again, unless everything he does is an attempt to find someone to love, long and permanently. When will he learn to absorb frustrations, to not be intimidated by failures, to not judge himself? It is one thing to declare in a speech that people are being lost, the way the land is being lost to the sea; it is another thing to grieve. If he would just try to *do* something about it, perhaps he would not feel obscured or subject to capricious laws of his own nature.

Where does he start the slow unmaking of himself? Go to Ortigas? Or turn around and see what can be done at the Fairview station of Radio Veritas?

"This way to the revolution, *Tito* Benhur! Did you just arrive?" Miggy and Joel are waving to him from the traffic island between the two military camps.

Benhur has to stretch a bit now, to be able to muss the boys' hair, his usual greeting to nephews. "Does your Mamá know where you are?"

"She begged us to come," Joel says. "Really."

"We saw Papá." Miggy, hands in his pockets, stands facing Benhur.

"Has General Ramos released the detainees in Crame?" Benhur faces the *aguho* and banana plants visible over the fence. What else can he say?

"Back to the teach-in for me," Joel says. "Will you join? Or are you riding Lord Godiva–style to the barricades? Save a tank for me, *Tito* Benhur."

Miggy waits until Joel has reached the group of young men in *sandos* who are listening to a seminarian. "When we saw Papá with Alex's mother—don't worry, I know all about his relationships"—he tries to crack another of Joel's jokes. "I wish I could go to a different school."

"No reason why you have to be together all the time."

"Mamá wants one of us to go to medical school. Which, she does not care. She wanted to invite *Tito* Vergel before, but did not know he was returning home so soon. A lawyer and a doctor is what Mamá wants, to make up for her sacrifices. Suppose I want to be a priest?"

"Do you?" In any way, would it help for Miggy to know what his father thinks? *Joel has elán; but Miggy is the better-looking, has the height, and if I were a woman I'd go crazy over him.* The psychology of sexuality fascinates Osong, who might draw the wrong conclusions, but can talk the subject to death with illustrations from his own experiences. EL, he calls himself. Eternal Lover. It's irrelevant, Benhur decides.

He knows the violent intensity that is, at the same time, terrible and beautiful; the rupture of darker feelings he senses in Miggy. Do maimed and mutilated souls speak one to the other?

Like fine sand passing through his veins, his helplessness hurts him. He's still where Miggy is; still maturing, for the rest of his life, perhaps. He does not look forward to anything, except for some final and severe mercy in the end.

People continue heading toward Ortigas, stepping over the barricades of ladders and tree branches improvised on EDSA. Friends stop to talk to Miggy. There is no need for Benhur to change the topic. He is grateful that Miggy will stay with him, give excuses and help carry the moment as far as it will go.

More people join the teach-in, stay a while, then move on to make way for others. "All Joel needs is to hear someone ask a question, and he pulls a seminarian out of the air to explain the reading. Maybe that's not at all what the question is about. Maybe Joel should be the priest." Miggy does not act interrupted in his thoughts. From time to time he looks up at the helicopter circling, capable still of simple wonderment.

Cory's Crusaders sweep by, one of the women hanging on to a little girl with a bag of chocolate kisses, some of which scatter in their hurry. *Is Cory here?* people ask. *Where?*

Some blunder through, rude in their conceit even if all they do is collect chewing gum on the soles of their shoes. Benhur has to give his arm to a woman carrying an infant when she is brushed aside. A tentative smile plays on her face.

"Are you looking for someone?" Miggy asks.

"I'm waiting for my parents," she answers, pointing with a nod towards a woman and a man hurrying along with a round tray of rice *bibingca* covered with wilted banana leaves. "We're from Apalit," she explains.

The mother smiles at Benhur as if she might know him. "They told us not to go to Manila because we'll only get robbed, but that has not happened."

Recovering his breath, the man asks his wife to offer the rice cake to Miggy and Benhur. "It is for the revolution. Offer some to everyone."

"I make it only for birthdays. It's his birthday." She looks at her husband.

"It looks better than those served in Manila Hotel," Miggy and Benhur say at the same time.

"It must be true then." The man helps steady the tray while his wife proceeds to slice the rice cake, placing each piece on a strip of banana leaf. While his wife serves, he starts talking about his family. "My daughter's husband is a soldier. Maybe we'll see him. He will defect. I taught my children to love their country." He has another daughter working in Taipei. "End of contract, she comes home."

"To stay," the woman adds. "I pray for that."

End of contract: beginning of life, again. Benhur knows of women workers abroad who have come under the mercy of employers who hold back their salaries, take away their passports, abuse them criminally. There must be more cases than those reported in the papers of women who have jumped out of windows, thrown themselves to death. Behind each cipher in the statistics is a human life and story, its luminosity visible in the universe—if Teilhard de Chardin is right.

Benhur feels he's in a different place from the night before; a different immanence faces him. This could be the most important event to happen in their lifetimes, and he is beginning to feel that he is in a place that has lost its name, that he has come unprepared—someone there by chance.

When Miggy comes over and places an arm about his shoulder—"Don't worry, *Tito* Benhur. Don't worry."—he feels he has been shown his own succession. Miggy might have called him *Papá.* They see through a single eye.

Runners come through: *General Ver's men are marching toward the Morato area; heading toward Nepa-Q; coming up on Aurora Boulevard.* Everywhere, running parallel to lightning strikes in the sky. How soon will the rockets come?

The sports headlines: *Lendl wins. Connors quits. Manubay rules RP Open Golf.*

Ferdinand Edralin Marcos is four miles away, in the other direction. The urban militia is in the crowd. The New People's Army of the Communists is on alert: where?

Equations: with the sun at its highest, forming dark hollows around the feet of the statues on EDSA.

Is the trophy *noble meanings?*

The Reformists are moving to Camp Crame.

Across the highway, parallel lines of civilians bridge the gates of the two military camps. Jeeps and cars are passing between, stalled by the rush of people trying to shake the defectors' hands, to press food, cigarettes and rosaries upon them. The sun has peaked in the sky.

Used to acting in his mind, reflex confined to thinking, Benhur is left behind by Miggy and Joel, who run forward to be ahead of the crowd.

Trying to see through the gaps that form and re-form like shadows of windblown branches, a nun standing on tiptoe cries: "It's deliverance. It is the Red Sea parting."

When the statue of the Lady of Fatima is seen being carried across, above the heads of the defectors, people rush to touch the statue. Soldiers are seen weeping. *"Umiiyak din sila,"* a woman says, surprised by the outpouring of emotion.

The chant comes—*Johnny, Johnny, Johnny*—when the Minister of National Defense walks across to join General Ramos in Camp Crame. Those up on the lampposts, or on the roofs of the waiting sheds along EDSA, even those on the overpass by the Farmers' Market are picking up the chant while cameras, like radar equipment monitoring heat or movement, are lifted above the crowd, snapping sight unseen in all directions.

"Please," a man holding two children asks Benhur to lift one of them so both can see the soldiers crossing over. "This is history. I want my children to be in it."

The child's thin arm soft around his neck, Benhur lifts her up beside her brother. Not quite two, she continues to suck an edge of her dress which partly covers Benhur's face.

"Wave," the father tells both children, holding up the arm of the boy. "Harder. So the Minister can see you."

The helicopter circles.

Impeded by the exuberance of almost half a million, it takes the four hundred Reformists close to an hour and a half to cross the highway. Surging after them, the crowd presses Benhur right through the gate and into Camp Crame. The child begins to cry.

Benhur pats the child on the back, pressing his face against her cheek. "It's all right. It's all right. There's your father." He steps out of the way of the people trying to find either General Ramos or the Minister.

Taking the child back, the man asks her to kiss Benhur. "Kiss Uncle. Again. Now we can go home."

Benhur pulls out his handkerchief to wipe off the wet smudges the child left on his face; but seeing her wave as they walk out, he smiles and returns the handkerchief to his pocket. The press of her tiny body against him has imparted a tender symmetry to the early afternoon. He hopes she will have a beautiful life because of what she has seen on EDSA, a happy life that he would wish for his own child, a questioning wisdom, some kindnesses and gentle care, work that connects her to herself and the world so she can use her talent to create what does not yet exist, some challenge, some healing when she needs them . . .

He can no longer see the child, so he turns toward the parade grounds almost wishing the same things for himself—a fresh start. The sentiment is pushed out of his mind by people coming in, looking for the Baby Uzi slung on the shoulder to identify Minister Enrile; the cigar, General Ramos.

It is impossible to hear Enrile and Ramos thanking the people for coming to protect them, but their voices carry loud on the transistor radios that are also alerting people to troop movements from Malacañang Palace: *Pincer movement. Six truckloads approaching. Cubao. General Lim.*

The crowd cannot believe it. General Lim on the phone saying "Yessir" to General Ramos. Has Lim defected? A voice is heard telling the soldiers not to hurt the civilians. *We are all Filipinos.*

The crowd hears itself cheering. Over the loudspeakers their voices float and crest with each new defection reported.

Now the sun is behind the statue of the Virgin on the guardhouse at the gate, behind the lilies white in tall vases. It glitters in the glass imbedded in the high fence of the camp like flowers budding out of bark, while radios on loudspeakers replay the hours since the revolution began Saturday night.

The comedians performing on EDSA sound the alarm: *Tanks coming from Guadalupe. Stop them before they reach Ortigas.*

Run. No longer someone who knows nothing about himself, Benhur runs with an energy that does not seem to come from him. No time to estimate the odds of coming out alive. The idea is to connect with the tanks. The vanity of this thought carries Benhur past a kneeling circle of nuns praying quietly.

Underfoot are dark glasses, bandannas, slippers, a Rayban, cups, biscuits, half-eaten corn on the cob. Carrying knapsacks, people hurry away from Camp Crame before the tanks reach the defenders. Benhur picks up a rosary, hangs it on a bougainvillea in the traffic island. Running in Reeboks, Topsiders, or Nike; running with Walkmans strapped against their ears, ears daubed with L'Interdit or Nina Ricci, cheeks fat with Perugina chocolates and Lindt; running with those who sleep under shrubs in the park across from Manila Bay and the five-star hotels.

A light drizzle falls.

While being carried in the arms of a woman who keeps looking back, calling out a name, a small child tries to catch the raindrops with her tongue. Bold, like brushstrokes, the sun scatters its pale brilliance.

In the rain, the running sounds like plunging into fire, takes the crowd over the barricades—sandbags, culvert pipes dragged out of the ground, street drains, limbs and branches of evergreen. Up ahead, men are driving trucks and buses into a line, toppling them on their sides or deflating their tires so they cannot be moved or rolled away when pushed by tanks.

Held aloft like little children, statues of the Virgin and of the Infant Jesus are brought forward. In daylight, they could be astral bodies, galaxies expanding.

Though he hears no distinct singing, powerful music beats inside Benhur as if the universe itself is taking part along EDSA. Across the lower sky, banners rip gently. Aware of landmarks—the guardhouse between Gates Three and Four of Camp Aguinaldo on his left; up ahead, the blue and red tile roofs of houses in the Corinthian Gardens, where Osong hopes one day to live; on his right, Barrio Fiesta and Kamayan, where he wants to bring his mother; banks, Slimmers' World, red and blue Pepsi signs, beyond the PX Securities Commission, the Tropical Hut open-24-hours, coconut trees—Benhur nevertheless is recalling the pictures of *revolucionarios* racing across rice fields overrun with Spanish soldiers and American sharpshooters who can pink the eyes of squirrels up ninety-foot pine trees; *revolucionarios* refusing to stand inside trenches but lining up on the mounded earth to meet assault at a standstill; trenches in which they will be pictured after the battle in rows across, just before they are covered with earth and long guns are pulled over them, in the chase after General Luna, General Aguinaldo.

Marines! General Tadiar; not General Lim, who, coming from the direction of Cubao, acknowledged General Ramos's authority.

Loudspeakers are giving instructions so the crowd will know the procedures to follow when the tanks start firing into them: *Keep infiltrators out. Don't let them wrest our revolution from us. Fight to the death.* The words run together like beads on a chain.

A young mother covers her infant's head with a *buri* fan. Schoolgirls are running hand in hand. As though on their way to the beach, some youths come, shoes laced across their necks.

It continues to rain lightly. An old woman comes with an umbrella under her arm, a folded handkerchief on her head. Bicycles weave on the outer edges, where medical relief tables have been set up by volunteers.

Announcement: *President Marcos has been trying to talk to General Ramos and Minister Enrile. Neither wants to have a word with him.* There is a second helicopter in the sky.

Now Benhur can see the barricade on Ortigas. A tractor has been pushed into the line of buses. A late model Mercedes is wedged between the vehicles. Those already at the intersection are linking arms, a second barricade of bodies. He is done running. As he arrives, Benhur finds arms locking into his. *Pare.* No time or reason for introductions. Juan or Juana de la Cruz. Body slower than his mind, Benhur is three lines from the front. All holding firm.

Say the act of contrition. The words of purification wash over Benhur, who tries to turn his wrist and see what time it is. Looking up at the pale sun, he guesses it to be close to four. He feels neither brave nor afraid.

They're here!

The helicopters' engines drown out the approach of personnel carriers airlifted from Davao. *They're not tanks. They're Armored Personnel Carriers that look like tanks.*

Benhur stretches for a look. Jungle camouflage, ammunition belt, and a bandolier of bullets shield the soldier standing on the lead vehicle. Benhur stares. He can separate the sounds of the wheels pounding with the force of the sea; he can see smoke spreading like a screen; then the sounds stop and the vehicles stand still just before crossing Ortigas.

What stopped them?

Benhur braces himself for the sound of the armored carriers revving up to cross Ortigas and smash into the barricades and crowd. He wants to stand by himself, to slip past the lines already formed, but the barricade of bodies holds firm. On either side of him, arms are locked into other arms, like a tangle of roots.

"What are we waiting for? Today is just as good a time as tomorrow to die," the man on Benhur's right strains forward. "If I'm going to die, I don't want to have to go to work Monday."

Some have approached the stalled carriers to toss cigarettes and candies to a soldier, who ignores the peace offering. A correspondent brings his microphone. "Are you going to shoot?"

Without answering, the soldier brings his M-16 closer to his body.

"Will you obey orders to shoot?"

"Don't do it," someone in the crowd calls. "Your sister is with us. Think of your mother."

Seminarians are walking through and among the crowd. "Let's avoid a firefight. Don't provoke the soldiers."

Similar exchanges float back and forth like wind across rice fields while TV camera crews continue to come at a run to record the moment of impact.

Time is both at a standstill and running.

The sound of engines revving up tears through the crowd like barbed wire. The ground trembles. Correspondents rush as close as they can to the Armored Personnel Carriers that begin swerving to their right, away from the barricades and the lines waiting to be run over, to smash into the wall fencing off the vacant lot on the way to Pasig, into the tall grass, missing a billboard: *God listens.*

Only briefly is the moment lost to disbelief. Recovering quickly from amazement, the crowd rushes toward the smashed wall, over its stones, hoisting one another up as they climb. Once on the other side, groups assemble with their banners, rosaries, transistor radios.

They find the Marines have jumped off their armored vehicles with 50mm machine guns that can hit targets a mile away. Armalites drawn, ammunition belts bristling across their chests, the Marines encircle their Armored Personnel Carriers, in the center of which can be seen an officer conferring by radio with some command post.

It's General Tadiar! Secret ultimatums?

The throttling sound of the engines shakes the ground. Black smoke belches out. A black gunship hovers above.

Benhur recognizes the men who had earlier been on EDSA with sportsbags containing weapons. They are sprinkled among the crowd. Can they disable the armored carriers? He remembers what they said: "We can't defeat them but we can reduce casualties." The surveyor next to his office once invited him to a guerrilla warfare teach-in. The 1980s Light-a-Fire Movement. *Makasuntok lang.* Fistfight.

The gunship starts hovering, then lands away from the crowd. *A Sikorsky!* Rumors flare through the crowd: *Regardless of casualties, General Ramas in Fort Bonifacio wants the Marines to ram through.*

"The Marines look so young," a woman marvels. "Just like my sons in high school. I pity their mothers."

A man with binoculars reports an exchange of salutes just outside the gunship. Several men come down. Someone with his radio pressed to his ear says General Tadiar is asking Minister Enrile and General Ramos in Camp Crame for a conference before obeying his orders from General

Ramas in Fort Bonifacio. General Ver has also called the Minister, addressing him as *Sir.* Is it a delaying tactic, some deployment maneuver learned from Vietnam? Are they being encircled?

Close to an hour of standoff brings young women, approaching the circle of Marines to offer flowers. Hands trembling, one places the flower refused by a Marine into his gun barrel. Emboldened, others come bringing candy and cigarettes. From the waiting shed on EDSA comes the singing of *Our Father.* A crucifix has been placed on the roof, while the rosary is prayed in all of its three mysteries. More belligerent cries puncture the air, daring the Marines in combat outfits and dark boots to do their worst.

Threading the lampposts on Ortigas, electric wires appear like barbed wire loosened from the barricades surrounding Malacañang Palace.

The gunship starts lifting up. One of the officers aboard is identified as General Kanapi. Benhur wonders if anyone has accepted the responsibility for a massacre. Who?

In another hour it will be dark. It is about twenty-four hours since Minister Enrile called for a press conference on Saturday. Who will the Marines obey? These are seasoned combat troops from Mindanao, battle-tested against the Moros in their fight to secede. Is Jainal there? Last Benhur heard, he had become a judge.

The black Sikorsky sweeps the sky. From its height what does it detect of the earth's luminosity?

A few minutes after it lands, an ultimatum is declared. General Tadiar to General Ramos in Camp Crame: *Will attack in thirty minutes. No quarter given.*

Thirty minutes. Benhur checks his watch to begin countdown. Attack will come at 4:50 p.m.

"We would have died of fright at home, not knowing what is happening," a woman says, a yellow ribbon draped about her neck. "'Let it be. We have to go,' I told my husband, and we brought our Santo Niño and children." They have just arrived since leaving Gapan upon hearing that Radio Veritas transmitters were destroyed on Ferdinand Marcos's orders. The loss is estimated at 50 million pesos.

The ultimatum brings other people from their homes to EDSA; brings would-be negotiators on their own, former cronies, socialites heading for the armored carriers to see who will make General Tadiar back down, who will talk him into surrendering. A bishop is seen on top of one of the carriers.

The front pages of newspapers map the state of the revolution, which some attribute to the Marian Year, 1985. *Quit and avoid bloodshed,* so *Malaya* reports Cory telling Marcos, who *Warns he may order tank assault* on what General Ramos calls *A Revolution of the People.* The *Inquirer* headlines Enrile as saying: *I'll never surrender,* and Ramos as charging: *President Reagan supports Marcos.* A front-page picture shows Ramos monitoring Marcos on TV, and plot-leader Colonel Greg "Gringo" Honasan in battle fatigues. Boycott Watch: Day Six. FM to Habib: *More forceful means to quell disorder. Cory "cabinet" set for takeover. Reform Group Expect Arrest.*

Sit. Sit down so General Tadiar can see how many surround him.
The order brings some to kneel on one knee, as in church. Others sit on the ground, in the middle of EDSA.

Over the public address system come the voices of those attempting to negotiate with the Marines. Nearby broadcast towers describe what Benhur is watching: a woman with a red scarf posing against the Marines and their armored carrier.

A bag of peanuts is passed around. *Energy for the revolution.* It is lifted up, offered to the Marines on the Armored Personnel Carriers.

We are peacemakers. Father Case touches Benhur on the shoulder. "Good job last night at Libis."

Designer weapons! Made to explode on impact, or delayed for maximum destruction. Different modes and settings for fuses: weapons so trigger-happy that air can detonate them. Moving air. Howitzers at Fort Bonifacio that can reduce Camp Crame to powder, bring walls collapsing on their foundations.

Is courage still relevant? Benhur wonders, hearing Marcos's arsenal described. What does it say about the minds that conceived and produced such weapons?

Benhur thinks too late of the questions to ask Father Case, who is walking past the Marines. Saturday night, on their way to Libis, the priest had said that politics is the place for contemporary man to seek holiness. Jesus Christ is a *revolucionario.* And Andres Bonifacio. And he?

Evening to evening the hours have run. Countdown. Off to one side some are singing *Pananagutan.* Not knowing the words, Benhur lets the singing flow over him while he looks up to where the moon would rise, if still it could. He feels proud that he has not run away, has not tried to protect himself. With God's help, the words say, human freedom will fulfill its responsibilities.

Are those the tanks? The Marines? Is Cory here? New arrivals squeeze through.

Fifteen more minutes to count down.

"It looks like Bishop Escaler," the man with binoculars says. "And General Tadiar has not stopped smoking."

Benhur gets up from sitting on the ground to move closer to the circle of Marines, starting a scramble to get right under the metal of the armored carriers, beyond the nuns kneeling. His head spins from lack of sleep; from suddenly rising.

"For God's sake, Sister, get out of the way before you're crushed!" A Marine comes to the edge of the crowd.

Some kneel with the nuns.

Another soldier is seen getting out of the armored carrier closest to the nuns. Benhur shudders. Tight spaces scare him, make him feel encoffined. He closes his eyes, swallows. Not all of them will die here. If God is God, how does He choose who will die? What about courage or love? When he was small he told his father he did not want to go to heaven. Mass is long enough adoration. His father told the story to friends and relatives: *Something will come out of this boy. He thinks.*

His head starts pounding. The same thing happened once in air flight. That time, he closed his eyes and willed himself, slowly, to feel well. Another time, he and his father were in Santa Cruz; it must have been September, for his father, knowing he liked the fruit, bought him a kilo of *lanzones* to eat in the bus on the way home. Exhaust fumes had made him ill, but he forced himself to eat so his father would not be disappointed. In his office he rubs his temples and his neck, pressing hard, whenever he gets a headache from working through the night, but in public he refuses to be seen tending himself.

It passes. He checks his watch. Three minutes past the deadline. Are their watches out of sync?

Sit down, people are being urged, *so General Tadiar will see we are not armed.*

A correspondent asks one of the Marines: "Whose orders will you obey? If you are ordered to shoot the people, will you?"

"I am not permitted to speak, Sir."

The correspondent turns to the man closest to the Armored Personnel Carriers. "Are you going to let them kill you without doing anything? Will you let them?"

The man presses both hands on the carrier.

"Will you pray for the Marines, Sister?"

"I'm praying for them."

One of the Marines thrusts an obscene gesture at the nun. The crowd jeers. "Please don't leave, Sister."

"No! No! No!" The crowd shouts in answer to a question Benhur did not hear. The chant is picked up, returns from the back. Benhur walks to the Armored Personnel Carrier to place both hands against the metal. It feels like a wall against which a firing squad might fire.

The trampled grass darkens. The sky is starting to grow heavy. The ground trembles as the APCs roar back to life, emitting black smoke. People rush forward to brace themselves against the carriers, which jerk into their bodies. Cameras start popping their flashes. 400-speed film can pick out the color of blood in the dark. On what will survival depend? Chance or fate?

Benhur coughs out the black exhaust. After this is over, what minor political officer in the United States Embassy will be credited with calling the shots?

Clear out and make a path. Let us through. We don't want to hurt anyone. Loudspeakers carry General Tadiar's request.

Time's up!

It's 5:30 p.m. The Marines on top of the APCs grip their Armalites. Those who had been posing for the benefit of the world press have jumped off. Benhur thinks of those who, in 1972, managed to have themselves jailed after the initial wave of arrests in order to have their pictures taken inside Camp Crame: the current patriotic immortality system. Has General Ramos freed the detainees inside? He wonders where his thoughts are coming from; or if he's only another fool multiplying words that reach no conclusion and have no significance; or if everything unleashed from the same source has no beginning or end.

His hands against the APC, a surge of pain runs along Benhur's shoulders and arms, spreading down his back. He makes himself recall that whatever is happening here is happening everywhere, to all; to his father, to Vergel. He is pushing so hard that his body starts to feel hollow. He wishes he could stand away, take a few deep breaths. From behind, many are trying to place a hand on the metal, to get their own handhold on the APC.

Contact with history. Handhold on time.

He can hear sounds, but it feels like silence. When he looks up, the open hatch is like the rim of a well in which water might suddenly rise. There is a well in Gulod, close to the river where, people say, the dead of the revolution of 1896 were thrown by the Spaniards, who then ordered it filled with stones and earth.

Benhur lays his face against the metal, digs his heels into the ground, willing to be hurt, recalling a book in an antique shop in Concord, Massachusetts, a waterlogged copy of Neely's *Photographs of a War,* the Philippine-American War of 1899, showing bodies of *revolucionarios* bloated by the sun, the finest and best of them dead in the first encounters. His thoughts connect him with those who have died, those who will yet be born as history and creation continue each other.

He feels out of breath. Pain shoots up and down his legs while the Armored Personnel Carrier's vibration sobs inside him. He no longer feels himself pushing back; only knows.

A man tries to reach between the bodies pressing against the carrier. "I'm doing this for my children," he apologizes.

The light-green patches on the Marines' uniforms remind him of the pepper leaves in his *Lola* Sula's backyard, heart-shaped leaves that she smears with lime, folds, then rolls around a sliver of *buyo* to chew as a soporific.

"The Virgin is protecting us. Let us not be afraid," a woman in white says. "Keep your places. Nothing will happen to us."

Looking for where the moon will rise, Benhur refuses to enter into what the woman says. What if the Virgin is really there, over them? In another hour the moon will be bursting its halo, rising.

The groaning of the APCs winds down to a low whine as the engines are cut off. The ground stops trembling. A cheer breaks loose, running over the crowd like wind over grass. Benhur stands away, but before he can stand free and clear he starts falling backward, is caught and held up by those in back of him, held upright until he slides down to sit on the ground, both hands covering his crying.

A second time the APCs come to life, throbbing. Benhur loses his place against the metal, moves aside for those dashing forward to push back the carriers. A nun's white hair is a fine net where her wimple has slipped.

It has become cool. Benhur recognizes some of those trying to touch the APCs. He has seen them earlier on EDSA and Libis, between the military camps. How will they recognize one another afterwards? No longer by blood, by school ties. Fraternity replaced by a new affinity: EDSA.

The heavy, oily smoke from the exhausts is on Benhur's face and hair. Away from the carriers, Benhur looks back on EDSA. There is a statue of the Virgin on the waiting shed. Might it be the one that in the 1750s turned back the Dutch fleet from Manila Bay, drove away the English after their brief occupation? He is thinking like someone recalling his own death.

The moon is rising with many halos.

"Make way! We are returning to Fort Bonifacio," General Tadiar exhorts the people.

Not willing to trust the announcement, wary of being deceived—the Marines might double back toward Camps Crame and Aguinaldo—the people follow the Armored Personnel Carriers through the breach in the wall, passing men lined up against it, staining the limestone.

Night to night, the hours continue to run.

On portable radios comes the news that a personal emissary from Ferdinand Marcos has contacted Minister Enrile, offering a show trial: a pro forma trial for public consumption. *No one will be punished.* Cory Aquino has not gotten in touch with anyone on EDSA but has talked with Cardinal Sin and U.S. Ambassador Bosworth. Enrile, replying, demands that Marcos step down.

Again the sounds all outside his body, Benhur wakes up—Monday, one o'clock—inside one of the barricade buses that had been rolled into place and its tires flattened at Ortigas, Sunday. He does not remember boarding the bus, entering to sleep in the back seat. Did nothing happen while he slept?

Five youths are huddled about the steering wheel. One is turning the wheel as if he's rounding a corner, releasing it to let it spin back to starting position before giving it a full turn in the other direction. If they had meant to rob him, his wallet would not be in his hip pocket. Were they in the bus when he got on? They could have stabbed him, too. Ice picks are a favorite weapon with youths who wait for taxicab drivers at night. In some cases, the police blotter reports: *Done in fun.*

In a manner of speaking, just sharpening points.

Benhur goes to the front, slowly as to cause no alarm. *"Para,"* he says, lighthearted in pretending he's a passenger getting off. No indication of an attack on the intersection.

"Cigarette, Boss." Wearing rubber thongs and pleased faces they offer him a cigarette instead of a greeting.

He takes the offer, lights it from the glowing end of the stub offered, then lets the cigarette hang from his mouth like a smile. Some men are asleep on the traffic island across Petron.

Through the door a family-size Coke is thrust toward the one pretending to drive. Laughing his head off, another youth comes up with a *bilao* of *pancit* and a bag of hard *galyetas* biscuits to eat with the noodles. "*Hatchet,* Boss," they invite Benhur to eat with them.

He sits just behind the driver. They might have been from Gulod, gathering to drink, to pass the time joking by way of dreaming, waiting to act big when the girls came around. Benhur watches as the driver, with a plastic spoon, divides up the *pancit* into portions on the tray, then, handing the spoon to Benhur, starts scooping the noodles with a *galyetas.* Soon their hands are moving in the pounding rhythm of farmers dropping wooden pestles into mortars carved from tree stumps, when rice used to be husked, not milled.

"Do you live around here?" Benhur asks, taking a swig from the bottle of Coke.

"Far. How about you, Boss?"

"Also far."

"You look as if you live around here. This morning . . ."

"Yesterday," the others correct him in one voice.

"Yesterday morning, we saw you walking with those who own the land around here. We heard them being interviewed. I would not want to live in the big houses. What if there's a fire? Steel bars on the windows. High walls. The gardens are imprisoned."

Benhur is surprised by the imagery. Imprisoned gardens. Something pristine from what he judged were abandoned lives.

"Just one day," the driver says, "it would be good to live inside those houses with blue palms." When he turns from the lights on EDSA, Benhur sees a scar running from the boy's right ear to the mouth, like a lopsided grin; but a rosary hangs around the neck.

That is also the wish of Osong: to live in a house in the Corinthian Gardens, surrounded by palms of all kinds—champagne, traveling, blue, red. He wonders if the youths realize one stalk can cost ten thousand pesos.

"What do you do? Where do you work? Customs?"

They have heard that after a year at Customs an employee can have a car. "Self-employed," he says, though his *Lola* Sula's ambition for her sons and grandsons is government employ. No slack season as in farming; no endangered profit as in business.

"If we win," says the one playing with the wheel, "Cory will be president and there will be no corruption any more."

"Let's light a candle and stick it on the hood," the one who brought the *pancit* suggests, pulling out a stub of wax from his pocket. "It came from the nuns. I didn't take it from any shrine. I was going to bring it to my mother."

"Better bring it to her," Benhur says, thinking of the gas in the bus's tank. He thanks them for supper, considers giving them some money—they could have harmed him while he slept and taken the amount he was going to bring to Gulod—but that would reduce them to mercenaries. Too crass. Indelicate for a revolution.

"*Ingat lang,* Boss," they call from the door, as if he had been their guest, which he was. "Careful, Boss. Some have plastic bombs in their bags."

The last thing he would have anticipated. Their telling him to be careful. He waves the Laban sign, fixing their faces in his mind in case they need his help in the future.

A payloader has been added to the barricade at Ortigas on EDSA. The darting light of candles is sharp, like glass shards imbedded atop stone walls, like the barbed wires in the steel barricades encircling Malacañang. Is Marcos watching them on his TV?

It's Monday. Second week of Lent.

Benhur is reminded of flagellants scourging their backs with spikes and pieces of glass attached to lengths of leather. On Good Friday a flagellant actually had himself pierced with nails and crucified, on the chance that his father, an American soldier, might see his picture and recognize his name. Others try to get rid of their demons. Might Sister Madeleine have one tempting her while she prays, heart upright, on bended knees?

He stands at the intersection where, ten hours before, he had stood to wait for the tanks coming from Guadalupe.

Omega/flashpoint! Yesterday never came. Might it still come? The Marines were seen last on their way to Fort Bonifacio. It feels as if he's wandering lost, all directions mislaid.

Marcos will attack us at 2 a.m.

Another hour.

A replay of General Ramos's earlier message to Marcos's troops: *Don't commit a crime against your own people. It's a violation of your military oath. Join us here at Crame.*

How come nothing has happened? EDSA can be strafed by aircraft from Villamor Air Base, formerly Nichols Field. It will take only two minutes. There are British Scorpion tanks that do not even need to leave their base to shell Crame and Aguinaldo.

Or are they, at that moment of apparent safety, already targeted? Flashpoint in seconds. Rockets, mortars, missiles; Sikorskys and Hueys with 20 mm cannons to blast civilians who have come to protect some four hundred defectors. The walking theology that Father Case talked about on Saturday night, or was it already Sunday morning? In the continuum, time has lost its measure; certainty, its direction.

Several children are asleep around a small bonfire, watched over by a woman who stoops over them as if her bones have crumbled into lace.

Improvise barricades. Those listening to a portable radio repeat June Keithley's announcements. *Repaired, Radio Veritas is now hooked up to a secret station. 8.10 AM Band. On back-up equipment.*

Others turn the dials on their radios. They have been listening to Keithley on Radio Veritas since election day, when she started a running tally of the votes. The real count missed her when the Malolos transmitters were hit with Israeli-made guns Sunday morning, and the Fairview Station was too weak to give a steady signal, until now. *Radio Bandido.* Location unknown.

Twenty truckloads of troops moving towards Camp Aguinaldo on Commonwealth Road.

Walang aatras. Those listening declare they will not retreat.

Benhur checks his watch. 3 a.m.

Lookouts with walkie talkies stand on the buildings on EDSA, reporting their spot observations to Keithley: Government troops seen in the vicinity of Horseshoe Drive in San Juan, behind Camp Crame. That's near the Moscoso home.

"It does not sound like Radio Veritas," a woman says, covering the children sleeping on the ground. "It might be a government radio imitating Veritas to trick us." Her husband believes it's Veritas in a building close to

Malacañang Palace itself, so the government has not been able to monitor its signals. "It's Keithley. Mambo Magsaysay is her signature. Listen."

It seems so long ago that he stood against the Armored Personnel Carriers at that intersection. The moon has begun its descent. On the ground, nuns are sitting back to back.

"Yes, I saw Osong," Benhur replies to his classmate Jainal, who has brought his sons to the barricades. Benhur is introduced to the sons, one a premed student, the other about to take the Bar. Benhur is reminded of Joel and Miggy, then of Colonel Moscoso and Cayetano. They are still all alive, perhaps.

"I saw him, too. Looking for twenty volunteers to command. And also for you." Jainal says. "He was encouraging me to resign, too, though he was not sure if he would. Typical Osong. But I've been thinking of resigning. For some time now."

"And?"

"Not right away. When the youngest son graduates from college, perhaps. I want to write. I can't do it in my place. People come at all hours to talk, for advice. I want to write the story of our family. I'm thinking many volumes, Benhur. Presumptuous, as usual. I've written only briefs and, lately, opinions, mostly in the minority. However, I have come to the stage in life where I must decide whether to go on as usual, or to tackle what the rest of my life I would otherwise regret not doing."

Benhur knows the general outline of those stories. Jainal's ancestors fought the Spanish and Americans, who never got a real foothold in Mindanao. He belongs to a royal house, a family of *datus.*

"My brother, you know, with all the forces of our family and its constituents, does not believe we can gain autonomy without firing a shot. But both of us want to put more than just cassava on the plates of our poor. For that, we need autonomy, peace and order. I especially want to show the young ones that leaders can come from any family, not just the royalty."

"Which will you do first? The book or that?"

"Maybe I'll end up doing neither, Benhur. That's what's frightening. Which? The books will remind the young ones of our past. Not *one* republic, but thirteen Muslim republics, each with its own administrative system, courts, and legislators. To continue our tradition we need factories and a balanced economy which will not come from the promises of politicians from Manila. I have a son going to school in Saudi, another in Lebanon. We have to unify our independence movements, reformists, and liberation fronts. Establish priorities. Inclusionary motives. No betrayals. What about you? Are you up to your neck in work these days?"

Beside Jainal's plans, even his most serious work pales. Benhur shrugs. "Same things." As usual? or similar to Jainal's? Let his classmate interpret it his way. Sometimes it seems that, no matter how hard one tries, nothing is accomplished. Should he admit to that? Betray his own failures?

"How's your family?"

"Doing all right." He does not know if Jainal thinks he has tied the knot sometime, or several knots. "The class seems to be doing all right, too." Benhur shifts attention from himself. "You must find it distasteful to see prayers mixed with revolution, if this is what it is." Qualifications, again. The word "distasteful" is grossly inappropriate as an apology for the statues of saints and the continuous rosaries being prayed on EDSA.

Jainal looks about, glances towards his sons standing with several Muslim students at the barricades. He never felt discriminated against by being referred to as Moro, and the term is gaining acceptance once more. "Not at all, Benhur. We pray during our own rallies. Prayer is the strength of politics, and politics is the arm of prayer. Freedom and God and Allah."

It feels like a state of continual desire, waiting for flashpoints: Omega. Runners announce a correction—the tanks that were reported approaching Horseshoe Drive from Greenhills are only garbage trucks. *Garbage is all the government gives us. Disinformation.* Shortwave radio operators are reporting what people are calling in, from wherever they are. The replays of pleas, troop movements, rearrange time too arbitrarily for Benhur to have an exact sense of what's happening. It's Monday already.

Ten past five. That time Sunday he was at the Libis intersection waiting for the Marines. Benhur decides to head there. He passes people still asleep on cardboards. In the uncertain light they seem corpses heaved out of the ground.

The proprietor of a ready-to-wear shop on Boni Serrano has opened his back room to anyone who wants to wash. Benhur buys himself a shirt on his way to the faucet where he washes his mouth and face, drying himself with the old shirt, which he leaves behind.

"The roosters have been crowing since one o'clock," the proprietor says, giving Benhur his change. "And several provincial commanders, even Presidential Security Command troops, have defected. Radio Veritas/ Bandido says the navy ships in Manila Bay have their guns aimed at Malacañang. But some groups are trying to take advantage of the situation. I think that's what Keithley is trying to say. To warn us. We're still on top of dynamite."

Benhur steps out. There are stars. He can smell *sampaguita* from the garlands wound about a statue of the Virgin, unattended on a narrow table except for candles burning down to their wax, and wonders what he did with the *sampaguita Mang* Genio's wife placed in his hands to give to the Virgin. He thinks of Colonel Moscoso and Cayetano, of his mother and sister, of the boys, of Jainal and his sons. What an experience Sister Madeleine is missing!

Beside a van, some people are watching a miniature TV. A replay of Marcos raving, telling Enrile and Ramos to stop the foolishness and surrender before he blasts them off the earth. Everyone with a radio has discovered Radio Veritas/Bandido's broadcast station. Reports warn of airdrops inside the military camps on EDSA: *Marines armed to the teeth.* Spot observers have seen troops coming up on Katipunan behind the camp. Benhur recalls those with walkie-talkies on top of the Soliven building on EDSA. He passed the Kamayan but does not recall seeing it. He must not be hungry.

It's cold. He should have accepted Jainal's offer of his son's jacket. People are asleep beside their coolers and portable grilles on which they had cooked supper and where they will heat their breakfast later that Monday. If Marcos and Ver could see the protectors at EDSA, they would dismiss them quickly.

Only a few stars visible. They might have fallen off the halo of the La Naval. Fallen up. Was she the one who witnessed the American fleet entering Manila Bay stealthily on a Sunday, blasting at the defenders observing the Lord's Day? He has read that during the revolutions there were no skirmishes between Filipinos and Spaniards on Sundays. In two/three years the Philippines will have twice the population of Spain. If that is some kind of revenge, against whom is it? Even if it succeeds, the revolution of 1986 will have to face the problem of overpopulation.

The only national problem to which he has not contributed.

One last look at EDSA before he heads down toward Libis. Floodlights are sweeping across the highway, lifting up the flags on lampposts, pulling a comedian out of the shadows, pushing together the roofs and crowns of trees.

He is walking to Libis with less strength than he had the morning before, or when he faced the Armored Personnel Carriers on Ortigas. Headlong into catastrophe.

A busload of people stand in his way. Carrying baskets of food and gas masks, they describe how they saw General Ramos jogging. They offer him coffee from a Coleman jug.

The Alma Mater song of the Philippine Military Academy is being played, making some cry. Both sides must have each other's frequency by now, and the broadcast information may be strategic instead of factual. Psych warfare—General Ramos is a master. So does Benhur believe the bulletin that Marcos loyalists at the old International Airport have captured troops who hijacked a plane in order to defect? or that ten Marcos battalions are advancing, and General Ramos is asking that foreign correspondents covering him inform their embassies if they are staying at Crame? In case a rocket melts them into a single mass?

Over loudspeakers comes news that government troops are arriving from the provinces to encircle EDSA. Many are being airlifted.

In the middle of Boni Serrano some children are playing while Radio Veritas/Bandido announces that the troops landing at the now Domestic Airport are really defectors. *They're ours. Talo na si Marcos. We're winning.* Enrile is supposed to have told Reagan by phone.

The announcements echo back and forth as Keithley asks people to turn their radios up to blare, to keep their electric bulbs burning. "The Meralco bill is your contribution to revolution at EDSA. Keep your lights on until daylight."

"You can't imagine the peace of mind this gives me," a missionary had once told Benhur on the Hong Kong leg of a flight to Los Angeles, as she took out the contents of her "contingency purse": an aspirin, a Band-Aid, a safety pin and a straight pin, a rubber band, a needle and white thread, two sticks of gum, a Chinese compass the size of a lemon drop, and a tiny bit of folded paper on which was written the Lord's Prayer.

The disco music being played in the street meets feeble resistance in Benhur's head. It is pure sound, like Father Case's litany on their way down to Libis: *We are called impostors, yet we are truthful; nobodies, yet we are in fact well known; dead, yet we are alive; sorrowful, yet we are always rejoicing; poor, yet we enrich many; seem to have nothing, yet everything is ours . . .* He never heard the whole litany the priest was composing as he brought them by motorcycle down to where the Marines, all 2,000, had been seen approaching.

Where are those Marines now? General Tadiar?

If they all died there, who would make it to the obituary page? *Vitaliano?* some commentator or correspondent will ask, *Is that a Filipino name?*

"Play 'Immaculate Mother' instead," a woman who has just arrived suggests to those playing disco music. Then she turns to Benhur. "This is my first time demonstrating."

A bullhorn is calling people to Libis. The Marines who retreated from Ortigas on Sunday evening have doubled back behind Camp Aguinaldo, and hotheads among the defenders want a fight.

The Philippine Military Academy Alma Mater song sets the pace for the run to Libis and assures Benhur that he is not going in circles. An unaccustomed feeling of fineness comes over him as he imagines the *revolucionarios* crossing fields not far from here to rush headlong at the Spaniards, or following General Aguinaldo against the Americans, whose long guns dropped shells that disinterred the earth. Acts simultaneous in eternity.

When he stops to catch his breath, someone brings a pail of water over to him. A bowl of already-halved *calamansi* is offered, too, along with pieces of cloth, along with instructions for preparing gas masks when tear gas is lobbed at them: *Squeeze the juice into the cloth after dipping it in the water. Cover all exposed skin.* They are also reminded to hug the ground. *Don't touch the canisters with your bare hands. Neutralize them by dipping them into water.*

A woman says, "The *calamansi* is my children's donation. They opened their *alkansiyas* for the revolution. It's only four fruits for a peso, and so tiny. After this I'm going to plant some seeds and they can start saving coins again."

Some streetlights are plugged into apartments and stores, shops donating electricity. A relay of ice in plastic tubs comes through the doors along Boni Serrano which are busier than bus stations with people heading for the bathrooms. Benhur is asked by a woman in hair curlers to bring a basket of boiled eggs to the nuns' table—"So everyone can have breakfast before the attack comes."

Without looking up, the nun tending the first table Benhur comes upon presses on him a sandwich already wrapped. "*Hijo,* eat. So that when you faint it will not be from hunger but from seeing her."

"Her?" Benhur opens the jar of mayonnaise with which she has been struggling.

"Are you the only one who has not seen her walking about? A woman too beautiful to be other than the Virgin!"

A security guard on a motorcycle unloads a box of *pan Americano* on the table. Other nuns start making sandwiches with the still-warm bread. No room is left, so the bread man on a bicycle starts distributing the *pan de sal* in tin cans on either side of the wheels.

"Please take some sandwiches with you," the older nun tells Benhur. "Share them with the Marines, if they're already down there. My legs are swelling, but if I sit down they will make me return to the convent. Only our old and sick are left behind, praying. The transmission is getting clearer." Pointing to the radio on the table, she asks Benhur to turn it up. "It's hard to hear with everyone praying and singing. Marcos cronies had the transmitters of Veritas destroyed. And the backup at Fairview is weak, only 10 kw."

"How do you know these things? Are the game plans cleared with you?"

"I hear things. I look. That's how God feels and sees. Through us. Can you carry all that? A few more? I apologize. You don't look as if you work with your hands, but this is revolution. And that is the last word from Sister Luciana." She assumes the rhythm of June Keithley. "You know, I made my vows forty-seven years ago. In three years I will have my golden. Why should I pay attention to these knees?"

Benhur hurries. People who have just arrived from the circle in Quezon City say they've come to fill the gap in the barricade. Instructions coming in on their Walkmans are directing them to the Logistic Command gate, where a lookout on a church roof has spotted a military truck trying to force its way.

Others decide to go along, and they all seem to be heading for the sun. What remains of the darkness is being isolated by the torches of fishermen burning like prods, like lightning rods.

Before he reaches the intersection where Father Case dropped him off early Sunday morning, Benhur is overtaken by a man wearing the kind of costume worn to Holy Week processions, his ears flattened against his skull by a Roman helmet. He gives Benhur a kind of salute.

On the other side of the same darkness Benhur sees the government troops; some of them are listening to Radio Veritas/Bandido reporting on their location; a few are singing as if on their way to church on the eve of Christmas.

Then a truck with a crucifix and a statue of the Virgin comes to a stop between the troops and the people watching them. A seminarian pleads with the driver to move on. "Don't separate us. We are singing and praying together."

Benhur walks around the truck to bring the sandwiches to the soldiers who, he learns, have come from Mindanao, commanded by Colonel Balbas. Until they saw the civilians, they thought they were to arrest some rebellious soldiers. They appear confused as the crowd cheers and insults them by turns.

We need bigas, not tear gas, the people taunt—*Rice, not bullets.*

Defect! Defect! Some shout General Ramos's phone number, announced by loudspeakers earlier. Others cry out: *Choose peace. Don't start a bloodbath.*

The noise peaks: *Don't attack the soldiers. Cover your faces. Stay low when the canisters come. Don't inhale, or it will feel as if your insides have caught fire.* And the singing: partly remembered words, buried, carried in the mind with the landscape of old hills. Then: *Keep your eyes on the flag. Follow it. Ram through.*

And headlights of the military trucks come on suddenly to stare down the crowd and darken the sky: "Get out of the way. We don't want to hurt anyone."

Blinded momentarily, Benhur looks to the side. It is as if the sun has come up directly into his face.

Screams come as dark figures run past the headlights, shoving everyone in their way. Falling, an old woman in long loose skirt and an *alampay* about her shoulders cries out, "Don't hurt the children. Lord of angels." Benhur pulls her out of the way; her shawl loosens behind her like hair, just as riot police with shields, bullet-proof vests, and gas masks arrive.

Take cover! Run! Utterances lose the distinction of words, become sounds echoing into sounds.

A rifle slams against Benhur's chest. He feels it like an aftershock. More screams, like wires being pulled through the flesh. The food tables are toppled, with dogs snatching what has fallen. During the revolution of 1896, his *Lola* Sula said, dogs fought over the bodies left in the towns. Did that happen to the villagers his brother Demetrio's company allegedly killed?

Demetrio was the brave one, was never afraid of the dark or strangers. He could dive into the river and not come up until everybody had climbed out and given up trying to locate his body. Demetrio's son Ryan is most like him, so Benhur feels a special affection for the boy; sometimes thinks of himself in terms of Ryan and Demetrio, who attracted girls, had only to smile. It almost feels as if together they are running for cover against the walls where candles have been set only moments before.

Just ahead of the headlights' reach he finds the woman he is leading has slipped through his hand. He looks back for her, sees the troops hitting their shields instead of the people, mocking attack.

Along with others who discover this, Benhur turns around and leads the troops who want to defect through the rough ones who look for trouble. In no time, reports of this turnabout are being announced on Radio Veritas/Bandido, over the loudspeakers and the walkie-talkies, over the transistor radios held to the microphones and public address systems. *Some of the military have chosen peace.* Cardinal Sin's blessings come over the air for all of them.

The running does not stop. It is impossible to stand still with sounds immediately overhead of helicopters, their headlights smudging the just brightening sky. Radio Veritas/Bandido identify them as of the 15th Strike Wing, headed for Camp Crame, where Enrile and Ramos are.

Sit down. Sit.

Where?

2,000 rounds per minute. No way to outrun zero hour, or get out of its way.

Past the main gate of Camp Aguinaldo with the water towers on his right, Benhur's running slows down to a walk approaching Gate 2, where Minister Enrile and the Reformers crossed over to Camp Crame, Sunday afternoon; but he keeps on going. Perhaps it's a numbness. Perhaps it's inherited courage. Out of stubbornness or disdain, *revolucionarios* refused to beg for their lives as they were being lined up for execution by the Spaniards and Americans at the turn of the century; the guerrillas and resisters, during the Japanese Occupation. It is not an absence but a suffusion of feelings, Benhur thinks; indifference to the enemy's power, or disdain for it, and submission to one's fate.

On the margins of a book he found at Harvard, in Widener, Oceania Collection, D level West, he refuted defamations that the Filipino goes to his execution without struggling, like a dumb beast. In pencil, then in ink for permanence.

Benhur is surprised at how calmly he recalls the anger that made him write in the books, his treatises reduced to conclusions in order to fit the margins, all the space he had to confront his own mortality.

6:10 a.m. by Benhur's watch. This is the second time the sun has come up in the sky since the revolution began Saturday. The sky no longer crouches over them but spreads out fully like a tree growing new leaves.

Another pass is made by the helicopters. The sun glints off the metal sides. The leaves of trees inside Camp Crame are whipped about. Black as night, five Sikorskys and one white gunship make a wide circle, their headlights cutting through the light fog like several suns rising. They seem not to move from overhead.

Through the cover of dust and fog, the helicopters spiral down and land inside Camp Crame. A moment of stunned silence lifts into cries—*They're ours. They're ours!*—and the crowd rushes toward and over the walls even as their radios and walkie-talkies describe them running to meet their new air force.

Two men are hurrying to the parade grounds with a statue of the Virgin, ahead of those helping one another over the fence. The rotor blades are still whirring when the first men reach the helicopters and start hugging those disembarking. On the tops of buildings inside Camp Crame, the Reformists slowly lower their rifles and an armed escort comes out to accompany the defectors to Minister Enrile and General Ramos at the headquarters building.

Correspondents are all over the jubilant crowd.

So recently ready for death, the thousands who scaled the fence surround the helicopters, over which, lightly, dust still floats; run their hands along the metal; pose for pictures.

"We're free! It's Independence Day!" Benhur joins freely in the loud exultations: *We will never fear our government again. God Himself set us free!*

Over a loudspeaker comes the announcement that General Fidel Ramos and Minister Juan Enrile are coming down to meet the people.

Day One, from zero. February 24, 1986. New Independence Day. A new sign now obscures the grandstand—*Welcome: Defection Center.*

Clearing, rising higher than the sun, the sky is the shade of blue after a hard rain. General Ramos's jeans and vest are green. *Ramos. Ramos. Ramos. Johnny. Johnny* the crowd chants.

June Keithley's signature song, Raul Manglapus's "Mambo Magsaysay," gives way to a 1960s song, "He's Not There"—to indicate Ferdinand Edralin Marcos has fled from Malacañang.

It's over!

The shouts pound with the rhythm of waves rushing.

While the jubilation jams the airwaves, Benhur enters the headquarters building to look for Cayetano and Colonel Moscoso. A few men are still asleep, sprawled on the floor. Yellow ribbons muzzle the rifles carried by the Reformists.

Benhur sees Colonel Moscoso sharing a headphone with an officer. On seeing Benhur, the Colonel says, "It's not over. Minister Enrile has just talked with Ambassador Bosworth. FM is still in Malacañang." He extends his earphone to Benhur. "We celebrated too soon."

On a walkie-talkie, gunshots are heard coming from Channel 4. Reformists and loyalists fighting over the TV transmitters, the government's Maharlika Station.

Still in Malacañang, the president is holding up Monday's edition of the *Daily Express* to prove he has not fled. Surrounded by his immediate family and General Ver and many generals fewer than at his Sunday press conference, Marcos is announcing that he will take his oath of office on Tuesday.

It feels to Benhur that he is asleep standing up. Over and again the government communications in Camp Crame's war room are being monitored and assessed: At 0930—just that morning—General Ramas ordered Colonel Balbas to fire and report compliance. *Fire three rounds; then confirm.* The order was given three times. Three times the Colonel asked to verify, calling General Tadiar, who told him to act according to his discretion.

Colonel Balbas's conscience will decide what happens.

The colonel has 800 Marines in Camp Aguinaldo, 35 officers, 90mm recoilless rifles, 81mm mortars, and V-150 armored vehicles with howitzers.

At this very moment the Camp Crame war room might well be centered in their bore sights. Hairline trigger. But no one leaves.

From Manila two F-5s are coming at Camp Crame again, streaking the sky like hot stars. In Crame's war room, headphones try to pick up the communications between Malacañang, Fort Bonifacio, and Villamor Air Base to see what the president is up to.

Benhur wonders if the president is following a script of lies to trap the country into surrendering. If the world were not watching, would he have held back his guns this long? Is it to his advantage that, as he sits in his study/war room in Malacañang, he does not see the crowd on EDSA—the comedians suddenly stopping their routines to sing the National Anthem? the crowds singing "Ama Namin"?

Benhur looks out to the tops of *aguhos* and acacias. A nun is leading some defectors through the crowd, to bring them into headquarters. Over in Camp Aguinaldo, Colonel Balbas commands the Elite Task Force of the government. Is this the same Colonel Balbas who retreated from Libis on Sunday night?

He glances over to the TV. General Ver is asking President Marcos's permission to disperse the civilian crowd on EDSA with force, to bomb Crame and immobilize the helicopters.

Does the decision still hinge on Colonel Balbas's discretion and conscience? Has he set his fuses for maximum destruction and dispersal?

Benhur surveys the televised room where the president sits listening to General Ver. What is the point of this scenario? Some officers are being introduced to the president while the generals watch. At Sunday's press conference there were several rows of seated generals. This time, they can be counted on one hand. Soldiers with white armbands stand at attention while the officers, followed by the family, withdraw, and Marcos starts talking, more like a sound-producing machine as he goes on, as if he is speaking someone else's mind. Or, tuned in to his own frequency, is he responding to his imagination only?

Then FM disappears from the screen. Channel 4 blanks out, but news continues to come on other government channels.

Radio Veritas/Bandido broadcasts the sound of gunfire identified as a firefight. *Rebels hit the transmitter. The government's Scout Rangers have surrendered. Channel 4 is liberated. And troops loyal to Marcos are sitting in their trucks immobilized by People Power.*

Thirty-nine hours of revolution. Channel 4—captured fourteen years ago by Marines with fixed bayonets when martial law was declared by Marcos—has been liberated.

Small explosions. Gray smoke rising.

FM's arsenal of TV stations is down by one.

Day Three.

"Benhur! Benhur!"

Benhur sees Bastian Canonigo running toward him, calling "Benhur! Benhur!" the same way his classmate Siso Feleo might drop the title of Attorney from their conversations. The informality has to be the result of Bastian's perception of the revolution.

Benhur will not take advantage of it by asking Bastian to run the errand he promised Colonel Moscoso: go to the house and tell *Mang* Genio to proceed to Angat so his family, unable to know what is happening, will not rush to EDSA like the thousands who come to the city because transmission garbles the news on radio.

"Benhur. I spat on Marcos's picture on Channel 4. We threw out Imelda's picture; out the window," he makes a gesture of flinging, "and those waiting below stepped upon it, and burned a hole in her. Right here." He points between his legs.

Always restrained in his emotions except with his family and a few friends, Benhur blunts Bastian's enthusiasm by asking who else is with him from Gulod.

"Not Siso. Nani is washing their clothes. But Marcelo, Hernan, Piling, two maids of Sally."

"Sally?"

"Mrs. Moscoso. It must be the revolution. We were standing at the highway, wondering how to go to EDSA when her car comes out of the driveway. You know how she never looks at any of us except to smirk. This time, she gets out to sit beside the driver, a maid between them, the other in back with us. No invitation. She just opened the door and we got in."

"And my mother, have you seen her?"

"She's home with Loreto. And all the boys. They were watching TV, last I saw them. Yesterday, across in the chapel people were praying and we were watching TV in your house. Your mother kept saying she wished you were there, too, so you could send for beer for us. We said it's enough to watch the revolution. We didn't know if you would be on EDSA, too. We looked for anyone about your height. Different people saw you several times but, of course, it was not you."

"Where is Sally?"

"We all got separated. She was looking for Miggy and Joel." Bastian stares ahead. "She was wearing her old tortoiseshell eyeglasses, and walking very fast. Usually she walks step by step as if she's the Virgin in a procession. I mean *Reyna Elena.* I don't think the rockets will hit her; she's faster than their speed. Do you remember when she campaigned in Gulod and washed her hands with alcohol after shaking hands with us?"

The Sikorskys are lifting off, pulling dust and leaves into the air, Children are covering their ears against the noise. The parade ground looks like part of a movie set for a war picture.

Even as the helicopters are taking to the air, headphones brought to loudspeakers are announcing: *Five Hueys have been dispatched from Villamor Air Base to bomb Camp Crame.* Overheard exchange between Ver and Ramas: *Throw everything at Ramos and Enrile.* A man coming from Libis is saying: *Colonel Balbas in his jeep asked the people to let him return to Fort Bonifacio.*

Disinformation? Attempts to turn victory into painless maneuvers? It is no longer possible, Benhur concludes, for one man to win a revolution, which is really about surrendering power, or wresting it away.

After the noise dies down and the Sikorskys become airborne, Bastian Canonigo says, "The Marines were coming by truckloads to Channel 4 and we were caught between gunfire. Grenades were launched. Yellow ribbons and daisies flew up in the air. Some were hit. It's good there were doctors and nurses." He pauses to take fried chicken and sandwiches being distributed.

Benhur wonders if he should go on to the Colonel's to tell *Mang* Genio to proceed to Angat, when over the loudspeakers comes the news: *Malacañang attacked. Rockets fired from Sikorskys . . . blue Mercedes part of casualty in Palace garden . . . tanks and soldiers fired back.* Persuasion missions and psych warfare? Benhur heard, up in the war room, that the ground crews at Villamor Air Base might be persuaded to foul up the circuits. But the Hueys were reported to have been dispatched.

A man with two radios tuned in to separate stations is saying that *only 8 percent of the military is still Marcos loyalist;* and that *Ver is ordering General Piccio to attack Crame.* Seeing Benhur unencumbered with radio or headphone, he tells Benhur: "Ver ordered the Operations Center to evacuate Edna Camcam and her children. I used to work in the bank with her, then she caught Ver's eye. It's now loyalist against loyalist."

"Have you heard anything about Cory?" someone asks.

"There's something coming up about Marcos's pilots." The man with a radio looks through the crowd waiting to hear his reports. "They might have defected already."

"How can he escape now?" asks the one who asked about Cory, looking from one to the other to see if his insight is being appreciated.

A jubilant parade of utility trucks and yellow Ford Fieras is going down EDSA. White birds floating on the aircurrents above Crame draw the crowd's attention from celebrities performing on flatbed trucks and barricades to the F-5 jets winging closer, just as someone is saying, "It might already be over. Channel 4 is ours. Let Marcos take all the loot he can carry as long as he leaves, as long as all the rats leave with him."

Bastian offers the last piece of chicken to Benhur who shakes his head. "I've had breakfast three times already." If he said he is not hungry, Bastian might take it as an assertion of superiority. A rich man is never hungry.

On a mini TV, the taking of Channel 4 is being replayed. "That's us," Bastian recognizes the crowd blocking the escape of loyalists guarding the government station, and holding back the firetrucks bringing reinforcements. A priest is talking to the loyalists who look helpless with the crowd watching, waiting to cheer the first sign of wavering and embrace those deciding to defect.

The man with two radios is repeating what he hears on the airwaves: *Four jeeploads and a couple of staff cars seen entering Camp Aguinaldo.* Colonel Balbas or his replacement? If his replacement, will this one obey orders to fire the howitzers?

"Don't just stand there," someone in the crowd reacts. "We're People Power. Let's move and barricade Camp Aguinaldo. Let's intercept them. They're only eight hundred. So what if they're the Third Marine Brigade! So what if they're anti-riot police!"

Many walk away from the mini TV showing Channel 4 burning. Others linger on the sidewalk to watch, check the screen against the actual sky over the area where the transmitting towers rise. The overlap of the burning and its picture on the screen takes the words out of a man who leaves his mouth hanging.

Hand-held for maximum viewing, a mini TV shows smoke rising like balloons from the transmitting tower of Channel 4. Those glued to the screen cheer the announcement: *50 percent of the military have defected from Marcos. The Philippine Military Academy has declared for General Fidel Ramos. Defections in provinces.* On the TV set atop a car, Imelda's portrait is being spat upon, dragged in the street to be pulled apart.

Replays take over, making events happen again and again and all at once, jumbling EDSA into overlapping images out of sequence. No matter what happens, Benhur knows it will be back to ordinary times. Let newcomers man the barricades. He feels like a drunk who hopes only to resist drinking, fully knowing the determination is not a promise, only the statement of intention. Scaling down his estimate of himself, Benhur admits to loving always short of risk, very carefully and safely. He has survived, hasn't he? Survived life with ample feelings of righteousness; nothing else.

It's only history acting on time. He and the rest who have not fled are only performing heroics, posing for home videos and foreign photojournalists, from one landmark to another, the new series of stations of the cross.

Some pigeons released on EDSA are streaking across the midday sky. No longer with Bastian who has run to protect Ramos and Enrile, Benhur thinks almost gently of the Gulod neighbor who raised homing pigeons once and raced them, whose pigeons landed on electric cables or trees, coming down only after the other birds landed; and until the birds touched ground, they were not judged to have returned. The pigeons might have carried drugs.

Benhur decides to head for Gulod after telling *Mang* Genio to go to the Colonel's family in Angat. He looks up at the headquarters building inside Crame. Somewhere there Cayetano is either monitoring government troops or attempting a persuasion mission. It never occurred to him to seek Osong's brother, once he found Colonel Moscoso. He wonders if Sally has found Joel and Miggy. There are no reports of the Sikorskys and Hueys clashing in the air. Are all victories ultimately false, no one permanently disarmed; so that revolutions are no longer possible to win?

It's just as well to trust only impersonal events.

"Where shall I donate these?" a man with a small crate of live chickens intercepts Benhur, just as the anthem is struck on EDSA. The sun is a hot star. The words wind through Benhur's thoughts like the movements of a dance—small explosions.

Just a moment before, the sounds irritated Benhur like the ticking of clocks and the ringing of bells; but he has been returned from ordinary times by the realization that his nephews should not miss EDSA—no one should be deprived of a first-rate experience of history—so he heads for the car. He will pick them up after delivering the message to *Mang* Genio.

A private jeepney has parked behind his car, locking it in; but when people see him get in his car, they push the jeepney out of his way, then push it into the space he vacates.

"There's a pot of rice to be picked up near Channel 4. Can you bring us there?" A man approaches Benhur. "Just as close as you can take us, and we'll worry about returning. There will be free rides, I'm sure."

Benhur unlocks the passenger side. Three men get in.

"That's my car," the man points to a car wedged between two vans with a truck in back of it. "Since Sunday it has been there, and no one has broken into it."

"The Filipino is honest again," the others add.

Benhur takes a look at them in the rear-vision mirror, decides to forgo introductions. Even without names, they will know each other if they meet again. He is already looking forward to coming back to EDSA, no matter whoever, Marcos or Aquino, is president.

On the way, they remember what they saw on EDSA.

They begin exchanging their impressions: Ramos jumping on top of the Fiera at the news—false—that Marcos has fled; the lookouts on V. Soliven facing EDSA; the canisters of Shellane gas in the truck that beat the Marines to the intersection of Ortigas. No way the Marines would shoot with all that fuel. Other checkmates occur to them; General Tadiar backing down when the crowd stood in his way . . .

It is as if EDSA has been won.

Their host invites them to wait for another pot of rice. "Have lunch while you're waiting," he suggests. "The *pancit molo* is about to boil." His wife brings out honey from Mindoro. "For the revolution," she says, adding they have not slept since three in the morning when neighbors woke them up saying tanks were coming and troops would be lobbing tear gas into the houses.

Benhur agrees that it would be better than winning the Sweepstakes to have seen Marcos's face when a rocket hit his mother's garden in the Palace grounds; hit the blue Mercedes, though that is just one of the many cars in Malacañang.

Radio announcements interrupt their conversation around the dining table. An appeal to reenforce the Ateneo students trying to hold

Libis; announcements of defections. Channel 7 is under siege by defectors. *Channels 2, 9, and 13 are still in Marcos's hands.*

Besides the rice, their hosts load them with *caimito* from the trees in the yard; some *lanzones* from Davao, not as sweet as those from Laguna; bananas. "One more day and they will be their sweetest," the wife says.

The husband tries to delay their departure, but they have to pick up roasted chickens on Panay, and eggs from Bohol Avenue. "I have been trying to think where we met," he tells the man on the passenger side. "Were we not neighbors in San Andres?"

"I have never lived there," replies the man, smiling. "Sorry."

"Okay. I just thought I had seen you. Okay, look out for soldiers flashing the Laban sign. Go by the flag patches. They're rotated 90 degrees each day. White armbands. Near Polymedic the loyalists tied yellow ribbons to their M-16s, to deceive the people. They're going through side streets to avoid civilians. I wish I were going with you, but the Mrs. has a bad heart, you know."

"Sorry," says Benhur. He gets out of the car to shake hands.

They stop for a ten-wheeler crossing Aurora. On board are men and women carrying signs to show they come from Blumentritt. "Our neighbors are cleaning the neighborhood chapel, in case we are brought back in boxes," the driver calls out to Benhur, saluting him for stopping.

The simple faith and courage remind Benhur of what Nietzsche said about finding strength in simple, mild, and pleasant people without the least desire to rule: *The desire to rule has often appeared to me a sign of inward weakness: they fear their own soul, slave soul, and shroud it in a royal cloak (in the end they become the slaves of their followers, their fame) and power.*

Messengers on motorbikes weave in and out of the foot traffic headed for EDSA. A large Philippine flag is being carried down the highway, its corners stretched by the hands of teenagers covering themselves from the sun.

Benhur drops the men as close as possible to the distribution point. He can't come any closer. Turning to thank him, the man in the passenger seat hesitates, then says: "The truth is, I did live in San Andres before I went to work in Australia. Before Christmas I was called home. My wife was found stabbed, the knife left in her chest. My daughter's boyfriend . . . she let him in . . . he was on drugs . . ."

"I'm sorry," Benhur says, turning off the ignition. "Is there anything I can do?" He wants something from God for the sake of this man struggling with the pot of rice.

Making a three-point turn to proceed on to Gulod, Benhur finds himself behind a van with a TV anchored to the roof.

"Channel 4," one of the viewers says, to explain the dove locked on the screen. "Not yet operating, but any minute now, unless the Marines coming from Camp Capinpin in Tanay have retaken the station."

Warn pregnant woman away. If Marcos suddenly appears, their children might look like dictators.

The dove disappears, making way for a home video of the revolution. People with guitars and women with their best smiles are entertaining those who have just captured the stations from Marcos loyalists. Benhur hears ballads he has not heard before, being sung by residents from Tondo; he sees tables heavy with food overturned along with candles on the ground, tear gas spreading like fog down mountains, students arm-in-arm facing off with Marines, crowds being warned of spies infiltrating Crame; he recalls the pictures of *revolucionarios* and soldiers fighting over the same riverbanks again and again, battles surging forward and back again over the same trenches, pictures pasted in a folder by Mrs. William James, side-by-side with letters to editors condemning the Philippine–American War, with soldiers' letters he found in the sub-basement in Widener.

Slowly like underwater scenes, or fast-forward, while hastily assembled crews try to work the control panels of Channel 4, the pictures stretch and blur, go in and out of focus.

Channel 4 serving the people again. First uncensored news in fourteen years. We're free again!

Benhur recognizes Ortigas's intersection with EDSA on the Sunday afternoon when Armored Personnel Carriers came at the crowd; the statue of La Naval overlooking the smashed walls and the circle of Marines in the fields while negotiations went on and flowers were pressed upon the soldiers; the crowd being asked to sit down and show General Tadiar they were unarmed; the Sikorskys landing in the parade grounds inside Camp Crame; General Ramos jogging; Minister Enrile and his men crossing EDSA to join forces; then back to the fields of Marines and the circle of APCs with people trying to push them back with their hands.

"Look! Look at the man crying!"

Benhur looks, then backs out as far as the crowd allows, driving off before anyone could see that the man is himself. He had not known he was crying.

He does not want to go to Gulod any more or see anyone. Once in his office he would call *Mang* Genio to deliver the Colonel's instructions. His mother can get canned meat on credit from *Aling* Maxima. No use in bringing the boys to EDSA, putting them at risk.

Driving down P. Tuazon to Aurora Boulevard he passes Magsaysay but turns, avoiding Legarda, which would take him to the Palace. He has had enough of revolution jumbled up in his mind through replays and interrupted sequences of events. It has become memory and act, and neither; back to hope that the anti-Marcos stance will mature into a vision and policy for government, with leaders fearful not for themselves but of failing the country. Marcos could have been a great president. Osong could have made a difference if he had dreamed beyond escorting the most sought-after women.

And what about him?

Instead of confronting himself, he plans his future. Once in his office he will take stock of what he has to sell. The surveyor down the hall might buy the desk, the typewriter, the phone and rights to Philippine Long Distance service. The books, if he has to, he'll sell to the used bookstores on

Recto, though he has always hoped one of the nephews would have use of them. As soon as possible he'll get his transcript of grades, so he can take the final semester at Northeastern or Suffolk or New England Law. Then he'll take the Bar and set up a practice.

Should that not be possible, and should his conscience permit, he'll get a fake license or just bull it. In the States he can take on immigration and citizenship cases without taking the Bar. He'll stay clean, away from the false claims and faked accidents one or two *compañeros* in California have discovered to be lucrative.

Once in the States he can ask Vergel and his family to come for residence in a top-rank hospital. If Vergel refuses—instead of an *anting-anting* in his back, his brother has a stubborn streak—he can find him some funding for a hospital in Kapalaran. German parishes are specially generous with donations.

If his mother were not needed by the children, he could have her and Loreto with him. Until then, once a year at Christmas he'll come to Gulod bringing fine gifts not available in Manila. Maybe he can find a match for Loreto, not an old-timer or just any white.

Will he let Osong know? Perhaps. The Colonel, yes, but not Sally Moscoso. Before he leaves, he would like to see again the teenagers in the bus as well as Father Case and the man who went with him to pick up the pot of rice. Maybe they would not recognize him; maybe Case is like the priest, a distant cousin who bought a house in Manila so he could live with the student he sent to school on funds he had collected for his order.

Up and down the streets people are walking, heading toward EDSA. He had thought no one was left in the city. They're not shopping, just heading for destinations that demand they hurry. Over the radio comes news that Nagtahan bridge is closed in both directions. He does not want to see the Marcoses anyway, nor to meet Osong and Ting Dolor, experts at playing both sides.

Not Seniong but a different security guard is at the entrance to his building. With others, the new guard is watching a small TV. On the screen some youths are shown taunting soldiers protecting Malacañang Palace.

The barbed wire barricades are taller than many of the youths who look full of the devil on their ragged knees. Nodding at the guard who salutes him, Benhur stops to watch a youth, then another, crawl toward the barricade, snip off a length of barbed wire, then run across the street where others are fashioning crowns of thorns from the wire they have previously cut. Lent and revolution. Unraveled barbs.

A few more attempts, then gunshots clip the air; and blood spills on the approach to Mendiola.

Freshly showered and changed, a bottle of beer in hand, Benhur starts the electric fan in his office, faces it against a wall so the air will bounce off and swirl around the room. Dust still grates underneath his skin.

Finishing his obligations, he pulls out a legal pad to write Osong's formal letter of resignation. He scans what he has written on the American bases—itemized discrepancies between the agreements with Turkey, Spain, and Greece, and that with the Philippines. From ally or enemy, the Philippines gets the raw deal. Even now, Philippine history has been revised to its disadvantage. While in the States, he and Osong sat in on a lecture by a scholar funded by the Japanese Government: *Japan had no plans to invade the Philippines in 1941; merely wanted to have the United States come to the negotiating table.* Then there was Sabah and the title to the islands the United States casually let go when it first occupied the country. Unfinished monographs.

No time to finish them now. And the resignation is not a priority—Osong never is able to commit himself.

Benhur decides to sort through his desk with the TV on. As he rummages, he sees flashes of scenes on Mother Ignacia street near Channel 4, on Panay and Bohol Avenues.

Did the folks in Gulod see the home video of himself? Perhaps it was a look-alike, but the shirt is unmistakable; a loud Hawaiian print, the only one his size at the tailor's. Because of that, perhaps no one in Gulod will think it is he, since they see him only in *barong*. Perhaps. Even now they could be saying, *Mababa ang luha ni Attorney.* Crybaby. He'll give them time to forget what they saw on TV. A long time.

It's still Monday.

On raw footage from some home movie, Channel 4 is showing policemen just watching the media near the Palace, with photo-journalists working the crowd. Another appeal for someone who can handle video cameras and control panels at the TV station. A view of Nagtahan bridge being closed by Marines and Presidential Guards; of the overpass where the First Light Armor Company is dispersing the crowd; some nearby streets being evacuated.

The military are wearing riot helmets and flak jackets; carrying Plexiglas shields the width of coffins in one hand; armalites or M-16s, used in Vietnam, in the other.

Then replay of EDSA—the three days there so jumbled that Benhur gets a sense of things out of control again. He turns his full attention to the contents of the top drawer while he thinks of the man who stopped listening to his transistor radio and gave it away.

The drawer emptied, he pushes it shut. Everything will have to be given away if not sold. The papers make a tall pile on the desk. He is trying to decide if he will go out for supper—the Bulwagan is down the street; the Barrio Fiesta up toward the park; it is past eight—when Ferdinand E. Marcos appears in a light windbreaker as if on his way to play golf. His family is seated on the handcarved chairs proper to presentation ceremonies, listening to the president promise a fight to the finish.

The last time Benhur saw Marcos on TV, Ver was debating him on strategy, urging an attack on Camp Crame and Camp Aguinaldo: *Splice through the crowd.* Which is the feint?

The First Son looks bored in his fatigues, probably thinking of the island he is supposed to have stocked with specimen African animals so he can go on safari anytime he chooses. He gets up to chase a small nephew back to his seat. Has he seen the crowd at EDSA?

In less than twenty-four hours, the president will be inaugurated in Malacañang, not in the Luneta as planned. Cory should beat him with her own inauguration.

The president's press conference underlines the circular character of developments—breakthrough, recovery, then restoration—back to the ideals of the revolution of 1896, then to the tenets of martial law, as if events themselves are afraid of resolution. So much for the earth's divinity, as Sister Madeleine would declare. So much for its luminosity.

The one who had the situation correctly tagged was the little boy sitting on his father's shoulders trying to pinch off the F-5 cruising overhead, as if it were a mere dragonfly.

Benhur pushes the papers and envelopes together. He might as well be listening to a broadcast of events happening overseas, or in outer space.

With no feeling of urgency, Benhur looks down at the pile on his desk and sees the envelope left by Terence Hugg. He stares it down into disappearing, then he picks it up and sits on the sofa, holding it by the top corners as if it has a will of its own and might bite.

It is Tuesday when he wakes up. 4:30 a.m. There is an appeal for wine and large hosts for Mass inside Camp Crame. Already Tuesday. *Prevent dawn raids on Crame and Aguinaldo. Say your prayers and come to the barricades. Protect Channel 4. The First Ranger Division is heading towards the bridge at Guadalupe.*

Out of focus on the small screen, the pictures seem far away and watery, with no power whatsoever to affect him.

The next time he wakes up, Keithley is still calling on people to come and protect Camp Crame. Tanks are reported headed for the Mormon Temple in White Plains.

Loudspeakers, as when he was on EDSA, are announcing troop deployments. On silk standards, students are carrying the likenesses of their patron saints. Cursillo standards fly under an overcast sky, with light rain falling. On the uniform of a soldier on Scout Borromeo Street, Benhur sees a medallion of the Virgin.

It is 7:00 a.m. Government snipers with white armbands are holding on to Channel 9, the last Marcos broadcast facility. When were Channels 2, 7, and 13 taken?

What about the battalions in the Malacañang Park across the Pasig? And those whom the president called, with their firearms, to assemble in the Palace when he appeared after midnight? Was that in his dream, with the moon's rising, beaming down on the light of fireflies and candles, joining them?

He tosses into the wastebasket a sheet of paper on which he has written: *People are violated by conditions of life where wealth is in the hands of 5 percent of the population, forcing them to live and be waked in the space between estate fences and ditches, shielded from view by leaves of banana and palm;* though he is not certain that EDSA has rendered those issues moot. Those concerns affirm any democracy.

Video and sound track alternate on the TV screen, showing people singing to keep awake, making him wish the revolution were over; wish for sleep from which he would not wake up tired. Trying to return to sleep, he recalls rock stars performing on flatbed trucks like the one that carried Evelio Javier's coffin through Makati, sees fireflies suddenly lighting up a tree, remembers the light rain while he was walking down EDSA toward Ortigas. The images reach clarity and purity for him.

With such images, Benhur is coming to sense that his life has entered history—emotionally and actually, in the way that thought is experience and will to which life submits; mostly because he has not gone after his own happiness, or lived his life to bursting—when a knock at the door intercepts his homecoming.

One more moment, and he might have been able to decide whose heroic act EDSA is: God's?—as Sister Madeleine would certainly insist—or the nation's?

"I have to decide which inauguration to attend, and I can't get you on the phone!" Osong cries, entering the office without ceremony to pick up the phone. "It's dead. Don't you ever check? No dial tone. Since when?"

Asking Osong himself to close the door, and giving him time to calm down, Benhur faces the TV where a tire is shown burning somewhere near Channel 4 and some joggers moving a barricade of trees to let traffic through. He is used to Osong's rage over matters that require deliberation, not outbursts. Panic is Osong's coat of arms.

"FM has been good to me," Osong sits down behind the desk. "Besides, he might not be finished at all. He has something in mind when he offered to be a figurehead. Didn't you hear? On the radio coming here, he was talking to Enrile about a provisional government. I would feel like a traitor if I attended Cory's inauguration."

"That's the answer then."

"But Ting Dolor wants to attend Cory's at Club Filipino."

"A private club for a public ceremony?" Benhur sits across from Osong. An exclusive club.

"Ting went to see Imelda last night; was there up to early this morning and called from the Palace. FM and Imelda called Washington. Monday afternoon in the States. The message from Admiral Poindexter and Senator Laxalt is: "Cut clean." She said they called from the bedroom, sitting on armchairs at the foot of the bed. The last message came at 5 a.m. That's when Ting decided on Cory's inauguration."

Benhur gets up to make coffee in the Braun Coffeemaker he got at the Harvard Coop. He learned to drink it black in the States. No sugar. There is nothing to go with it. Even if Dulcinea were open today and serving pastries, *churros* with chocolate, the place would still be closed yet.

"Shultz gave the same advice. The French are leaning toward Cory. The German and Australian ambassadors will go to Club Filipino, Ting guesses. Only the Russian ambassador has opted for FM. So where do I go? This coffee is dreadful."

Benhur is not surprised. The daughters of past presidents were reported to be going to the foreign embassies on Cory's behalf. "A battle between secular gods and goddesses."

"What?"

"In case you need a speech. Politics as a vocation, a calling; not a power game or a photo opportunity."

"Be serious."

"I'm serious. Hunger is not ennobling, and the obligation of rulers is not to reelection but to the country. That is how to decide. Not nouvelle cuisine but crispy *pata* and beer. *Bulalo. Taho.*"

Osong is watching the screen, mouth open as though to clear his sinuses. Channel 4 is showing the helicopters that ferried Enrile and Ramos to Club Filipino. Applause greets the elites going up the driveway. Cameras are banked several deep along the curb. Loudspeakers crowd the front lawn, and the Unimart parking lot is filled. Those not cleared to enter the club are listening to car radios.

"Too late to attend this one," Benhur says.

"Ting said Justice Teehankee is going to swear in Cory. He must be inside by now. It's two hours past the schedule."

"Almost ten. Who's swearing in Marcos?"

"Ting saw Monching last night at the Palace. Chief Justice Aquino."

There is a shot of the club pool and the balcony. Enrile is wearing a rose-colored shirt with stripes. Ramos has his cigar, and a tricolor patch on his left shoulder. Napkins on which names have been written are being passed from hand to hand, so they can be read off. Some record of attendance!

"Go with me, Brod."

"To?"

"FM. I think I should. What options do you suppose are still open?"

"For the president?"

"For me."

As a last favor, before they go their separate ways to be surprised by life according to the heaven they hope for, Benhur is willing but Osong does not get up from the desk.

"Try Channel 9."

Benhur switches from the video of Cory saying she will not pursue charges against Marcos—"I can be magnanimous in my victory"—to a transmission from Malacañang Palace where a general is reciting a list of credits for Marcos. Too late even to attend the noon inauguration.

Osong watches tight-lipped.

"At least you stayed away from both," Benhur consoles him," and if Ting Dolor asks, you can lie. It won't matter. She might have stayed home herself, or she would have stationed herself in front of the cameras at Club Filipino, wearing clothes that set off her figure. Or she might have gone to the Palace."

"And now, the moment we are waiting for." The Channel 9 newscaster announces the president.

The screen blanks out.

Osong leaps up to change channels.

Instead of Marcos, Channel 4, newly liberated, is showing a puff of smoke spiraling from the tower of Channel 9 on Panay Avenue. One of two soldiers is hit by a sniper from a rebel helicopter. Another burst of fire and the soldier with a walkie-talkie goes down, hit in the head. His cap blows off. His rifle drops. He hangs like someone burned down to the bone.

The picture of the loyalist soldier dangling in the air as he is lowered from the captured TV-transmitting tower crowds out everything Benhur recalls of EDSA since Saturday night. It demands that he know, for himself, the ultimate purpose and end of existence; what he should want from life. Suppose all there is to expect is what Osong wants?

The possibility makes him look at the window, staring into himself while pain comes, exactly as if his own head has been blown off and he is seeing nothing.

"It's like a war zone," the taxi driver tells them; but Osong has to see for himself the tanks and APCs blocking the Nagtahan bridge approach to the Palace, before he will agree to go over Ayala and then to find the way in back of the universities. In Sampaloc, streets are blocked with burning tires, trees hauled across, rocks. Radios pressed to their ears, people look down Legarda from the overpass.

When Benhur and Osong decide to walk down Recto, to chance it with the crowd still pouring down, some arriving from EDSA through Santa Mesa, the taxi driver refuses to be paid. "Be careful," he tells them. "This morning when I brought someone for the president's inauguration, people banged on the hood. On my way out the taunts had turned into rock-throwing. *Ingat.*"

Unprepared for what they may find at Mendiola—before martial law, students had mounted demonstrations there that saw the first martyrs against Marcos, a secular martyrology—Osong's sense of obligations and confidence are at odds with reality. Benhur looks up at the gray house rising from the sidewalk with its iron gate and *caimito* in the courtyard. He often wondered how it would be to enter that gate and walk under the tree. His mother had a similar tree cut down from the front yard because neighbors told her someone in the family would die if the roots reached the front door. His father died anyway; then Demetrio.

The movie houses where students passed the hot afternoons, enticed by cold air blasting out of the entrances, have lost their billboards to the barricades pointed like broken fingers in several directions.

Something reminds Osong of being stalled across all the lanes on Jones Bridge. "You were driving," he accuses.

"You were," Benhur argues him down. "It was Quiapo."

"Lately, I've been dreaming that I'm driving and the brakes fail. There is no wall or tree into which to crash, so I go off, straight into space."

Benhur resists countering with his own dream.

"What do you think of it?"

"Good movie sequence. Manuel Conde, Jr., starring."

"Let's stop for beer," Osong says, sitting down at a counter between the movie houses. A TV blinks against the light coming in from Recto.

The man behind the counter comes around. "It's a *rigodon.* Now we have two presidents inaugurated. The country is as confused as a weed. Just beer?"

They nod without speaking. Almost at the Palace, they seem hesitant to reach it, the way people who run for office become paralyzed by victory if winning is their only goal.

"Anything else?"

"Ice," says Osong, tipping his glass as he pours from the bottle.

"My sons have been back and forth, bringing souvenirs and boxed lunches." The man points to crowns of barbed wire, pink styrofoam containers. "I told them to look for chicken, not empty containers. They said that when the president and Imelda came out on the balcony at noon, they did not know Channel 9 had been captured. Just as FM was about to speak . . ."

Having brought the ice in a glass, the man lingers, then goes over to the counter, returning with two miniature crowns of barbed wire. "On the house."

Osong lays his crown on the palm of one hand, counting to see if any barbs are missing. Then slowly baiting Benhur, he asks: "What keeps anyone from making these to sell to Filipinos in the States? Give them a sense of the action here. Might make a million easily. Dollars, too."

"If you have it made in the States, you'd save on shipping costs," Benhur mocks Osong.

"Brilliant. Brilliant. Let's go tell Ting Dolor. She might be in her grandmother's house, across from Malacañang. You know, she'll wish she thought of it."

Fortified by beer and serious prospect of profit, Osong hurries Benhur down Recto, looking neither left nor right, impatient when Benhur stops to retie his shoelaces.

It's not the same crowd as at EDSA.

Ting Dolor is crossing J. P. Laurel from her grandmother's gate, followed by more photo-journalists than Imelda herself can attract. The guard at the entrance recognizes her and opens the gate, letting in the correspondents as well, and Osong who sprints across, forgetting to wait for Benhur, who just makes it through.

They cross the newly laid lawn, already curling at the edges, into which hand flags are stuck in random pattern by those who had waved them during the inauguration. Up to 3,000 are still waiting for something else to happen: Imelda to come out again to sing; Marcos to declare anew that he is not stepping down; or the Reformists to come escorting Cory to the Palace. It's touch and go, with leftists ready to provoke bloodshed and a firefight.

Ting Dolor walks into the Palace, defying gravity in her long white dress that makes her appear thinner than a shadow. Her hair is braided down her back; her ankles are as thin as wrists. She's no Imelda or Cory clone.

Osong follows right behind the correspondents who trail Ting Dolor.

Benhur stays on the grounds facing a platform built for the inauguration but not used. Children are stomping on the boards. Some are asleep under the shrubs. Benhur recalls the correspondents asleep on table tops in Camp Crame.

He tries, but cannot figure out Ting Dolor's motives in sending Osong to Cory's inauguration while she elects to be at the Palace; in her telling Osong that the President has asked Enrile to stop the provocateurs from firing into Malacañang, and also to get a security escort from Ambassador Bosworth for the presidential party. Are they still inside or have they fled? He can hear the hum of tanks and APCs. He looks up at the balcony where, on the ledge, soldiers with M-16s stood while Marcos and Imelda greeted the people on the lawn. Only five hours before, at noon.

The crowd outside is closer to the fence than they were when he and Osong followed Ting Dolor inside the grounds. Is it the same fence, he wonders, at which General Lawton some eighty-six years ago stopped on his way to face General Geronimo in Pasig, namesake of the chief he fought during the Indian Wars? Accounts state that Otis, commanding general of the American forces, did not come out then, nor in the afternoon of that rainy day when Lawton's body was brought back past the Palace by the Pasig. Plaza Lawton, named after the general who distributed the rice he captured, but burned all the documents in the Filipino camps, is now Liwasang Bonifacio.

Wearing a Marcos/Tolentino badge, a young father watches his little boy smudging the tank with his fingers. Has he brought his son to the same history as did the one who carried his son on his shoulders to shake hands with General Ramos? As the crowd outside inches toward Mendiola bridge, their cries hang like static in the air. Those who changed their minds about protecting President Marcos have somehow managed to leave.

Red, white, and blue predominate on the grounds; not yellow. A picture of the young Marcos flutters from the branch to which it is taped. Across the white triangle on posters and banners VICTORY is printed bold. Benhur thinks of the old man who walked his way to EDSA, taking eight hours, because Cory promised land reform. "She will give her hacienda to the poor like me and set the example for those landlords in the government." And of the woman who cried during Mass because she learned that her father's name means God's friend: *Teofilo.*

In the garden raked earlier by rebel Sikorskys, Benhur hears people saying President Aquino was not really inaugurated. "It's just a tape to fool us," says a young girl who resembles Rio Locsin in *Paano Hahatiin ang Puso,* a movie Loreto saw four times, perhaps seeing herself in the story of heartbreak. On her insistence, Benhur saw it with her and their mother; fell asleep.

Looking up to see if Osong is at the window, Benhur sees a man coming toward him, taking out the two cigarettes in his shirt pocket. It can't be matches the man wants, thinks Benhur.

"Attorney. I'm the *vaciador.* Have a cigarette."

"Thank you. I stopped smoking."

Returning the other cigarette to his pocket, the *vaciador* lights up from Benhur's proffered lighter, cupping the flame with both hands.

They stand, looking about, away from each other. The *vaciador* is tempted to remark that hungry men smoke to deceive their stomachs; and Benhur restrains himself from asking about the *vaciador.* He has no room in his brain cells for any more information.

"You have not seen my son." The *vaciador* pulls out a thin plastic wallet from his hip pocket. "The only picture I have of him."

Benhur holds the much-handled picture by one corner, handing it back at once for it makes him recall the head of a foetus floating in formaldehyde.

But freeing himself for a moment from his grief, the *vaciador* allows Benhur to hold the picture while he looks at his young child in a makeshift coffin. When he takes it back, he wipes the surface with his palm and says, "If he had lived, he would be twenty-three. Twenty years ago. And two months. A week. But I have to be happy for him. He could be one of those children living on Smoky Mountain off the refuse of good lives, their lungs seared by the vapors rising from decaying garbage while they pick up used plastic to sell or rotted fruits to eat. Just so many piles of bones actually; like the mortuary in Paco. Who makes the choice, Attorney? Who will live in Forbes Park? and who will live on Smoky Mountain?

"That's a million-dollar question," Benhur starts to say, but he can no longer take it back after he realizes how offensive the remark is. Sister Madeleine should come out of hiding and answer these questions; ask it of her God during her prayers. Whose choice? The doctors of her Church should have faced that *vaciador,* answered him. Thomas Aquinas. Not the persons in God, but the people in God. Will it make any difference if he manages to emigrate and live clear of the *vaciador,* just another person tying him down to Gulod, the way Gulliver was pinned down by the ropes of those Lilliputians?

"My son would have marveled if he were standing here instead of me. If he could see inside the Palace. I'm here for him."

The sun pulses weakly in the sky, already darkening. Benhur places a hand as casually as he can inside his pocket, folding a hundred-peso bill.

The *vaciador* catches his hand as he extends it. "No. Attorney. Thank you."

Benhur leaves him there, standing on the browning sod laid down for the inauguration originally planned for Luneta. Some things revolution will not heal. In what speech or policy statement can he reveal that truth?

From the balcony where Marcos spoke at noon a large flag hangs, its white triangle pointed to the ground as in the victory signs still hanging from the trees. Benhur thinks of the banners bearing the names of provinces from which people have come to EDSA; the silk standards of saints and of the Virgin who turned back the enemy in Tetuan, Lepanto, Manila Bay: victories commemorated on the facades of churches. He wonders if majesty returns to its source when it is elsewhere undeserved. And comes again.

"They're now fifteen meters from the soldiers," a man wearing a *Marcos Pa Rin* T-shirt climbs down from the tree with large leaves. He stands as if he's on fire. "The Virgin is coming down Mendiola with them. You can hear them praying at the barricades."

Benhur looks through the fence. The people inside have moved away from it and no longer walk about as if they are in a park, or sit on the grass. Some have thrown away their flags.

"They're coming," another man drops from the tree. "Carrying pieces of plywood. From Mendiola, Santa Mesa. Arlegui. It's rush, retreat. Flashbulbs as bright as lightning."

Benhur hears what could be shots or firecrackers.

A woman holds a child between her legs, covering him with her hands. The man with her has thrown away his Marcos badge. "What will happen if the barricades fall?" he repeats a correspondent's question?"

"What do you think will happen?" the correspondent asks the others who have gathered to listen. "What if the president leaves? If he has left by the back door, through the Pasig?"

"He won't desert us," a woman says.

"The soldiers will protect us with water hoses and tanks. The fence is tall. No one can climb," another says, as a rifle shot whistles through the trees.

"We will protect this place until the president returns. He will not leave. Look! The chandeliers are blazing!"

The correspondent says: "Duvalier fled. The Shah of Iran fled."

"The president will protect us. President Marcos loves us."

Lights have gone out in some streets about the Palace. The haze of streetlights has gone out over parts of the city and, for no reason Benhur can imagine, someone has begun cutting off the overhanging branches of trees. None of the soldiers intervenes. On top of a car some young girls are still dancing.

Open the gates! Cries are heard on J. P. Laurel outside the fence. *Open!* Some stones land inside the grounds of the Palace, while in the street firecrackers are writhing among the stones and pieces of glass.

A man brushes against Benhur, running. "There is a dead man in that building. Over there."

High above the river in back of the Palace, the moon sails clear of the trees. It is nine. Church bells toll the hour. Flashbulbs are popping outside the fence that some are already attempting to climb.

Benhur sees the helicopter blades against the moon before he identifies their roaring. He cannot tell if they are lifting up or descending. The sound is the staccato rush of unintelligible words. Too dark to make out the presidential seal on the French puma. But weren't the president's pilots supposed to have defected Monday?

Sssssssst!

The low hiss draws Benhur's attention. He is in through the side door before anyone else sees it open, then immediately close.

A guard sitting in front of the TV looks up and then returns his attention to the screen: firecrackers are going off against the walls of Camp Aguinaldo; people carrying candles are singing "Purihin ang Panginoon."

The man who had opened the door to call to his companions walks up the backstairs alongside Benhur. One of the staff stops halfway down with a box, turns around again as if at a loss for instructions.

"Ma'm took the ones closest to her. The rest of us she gave brown envelopes with $500. After she left, the envelopes distributed had only half that inside. Madame stood on the stairs, crying. My heart broke seeing her cry."

"What's down here?" A correspondent who had been able to enter another way is anxious to see what the ground floor holds by way of surprises. He finds a barbershop and a beauty parlor. In what looks like a clinic, he starts taking pictures. "Was President Marcos operated on here?"

The guard and the woman staff look up but say nothing.

Benhur takes the stairs. There are signs of hasty packing interrupted: suitcases with lists of contents taped outside, vases, trays, attaché cases, boxes. Retainers are walking about scanning one another's faces. In the chapel Benhur sees some of the staff praying.

He has never been into the private quarters, and he hesitates, walking around until he finds himself in some kind of balcony over a courtyard, looking down into the fountain surrounded by crates larger than coffins. Lights of many colors weep into the fountain.

He overhears two saying that the president and Imelda left with eighty-nine staff and relatives, friends. They were preceded by the security force in plain clothes, headed for Clark Air Base. The two stop talking when they notice him.

There is no sign of Osong or Ting Dolor, or of anyone who is not staff, correspondent, or, like him, intruder. Until he gets to the study. There a young man as tall as Miggy is standing in the doorway, hands in his pockets, scanning the radios that are still transmitting. An M-16 is against a chair. The floor glistens like paneling. There is a board where a map of Camp Crame and Camp Aguinaldo has been chalked in white, with lines indicating the surrounding streets. Reformist positions are noted with estimates of strength.

This is where, Benhur thinks, the country has been ruled by imperfect men for centuries; from where it has been, up to now, occupied. He recalls that he wanted once to become president, had always run for student office and won, was voted most likely to succeed. Had he taken the Bar, he would have placed in the top ten. He could then have had his pick of government or corporate appointments. He thinks of this without bitterness, finally. After twenty years the regret has gone out of him. Almost without anger, he thinks of the dying man who clung to the presidency until an hour before; going from relapse to remission, from almost dying to almost recovering, then sliding towards death again.

This is the point in life when Plato comes in, he thinks. When she was Elen Rodrigo, Sister Madeleine believed reason is everything. *Time,* she will now quote as if the ultimate answer, *is the moving, unreal reflection of eternity.* He was reading the *Dialogues* instead of the assignment for Tuesday morning in Constitutional Law, to be able to argue with her.

Well, now he can tell Plato that life is about death. In that Palace, a dying man faked life; his wife tried to be beautiful forever. Life is only a fixed duration. And luckily so, because the world of cronies and decrees by letters of instruction, obfuscatory rhetoric to discourage resistance and to encourage assent and conformity, must sometime come to an end.

Light from the chandelier floats on the deeply polished floor.

Benhur moves on.

A servant comes out of the inner room, points to the secret door leading to the garden. "They went that way," she tells the reporter following her.

"Unbelievable!" the reporter glances up as Benhur walks through. "He sleeps on an electric-powered hospital bed with a magnetotherapy machine for degenerative diseases, oxygen tanks nearby with masks, glass pyramids in the ceiling. Was that a scanner beside the air purifier? A dialysis machine. Shelves of medicine and enough equipment for a hospital . . ."

When his father was ill, Benhur recalls his mother going from pharmacy to pharmacy for the medicine prescribed. The one needed after his father's blood pressure dropped precipitously required refrigeration. All they could afford at P132 a vial were three to inject into the I.V., replaced every four hours. A man whose mother had just died in the ward gave them what she was not able to use, and refused to be paid.

He recalls these things while he steps into the bedroom. There is a World War II helmet, a black suit among several white barong Tagalogs. He does not go into Imelda's room, which another photo-journalist is recording for posterity: sunken bathtub, mirrored ceiling, gallon-size perfume bottles to freshen the foul air sealed in by bullet-proof glass, Persian rugs, grand piano, jade plates, stereos. And the inventory does not include the gold chains and jewelry with receipts from Van Cleef and Arpels, Winston . . .

Several cameras hanging from his neck, the correspondent heads for other rooms.

On his way out, Benhur thinks of the sign outside St. Paul's in Cambridge, the summer he and Osong were there: *Abstain from what you do not need.*

The same young man Benhur saw in the study is looking silently at the portraits of FM and Imelda in the blue drawing room off the reception hall.

Benhur walks quickly through. No one has bothered to turn off any of the lights, or to gather the receipts and letters scattered in the hall containing the podium and throne chairs.

The servant who pointed out the secret door through which the Marcoses escaped has opened a side window. Through the grilles, part of the grounds can be seen. As if he has just come from sunlight, all Benhur sees at first is darkness. The opaque glass pulses like membrane from the movements of people trying to climb the fence from which the soldiers have hastily withdrawn. The soldiers are changing into polo shirts; one still holds his armalite.

The scene outside excites the servant who tells the reporter, "I have to go. I live far from here. I don't know if the bus that took us here is waiting. We were stoned reporting for work this morning. The door of the bus was hit several times. I thought this is democracy. My father works here. He has been gardener for four presidents. I don't know where he is. I have to go."

"One last question. Do you know where the icon is? The solid gold Santo Niño with a diamond pendant? Did you vote for Marcos or Cory?"

"*Aling* Cory? They make fun of Madame kneeling at prayer but *Aling* Cory has a picture kneeling, too. If we are not fair, we are not just. That's all I know. I can't answer any more."

"Just one more question. Are you afraid of being killed?" Not getting his answer, the correspondent turns to Benhur. "What is your name?"

"Juan de la Cruz," he answers, not stopping for questions.

Flashbulbs popping like a lightning storm, the journalists zigzag through the crowd surging up into the ceremonial hall. Once up the stairs, the people take turns sitting on the throne chairs where FM and Imelda and their guests once sat, falling out of the seats with laughter as they conduct mock interviews among themselves. Sending documents flying out the windows, tossing letters and decrees and receipts that have fallen out of crates carried to the helicopters, the crowd runs towards the family quarters, through the study.

"Don't break anything," Benhur calls to them. "This is your Palace now." He would have added, "May not another tyrant sit here!" but no one is listening. Anyway, he thinks, democracy can survive the destruction of buildings but not the loss of integrity.

Before he reaches the end of the stairs, Benhur hears someone at the grand piano playing "Bayan Ko." Plaintive and slow, the music cuts across the screaming and the rush.

On the grounds some youths are trying to dismantle the cannons by hand while others are jumping up and down from the tanks. A man runs out of the Palace holding the black suit aloft. Papers fly down, part of the inaugural speech, like white ashes from the portraits being torched. FM's picture is hit again and again with sticks until it becomes the likeness of someone who has been savaged by police.

Some students are forming a barricade with their bodies at the entrance to the Palace. *Don't destroy. Don't take anything. Only Marcos is the thief. Only Marcos and his cronies steal. Don't destroy our revolution.*

A soldier watches, hands in pockets, while two men struggle with a crate of ammunition. Another soldier lets his rifle be taken from him without protesting.

Too impatient to wait for their turn through the gates, many are still climbing over the fence, standing on top of each other, then pulling each other over. People pour into the Palace; scaling the walls of the balcony where FM and Imelda appeared at noon. TV cameras fix them against the red of the large flag, which a man is attempting to kiss.

And a statue of the Virgin enters the Palace grounds with flashlights held like candles, bringing down the stars through the branches of trees while, from the buildings on the grounds, shredded documents continue to float down like pieces of sky.

Everything is moving and lit.

At Gate Four, besieged in the seventies by student demonstrators, a TV camera now scans the crowd from where guards stood only hours before. A man picks a pebble on his way out. "To show I was here," he explains. Some are carrying away branches, or flags that had been used to anchor the curling sod. Some with crowns of barbed wire are stepping among the firecrackers ricocheting across J. P. Laurel, which used to be Aviles.

From all over Metro Manila, church bells are ringing. Car horns are blasting away as if it is New Year.

We're freedom fighters! We're as brave as the Poles! Happy New Year!

Headed for Mendiola, then Recto, Benhur looks back. The Palace is lit inside by chandeliers; outside, by TV cameras. The moon looks like a bird flying in place. Is it Paradise? The Paradise that is lost as soon as it is found, sullied as soon as it is touched, that ceases to exist on being claimed;

but that is capable of renewing itself—its nature like that of truth, to be hidden, to be lost and sought again—of making promises to all alike, even to the restless hearts of those who wish to walk both sides of a river simultaneously.

In front of San Beda some are praying before a statue of the Virgin, holding their beads with eyes closed. Benhur bows but does not genuflect. Going on his way, he feels in his pockets for the rosary Father Case gave him on their way to Libis. It must have dropped when he changed shirts in the tailor shop, though it might still be in the shirt pocket. He tries to recall taking it out, to assure himself it is not lost.

Coming up toward Mendiola, the new armed forces greet people with cheers. Yellow armbands gird their sleeves, and people cheer back.

"Hurry," Benhur tells them good-naturedly. "They are throwing books at the walls of the Palace and ripping out the pages."

Don't shed blood. The old regime is over.

Even as the men in camouflage fatigues are marching by, a loyalist is caught by some youths, who start beating him. A priest in cassock rushes to break them apart. His cassock is quickly soaked with blood as he carries the injured man.

"There are doctors at the corner of Morayta and Recto, Father." A man in a car slows down to bring them to the volunteer medical station.

Benhur only then recalls someone telling him, back in the Palace, of a dead man in the lobby, stabbed with an ice pick. He helps clear the street for the car to pass through the crowd, then looks toward Malacañang.

Malacañang is no longer visible, except for the haze of lights above the trees and roofs—and the cries humming in his head.

"It's there. Still there. It's moved deeper." The cries of men on their knees, trying to pry loose large boards on the sidewalk, draw Benhur to a stop on his way home down Recto, which used to be Iris, then Azcarraga, connecting Manila Bay to the Palace across four tributaries of the Pasig River.

"Get a flashlight and see what it is."

Legs jerking off the sidewalk, a man lies on his belly, one arm reaching as far as he can. "It's alive."

"A cat?"

Crowned lightly with barbed wire a man comes running through the bystanders. "It's my flashlight. Let me do it." He swings himself through, drops down to beam the light beneath the boards, past heads scraping the sidewalk to be able to see what the flashlight will disclose. The light cuts across the sky like lacerations, as other men grab at the flashlight.

"What is it?"

Those standing closest draw back as something dark comes out, between the wildly streaking light, stumbling on the men trying to be the first to see what the light hits.

"It's a girl. A girl!"

Benhur sees a scraped knee just below a skirt ripped at the pockets which catch the men's hands. Four or five years old, the size of *Aling* Dionisia's granddaughter when they first came to Gulod, the child stops to cry.

Straining to break free of the hands pulling and pushing at her, feeling her all over, she drops down to crawl away between the men's legs, through their hands digging into her. It looks as if she might rip.

"Let her go!" Benhur shouts. He is pushed back by hands as hard as belt buckles. "Run!"

Without looking up, she runs.

The men turn on Benhur, one locks his arms about Benhur, another kicks him. Then all run after the girl while those watching pull Benhur to his feet.

The sun will get cold before those men will do something good. Better leave before they return. Dali. What has just happened on Recto is explained to those arriving from EDSA with candles and rosaries.

A chill, a feeling of bloat and rupture comes over Benhur. Some of the people steady him until he can walk off on his own; until it no longer feels as if his head has been knocked off. A woman offers him her wet handkerchief, to wipe his face.

As if coming from both ends of Recto at once, many thoughts occur to him. He wonders what God wants for that child, wants for him . . .

"Can you walk?" Some teenagers offer to go with him, against the flow of people celebrating.

Benhur thanks them, starts walking as erect as he can down Recto. Past the beerhouses and movies, the bookstores selling answers to tests, selling term papers and graduate theses; past newsstands and fast-food counters, copying machines and tailor shops, boutiques and apartments that rent bed space to students attending the twenty-odd colleges and universities in the area, Benhur walks slowly, stopping to look deep into the alleys.

Though he did not see her face when she ran out from under the boards, he sees it now as a reflection on the moon, an image coming into the light which might have fallen up to the sky; opening.

Part Three

1986-1987

Where the patent-medicine man had stood selling his snake oil on EDSA, Benhur returns early Wednesday morning. A choice of parking makes his decision difficult. No more than 2,000 are on the highway.

For most of the seventy-seven hours since Saturday night, he was part of an estimated one million defending the military Reformists against attack from the Marcos government. Expecting the intensity of those hours to be preserved in the very air over EDSA, Benhur starts to feel that he has lost his way.

It looks like a different sky.

Where once they stood waiting for the tanks to crash through the barricades; where candles were set on the ground, illuminating the singing; where sandbags lay softly in the shape of bodies huddled together for warmth in the cool nights, and branches of the felled *aguho* caught the moonlight on its needles, and wax from the melting candles marked where the statues of the Virgin and the Sacred Heart and the Santo Niño stood, cars are now dodging the debris of the revolution.

Running after vehicles, like vendors who must sell out before the rice cakes turn cold, newspaperboys hold up the headlines: *FM in Hawaii; Cory in Malacañang.*

Benhur considers parking in Camp Crame, where the helicopter squadron defected, or Camp Aguinaldo, which they tried to barricade against Marines whose truck headlights pushed back the sun coming up over Libis.

Several hundred are now attempting to clean up the highway, the sidewalks. Some soldiers join in, stacking their rifles against the guardhouses, sweeping the rubbish into piles for trucks of the Industrial Engineering Service Corporation to pick up. Work crews from Boys Town and the Himlayang Pilipino, where his father is buried on a plot donated by Osong, are shoveling the trash into the trucks. Wearing brimmed hats, with towels across their shoulders, Metro Aides in their red and yellow uniforms have spread out between the two camps. Mud and stains from cooking fires cling to their brooms.

Men sent by their companies to help are using water hoses on the walls of the camps. A photo-journalist takes pictures of men with their company's name on their uniforms: Gramesco International.

The sign of the revolution is on the people who have come to clean EDSA, Benhur thinks, and he parks his car so he can join them. If Sister Madeleine were there, she would know something has been made holy beyond forcing a dictator to flee. Something has been restored. The marks are not visible on their bodies.

A nun with a dustpan and broom refuses to give them up to Benhur. "I want to do my part. There's a woman with two brooms over there."

Benhur recognizes the woman who let them wash in her apartment on Boni Serrano; who boiled eggs for the Sisters. "Long time no see," she laughs on recognizing Benhur. "Take the newer broom. My husband is making coffee to bring here." They talk as if they're lifelong friends. "I didn't think we'd still be alive, you know. I think those colonels who disobeyed commands to fire into the crowds are the real heroes of the revolution. My husband says so. Cover your face with a handkerchief so you won't breathe the dust."

Benhur pulls out a handkerchief. "I have not yet started," he tells the occupants of a car that stops to offer sandwiches and drinks. "Later on. Thank you." The handkerchief does not stay in place and Benhur ends up holding his breath while the dust rises.

"*Sipsip!* Bootlickers! Cory does not even know you're here!" people call out from a passing car.

Benhur's ears burn and he stands up to return the taunt, but the nun goes up to him, lays a hand on his arm.

"And you, Sister. Go back to the convent!"

Benhur feels like the man in the circus who can spit out fire from gasoline held under his tongue but cannot swallow. He wants to hurl his broom at the car as it runs full tilt into a pile of debris, scattering what has been swept together. Instead of a beacon, was EDSA only a comet streaking across the sky?

"Let them," the nun says. "God knows. Let's keep cleaning this place where, for three nights, the Lord kept vigil for us."

They return to their brooms, looking up each time a car passes. Squirming like a snake, a water hose careers across the highway, spraying the workers and causing much laughter. Besides dislodging dirt and stench clinging to the cement, the water releases their hurt feelings and they throw themselves into the work, raking paper from the shrubs that had served as comfort rooms during the revolution.

Unused to work that stretches his arms, Benhur soon is out of breath. He leans on his broom while shovels grate on the road and the water runs along the islands dividing the highway. He watches youths moving the barricade of rocks and wooden planks, sweatbands across their foreheads and around their wrists as if they are tennis players in a championship match. They race across, picking up sandbags and rubbish that have escaped the brooms and shovels, their Nikes still clean and white. One catches his sleeve on the thorny bougainvillea planted to discourage jaywalking. The others playfully make the rip bigger, pulling at the shirt. They weave in and out among the lampposts.

Another car comes, runs over a pile of newspapers a couple has been collecting to sell. The man and his wife bring their scattered pile to a waiting shed.

"Smart! Long live democracy." A Metro Aide working near the shed gives the car a long glance. Seeing Benhur, he says, "They must be burning off their happiness. Some people have too much of that. Long live EDSA!"

Benhur resumes sweeping. The remark impresses him, especially since the Metro Aide can only be someone from whom God wants nothing. He is immediately sorry for this thought.

The Metro Aide pulls the towel from his head to wipe his face. He looks down EDSA toward Cubao, then toward the Ortigas intersection where the tanks came Sunday afternoon after Enrile crossed over to Ramos in Camp Crame.

A woman, her legs as heavy as the wooden paddles used to beat laundry against rocks, walks by, running her broom of coconut midribs behind her. Youths with portable radios are calling out the news as they hear it.

"Are you a professor?" A young woman wearing jeans and a yellow T-shirt asks Benhur as she offers a large paper bag of still warm *pan de sal.*

"I'm many things," Benhur answers. "Why not a professor?" He pulls out a bun as the girl walks by.

She returns from the Metro Aide to ask, "What many things?" Her teeth are as white as the daisies set in vases before the statues on EDSA. She must have been there all weekend, for her cheeks are sunburned, like someone who has just run in barefoot from jumping in the surf.

"I would not be surprised if your name is Daisy." Benhur takes another *pan de sal.*

"Ugly name," she says, looking back as she walks away with the bag of *pan de sal,* tossing her head to make her hair glisten in the sun.

"Wait," Benhur calls. But she does not.

"What is the life course of miracles?" The Metro Aide faces Benhur. "A miracle is supposed to have happened here. In other words, in whose bodies did the revolution take place? And what exactly was won? Do we gain in the next world what is denied here? Even stars die, you know."

Those are Benhur's own thoughts, but expressed forcefully and simply. Benhur lapses into vagueness to give himself time to figure out the coordinates of the situation. "There's always a pool of opportunities and possibilities." He should have said, pool of responsibilities; but does it matter? Benhur, you have met your match.

"Shall we say something more than freedom was won here? Or shall we just set fire to EDSA?" The Metro Aide offers Benhur his other bread. "Turn it into another Smoky Mountain."

His full attention now engaged, Benhur wonders if the man posits salvation and freedom. The free association of words brings him to wonder if God Himself was saved at EDSA. Is He not affected by what people do? But why would such ideas occur to a Metro Aide?

"Then there will be only ashes that the wind can blow away," the Metro Aide wraps the towel around his head, preparing to start sweeping. "The cost of energy, human fuel included, is what determines economies around the world. Perhaps around the universe. We're farmers. My mother's father was swallowed by the earth in Nueva Ecija."

"How did that happen?"

"He was plowing. Without warning an earthquake opened up the field, and fissures ran in all directions, wide enough to swallow him, his carabao, and the plow. The way I see it, poverty and lack of opportunity are slow-action earthquakes that swallow up people, countries. What do you think?"

The man is using images from geology now, having pulled them from political science and economics; and implicating faith as easily as Case. Father Case. God People Power Revolution: that is the priest's phrase for EDSA. Is the Metro Aide repeating the sermon he himself did not get to hear Sunday?

"Those are sharp observations," Benhur admits, while refusing to be drawn into his own. "You and Sister Madeleine could talk off an afternoon." Perhaps he should introduce them.

"For a Metro Aide? I'm not offended. I'm a lawyer, actually."

"Diploma and Bar?"

"Both. But a diploma is only paper, something to fight over. My mother wants it in our house; my wife, in the room we rent at 400 a month. Do we sleep or do we eat? Hard choice. When I was small, people called me a philosopher because I could already carry thoughts around in my head. It made it difficult for me to hear what people were telling me. Thinking helps pass the time. Makes one forget the permanent state of one's hungers. It is a kind of experience, but not the useful kind. Is understanding useful?"

"When did you graduate?"

"Three years ago. Going on four. I waited outside our governor's office until the letter of recommendation from our mayor had become smeared from the hands of so many secretaries and clerks to whom I presented it. Almost every day I went. A diploma should have been sufficient, but no, a letter of recommendation is required. I carried my lunch in a plastic briefcase, like an influence peddler. After three years, three months, and twenty-seven days, it was my turn, and the only job available was Metro Aide. I took it. My father and grandfather mortgaged the small family farm for my law school tuition, so I can sweep the street."

"Your time and chance will come," Benhur says.

More people have arrived to help clean. Others have left. It is almost noon. Over the portable radios comes news that Metro Manila police have intercepted a truck registered to a Marcos crony and loaded with crates of newly minted pesos. 130 million.

"Not enough chances to go around. My wife thinks I work in a bank. She also thinks I have another wife because all the lawyers she knows, even the governor's drivers, have several wives. It's the reason men work at so many *diligencias.* The reason for corruptions. I let her think so because it allows her to feel she's married to someone sort of big. When I go home on Saturday, she thinks she's special because I spend the weekends with her. I'll always be a Metro Aide, and also a philosopher. Revolutions will thunder and lightning in the bodies of men like me and bring into office those who keep themselves from danger. Equality does not follow from democracy, if that it what we won here."

"Cory will clean up the government the way we're cleaning the highway. The Communists will surrender to her and once there is peace and order . . ."

"She says two NPA commanders will surrender to her. Let's see." He holds up a hand over the broom and Benhur notices the bandage. "I burned it yesterday, putting out some cooking fires. When I saw that soldier's body dangling from the TV tower Tuesday, I thought of deer tied to a tree so the blood will drain out. Is it alright for that soldier to die? God of love, my wife's mother says. Not *Susmariosep.* How can I believe it will get better for me?"

"You might be surprised."

"I would like to be surprised, Professor. How about next year, at this time, we meet here on EDSA? By this waiting shed. Now I have to work, or someone will report me and I will lose even this job I do not want. Next year. Don't forget. Here's my card."

Benhur glances at the card in his hand and almost cries. Siso Feleo, when he thought Benhur had graduated and passed the Bar, brought a box of imprinted calling cards to the house.

"My brother had that made in the *imprenta* where he works. He designed it himself. Every year he gives me another hundred. One time, I distributed them through Manila. Just left them on counters, in jeepneys, stores. No one ever found them. I never got a client. Next year, Professor. We'll see if I'm wrong."

The card is a summons to confess his own failure, but Benhur lacks the courage. He leaves his broom against the shed and walks to the car. Appearance of success. The Metro Aide even has what he does not possess: a diploma and a license to practice. What finally matters? What if he hangs himself outside Sister Madeleine's window? Will her faith save him, or will his disbelief condemn her as well?

Youths who look as if they had boycotted Magnolia products during the elections, up to the revolution, are drinking Coca Cola at the corner store. San Miguel stocks must be soaring now that patriots have been released from their pledge to boycott crony products. Each day of trading will set new records. New fortunes are already being made.

About to leave, Benhur walks away from his car to head down Boni Serrano towards Libis. It can still be counted in hours, since the early morning he stood there against the Marines . . . He wonders what the true vocations of citizens are. Wonders if all occupations require the highest demands from the self: a consecration of the mundane, so—in Sister Madeleine's thoughts—humanity can be holy. Would she agree that operating a travel agency or a driver education school should demand the same ideals as being, let's say, a teacher? A nurse?

What chance has he of finding out if salvation and freedom are the same; are impermanent states like emotions? What saves lives such as his?

Used to pouring out his thoughts to himself, he walks without seeking anyone he recognized. Thoughts as powerful as feelings tear him apart inside, darkening his face.

He walks quickly.

The owner of the tailor shop where he changed clothes is running after him. "Are you looking for this? You left it in the shirt pocket. I knew you'd be back."

Benhur clasps Father Case's rosary. How will he return it himself? What obligations are imposed by this revolution that took place less than a hundred hours ago? Why should people act as if they can now live in safety anywhere, as if this revolution enables the sun to enter rooms without windows? If God does not exist—to whose longings his heart beats, according to Sister Madeleine—would he be free?

Might as well go back to the waiting shed and admit to the Metro Aide he is right. Why wait another year to concede? The Metro Aide failed to point out that Marcos's Minister of National Defense is now Cory's. And the *Inquirer* reports that Cory's cordon sanitaire have been acting like Imelda's Blue Ladies. Marcos has been gone no more than twenty-four hours.

People are greeting one another in the streets, in front of the dress shops, the water towers, Imelda's Mini Park, the Superior Mami House, Maria's Carinderia. Are there no strangers left? Someone waves to him from Nerin's Store, from the Body Part Shop, from Capitol Bowling. He remembers his mother complaining that the boys cut classes to play billiards in Gulod. He should talk to them, she says. He wonders if he should go home now, buy bread from the Santo Niño Bake Shop first.

As soon as he goes down to Libis, he'll go to Gulod. He nears the Little Star Tutorial Center, the law offices beside the Abacus Air-conditioners. The white fence of Camp Aguinaldo stretches out to his right. There is the side gate. Now he can see the intersection with Katipunan, the three Caltex stations that gave out ice during the revolution; Kameraworld, where Miggy and Joel had their films developed.

Where are the tracks of the Marines who retreated on Sunday? the students and seminarians and nuns who held that intersection while candles flamed on the ground and on the fence? Is EDSA simply a spectacle, a sensation, a world-stopping event? Is the government asking too much—to claim that 90 percent of Communist rebels will soon surrender, so that, therefore, nuns should go out to the rebels, though no guidelines have been formulated? Surrender on faith.

Everything that has happened begins to rush his mind. For whom is he responsible? Might freedom not be having to answer for no needs other than his own? Even the man who carried on his back the bed he made is part of his bad dreams. The little girl in Recto whom he could not protect has kept him awake all night. For what is he responsible? The Metro Aide who carried thoughts in his mind the way other children carried slingshots? Is it a sign of being saved that he has thought of finishing his studies and taking the Bar?

A fire is beginning to go through him, a sense of God, though he does not recall having felt him there. Sister Madeleine would say, *But he saw you, Benhur!* Was He there wandering among them? The life expectancy of miracles!

"Hallucinating in the middle of the day!" Osong intercepts him. "My arms got stiff waving to you. I thought you would be at the demonstrations in Malacañang. Already started, but polite and quiet protests. *Free all political prisoners.* Where are you going?"

"It's good to see you."

"Good to see me! I never thought I'd ever hear you say that, Brod. What's happened?" Osong play-acts.

Benhur checks himself from saying, You kept me from weeping again. The questions he had been asking himself were about to choke the afternoon sun. Osong has kept him from self-destructing.

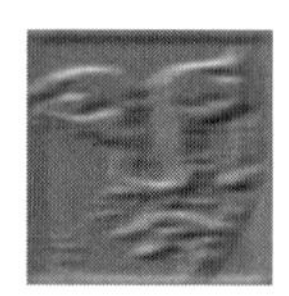

"While you are out here playing Metro Aide, Cory has been putting her Cabinet together," Osong accuses Benhur. "Every minor fundraiser and adviser has been awarded a chair and a desk, and I have gotten no promise or illegible signature. Ting Dolor thought you might have gone back to EDSA to clean up because you're sentimental. 'Sweet and exasperating,' is actually what she said. Let me just tell my driver to go back. Better gas up."

"What is it exactly that you think I can do?" Benhur heads for the Caltex station, letting in other cars ahead.

"Suddenly, everyone is so courteous. A new excuse for being late at the office. 'Sorry, Boss, we couldn't decide who should go ahead.' I'll be happy to get whatever Cory wishes me to have. Anything at all to serve the country."

"Give me a reason why Cory should appoint you. Ongpin denounced crony monopolies; Concepcion monitored the snap election and pinpointed the cheating; Gonzalez . . ."

"I know all that." Osong throws a five hundred peso bill with Marcos's picture on the dashboard. "I'm using these up before they're banned. Cory will certainly refuse to have Marcos around in any form or shape. I hope the president can weather exile. He might come back a hero, you know."

"Tell me the worst."

The sarcasm escapes Osong, who is focused on what he is trying to grab. Women with minds and money of their own free him to indulge himself, and Benhur always bails him out. Between them, there is only pure unadulterated need. "The worst is that Sally might not be home."

"Sally?" Benhur cannot recall the last time they went together to Sally. Long ago they stopped speaking her name. In front of the gas pump, he turns off the ignition.

"Sally!" Osong looks in the windows of department stores that have reopened. "You have any idea what we can bring her?" He picks up the change Benhur has placed on the dashboard.

On the overpasses, pedestrians are flashing the Laban sign: *Free-dom, Free-dom. Ra-mos! En-ri-le!* Movie marquees are banners of a different kind.

"What about Ting Dolor?"

"She's going to pick up the videotapes of *Dynasty.* Philippine Airlines resumed scheduled flights today. Anyway, it's Sally who is an Aquino on her mother's side."

"Cojuangco would be a better connection," Benhur heads down EDSA toward North Avenue. "How do you know Sally will help? She's become tough."

"She'll do it for the boys. Make that clear to her." Osong pulls down the cuffs of his blue *barong,* darker blue embroidery down the front.

"I? I was going to see my mother."

"You know how to do these things, Benhur. I don't. One word from me and Sally will balk. Let's get some newspapers. Someone should buy these up for souvenirs. Should be worth their weight in gold some day. See. Two commissions are being created. Good government and reorganization. We'd better get to Sally before they're all spoken for. Marcos diehards are passing themselves off as Cory partisans, having shred the records in their office. Make it very clear to Sally. Time is of the essence. Whatever she asks for in exchange, give. And ask for yourself, too."

"I'm not interested, Osong."

"It's your chance. Why not?"

"I'm saving my loyalty."

"Your loyalties? For what?"

"Loyalty. Singular, Brod."

"Sounds like a woman saving her virginity for marriage."

"That's the idea. By the way, did you stay with the president last night until he took off?"

For a moment Osong looks blank. "Oh no. As soon as we could, we left to go to Mandaluyong. Ting Dolor wanted to be among the first to congratulate Cory. You've done that, haven't you?"

Benhur does not bother to answer. He's thinking of a postcard he bought. Picture of man-size saguaro cactus from Arizona pumped full of buckshot. It is stuck over a picture of himself on his desk. Update.

Surprised by the popping flashbulb,
Ting Dolor looks up from the open drawers in Imelda's bedroom to the camera still aimed at her, giving her no time to decide if she should turn on the wild-animal-with-power-to-devour look or the wild-animal-willing-to-be-tamed. The taste on her tongue is that of burnt pineapple.

"Keep working," he says. "The crowds are restive at the doors, waiting to tour the Palace." He starts moving around her, snapping as he talks. "Hold it. Now, look over your shoulder. You should become a professional model. You have the bone structure. How about just inside the bed railing? With part of the canopy showing. By the bed. Good. Good. One more, then you can return to taking inventory before the rush."

"No bathroom shots?" Ting Dolor recovers on hearing she has been mistaken for one of Cory's Crusaders preparing the rooms for viewing.

"One in the music room would be good? And with the soldiers keeping the lines below. Background shots. I've taken the grounds while waiting to be let in; and the remains of lunch or dinner on the dining table when the First Family left. Did you know them? Would you care to climb on top of the pile of anti-riot shields on the roof of a van downstairs? Stunning angles there, against the balcony where Imelda sang for the last time. What is her song again? Theme song? *Dahil Sa Yo?*"

"You've taken quite enough, thank you," Ting Dolor snaps. "Take the crowd and the volunteer ushers. Usherettes." She places both hands inside her deep pockets to camouflage the bulge of the heavy pieces of jewelry.

Without a pocketbook, handbag to the locals, she will not have to go past the guards.

He stands in her way. "Just one beside the river. By the porte cochére, which I understand dates from the American Occupation."

She shakes her head, going past a sign: *Marcos the Winner;* past the mirrors bouncing off each other's reflection.

"I'd like to see you again. I'd like you to have copies of the pictures I took of you."

Against the lines starting to enter the hall of murals and the Czech chandeliers, Ting Dolor hangs onto him. Unwittingly, he is giving her the chance to escape search at the door, allowing her to vanish into her car, leaving him behind. But he follows her right up to the fence and past.

"I'd like you to see the pictures. Where can I send them?"

Her driver in uniform opens the door for her.

She motions him over to the front seat, beside the driver. "My husband has a darkroom in the house. Show me the pictures there."

"He won't mind?" He cradles the cameras as he sits.

"He's in Australia, on our ranch. He has no time to take pictures."

"That's the life," he says, introducing himself to the driver, telling him, "One minute last night, the barbed wire was holding off the crowd; the next, the crowd was climbing over the tall gates of the Palace and snatching ammo belts from soldiers who didn't know what hit them. Then in the chapel, a maid was crying. She said Madame sent her for something, and when she returned, the room was empty. Madame had left."

The pictures better be worth her taking the photo-journalist home, Ting Dolor thinks. The driver, Roger, is probably thinking of how he will report this to German's mother, who will then call up German in Australia: *I heard Ting brought home an American.*

They pass by the Lorenzo Ruiz Student Center on Legarda, then the Santa Catalina College. Ting Dolor loves the Franciscan monastery that used to be there. Did the American see her take anything? When he admitted he took a towel for a souvenir, was the admission to make her confess her theft? She shrugs off the possibility. He could not have seen anything suspicious. Anyway she'll have the stones reset in Malolos, then bring them to Hong Kong and even New York for redesigning. No trace.

"What's your name, did you say?" She leans forward, feeling him out for weaknesses. Benhur can't be made to lose control over himself; does not appear to suffer from what she does or says; does not do or say. Sometimes, she thinks Benhur has the cleanest sex in the world, all emotional release. All in the head.

"Steve. Stephen Hynek. Polish. Part of me was also in America before Christopher Columbus."

"Ha?"

"American Indian. Blackfeet and Crow. Many in my family died in Auschwitz. Maximilian Kolbe? The priest who took the place of the man with children?"

"I thought only Jews died there."

"Catholics were attacked for resisting Hitler. Priests and nuns were sent to death camps. People who hid the Jews were sent to Auschwitz years before the Jews were sent there. There were different colors for gypsies, other minorities . . ."

"Do you play the guitar? We just passed the place where first-class instruments are sold. From Pampanga."

"I saw. People brought their statues or guitars to EDSA. I would have been sent to Moscow to cover the 27th Communist Party Congress. 5,000 delegates. Then EDSA happened. Developed fast, too. Think what I would have missed!"

"How old are you?" It used to be that doctors, policeman, and men who wanted her were older than she. Before she can ask again, they are at the house. The guard at the gate throws it open.

She never looks at him, nor at the maid who is at the door in uniform and bare feet. In the entry hall the Igorot maid, life size, which German ordered carved to tease her with its full and rounded buttocks is turned to the wall, causing Steve to miss a step, turn to Ting Dolor, who goes up to the staircase, along one steep wall papered with yellow, bell-like *campanillas* clinging to woody stems.

"The darkroom is through the library. Take your time, and if you need anything, ask. Tell the driver when you're through." It's just as well he's so young—maybe no older than her son Alex who wants to go to NYU. Men older than she, or even her age, expire from the effort.

On her way up, she sees him follow the maid from German's mother. Did he notice the white cushions with lace on the wicker chairs off the patio, long stems of white flowers setting off the green square pots? She likes pottery of all sizes and texture, ridged or slashed with overlapping strokes, free-form or precise rounds—the shape of seated women—instead of figurines, which she has had hung like portraits among the empty bird cages built like cathedrals with cupolas. Because he kept tripping on the pottery, she allowed German to choose the wallpaper with the ugly bands of entwined garlands, nineteenth-centuryish.

Light coming in from the tall windows purrs like cats, as shiny as the surface glaze on thin vases.

Inside her room she practically tears the clothes off her body, impatient with zippers and buttons. Facing herself in the mirror she wonders how Steve Hynek sees her. Is he already in her power? And what can he give her she does not already have? Of course, in ten years he could be a Dan Rather or Koppel. So? When he was not yet a name star, Chuck Norris came to Manila to shoot a film and she did not try to charm him. Now, he's box-office. Alain Delon also came, before he was every woman's heartthrob. She didn't see him either. Her companion then was a producer, he said he was, and wanted her to star in a Philippine-American War epic; but he could not find a script.

A light knock at the door startles her into taking the jewels from the pockets. Under the pillow would be too risky. The vault? Will take too long. She wraps them in her kerchief and drops them into the vase filled with silk flowers, on the reading table with the books she meant to read this past year. "Come in."

"Sir called. Said for you to call him as soon as you get back. He asked if the children are with *Lola* Mamá."

"Bring the American beer." Ting Dolor dismisses the maid. "I'm going to rest, then I'll call." Is Steve Hynek one in whom it is worth her effort to arouse powerful feelings; who can be made to suffer, to think he's dying if she refuses to see him again; who will die differently each time? Not a Benhur Vitaliano! She likes the awkward way he walked past the guard; as if there were stage directions on the driveway and he could not tell which chalk marks were his.

"Ma'm?"

"Go, already. That's all." The impertinent one even comes in when she's in the middle of a douche. *Bruja.* German's mother will send her a witch, of course; snooping through the maids.

Should she call Cora? Break up her encounter group with: *Cora, an American fifteen years younger, is waiting for me to ask him up. Should I? If you can make it in ten minutes you can meet him certainly. Just cuidao. Hands off. He's mine.*

Very psychic, Cora gives inspirational talks about men and women, women and offspring, exuding and transmitting sexual powers. Scarves of many colors layered on her head, Cora winds and unwinds the ends as if she's peeling off her clothes while she talks. Very expensive and chic, she can have a following in any city. Just name it. Friends of Ting Dolor's ask for advice they don't need just to hear Cora speak, talk about the eternal position of all things. Cora emits. She can make the sun writhe and lead you to places reached only through violent desires.

Her temples are swollen again, the way her mother's pulse whenever angry or excited. Her doctor can't tell what causes it; suggested she measure her head before and after, or see him while it's swollen. "It swells while I'm in bed. Will you come then?"

A moist and spicy taste spreads down her body while she showers. An aunt who, until she died at ninety-one, drank wine in order to fall asleep could tell if a man was walking past the house, even with the windows closed. She never married, though she had several prenuptial honeymoons. And when she died her face was unlined, stretched like a bride.

There's a bruise on her right thigh the size and shape of a bullethole. Would that be interesting in the news report Steve Hynek files? The water runs down her legs, swirls around her toes; thin and slender like fingers. German says her toes are like his mother's.

All the men she knows are immature. Immaturity she can handle. No matter at what age, whether emotional or psychological, from too intense a desire.

Close to her head, wet, her hair makes her look like a young boy. No mascara. Just blush lip color. Light swabs with the blush. Looking at herself makes her feel a needle is being jabbed tenderly into her.

Another knock. "Ma'm?"

"Is the American still there?" she asks, faking indifference with her voice.

"Yes, Ma'm. Reading."

How does she know unless she peeked into the library? "He's waiting for the film to set. Don't bother him. Remember to tell him he can use the car to go home."

"Ma'm. *Tita Madre* wants to talk to you."

"All right. Hang up downstairs and I'll talk to her." She has to insist that she hear the phone click off before she starts any conversation. "Yes, *Tita Madre.* So much happening in the country." She speaks slowly picking up the slow pace and accent of her aunt who has to get her Prioress's permission before she can call out of the convent.

"Did you pray? On your knees, *hija?*"

Ting Dolor plays the same smile on her face she used in their high school dance program, years and years ago, when just before the Agnus Dei sequence, part of the chorus, she lifted up her face, her neck powdered white and throbbing; arms as thin as spikes with which to impale. From starving herself she's still that thin. Inspired by the devotions in their Bontoc mountain missions, the Belgian sisters who crossed over in a cargo boat after World War II, encouraged dance as prayer. Pure offering of self, of one's talent to the Lord. In thanksgiving. Before the War, ballet was considered pagan and indecent in Manila's *colegios:* punishable by expulsion.

"You received permission to listen to the radio during EDSA? Then you did not miss anything, *Tita Madre.*" Ting Dolor waits till her aunt finishes the sentence, then lays the phone between the pillows. On cat's paws she walks down the hall and the stairs, startling Steve Hynek in the library.

"How long has the film been in the canister?"

"Ten minutes." He gets up.

"I'm supposedly on the phone; the maid is next door telling the neighbor's maid the news about you in the darkroom. When she's gossiping, she loses track of time." She rubs against him the way women rub their bodies against the crucifix in Quiapo, tilting her head back until she can feel his body swelling into her. It's good. As good as Benhur swimming beside her to Pigeon Rock where red pigment, blood from pigeons, ran from the cracks. The first time, a dark shape appeared below, following her and she started to race for the Rock, reached it out of breath with the waves beating inside her. Sometimes, to bring that back, she bites her lips to draw the pain of the dark shape below; rousing pain, large with expectations.

He licks her ear. An ache deeper than happiness goes from the top of her head, down her body. Pleasure has nothing to do with it, or love. Benhur might love her, but what good does it do her if he stays away? All she needs is to stun.

But suppose Hynek writes of her, in his tale of Asia, side by side with washerwomen? She pushes him away.

"Why?"

She arches her back to transfer his weight. "*Tita Madre* is on the phone. I'll say a few words so she won't think I fell asleep." She looks down at her body while she picks up the phone by the sofa. "Mamá said he looked dead on TV. Good he's gone. Are you sure, *Tita Madre?*"

He lies there, licking her fingers now. God, he's young, Ting Dolor almost cries into the phone. God of love. What does he think of her?

"Am I giving you pleasure?" He wants to know; to be told. "Am I?"

She thinks of Alex in New York wearing a black pigskin hat and boots of elephant skin. Stuck to the crown of the hat is a toothpick with tassles.

He's sixteen, but at three he had a mind of his own. German wants him to become a rancher!

"Am I?"

"Yes," she says though she feels something has collapsed, no longer swells. She wants to get up and shower herself with Roger and Gallet's Santal. Strong enough to mask odors. Drum out the pain in her head and the empty hole in her body. "Isn't it time to give the film a water bath?"

"You're right." He steps on his clothes, walking to the dark-room.

When *Apocalypse Now* was being filmed, she met an American for every state in the Union; some on location, some in Forbes where an aunt rented a house to the crew. They all wanted to know the names of things. She wants what she can't see, can't possibly know or recognize; wants wanting.

She thinks of listening to *Tita Madre* but walks instead after Steve Hynek. "How long will it take?" she asks, tying her belt as tight as it will go, most expectations gone, but willing to revive them.

"I'm about to test a strip."

"Is that how you do it?"

"Yes. I want to know how much exposure I want for the rest of the film. One minute is all it takes. Then into the stop basin for twenty seconds. Water bath for fifteen minutes. Then it can be brought into the light. I thought you knew how."

"Barely." Waiting to see the pictures of herself at the Palace, Ting Dolor feigns disinterest. "My mother always wanted a party in the garden with the full moon to light it for the guests, but my father could not bear to have other people in the house. When anyone came, he took a nap or studied his ledgers. In everything else Mamá had her way. She wanted Spanish *yayas* for us."

"Yayas?"

"Mary Poppins!" She exclaims to his ear, biting. "*Mestizas* wouldn't do. Half-breeds! Had to be pure Spanish, like the brides some Spanish families in Manila insisted upon for their sons." For some reason that irrelevant fact matches her feelings to the moment, making her happy.

"When I was growing up, I played with a boy, Benn, who later held up people coming out of the movies at night. His father hired the best lawyers but even they could not keep him out of jail. Broke his parole each time, too."

"Why would he do that?" She composes a sad face for Hynek.

"They had money. I don't know. For the excitement, perhaps. One time I was home for a visit and was sitting in the neighborhood bar when Benn comes in wearing prison clothes, orders a beer at the counter. Leon the bartender recognizes him but gives him the beer in a glass mug. Several policemen who know him come in, order drinks, and leave. Finally I get nervous for him and go home and bring back a shirt for him to change into. They picked him up the next day."

She laughs, as if she has discovered family resemblances between them. The laugh expels all the sounds buried inside her. She feels light and new.

"You did not tell me. Did I give you any pleasure?" he asks, rubbing her back with both hands. "Why do you smile?"

"No one asked me that before."

"Where would you like me to touch you?"

"Where?" She lifts her shoulders away from his hands. "Where? I don't know. My soul?"

"Where is the door to your soul?"

"I'll be back. Make the pictures good." The dark marble floor is cool. Halfway up the stairs, the aqua sandals in her hands, the *bruja* maid comes out of the kitchen. Ting bends down quickly, as if to pick up something she dropped. When she straightens up, the maid is headed downstairs. "See if you can dial Australia after the American leaves. Has he left?"

"No, Ma'm. He locked the door."

"Let's see," Ting Dolor tells the maid, her tone challenging. Just as she is about to knock, she commands, "Bring some *merienda* on the good plates; and juice with lots of ice, to eat while we view the pictures. Hurry." Ting Dolor wonders why she would describe the plates as *good,* so out of character for her since they have only china in the house. Strange redundancy. Perhaps it is she in whom powerful feelings have been aroused?

But she feels perfectly lovely, able to stop the heart of anyone she chooses; with no need, for years to come, of injections of tissues from aborted foetuses, as Cora has had.

When she was sixteen she vowed not to live past twenty and the bloom of youth. Now she tells herself, one more year, and that is it; but every year brings an improved version of her at sixteen so that even her feelings have become photogenic. Will that show in the pictures? It had better.

All this, she thinks, knocking at the door as if she is the guest in that house, is at no cost to her. *No cost,* as her Spanish *yaya* liked to say to everything, to her own playing of the nose flute from Baguio, to time encroaching on pale afternoons.

But at whose cost, if the pictures catch what he wants?

"It's only Luis!
I can do this myself, Benhur," Osong says, stepping in front of Benhur into the temporary offices of the government in the Cojuangco building. "We won't wait for Sally."

Good, Benhur thinks. *About time you did something on your own.* Avoiding the crush of people waiting for a chance to be interviewed for any position, Benhur walks down to the cafeteria for a cup of coffee. No reason for him to see Louie.

A waiter brings out the sugar and powdered milk, takes these to another table when Benhur shakes his head. Four aides from the reception and secretarial pool fix Benhur with superior stares for occupying a table for four. He would have given them the table, but not after the snub.

"Saving these seats?" a man in *barong* asks, pulls the chair across from Benhur, and orders beer. "Lots of ice will double the tip," he teases the waiter. "Did you get what you want?" he asks Benhur as if they know each other.

"Not me, but a friend. He's being interviewed."

"Must have connections. It's a madhouse there. Worse than having the voter registration list scrambled. People pulling all kinds of tricks to get ahead of the line. What lines! But it can't be helped, I suppose. Can't be helped. Tell your friend to demand a written appointment. A cousin of mine came home thinking he's going to be general manager of the railroad, broke the news to another cousin who told him the job is promised to him.

Then there is this professor who thought he was appointed to some commission, read it in the papers. He went to check and no one had heard of him in the office."

"Horror stories," Benhur says.

"It will get worse tomorrow. The cordon sanitaire in there beats Swiss guards twice their height. I suppose they have gotten the pick of the appointments for their spouses. Marcos defectors and diehards are in there, too. Wild. Free-for-all."

The aides throw sharper glances at their table.

"Look at that," the man in *barong* says. "Look-alikes. Cory clones. If Marcos gets back from Hawaii, how will the loyalists know which is the real Cory?"

The aides get up, walking very close to Benhur's table to express disgust.

"I was getting airsick back there, you know," the man tells Benhur. "Yellow all over. Too much. Yellow-rimmed spectacles, short curls. That's better. Less yellow. By the way. You didn't tell me. Did you get what you asked for?"

Benhur defers the question to Osong who walks directly to the table. "What did you get? What did Cory give you on Louie's recommendation? What did you ask for?"

"Nothing to all three. Louie was called away."

"You might have to return tomorrow," the man in *barong* says. "I know a man who got his appointment, written and signed, but he could not find his office and staff."

Osong looks from Benhur to the man.

"He's waiting to be interviewed, too," Benhur explains. "Have coffee, Brod. When Sally appears, try again."

The man sharing Benhur's table has more advice. "Say you'll take anything. Once you're in, you can bargain for what you really want. Do you know the head of the presidential commission on good government?"

Benhur shakes his head on behalf of Osong.

"What I say is, forget the issues for the moment. Let's get past the appointment of officers-in-charge as against electing replacements for Marcos officials. So, documents burned in scattered bonfires. So, the Batasan election returns were tossed out of the windows by the crowd celebrating Marcos's flight? We have to start from where we are now . . ."

Without a word Osong gets up. Benhur leaves fifty for the coffee, does not wait for change.

"You can't get a word in," Osong says. "Like the nut in there says, everything is being settled all at once. First, Cory will have to decide if her government is revolutionary or constitutional. People Power or Constitutional Power."

"A debate on that could outlast this government. Might need another election if the Batasan results are gone," Benhur says. "But didn't Cory say at Club Filipino that she assumed office on the mandate of the people?"

"The Justices have been asked to resign, and the Constitution says they are appointed for life. Offices are being reorganized which might mean the civil service will be dismantled. Caput! Like Marcos, who violated fundamental laws 'legally'—see, I remember the speeches you write for me—Cory will do the same by *revolutionizing,*" Osong walks slowly back to the offices. "I'll give her two minutes to show up."

Benhur does not think it wise to crack a joke—that Osong could choose to wait for Marcos to return and Arturo Tolentino to seize power in Marcos's name.

They stand about, waiting to be recognized, then Osong says, "Let's go, Brod. Let Ting Dolor handle it."

It makes no difference to Benhur, yet he obligingly attempts to make the slight bearable for Osong. "You remember Terence Hugg, don't you? He said that the best ambition one could have is to hope to drink oneself under the table. No one will fight you for that. All you need, Hugg said, is a moderate income. Lacking that, you need just a few friends willing to pick up the tab occasionally. You don't even need a good woman, because she'll only try to help you recover from drinking, when drinking is the whole point. Under the table, you will be in complete peace. No one will try to edge you out, because, Hugg concluded, Filipinos want to be at the head of the parade."

"Hugg missed it entirely. This is not a question of drinking," Osong says, giving Benhur the empty look of someone disappearing in slow motion.

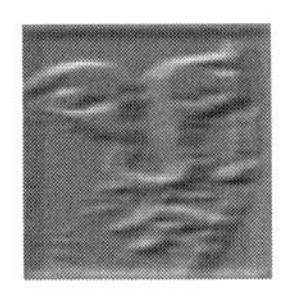

Benhur breaks away

from the gathering at his mother's house. The questions neighbors ask him have no answers. Hernan Sipalay presents the letter signed years ago, now dogeared from unfolding and folding since 1984. Signed by several dispossessed of their land like him, it asks the Minister of National Defense Enrile, now Cory's own secretary, to protect them against vigilantes. Will Enrile now listen? Benhur remembers the part of the story about Sipalay, hidden, watching vigilantes torching the houses in Santa Catalina: *Before they ordered us to yield our lands, they strafed our houses; first taking everything we owned; portable radios, tools, livestock. Every six hours they set a house on fire. Armed by the military, the vigilantes arrested and tortured everyone who went to the Social Action Center to complain.*

It is easier to be asked for money than for answers, which would force him to feel their hurts.

EDSA of the past week was a NO to injustices and inequalities; to humiliations. The common act of those who obeyed their instincts, who made history happen while it was happening to them, EDSA belongs to all: to those who acted and to those for whom they acted.

How will it save Dante Filemon's sons, who beat their heads against the wall to stop the pain between their ears, recurring pains from diving so deeply without gear in order to drive fish into nets that could trap *them* if they do not swim fast enough through the tight escape hatch. What does it hold out to *Aling* Dionisia, who thinks that her grandchildren will be returning home now that Marcos has fled?

Because of EDSA they now have large expectations, including a government that will incur guilt for infidelity to those expectations, and leaders who do not think they are more than what they are. Because they have seen the Virgin praying on her beads, some want immediately to go past the wounds that dislocate their lives, want all hurts to cease.

"I can't believe the Prime Minister of Sweden can be assassinated," Bastian Canonigo says. "I thought that happens only in underdeveloped countries."

"What I want to know is where the presidential yacht is, with all the gold bullions?" Siso replies.

Without a word Benhur returns his empty bottle of San Miguel to the case set in the shade of the *ylang-ylang* his father planted along with *sampaguita* shrubs; he walks toward his grandmother's house.

Patro comes after him with a bunch of the grapes he brought, ten grapes clinging to the dried stem inside a bag made from old newspapers. "So you won't arrive empty-handed."

"I've never asked without his helping me," Siso Feleo says. "I don't even have to ask Benhur. He knows when I need."

"He's not embarrassed to carry packages," Dionisia says, joining in the appraisal of Benhur as if he were a candidate being recommended to them for election. "*Aling* Cory should appoint him instead of the turncoats who have more sides than a *balimbing.* And if I can choose between *Aling* Cory and *Aling* Patro, I'll elect our Patro."

"Benhur's modest." Siso Feleo will not be sidetracked. "When we were in school he was just like one of us, though he was our valedictorian every year. He got along with everyone. *Magaling makisama.*"

The labor leader Bien Sotero expands the subject, "I can't understand some of the appointments Cory has made. Officials who enriched themselves under Marcos. I can't see what good having an upright leader is if the appointees are crooked. The good thing so far is the release of political prisoners. Some . . ."

"The big names," Siso says. "Nani's brother Canlas is still inside, though he cannot spell *communist* if his life depends upon it. And those employees who will be terminated I pity. How will their children enroll in school?"

"The thing to do is make a lot of noise," Bastian Canonigo says. "Then you'll get an appointment."

"I make a lot of noise, but nothing has happened to me," Siso says, making the others laugh. "I won't even be lucky enough to go to the Palace and see Imelda's bathroom so I can judge if oppression is the same as opulence."

"They've been washed," Benhur lays the grapes on the sill beside his grandmother, then brings her right hand to his forehead. "Next time I'll bring you more."

"Take them back with you. You don't remember when I went to market in Dulong Bayan. Either there or San Andres for fruits. Nothing forced to ripen in *carburo.* Rice that did not require *pandan* leaves to give it fragrance. My husband gave me his paycheck every week. 'Here,' he would say. And the envelope would not be open. Off to the market I would go." She takes another look at the grapes, which appear to have dried in her presence. "Now, it's hardly worth sitting down to eat. I used to throw away what I have to eat now."

"Where's the electric bill, so I can pay it?" Benhur sits across from his grandmother who sits with her feet on the front edge of her chair, covered by the hem of her loose and long skirt. "Let me have it."

"Let Meralco cut off the electricity. It charges a fortune for thickening the skin into dark leather."

"*Si Lola* Sula," Benhur exclaims. It is useless to argue.

"When we were young an aunt gave us little doses of a white powder. It was to whiten our skin. Our veins were like faint tracings on rose petals. She also gave us lavender soap which she said is how heaven smells."

Benhur smiles. He leans back to watch her. Heavy bands of gold pull down her ear lobes close to her head until she looks like a museum piece, a folk sculpture of lost ancestry. No more are loose blouses and long skirts with deep pockets worn by old women, whose loose housedresses reveal their skinny legs, unless they are rich old women who wear pants and gowns to take dancing lessons from instructors young enough to be their grandsons or great-grandsons, for whose undivided attention they quarrel among themselves like cats.

"Why don't you come to the house?" Benhur entices her to go with him. Patro tells him that Milang, the other daughter-in-law, plays *mahjong* all day and most of the night; returns only to ask for more money. When her children were small, Milang would give them a *pan de sal* each, and strict orders to say they had had supper when anyone asked.

She continues to suck her gums, looking at the sky between the branches of trees. Patro says that Sula no longer cares to chew, asks only for *lugao,* the grains of rice translucent from the water they have absorbed through long cooking. Vergel says she suffers tiny strokes while she sits there by herself, facing the tamarind tree with its trunk leaning backward like a woman heavy with child, around which molasses used to be poured to make it bear sweet fruits. Ants came from all over Gulod.

"Let's go to Luneta."

"How will I get there?"

"I'll bring the car as far down as it will go, so you won't have to walk far. I'll carry you to it."

"And what will the curious say? No thank you. They will say I fell or died. When a road is built to my door, I'll go to Luneta with you. I've been there many times. Besides, cars do not impress me. My father had a Packard."

"Yes?" He does not recall hearing this before.

"We had pictures of us sitting inside, my father in the driver's seat, though he never drove. We had a chauffeur with eleven fingers, so we called him Eleven. Onze. He could pass another car on the road so close without having an accident, barely lifting up the paint! It's just as well we had the pictures taken."

"Why, *Lola?*"

"*Naremata! Itay* lost it by missing one payment. That's how my mother found out he did not pay cash. *Escandalong malaki.* Installment payment then was the same as *estafa.* Nothing convinced her it was all right; all the rich were paying the American way. Suppose the debtor died? How would he know his children kept up the payments. Wouldn't he burn in hell then?"

He waits to be told more.

"My mother and her sisters embroidered *mantons.* Manton de Manila was the craze in Madrid then. Flowers as large as cabbages on the shawls. When the Americans came, they made as much sewing buttons on uniforms. Then they sewed infant wear for an American who bought out the Spaniard who returned to Spain. El Diablo, they called the American. He had this habit of walking behind them as they worked at a long table. Soon enough, one of them would feel his hand under her *alampay,* moving like a caterpillar on hairy legs. Just as itchy, they said. He didn't need a tail. Nose was long enough and hooked."

Benhur looks down at his shoes. Still uncomfortable, he turns his chair about to sit the way his uncles used to sit when they came, arms propped on the back of the chairs: after dropping a coin in each child's hand. The look of gratitude on his nephews' faces when he gave them money recalls his own.

"They wore beaded skirts, *sayas* splendid enough to wear to receptions, when they worked. Overskirts beaded, *de cola,* as if they were ladies of leisure still. They wore their *serpentinas* pulled up and over an arm to free the ends from dragging when they walked. As if there were servants to attend them."

As unbearable as loneliness, the story fills him with dread. He wants to interrupt her. What laws did they break with their bodies? What signs of love came to them and did not die? The air between him and his grandmother is sputtering, forcing him to face mortality in the stories of people he never knew—aunts and uncles, cousins; that American, wherever he was for trying to crawl under the skirts of the women who worked for him, grabbing from behind. Whom did those aunts' first-borns resemble? Too late for him to protect, the places of their virginity were just one more foreigner's handholds: their lives the early counterpart of those children who lived in the streets of Manila and in the outskirts of resorts, offering themselves to foreigners who came precisely for that purpose. How many ever escaped the dark spectrums of life?

She sits there now, sucking her tongue as if it is a sweet fruit and looking toward the trail as if someone expected is coming to visit. The pitch of this thought is of inescapable curse. It brings to Benhur the possibility that the place or state they called Paradise is several and different, existing actually, only in dreams.

Her silence makes Benhur think she is waiting for a star to fall.

"Lola," he calls, before her silence twists his heart into grieving. But he has it, too; that familiar lapse into thinking so deep, it renders him inaudible except to himself. He caught it from her; from her through his father, who used to stand overlooking the river, in rapt attention to his thoughts while the shadows of clouds passed over him, moving the ground at his feet. He has no one to whom to pass it on. Not all sons become fathers or all fathers know their sons.

She does not turn.

"Lola?" Is it the same silence to which Sister Madeleine is called? A gathering forgetfulness? "*Lola.* I remember a tree with chains of gold flowers in back of the house," he tries to pull himself out of darker thoughts. "It bore flowers in March and bloomed as late as April until the leaves started to come out?" The same kind of tree he saw in the States. Rain tree it was called there. Golden rain tree, fixed in sunlight.

"All I remember is a tree of Paradise. We are born looking for it, don't you know? Life is a journey to look for it. My mother thought she was giving birth to angels, so she did not mind the pain. I asked her when I was a little girl, and she told me. She was very beautiful. When she was old and heard someone talking to her, she would say it was God keeping her company for bearing thirteen angels. Not one died at birth, you know. All her pictures were lost in the fire during the Japanese Occupation."

Benhur gets up, swings the chair around to set it in the place where he found it, coming into the porch.

"Are you leaving? Why, you have just come."

He sits down again, slightly off to one side. For some time they sit, exchanging constancy in their silence, while the sun moves its shade across the doorway, and she sits on her bones; someone trying, and failing, to escape a hungry season. The light is clinging like a scent to her hair.

"Lola."

"How did you know? Everything was lost in that war. In that fire. Children slipped out of their mothers' hands and were lost. In front of me one woman was carrying an *orinola.* She had picked up the chamber pot, thinking it was her child. My husband tried to carry me. My left side—arm and leg—was burned, but I did not feel it until we reached the fields and I felt burned by the wind. It was only that my flesh had melted. The doctor said I would not live. For a year in the mountains I lay on one side. This side was just like the membrane covering a stillborn child. Two children died and were buried in the fields there. The doctor could not believe I was still alive when I returned a year later, after the American bombs drove out the Japanese. The doctor began to court me. I was forty. He had a wife. If you ask me, I would prefer to be a *querida* instead of a wife. A mistress does not lose face. But I did not like him. There was always a fighting cock over his arm. And he was a collaborator and had begun to smell like a dog. A dog's saliva exactly. That's how people could tell he collaborated."

Ricebirds drop through the branches of a *camias* tree, through the hibiscus branching without thorns, bearing red and yellow flowers.

"Bring me a bottle of the perfume I use, Benhur. I asked Milang to get me one and it does not smell the same. The contents might have been siphoned out and the bottle refilled. I need perfume when I have a headache and feel ill."

Pleased to have his grandmother particular about her luxuries, Benhur paraphrases what he recalls her saying. "Perfume reflects the quality of a person."

"No, Benhur. Jewels reflect the quality of a woman. You mustn't change the words." Gratitude does not restrain her. Benhur might pay for her new roof, the room added for Milang, jalousies so the windows will be burglar-proof, but she will not let him get away with even inconsequential matters.

Benhur does not resent this. A moment earlier his grandmother had appeared scattered, but now her thoughts are fully gathered again. "What else would you like?" He had in mind *corchos* to replace the worn-out slippers under her chair. Once when he had asked that question, offering to get her a chair with a seat that vibrated, she had shot back: "What! I'm too old to be aroused. Besides, there are no good men in Gulod."

Again she sits with the confidence of someone used to flattery. Could she have been speaking of herself in the women who sewed buttons for the American? Ingesting arsenic? The admission can uncharitably identify her with the professional beauties in Manila, who offer themselves up as a man's ultimate and personal decoration, hanging onto his arm like the flower on his lapel, arousing quick and impermanent passions.

Benhur notices that the gold band on her finger has worn down to the width of fine thread. If he offers her a new ring, what emotion will it set off in her? "What was *Lolo*'s name?" he tries to get her talking again. Her silence frightens him.

"You have forgotten? Jeremias!"

"Who was Flaviano then?"

"His brother. They were often mistaken for twins. Their sister's name was Agrifina; and her daughter, Columba. The name came from Irish missionaries. The mother of Flaviano's wife used to give us picnics in San Jose. Bancas would take us to the sandbar in the middle of the river that comes down from Cagayan. This was in the summer when the water was low. We waded. Food was brought to us in their cooking pots. There was all the fruit we could want or eat. On the banks there was a *camachile,* prickly with thorny leaves. Sometimes we picnicked in the dam area. On the way home we gave away the food to those we happened to pass."

Once more fat with memories, she sits in her doorway like a formal portrait of her young self. This time she does not speak of the dam suddenly being released above, of a niece and cousin being swept away, holding on to each other.

"You had good times."

"There were fiestas all year round. When we arrived, people would say: 'Here come the beauty queens!' Young men waited outside, in case we looked out of the windows, so we could see them. We merely peeked . . . It was improper to be seen looking . . . The young men lingered and lingered."

"And your noses got stuck in the sky." He imagined them walking between candles and admirers as if they were Magdalenes fleeing the Cross with demure smiles. The *elenas* he escorted when he was young—because he was tall and indifferent, each tried to be the one who made him smile—pretended to ignore him, too. That was Patro's advice to Loreto while dressing her up for the May processions, fitting a tiara purchased in Villalobos while Loreto fidgeted. He recalls the young women's breasts were as hard as *santols* under copies of couture gowns. Villalobos on Plaza Miranda was where Patro bought *corchos* with *abalorios.* As women aged, they chose high colors like maroon.

"Everything was proper then. Girls did not have a coming-out party if they had already been seen in public. There were no more beauties among us than among other families, but there were fewer ugly ones." A hint of cat and mouse creeps into her voice. "Where do you suppose you got your good looks? My brothers used only imported brilliantine on their hair. On Sundays they visited us in the convent schools. The other day I dreamed of Vergel. He had come to tell me someone died."

Benhur quickly changes the topic. "*Lola,* do you know who's president now?"

She sits, refusing to answer; as if trying to keep the place where God has set her down, where He would return for her; as if she has not just told him that young men waited for them to alight from *calesins* drawn by frisky horses and having just enough roof to keep out the sun and direct rain; young men waited to catch sight of their insteps as they lifted their skirts, practising the devotions they would later on dedicate to the statues of saints.

Benhur wants only the stories that make him co-exist with cousins, aunts, and uncles in the bloom of their lives; stories his grandmother used to recall when they would lie next to her in bed after supper, spinning them with the same words each time, beginning and ending exactly as before; stories that come to him sometimes as the day ends in his office on Maria Orosa; stories that are his lifeblood, his bloodlines and spiritual genes which, now, make everything he sees in that garden a part of what he feels, of what is stored in the cells of his body; stories with which to fight failure and illness and loss; stories they each brought to EDSA, making it possible.

It feels as if she has moved away, joining the distance of other and many lives, prompting him to call out.

"*Lola.* Marcos has fled to Hawaii. Who's the president now?"

The line along her neck and arm lifts with the late afternoon shadows stretching. She looks toward him. "I won't tell you," she says, ending the easy flirtation of their thoughts.

They come at him

in a rush, their voices tumbling as they race to be the first to reach him; and Benhur, surprised by the fury of their welcome, almost falls backward from the force of their coming. They can't all be Vitalianos, he thinks, trying with difficulty to sort them.

"*Tito* Benhur, buy me a robot," Pitong begs, surprising the others with the request, so that they fight even more intensely for Benhur's attention, making their own demands.

"What kind?" Benhur asks, happy enough not to think of houses burning on both sides of a street, forcing people to run to the center, to run between the cracks of the flames that ooze, it appears, from the sky. "What kind?" Aren't they too old for toys?

"Mega Motobot," Ryan says.

"Diakron, *Tito* Benhur," Pitong pulls at Benhur's hand. "It can be converted into attack vehicles."

"Govarian can be converted into a tank," Atlas nudges his brother, and calls off other names: Killer Spider, Destructor Beetle, Laserobot.

Atlas tells Benhur the movable parts of the robots are interchangeable. "Get those equipped either with action guns or swords and shields. Get space-cutters, *Tito* Benhur. I want Cosmoboy with radio-control antennae. Not the miniature ones from Taiwan."

"I don't want Laserobot," Atlas changes his mind. "That's only die-cast metal. I want the one that costs a thousand two hundred. I saw it. A friend in school."

"You don't need violent toys," Benhur says, recalling that Marcos banned Japanese-made cartoons to protect his grandchildren from the aggressive behavior of the characters. When he was home during the snap elections, the boys came in from playing basketball only to watch Voltes on Channel 4.

"How about racing cars, then?" Ryan asks.

"They are more expensive," Atlas says. "My classmate's father built a realistic endurance course for his radio-controlled cars. *Tito* Benhur, they cost six thousand each."

"Your friend's father?" Ryan asks. "I didn't know you have a rich friend."

"I said my friend's father works for a man who has a miniature course in his backyard," Atlas says. "Cars can go sixty mph. Dune-buggies are controlled by an electronic beam. He said he watches those racing cars collide in five-minute heats. It's like real driving. You need sharp reflexes and good field intelligence."

"Not your friend's father. Your friend's father's employer," Ryan stresses the difference. "I can learn to drive later on. I want a Mega Motobot, *Tito* Benhur."

"Instead of robots, I'll put the money in the bank. In your names," Benhur offers. "You can save the interest and use it for your studies."

"Oooooh." They groan simultaneously.

"I did not have any money in my name until I was in college," Benhur says. "Not my own bank account." The offer, he hopes, will give them dreams beyond making a three-point shot at the basket; beyond running to town, riding free in the jeepneys of drivers from Gulod; beyond merely existing in brief thrills; beyond the downward spiral toward addiction, stealing, or sex. "You can go to the bank with me. Not now. Next time. And we'll apply for the accounts."

They refuse to be saved from destructive impulses that can rob their future of direction. "Nooooo." They shake their heads, dogmatic in their determination.

"Let's go home and talk about it with *Nanay,*" Benhur leads the way to his mother Patro, an arm each around Pitong and Atlas. How can he be offering the boys banks accounts when he has been desperately figuring out how to get enough dollars to go abroad on his own? Sixty thousand dollars can get him a trader's visa. No questions asked at immigration. Even if he were to ask Osong, his friend could not manage it.

"How much will you put in the bank? For each of us?" Pitong asks and the others wait for Benhur's answer.

"We'll see," Benhur says. "Enough. Don't worry."

"That's where I live," a small boy points, tapping Benhur on the arm. "My mother has a baby."

"He's lying," Ryan pushes the small boy away, stands between him and Benhur, who has stopped to listen to the boy. "He lives with the nuns. He's a *pulot.* He has no mother because he was just *found.*"

"I have a brother," the small boy says.

"You were found on the railroad tracks by Mandaluyong, and he brought you to the nun who grows herbs and dries them for medicine for the poor," Atlas says, picking up the boy and carrying him alongside Benhur. "Come with us. *Lola* Patro has *lumpia.* She'll give you one."

"It's not meat but fish she mixes with the vegetables," Ryan makes a face. *"Dalagang bukid."*

"What's wrong?" Benhur asks, trying to keep his balance as the children push him along, each trying to stand closest to him.

"Ryan eats only meat," Atlas says, setting the small boy down. Running behind Benhur, he slips between Ryan and Pitong. "If there's only fish, Ryan will eat just rice and *toyo.* Soy sauce on everything. That's why he's thinner than a dragonfly."

"I'm not." Ryan hits Atlas with a left hook. "If I really hit you, you wouldn't be able to get up."

Benhur intercepts the next punch. Ryan reminds him more and more of Demetrio, who did not talk much. At the table Demetrio ate quickly. *In case there's a war,* he used to joke. When they were still in short pants, Demetrio would bring leaves to *Lola* Sula. *What will I do with it?* she would ask, amused. *Am I to play house and cook the leaves in a toy pot?*

Loreto said one of the boys was given fifty pesos by a man. No one could get him to say why, but he has been taking a bath every time the drums are filled. As if he's itchy. Immediately, Benhur felt violated, personally challenged. But, so as not to alarm his sister, he merely said he would talk to the boy. With the nephews running about happy, Benhur feels even more afraid for them, as if they are land being lost to the sea; beyond redress. How can he go to the States with the boys needing him?

"Mandaluyong!" the boys whisper as a man with a heavy face and collarbones jutting out like elbows walks toward them on the trail. Something closer to awe keeps them from making fun of him as he walks all over Gulod planting *ampalaya,* okra, *upo,* eggplants, beans, *patola* which he never claims or harvests. At night he sits with the men at the outposts, performing *zona* so thieves and druggies will keep away. People in Gulod leave him alone. Some throw bread at him; others allow him to sit in their yards, or doorways. It is said he has a good voice and used to sing in church, at the Opera House, in vaudeville.

Benhur waits to greet Mandaluyong, but the man does not look up. It seems he has just come from Bastian Canonigo, who saves a jar of coffee in which to serve Mandaluyong some drink.

"Come, see my roosters," Bastian Canonigo waits for their approach. "Benhur, those children look as if they have different mothers? Are they all yours? All first-borns?" He teases.

Without entering, Benhur looks over the fence at the roosters staked to the ground on T-posts, their feathers exceeding the iridescence of beetles' wings, their wattles brighter red than *macopas.* He chooses not to reply to Bastian's remark.

"This one is worth a thousand," Bastian says. "And that one is even more expensive . . ."

"Who owns them?"

"A Chinese millionaire from Binondo, who farms out his roosters among several of us so a pest will not wipe them out. These are better fed than me. They get fresh eggs, and vitamins, and a special white powder."

"Opium?"

"Perhaps. They have their own doctor, too. But when they lose, into the pot for them."

"Do they taste like a thousand pesos?"

"The way Meding cooks . . . with Chinese pickles. The next time, I'll send you some." Bastian picks up a rooster. He lifts it up, then holds it on his arm, close to his body. "I lie awake every night because just one rooster stolen . . . with my hard luck. Did you hear about the coffee plantation I almost had?"

Except for Ryan and the small boy, the others have left. Benhur remembers himself small, his treasures contained in a Guitara matchbox: beetles, spiders. "What plantation?"

"It's a long story," Bastian says. "Calero and I were going to be millionaires. Instead of taking care of someone else's roosters, I would be the one going to the derby with thousands of pesos. I would be a millionaire, but not cheap. I would give out *balatos* when my roosters win; not like my boss. I thought the roosters would provide tuition for my sons. Am I wrong! A few pesos is all I get; and promises. *If that wins or this wins.* This one—look at the scales—has won three times. Meding has my son's, the younger one's, test papers. All perfect scores. But do you think my Chinese boss will give him *balato?*"

In answer, Benhur smiles and shakes his head. Men always persist in something, live in hopes of when they can break away. Or they dream of saving everyone and fail to see someone begging.

"I should just get Magnolia day-old chicks for P14 each. In two months they grow to two kilos. At fifty a kilo now, that's already a profit of 86 pesos. If I got a few, say 100, that's P1,400 capital. Do you think the Chinese will lend it to me?"

"Don't forget, there's also chicken feed to buy," Benhur reminds Bastian, but he does not tell him to make allowances for deaths among the chicks. He remembers when they had a hen. Her brood always tried to come into the house and some would get caught in the door, instantly dying.

"The younger one wants to be a lawyer. Like you. He wants to work at McDonald's at night and save for his tuition. Even the rich kids work there, he says. He's waiting for an opening. P9 an hour is not bad."

"That's good. There's also Wendy's and Jollibee."

"He's bright. Took after Meding. You should see his medals from debating! If only I could drive again. Get my license. But everything is beyond my reach. The only cheap thing in the country is a Filipino. There's so many of him, that's why. No wonder we're a banana republic. But we can't even afford bananas."

"Siso also wants to drive," Benhur says. If Benhur could afford to buy a jeepney, as Siso imagines, he'd buy one and let Siso take it out for a boundary. Siso offered him P130 a day, figuring his daily total at P200. He would make P70, and Nani could stay home.

"Maybe the roosters will also lay eggs, Benhur," Bastian says. "Maybe I'll just hold illegal cockfights at two in the morning. I have a good sense of smell. I can smell the police. At night I can smell robbers planning to steal the roosters and I'm at the window in time to foil them. I turn on the lights and light a cigarette. That's the reason I can't drive jeeps. I'd die from the smell of armpits."

"Bastian, come to the house for beer," Benhur says. "*Nay* has only people who take a bath once a day. At least."

The remark sends Bastian laughing, bringing Meding to the window to see what is going on. "You didn't serve Attorney anything, Bastian. Ask him in."

"Thank you. I'm expected home. The boys are waiting for me. Another time." Benhur latches the gate, catching the *malvarosa* that throws off its spicy scent as he brushes against the branches. "Come to the house. There is a little *salo-salo*."

"Do you like school?" Benhur asks Ryan who has been waiting for him, along with the little boy who lives with the nuns. "It's always good to get a degree."

"Just like it's always good to be baptized?"

Surprised, Benhur can only ask, "Why do you say that?"

"Because nothing is any good. My friend Elias studied until the books were coming out of his ears, but even if he gets through, how many years will it be? And what job will give him enough? Not even if he starts working now. There are some whose walls are lined with diplomas and they are jobless. Unless they go to Saudi and risk getting their hands cut off."

Benhur has forgotten the impatience of the young. Once, he himself felt life was too many years ahead. Out of reach until too late. Long periods of thought must have formed Ryan's reply. Perhaps he is the one who inherited their silence, the brute anguish, the anger that frustrates and makes him wish not to have to wake up in the morning. Not Ryan who eats at a run, climbs the monument of Rizal in the plaza and once was caught trying to climb the church belltower from the outside, hanging on to the stones as to a cliff! Is this the one he is supposed to talk sense into? to save from the movie producer who wants him to star in a film if Ryan will live with him? What advice of his will Ryan take? *Go to school and get a job? Say a Hail Mary? Take ginseng or some other impotent magic for potent wounds?*

"I was baptized." The little boy tugs at Benhur's hand. "Everyone has to be baptized because everyone dies."

The statement sounds so like a plea that Benhur presses the tiny hand. If the atoms that exploded into stars when the universe was created continue to exist in his body, in Ryan, in the boy, are they each other's co-heirs? That's a more intimate, ultimate relationship than bloodline; a genealogy that predates Christian times, history; entailing obligations outside and beyond laws; before man legislated. All answers too heavy to be spoken.

"*Tito* Benhur, let me see," Ryan faces Benhur, walking backward on the trail. "When did we win the Asian Interclub title? The Asian Basketball

Confederation title? How many games apiece do we have with China? What about the World Cup Championship? When? Where?" Rapid-fire questions. "The years in order, *Tito* Benhur. The years we won the SouthEast Asia games."

Unable to give any answer, Benhur finds himself being arm-wrestled on both sides; he feels like a boy with them, unscathed as yet by Tuesday morning in Constitutional Law . . .

"Did she eat the grapes?" Loreto asks Benhur as they come into the yard. "She won't eat while you're there, so she can say she feeds it to the cat. What cat? Milang never cooks. If we did not send her anything, she'd starve. But is she grateful?"

"There, arm-wrestle with *her. She's* the tough one." Benhur tries to unload the two boys on his sister while deflating her bitterness. "She said you're the one who never forgets her."

"Liar!"

"Go ask her." Benhur is frightened by the silent way Loreto looks while she talks tough. It is an admission of giving up her right to be in the world, of her willingness to be trapped in Gulod to please her mother. Under the shadow of leaves Loreto still looks like a child, as young as Anya who stands aside smiling, not yet tainted with broken willfulness. Loreto already has the face she will have when she grows old. When and where can she begin again? With him in the States?

"People thought you had left. Come and talk to them." Loreto leads Benhur inside as if he's a guest.

Benhur places an arm about her. Should he take her along? Would she leave their mother? It was not so long ago when she would be standing, and suddenly she'd fall, foaming at the mouth. They learned to foretell the onset. *Patay ang tingin.* On noting the glazed look, they would pinch her nostrils to make her fight for breath and stop the seizure. If that did not work, they tried to insert a spoon into her mouth so Loreto would not bite off her tongue. Vergel prescribed medication. Stress, tension, and worry supposedly could bring it on. But Patro has not reported any fits lately.

Benhur greets those who arrived after he left. He sits among various neighbors and relatives under the shade in the front yard while Loreto walks into the house. Sister Madeleine is certainly luckier than his sister. Elen Rodrigo chose the better lot. Like a father, Benhur wishes Loreto had married, that she had good children and a comfortable home, a steady though modest income. Who in turn will wish for him? Sister Madeleine? What will her wish be for someone who leaves his clothes at the cleaners, picking up only a change of clothes each time; whose belongings will fit into suitcases? His obituary should be interesting; all three lines of it.

Patro comes out after Loreto takes her place in the kitchen. "Did she like the grapes?"

"She did," Benhur lies. How does anyone ever know what another person likes? He feels blurred. With so many loyalties struggling inside him, he can't respond to everyone's expectations.

Aling Dionisia waits until Patro has seated herself before speaking. "I want to say to *Aling* Cory to make us whole again. *Buuin tayong mabuti,* so we can forget Marcos. So my grandchildren will think of coming back. This country is even more torn than my clothes."

"I thought EDSA would go on for months," Patro says when *Aling* Dionisia looks in her direction. "Who could have predicted we would live through it and still be here."

"It might turn out to be just another rumor," Siso Feleo says, holding his youngest child between his knees as he sits next to Benhur. "It's like tomorrow. If you see the sun, you might think it's morning and tomorrow. Maybe it's not. It's like just because the banks are open and PAL is flying to California again, we think EDSA is over and we won."

"Filosofo!" several of the neighbors say good-naturedly. "Siso, you should be a senator so you can round our heads like a ball. That's all politics is. *Bilugan ng ulo.*"

"Look. Nani said bananas are still one peso each. *Aling* Maxima sells them for 90 *centavos* when they get bruised. *Galunggong* has not gone down. Cory should make the prices go down so the poor can eat." Siso allows the child to take the bottle of beer; does not see it sip.

"Don't worry," Eliadora Guzman says. "Cory will take care of us. We are her family now. She will fight for us as she fights for her children. You will see. Bus fares will go down; land titles will be given to those who have no land; jobs to those who want to work. Imelda's Bliss houses that were abandoned after the contractors got paid will be fixed, and we can apply for housing there. We can have milk in our coffee. We are lucky to see this happen. The Communists will surrender and all will be peaceful again. No NPAs."

Bien Sotero, the labor leader, looks across to Benhur. "We'll see. Why should the Communists surrender without a program of reform? Cory is considering declaring her government revolutionary. Will that not give her more powers than Marcos?"

"She will use it with restraint and for the good of the country," Patro says.

"Our heads are turned by the victory parades," Bien Sotero says. "Thousands marching with banners: *Free Again.* But hundreds of political detainees are still imprisoned. Only the big names are being released, being feted by the socialites. I'll wait. Doing a Marcos to get rid of Marcos is no help to the country. The traditions and precedents must be set right. Don't you think so, Attorney? Without reform, no revolution took place."

Benhur knows Bien Sotero means that Marcos used democratic principles to establish a dictatorship. Can dictatorial principles establish a democracy? Restore. Recover. If the difference between the two administrations is that between hard and soft pornography, what has been achieved? Government reduced to seductions and impersonations. "Yes, Bien. Marcos is not the measure of what is right, or wrong."

"Look, Attorney. If we are against the bases of the Americans, we are called Communists. If we are not enthusiastic about Cory, we're Marcos loyalists. What happens to the independent?"

"The one for the country, you mean?"

"The Japanese will come in if the American bases go," Siso Feleo says. "In fact they're all over already. But I will die for Cory. Too bad we can't live on rumors. When I heard Thursday that Marcos died, I jumped up, forgetting our ceiling is just my height. Twenty minutes later, the news was denied. I will die for Cory any time."

"If I have to die, I will die for the country," Bien Sotero says. "I will believe Cory if she releases us from poverty and takes care of our foreign debt. $26 billion! And no more corruption. Protection of workers' rights."

"Your list is growing, Bien," Siso notices.

"Only what we're entitled to."

"Benhur," Siso calls, "what I'm afraid of is this Snap Age. We had a snap election. Then a snap revolution. This might be a snap government, over before we know it. Don't you think so?"

A silence falls upon them. It would be far better, they realize, if Siso Feleo were just being clever instead of prophetic. They sit as if they do not want anyone else to know that roots are bursting through their bodies from the sun humming through the trees, spilling seeds and birds.

Loreto, trailed by Anya, comes out with a plate of spring rolls stuffed with fish; tells Anya to return to the kitchen with the empty dishes; then stands in the doorway white with fragrance, looking down the trail and up again. "Estong is coming. He is late with the mail."

"The *novios* come," Patro gets up to greet Sabel Martinez and her husband, walking arm-in-arm down to the gate.

"We used to be younger," Araw Martinez explains. "Now it takes us all day to arrive. We used to wear shoes, too; but we save the pairs we have, for when we go to Manila about our recognition."

"They all know about that," Sabel Martinez says, smiling at each one, taking Benhur's seat only after much hesitation.

"Benhur was still a law student when he went with me to Malacañang, after I found out that the Guerrilla Recognition Program is a government-to-government negotiation. It was ordered closed in 1948. Many of us were still fighting in 1945 when it was established, so we were excluded from the records." Araw is wearing a pale blue shirt over *maong* jeans—and too-large rubber thongs.

Sabel Martinez places a hand over his. "They've heard all that before." Partial to pretty things, she is dressed in a shift with flowers, lifting a hand to her mouth when she smiles in order to hide the gap in her teeth. She used to wear shiny material, the kind that looks like metallic thread, clothes more proper to wear in the evening. And beads on her slippers and handbag. Curved combs with rhinestones.

"Cory will help poor veterans like me get recognition," Araw Martinez adds to the hopes being exchanged in the Vitaliano yard. "She understands the poor."

"His pension went into our transportation, going from one government office to the next. To Congress. It went into stamps for the letters. I used to list down all the expenses in a notebook until I had it filled to the covers."

"Sabel wrote letters for all the men. Some forgot already the names of their officers and comrades." Araw studies the bottle of beer Loreto gave him. "Many never knew the official names of their units. But she wrote many letters, copying the one Benhur wrote, I don't know how many times. She studied with the nuns, so her handwriting is good enough for formal invitations."

Her smile slips. Tears fall down her face, over the mole the size of a kernel of corn.

"*Aling* Sabel," Eliadora Guzman leans over to pat her hand. "You must have that mole removed or you will have more griefs than you can count. It is directly in the path of your tears."

"An American congresswoman, Edith Rogers of Massachusetts, wrote back to me," Araw Martinez says, his voice clinging to his wife as he looks at her. "This Rogers sponsored a resolution setting up the procedure for reopening the program. Government-to-government. Then martial law came and Congress was abolished. I have gone to wait outside the offices of four presidents. Magsaysay, Garcia, Macapagal, then Marcos. Now the hope is on Cory. Marcos abolished Congress so I could do nothing while he was president."

"Limping, we still went to the newspaper offices with press releases. A veteran who died at the Veterans Hospital, that's where his crutch came from." Sabel Martinez touches the crutch between them. "It's a one-man lobby. It's slow work."

"Xerox costs 70 centavos a page even if it is so faint," Araw says. "Ten copies can buy a kilo of rice. One time, we went home by way of Echague. Where they have the Chinese groceries. We could not afford the ham, not even one gram, but I looked. Then I asked the *despachadora* for a taste. 'That sliver,' I pointed to a piece of fat on the side of the pan. She gave it to me when the owner was not looking."

"I was embarrassed," Sabel says. "And he even asked me if I wanted a taste. It was so transparent, I could not see it on the end of the knife."

"The words just came out of me, without my realizing I was begging." Araw looks surprised at himself.

"Many times I thought of doing that," the man who used to pan for gold admitted. "Maybe next time, I'll make myself brave and ask." His hands white from kneading mercury into the particles of sand before squeezing the amalgam through the cloth and boiling this until the mercury vaporizes, he rests his elbows on each knee as he sits forward, exactly as if he's holding the wooden *pabirile* or *pusod* where particles swirl and settle as the water ebbs.

Benhur gets up. He finds it painful to be in Gulod where people seem to have lost even their names, have become bodies roped together with barbed wire, throbbing like moths. It is worse than the camps housing Vietnamese refugees on their way to the States. For them he used to think he would be brave and wise. They astonished him with their enduring will to live. Simply out of respect, he should stop thinking about Tuesday morning in Constitutional Law.

At the gate he waits for Estong Calero to reach the house. People he does not recognize walk past, asking permission to pass the house. He would ask them in, except it would offend those they knew from the beginning, to be entertained with those who have appeared in Gulod so suddenly, almost as if they have simply fallen to the earth.

A moist and upright spectacle, the Black Forest cake shimmers past the neighbors in the Vitalianos' front yard, stopping all conversation. Breathless behind the maid carrying the cake, Sally Moscoso asks immediately for Benhur. "An important matter," she tells Patro and Loreto, who follow her inside the house.

"He has just left," Loreto says, wondering if Sally will leave the cake after that information. "He was here just until a while ago. You didn't pass him on the trail? I'm surprised."

"He and his compadre stood me up yesterday."

"Osong?"

Sally's anger returns full force and it almost slips through her own words that the cake was brought by Osong Wednesday when he and Benhur came to ask for a favor. "Who else? Osong wanted me to get him an appointment but where were they? It was embarrassing. I went to the Cojuangco building for nothing." She even had her hair done. A fresh manicure and a quick facial she didn't need until Sunday.

"Stay for supper," Patro says, coming out from having hurriedly prepared the ingredients for *morcon,* which she would have already prepared if Benhur had stayed. All she has to do now is slice the piece of beef—about as big only as her hand, until it unfolds, the size of a large man's handkerchief—stuff it and tie it up into a roll. "Have an *okoy* while you're waiting."

The golden fritter of squash topped with tiny shrimps entices Sally but also makes her think of the party she had planned on Osong's birthday which EDSA simply blew away. Here, the Vitalianos are having a party without having invited anyone. However, it's the quality of the guests that counts. Here there is no one she would speak to or even greet.

"Vinegar and garlic?" Loreto sends Anya for sauce to go with the *okoy.* "Anya, turn up the electric fan for Sally."

"I'm on a diet, you know." Sally turns the plate around. "No vetsin. No white sugar." Since she discovered the Healthy You in Greenhills, she has been into ginseng, royal jelly, and bee pollen. For the boys, brain-power vitamins. She has been spending as if the choice is between money in the bank and good health. "Okay. Just one, though."

Loreto places another *okoy* on Sally's plate. "Your skin is drying out from eating only health food, Sally. Didn't you see the survey that said the low-income diet provides more nutrients than a meal in an expensive restaurant? It was on TV."

"No more after this," Sally says. "And don't send some for the boys because I'll end up eating the food!" She anticipates their hospitality.

"Have you tried the new method of losing weight you were telling me about?" Loreto sits down across from Sally. "You know—thermal waves to accelerate the biochemical processes and enzyme activity so body fat is dissolved without exercising."

"I haven't had time. There was the party, then EDSA. Now, Osong. Let's go together. The first consultation is free. Marce France Bodyline International. I'm sure they will give franchises. Can I have a glass of Coke? Let's diet together, Loreto."

Loreto asks Anya to get the Coke. "Me? Diet? Hadn't you noticed? Everyone in Gulod is on starvation diet."

"You're always joking, Loreto. It promises no hunger. No pills. No exercise. I'll send for you when I go. Next week probably."

Just outside the window a spirited discussion about brewing *lambanog* cuts into their conversation. Bastian Canonigo is saying all it takes to make something as good as the American White Lightning, as good as Batch One Rare Whiskey, is a piece of bamboo, a chopping board, coolant, and an aluminum buoy to act as condenser. "What comes out does not burn the throat but goes down like grease. Melted butter."

"No wonder Benhur did not stay," Sally says, getting up. "Don't serve the cake. It's just for the family. Already I feel like a padded clothes hanger from the *okoy.* That's my supper. *Aling* Patro, thank you."

"It's only *okoy,* Sally. Thank you for the cake." Patro has brought out a plate of *okoy* for the boys.

Sally engages Loreto in conversation up to the gate in order to ignore the neighbors in the front yard. As soon as she's past hearing, she knows they will make fun of her, especially that Siso Feleo, who never stops telling people he and Benhur were classmates. Once she asked her brother to let Siso drive his passenger jeepney on Siso's promise of P150 each day. Soon enough there were excuses: the tire got flat; he caught TB; his children were sick. Then he got more imaginative. He could not drive because a passenger threatened him for not taking him to the hospital. Then another passenger was mistaken for a hold-upper and was stabbed by the other passengers and the victim's relatives were looking for him.

"Mrs. Moscoso." Siso Feleo greets Sally from his seat.

Sally's first instinct is to pretend she has not heard him, but she recalls Siso rounded up his friends in Gulod when her TV antennae blew down in a typhoon. Then there was that fire that almost jumped her fence, and the neighbors beat it down with rice sacks. Still, to put Siso in his place, she gives a general greeting to everyone. *"Mauuna na po ako sa inyo."* The deferrent *po,* used for elders and higher-ups in position and class, is for effect.

"Who is *that?*" Sally asks Loreto, outside the gate.

"The mail-order bride. She wants a white. Dollars." Loreto walks alongside Sally as the men nearer the gate begin to throw their comments at the woman.

"Malayo pa humahalimuyak na," Siso Feleo is saying, alluding to flowers that from far away attract bees with their fragrance.

Sally does not look back at the woman's hair, a tumult of curls, like produce she must keep balanced on her head on the way to market. She looks up only when Sister Laura comes walking down the trail. "She looks so young," Sally tells Loreto after the nun passes them.

"She comes from a rich family," Loreto says, "and gave up many suitors to become a nun, and to live here in Gulod. Of all places. Sally, can you imagine? But since the nuns came to sleep on the floor of two rooms, near *Lola* Sula, people have stopped quarreling. She was stationed in Tanzania before."

"Really? She's the one who speaks Swahili?"

"Yes. People won't fight in front of her."

"Where do they fight then?" Sally asks, pleased to see Loreto has no answer to that. Why Gulod, of all places? Just misery and poverty all over. Maybe Osong should be asking for that ministry. Ask Cory to create a Ministry of Poverty and name Fructuoso Moscoso as commissioner!

"Why are you smiling?" Loreto asks.

"Nothing. I just thought."

"Thought what?"

"The next time they come to ask a favor, I can make all the choices trouble."

Regretting that she has allowed Miggy and Joel to talk her into attending Thanksgiving Mass at Luneta, Sally Moscoso keeps track of the irritations they will have to make up for.

She is sick of the self-congratulatory tone with which people, all one million of them it seems, recount what they did and saw on EDSA. It's like watching the replay on TV, the sentimental music and messages, the pictures floating and sliding across the screen. So they saw the Virgin stop the Marines on EDSA! When she was young she believed the Virgin touched the *lanzones* and left her fingerprints on the pale fruit to let beggars know it was no longer poisonous.

As part of the celebration of democracy, People Power, and God, entertainment numbers are being performed before Mass. She does not see anyone she knows.

She tries to smell the waves beyond the grandstand. Once she swam all day, but now she is afraid of the sea as containing only sharks and drowned bodies from overturned ships. Each time one of the interislands sinks, she forbids the maids to buy fish.

Then there was the young man Miggy and Joel brought home one night who, without any embarrassment at all, said he lived in Rizal Park. At breakfast he told her, "I shower in the hotels and keep my clothes at the dry cleaners. The only problem is the police. I keep losing my money and watches to them, so I spend everything I make. One of these days I will be in a movie, not just for Betamax, where for twelve hours of shooting one gets paid only fifty. I get more from my clients."

The people whom one meets at demonstrations! "Clients" must mean the Europeans and Australians who come looking for sex, any kind. Recalling this, she looks away while the boys talk to someone resembling that young man, who ignores her until the boys introduce her, then greets her only half-heartedly.

She is glad enough to have the Mass begin so that people are drawn forward in recognizable lines. Still it is hard to breathe, and her attention keeps darting away to anyone who looks as if he might create trouble by throwing fire bombs or knifing someone.

Miggy and Joel stand behind her. During consecration they look for where they will receive Communion. There will be several priests coming down to the people. Lines form like walls. Will there be enough Hosts?

As a child she used to wonder how soon after receiving she could eat ice cream. She did not want Jesus to shiver. Now, many things have changed. Just one hour of abstinence instead of from midnight. One can receive on the hand and touch Jesus. One can receive from lay ministers, which she never does.

The lines are long; the light reflected from the sky and the sea give her a headache. Faint and sick, she cannot formulate her own prayers.

"It's too hot." She turns to the boys on either side of her. "And it's only the second of March." She has forgotten to bring her fan.

"Mamá." Miggy and Joel guide her forward.

"Let's go up ahead. The Host is bigger toward the front. They're already being broken small and smaller here." She breaks free from their hands at her elbows.

"It's the same," Joel says. "A crumb also contains Jesus; all of Jesus and each of us and the saints. It's Communion."

The singing goes through her head like prayers that fail to catch her attention, like commercials on TV from which she recoils and closes her eyes. She will be receiving Ting Dolor as well?

Two more, after interminable waiting, and it will be her turn. She swallows, wets her lips with her tongue. She has not received since Christmas, when she and the boys attended at the Cathedral. Even there, some were receiving on the hand.

Preparing to receive, she closes her eyes.

"Mamá," Miggy says, alerting her.

Just as her turn comes, a young woman cuts in front to receive what is being lifted toward her, as if they had passed through the same history separately.

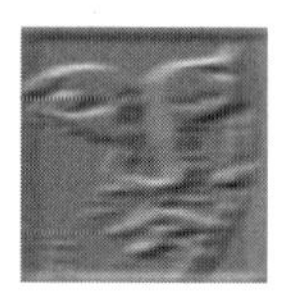

After four weeks

Dionisia stops counting the days since EDSA and, though still waiting for it to reach Gulod, to find her, to bring back the grandchildren with their mother, she decides to go on with her life.

Very early she pulls up the bench on which she sleeps, to bring it to the table, the only other piece of furniture in her shed. Then she shakes the cornstarch paste in the coffee jar, takes it along to *Aling* Patro so she can ask for some hot water to dilute the paste.

She is at the Moscoso house just as Miggy and Joel are leaving. They give her the old newspapers piled in the garage, whereas their mother would have charged almost as much as the rag buyers would pay. Five pesos a *dangcal;* the length between her thumb and little finger.

The boys are driving out in a new car, given to them by the commissioner, their father. "Free ride to Makati," Joey offers. But Dionisia is anxious to start making paper bags from the newspapers, especially since whatever *Aling* Maxima pays her will be all profit.

Looking across to Sula Vitaliano at her doorway, Dionisia starts ripping the pages neatly, folding each section askew at an angle, so that on each side a long, narrow triangle is exposed for the paste. She works quickly, running the side of her palm across the edges while reaching for another page.

She finds an old *Mr & Ms* magazine and sets it aside to return to Sally after reading the "Agnes of God" serial inside. Sally saves the magazines Loreto borrows. Inside the February 23 *Bulletin* is a "Panorama." On the cover page, neon signs appear like fireworks: The Dazzle of Restaurant Row. The sign in the shape of skewered fish intrigues her. As she puts it aside, the ad on the back cover makes her smile: Peach Lux for oily skin. Sharon Cuneta, who looks like her Maria Josefa, has two poses; one saying, "Gabby says there's a nice, teasing scent about it." That's strange, Dionisia thinks, because she read somewhere the actress and actor were separated.

If she finishes making the bags before noon, she can wash blankets for the Lunas. She hurries and almost rips apart a page. Working slower, she catches the ad for Ligo sardines on page eight. Above it is an article, "How to Betray the Noblest Profession." She folds that inside so no one can read it. On Recto where the movie houses are, young girls offer to go into the movie houses with men. She shudders, thinking of Ineng, who is almost that age now.

She lingers on the page of models wearing new fashion clothes. Patro, who once went to the Philippine Plaza, on reclaimed land fronting Manila Bay, said that tourists sat in the lobby to watch wedding parties parade into the reception rooms. Patro heard the tourists asking each other: "I thought this was a poor country?"

Because she went to school before the war, her English is better than most college graduates. She has no trouble with long words or new words, merely guesses the meaning from the way they're used. She takes the time to read "The Declaration of the Coalition of Writers and Artists for Freedom and Democracy." There is a complaint about the sloppy English used in the Declaration.

Dionisia looks up again at Sula Vitaliano sitting and chewing her gums. If the old woman needs something, she calls to Dionisia who walks around to the back of the house to enter by the back door. The old one is looking away to the man coming down the trail to the river. Dionisia recognizes him as the one who came from Samar because his sons were getting old enough to be conscripted by the Communists. One day, Dionisia met him coming home from standing in line at another factory. Casual workers are fired every six months so they do not accumulate any rights, and each time they need another NBI clearance.

Someone, Dionisia thinks, has to right all those wrongs. The way the nuns do, in Gulod.

"Portrait of a Tragedy" is about the space shuttle. There is a picture of the Challenger crew all wearing the same kind of jumpsuit, even the women. Dionisia wonders how to pronounce one of the names: McAuliffe.

The bees are going crazy over the hibiscus, which have grown thicker than walls on two sides of her shed. She used to have gardenias on the table but the scent was too strong, it took her breath away at night. The cuttings came from Sula Vitaliano, who continues to talk about the shrubs as if they still belong to her.

Dionisia rips, folds, presses, piles. The sun is no longer in her eyes. She can hear the television in the house to which her shed is attached. Because they're distant relations, Angge Bermudez charges her only thirty pesos a month, though when the shed was used as a store, she charged one hundred: according to her.

Another magazine escaped Sally Moscoso. On the cover a little boy is lighting candles on some rock. On the same page as an ad for stoves is a picture of Cardinal Sin: "The Moral Dimensions of the Political Crisis." The juxtaposition of letters on the page makes Dionisia think that, perhaps, Maria Josefa is in Italy or Canada and plans to send for them when she has saved enough for their fare.

The coming Sunday is already Palm Sunday. *Domingo de Ramos.* Then comes Easter Sunday. *Pascua.* She stops working to think of the time, long ago, when they were brought to church decorated with palm. Ribbons and flowers were attached to the *palaspas,* which they waved at the Alleluia, when the priest came down the aisle to sprinkle holy water on the palm fronds. Every year until the children disappeared, she brought *palaspas* which, after they were blessed, she tied to the outside post. If she had a window, she would place the *palaspas* in it to protect the household from illness, lightning, and thieves.

She thinks this while staring at the picture of pilgrims. *The Calvary at Mt. Banahaw.* Turning the pages, she comes upon an article about the church in Betis from which her mother came.

She hurries.

India general strike, 1000s arrested. She folds the page without reading the news item. There is an ad: "4 days and 3 nights in Singapore for only $448." Some people just won't get to Singapore. Herself and those in Gulod, except the Vitalianos, the Lunas, and Sally Moscoso. On TV, Cory said that, according to her cook, *galunggong* is only P5 a kilo. The rich must go to different markets and pay cheaper, because in town the fish costs P20 a kilo. The fish vendors must smell poverty and jack up the price.

Hurry, she tells herself. If she did not know how to read, she would be able to work fast.

Ineng could read when they disappeared, but Totoy just looked at the pictures. Totoy, however, is musical; even looks like Freddie Aguilar, whose singing makes her cry. One of the magazines has an interview with Freddie, who sings about justice and a father's dreams for his children. His "Magdalena" always makes her think of Maria Josefa. According to the interview, Freddie used to live in a project but is now a millionaire. Maybe Totoy will be another Freddie Aguilar. How is she to know, if she's dead by then? What did the priest mean, one Sunday in the chapel across from the Vitalianos, when he said everyone, all of them, are gathered in the Host?

She cuts and pastes the sports pages without reading. There's the Eskinol ad again. Sometimes she likes the actress in the ad, Vilma Santos, better than Nora Aunor.

Rioting dies down in Cairo. Acid rain threatens ASEAN countries. She thought rain was good for crops. She folds the items inside, does the same with the page containing news of an ambush: *14 cops, 2 others killed.* Cory claims the NPAs would be surrendering to her. Why does fighting go on in the countryside?

Shakey's Bunch of Lunch is P24. She reads the special offer: spaghetti in a skillet, crisp chicken, and a hot hero sandwich. Totoy can finish all that. The man behind Arsenio Grande who led the Marlboro Marathon Cycling eliminations looks very much like Benhur Vitaliano. Could it have been him?

Another sports page. Dionisia does not quite get the references behind *Phoenix rises above injury-plagued Lakers.* The glue is hardening on her fingers. The last time, she had a stick with which to spread the paste. *Local execs defy Cory.* In Quezon City, 500 gathered to demand the retention of the mayor. Minister for Local Government Pimentel cites a law passed under Marcos to support the ouster of elected officials. In Navotas, a group outnumbering his supporters demanded the ouster of the mayor.

Dionisia is getting confused about the sequence of news that has already happened and, from several newspapers, continues to happen. *Batasan to be abolished* she sees for the third time. She reads Louis Beltran's "Straight from the Shoulder" in the *Inquirer.* She liked his gutsiness in standing up to Marcos. Now he is saying that "through the appointments to local government the administration is inviting political appointees to transform provinces into the distribution centers for political spoils." She herself does not think the government should fire elected officials and replace them with officers-in-charge. Bien Sotero said it would restore the Spanish custom of bringing in new government employees with each new governor general.

Persons with invalid media-IDs demanding rooms in hotels. *Villagers confirm massacre: 90 killed in Maco.* She folds that news inside the bag she is making, so people will not get discouraged. *Amnesty body set; Reds defiant* comes out on the outside.

A cartoon shows Juan de la Cruz loaded with sacks labeled special taxes—income tax, gasoline tax, real estate tax, etc.—telling Cory: *You promised to lighten this load. Jewish Mafia from Old Manila.* The Bernsteins "fronted" for the First Couple in their Manhattan realty deals. *Passports of Marcos, relatives, cronies revoked to block their return to the Philippines.* Panama is reported to agree to have Marcos and family live there for $150,000 rent a week on Contadora Island. Panama gave the Shah of Iran asylum in 1980. *Marcos brought $5 to $10 million to Hawaii.*

Metrocom raids home of Marcos deputy Minister of Human Settlements, gets suitcases filled with P2 million and $64,000. Minister claims he can afford to have such amounts at home.

Dionisia takes out of her dress pocket one of the Halls candies she bought from Maxima's store. To save on food, she drops one of the candies in her mouth whenever she feels hungry. It's not as expensive as smoking, since each candy costs only 25 centavos. If she sucks, they last longer than if she chews.

Instead of using dynamite to blow up Marcos's cement bust in the national park built on Ibaloi land, the tribesmen exorcised it with the blood of a pig they slaughtered on the spot. The blood, drying, looks like a livid birthmark.

Dionisia makes the sign of the Cross as she comes upon the report on the Challenger spacemen. *Remains recovered.* Ocean search continues for more body parts and debris of the cabin. Her thoughts go to those found dead in Gulod, tied to one another by barbed wire; found floating in the river; each death more gruesome and permanent.

The candy has melted to the thinness of paper. She can taste its very transparency.

Payatas squatters resist eviction; clash looms. If Cory knows about that, she will not let the poor be evicted. Dionisia recalls, the other time she made paper bags from newspapers, coming across a news item about a former commissioner in the Bureau of Internal Revenue who had sold fake certificates of titles to unclassified public forests in Quezon. She later read in the *Noli* that farmers were marched through several towns to jail for resisting the confiscation of land to which they had no title, but which their ancestors had wrested from the forests. Right by possession against right by title. By law.

The appointment of an alleged Marcos loyalist to the Ministry of Waterworks has caused a walkout of employees. Dionisia scans the picture for someone she recognizes. Weeks after the release of top Communist leaders, *596 detainees remain in jail for political reasons.*

A newly organized alliance objects to the government's use of fanatical religious and paramilitary forces in its counter-insurgency drives. Dionisia looks up. She was sitting exactly where she is, very early in the morning, when secret marshals crouched outside behind her hibiscus to waylay

Tomas na hilo, who might be lazy and good-for-nothing but had not committed any crime in any book or code of law. Later on, it was admitted he'd been mistaken for a labor leader. Probably Bien Sotero. They're the same height.

Government deficit up from $365 million to $950 million. Dionisia wonders how that amount is counted. Siso would say someone with a million fingers must do the counting. Millions always make Dionisia think of sand. A briefcase containing documents was stolen from Jovito Salonga, former senator, now head of the Commission on Good Government. In Manhattan. So there are thieves, as well, in the States.

Libya clashes with U.S. Surt, 400 kms east of Tripoli, has been shelled by the U.S. fleet. Dionisia wonders if those ships came from Subic. The Gulf of Sidra. Dionisia smiles on reading the name. Sidra is the name of her grandmother. Isidra. She was very fair and her eyebrows met above her nose. Isidro is the patron saint of harvest, celebrated May 15. Washington says Libya fired at least one surface-to-air missile at U.S. planes that crossed Khadafy's "line of death." Then there is the Tass version of the attack. *U.S. Congress talks on Contra aid fail.* Dispatch from Paris: *Train blast, nine hurt in Lyon-bound express. 42,000 state employees strike in Finland.*

Dionisia stretches her back, lifts up her neck so that she is looking at the overhead light bulb, which has burned out and which she has not replaced since she never turns it on, to save electricity for Angge Bermudez and her family. She also runs errands for them and on occasion, when asked, cooks for their parties.

Raise food for your family. For P200 one can attend a seminar that teaches snail production. Each participant receives twenty free *kuhols*. The river used to yield snails with white shells. In less than an hour she used to be able to gather enough to boil in coconut milk and spice with *labuyo.* Though she is not a Bicolana, she has learned to like the tiny red hot pepper.

Diokno named to probe tortures. Dionisia folds the page without reading.

The next page has a picture of Bangsa Moro members holding a prayer rally in Malacañang. It makes her think of the picture of Cory kneeling in prayer and of the nuns in the school in town selling Cory calendars to the students. Siso Feleo said he asked his daughter to return the calendar because they did not have ten pesos.

She has folded to the inside the page about the probe of tortures, but she continues to see it in front of her. "Lines of death." Are they like the longtitudes and latitudes on the map? She used to help Maria Josefa trace maps on thin onion-skin paper.

Dionisia returns to the picture of Malacañang; is tempted to save it. But where will she keep it? All she owns fits in a cardboard box *Aling* Patro keeps for her. Her shed is open to everyone, as well as to the weather. It's a wonder she herself is not stolen while she sleeps. Cadavers must be more valuable because they are always being stolen to sell to medical schools. She sets aside the picture of the Palace by the Pasig. Her schoolbooks showed pictures of American officials, sturdy in white suits or khaki; of President Manuel L. Quezon and his wife, Doña Aurora, in Malacañang. People kissed their hands, if they allowed it. Now some of the rich candidates wash their hands in alcohol after shaking hands with the poor. If they wish not to be touched, why shake hands?

Estong Calero walks by, talking to the *barangay* captain about a letter he cannot deliver.

A news item about Syria reminds Dionisia of the sweets her mother taught her to make for the rich in Betis. Her father could sing all the parts in a *zarzuela.* Sometimes, the melodies of the *awits* her father used to sing wake Dionisia up at night. And she cries, because it seems her father is still singing back in Betis.

Soon enough Bastian Canonigo comes up hurrying on the trail. He listens to all conversations in Gulod.

NPA demands army pullout. There is a picture of Gringo Honasan with General Ramos about to parachute over Sagay, Negros del Norte to inspect the troops on the general's fifty-eighth birthday. *Colombia guerrilla chief slain. 14 killed in NPA raids; truce failing all over.* Dionisia scans the picture of employees of the soon-to-be sequestered *Daily Express,* protesting government takeover. *Quezon City policeman shot dead, killers unknown. Hundreds face lay-off at MMC. Cagayan mayor slain in ambush.* The rebels burned the jeep before fleeing. *Rites for Our Lady of Peñafrancia, patron saint of Bicol.* It will be held in September, to coincide with the fluvial parades in Naga.

She skips the obituary page. No one she knows will appear there. It costs thousands to have the announcements published. There is a picture of Freddie Aguilar singing "Bayan Ko."

Batasan abolished; new charter planned. Cory recalled promotion of colonel after it drew objections. 1000s stake out lots for themselves in Pasig. Dionisia studies the picture of people joining corners of lots with twine. Inside the area closed off are their belongings and children. *Dovie Beams deep in debt.* Didn't Marcos provide for his mistresses?

Dionisia looks towards the river past the house of Sula Vitaliano. *Lola* Sula is almost dozing in her chair, her chin hanging over her loose blouse. It would be good if, before she dies, Dionisia thinks, she could own even a square meter of land. Then they could wrap her in a mat and bury her.

Mitterand might resign. If the Right wins a sweeping victory, the French president will leave office. *S. Korea faces dangerous era.* All over the world there seems to be trouble, only it's worse in the Philippines. *Bangladesh general strike set.*

Luis Mauricio has a column on political appointments. "The major portfolios in the Aquino cabinet were first distributed to Laban leaders . . . to the darlings of the clerical mafiosi. To the UNIDO were thrown the crumbs." She has noticed that the vice-president's pictures are scarce in the newspapers.

Third-degree malnutrition watch. Children are dying of malnutrition in Bacolod. "Lycel Obligada, age 2, was brought home dead from the hospital, wrapped in a blanket like a sleeping child against her mother's shoulder so the driver's suspicions will not be aroused." In the other picture, the father is kneeling, taking a tape measure to the child for a coffin. "Lycel was taken to the hospital as a last resort. As death approached, the nurses packed hot water bottles against the little legs and turned on the floor lamps to warm the doomed child." It reads like the story of her own life.

"The hopes for a better government were not to be," Jess Bigornia writes in his column." Already the arbitrary actions of key officials are symptomatic of a relapse to the practices of a repudiated system. Still, Cory is better than Marcos."

There is a "watchlist" prepared by the Presidential Commission on Good Government. As a gesture of goodwill to the new government in the Philippines, *RP captives in Angola allowed to begin 800M trek to freedom.* In 1984, UNITA rebels captured, then released a hundred Filipinos working in the Kafunfo diamond mines.

Who in the world has time to read all the news as it happens? Everything she has read soon blurs in Dionisia's mind, giving her a sense of peacefulness in that, since the blight reported has happened in the past and elsewhere, it can no longer threaten her. She looks up toward the distance, toward something green to rest her eyes. Two mothers with curlers in their hair are taking lunch to their children in school, which she used to do for her own.

The memory makes her get up, starts her walking from a darkness neither faint nor clear. It has been almost twenty years since her husband died and she has had no way of knowing if something is wrong inside her. Afraid of pain she cannot feel, Dionisia forgets to place a rock upon the paper bags so they will not scatter on the trail she is following away from herself. She tries, but she cannot remember herself singing.

It is in her sleep
she has been singing, since Sally Moscoso asked her to chant the Passion from Good Friday to Easter. Angge Bermudez, her landlady, pounds on the wall to wake her up. "In God's mercy be quiet, Dionisia. Allow us to sleep. *Patulugin mo kami.*" Sula Vitaliano, across the way, shouts her down. "You Catholics even pray in your sleep. *Sus!*"

Afraid she'll fall asleep and start singing again, Dionisia walks out onto the trail. It is still too dark to see the trees against the sky. A cat comes out to rub against her leg. Shush! She pushes it away but it follows her, tail upright like a snake. A dog barks. It sets other dogs howling on both sides of the river. The sound flushes the birds quiet within the trees.

Those who rent the ground floor from Angge, who hit their heads on the ceiling because it is too low to allow them to walk upright, who take this out on Dionisia since they cannot blame Angge, have turned off their lights, giving the wall one last bang that chases Dionisia down the trail.

She walks sideways against the darkness, as if she is stepping into the wind that howls from the river and threatens to scatter her, until she meets Siso Feleo, the volunteer nightwatch in Gulod, who is making the rounds of the *zona.*

"*Aling* Dionisia, don't stand under the tall trees or the *tikbalang* will reach down and pull you up!" Siso Feleo calls out, warning Dionisia as if she were a child. He tells this to his own children to frighten them into staying inside the house. "The dead might still be walking around."

"The dead can't hurt me, Siso. It's those who still breathe I'm afraid of." Dionisia keeps to herself just who it is she's afraid of, those who charge her with worshiping wooden statues she knows are just representations of God in heaven. When she kisses the pictures of the children, she knows she is not kissing them but her memory of them.

"Walk with us," Siso says, beaming his flashlight, a gift from Benhur, on the road.

"I'm just trying to get sleepy again, Siso. Your shirt is inside out, did you know? You must have been in a hurry."

"So I won't get lost. Just a precaution. I'll have to catch up with the others, *Aling* Dionisia."

"Go ahead."

Once more by herself, Dionisia wonders what she said in her sleep that people would have heard. She might have been chanting the *pasyon,* the life and suffering of Christ. It is years since she last sang in the *pabasa.* It used to be that, right after finishing the *pasyon,* she was contracted for the following year's Holy Week. Like her father, she was very much in demand, but she never sang the *pasyon* during wakes, nor had she made a vow to sing the Jesucristo's life and death each year; nor accepted payment.

Only after her father had died did she find out that he made his *panata* as thanksgiving for her getting well after an illness from which no one had expected her to recover when she was three. Some vowed to dress as the Nazareno or to flagellate themselves on Good Friday or be nailed to the Cross in order to expiate sins. She remembers that those dressed as Nazarenos were always given a boiled egg to eat. Others were served ordinary food.

Her chest tightens, thinking again of the family renting Angge's ground floor who taunt her into throwing away her beads. It is useless to tell them: repeating prayers is intended to clear the mind and open it to God; to reach a forgetfulness into which God enters.

Without realizing it, Dionisia has begun chanting: *O Dios sa calangitan / Hari nang sang calupaan / Dios na walang capantay / mabait, lubhang maalam / at puno nang carunungan* . . . In all there are 2,660 stanzas from scripture, *aralins* and moral teachings that apply the Jesucristo's life and death. Her father knew several ways of singing the verses and could reach the highest notes without straining.

An infant cries. From the softness of its wail, Dionisia guesses it's a newborn. Another angel for the devil to try to lead astray. Brought to term, stillborns also are angels; but how about those aborted before they're fully formed?

If she were not singing the *pasyon* that day, she would have gone to Quiapo to listen to the sermon on the Last Seven Words; to follow the procession of the Santo Entierro in His glass coffin.

Sally said she would get a guitarist, have a sound system broadcast the singing in Gulod and across the highway. Suppose her voice cracks? Suppose the guitarist plays too fast? She and her father always sang *a capella;* never tried to outsing others or try to get praise. If there are professional singers—Sally had said she would try to get some—it could become competitive unless they all have the right attitude.

She will sing as if it is her vow. A *panata.* She will keep her eyes to the text. But she knows only the Casaysayan version. If a different text is used, she will have to improvise the notes when she takes her turn, because she does not have eyeglasses. She will make mistakes and Sally Moscoso will be embarrassed and regret having asked her.

Dionisia turns around on the trail, bothered by occasions of failure, which doing her best will not avoid. If only she had thought of excuses, though once Sally makes up her mind, nothing can change it. She tries to recall the different texts. Her father sang from the first *pasyon* ever written, around 1703; knew the history of the several texts, the last one being printed in 1852.

Suppose she faints? Like her father, she will not eat until the entire *pasyon* is sung.

"Jesucristo." Dionisia begs for help. The Jesucristo, her father said, would have fought for the people's freedom and independence because that is salvation on earth. There are two kinds of people: God's people and the world's.

Against the sky, Dionisia begins to see the tops of trees and Good Friday. She heads for *Aling* Patro's, where she washes and changes. Patro even asks her to sleep in the house. During typhoons she sleeps over but returns right away to the shed in case the children come looking for her. In exchange for the favor, she offered Patro the only valuable thing she has, a German knife from her husband, but Patro would not accept it. The *vaciador,* who complains that knives in Gulod have no edges left to sharpen and are so thin—"All I can give back is metal dust if they insist"—says the knife is top quality.

Loreto opens the door before Dionisia can knock. "Here comes Sylvia La Torre," Loreto teases her with the name of the singer. "Come and the *sinangag* will be ready."

"Just coffee," Dionisia says, watching Loreto stirring the fried rice into which she has added sausages diced into bits barely larger than pepper flakes, but it colors the rice frying in the pan.

"Dionisia, I have a dress for you to wear to the *pabasa.* Take off that one and see if this fits."

The dress fits. It has eyelet pockets. Sally will not be able to accuse her of stuffing her pockets with food. The new dress makes Dionisia happy. It makes her think of the church in Betis with scenes from the Bible painted in the ceiling. Lots of angels and blue sky have been painted on the porous limestone and miraculously have not flaked off. When she was making paper bags for Maxima, she read that the church in Betis is a miniature Sistine Chapel. All these make Dionisia feel she has been saved.

A man and a woman are standing at the Moscoso gate when Dionisia arrives. She is frightened again. Suppose these are the professional singers who will embarrass her with their excellent voices!

The maid lets in Dionisia but not the other two.

"What about them?" Dionisia asks inside the house.

"Ma'm can't decide. They're offering chairs from Imelda's house. They're her caretakers, they say; and they want Ma'm to promise to sell the chairs back when Imelda and Marcos return."

The candles are not yet lit on the altar in the living room where chairs are arranged in rows for the visitors; but the calla lilies from Baguio resemble lit candles with their yellow stamens. Dionisia kneels. Closing her eyes, she prays to the Santo Niño and the Immaculate Concepcion on either side of the crucifix. Jesucristo. She is seeing herself the way Patro describes seeing herself when she is thinking of all their lives: coming from a long distance on the trail. Except that Dionisia sees herself walking away.

Recalling herself being tossed in the air by her older brothers, remembering everyone leaping up towards the strength they believed was coming from God, like rain, on Sabado de Gloria, Patro hears the bells before they are rung on Easter Sunday.

Everyone is still asleep. She looks out of the window in her room and sees stars still in the sky; and time. The stars remind her of the dove of peace on the Channel 4 screen after it was recaptured; of Dionisia's singing the *pasyon* at Sally Moscoso's house. Her thoughts go back and forth from the singing, more mournful than at a wake. Unspoken and unasked for, her thoughts are those of someone buried beside the road, to whom dreams come too late.

"*Nay.*" Loreto comes out, places an arm about Patro. "I dreamed of Father. He was standing by my bed, telling me to go to church with the children."

"You should go then," Patro says.

"*Lola* Sula will know."

"I made the promise to become Iglesia for myself, Loreto; not for you, or for the children."

"We'll go to the church in town."

"Yes," Patro says, waiting to be asked to come, too.

"And will I take them to *Lola* Sula afterward, to kiss her hand and get her blessing? I don't remember. Does she still bless? *Nay!* What's the matter? Did we have the same dream?"

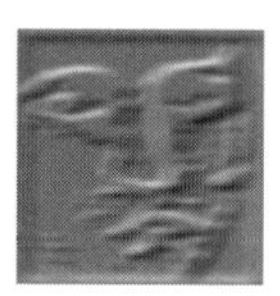

It starts out as a prank,
the kind that seizes Osong's imagination and will not be reasoned away until it spins itself out.

"What if," Osong calls Benhur in the office, "we dress in Cayetano's fatigues, yellow headbands and, with a warrant from the Philippine Commission on Good Government—fake, of course, you can improvise one—demand to search Ting Dolor's house? It will be only the maids. Ting is never there on Tuesday."

"What if the maids recognize you? And what's the point?"

"You and I each possess a point, but we don't have time to compare them. We'll be incognito. Dark glasses. Caps. Oak leaves or whatever on the shoulder. The shock will drive the maids too crazy to think straight or recall. I'll be there with Pete and Artemio and whoever else I can drag out. Sit tight."

Pete has gout in both feet. Artemio offers the use of his military-looking car in his place, and no one else answers the phone. Nevertheless, a military radio in hand, Osong dashes into Benhur's office as though at the head of a platoon.

"The security guard didn't recognize me. It will work, Benhur! He didn't recognize me at all." Osong confronts Benhur across the desk, gloating as if everything has already been accomplished according to plan. "'*This* is a raid! This is a *raid!*' Which sounds authentic, Brod? Wait till they hear about this at the next reunion. No one will believe it. Which is more real? I stress *This* or *raid?*"

Against his good judgment, Benhur goes along. Osong has cracked from not hearing anything about his appointment, but the sight of Ting Dolor's gate will bring him back to his senses. "What about the guard?"

"You're right. We won't wear the fatigues. We'll say we have an invitation. Then wear the disguise as soon as we get in. If we're recognized later, we claim it's mistaken identity. There's any number of people who look like us, Benhur. That's the basic fact of coincidences. Have you not met anyone who looks as if you have a twin? Not someone younger, because that can be your offspring."

One last escapade before he emigrates: Benhur tries to calm himself. Ting Dolor will be there and they will all laugh together.

"This is a raid!" Osong surprises the maid from Sorsogon who comes to the door in hair curlers, a sign that Ting Dolor is not home. "Down on the floor."

"This is the government sequestration team," Benhur corrects the dialogue. "Please stand against the wall and no one touch the phone." Unscripted, the scenario deteriorates into a police raid he has seen on TV and becomes even more unreal to Benhur.

Another maid, the one Ting Dolor calls witch, *bruja,* screams into a faint, the keys at her waist like dead bones protruding from her body. The others stare at the door that has closed. Having just read of the raid on the deputy Minister of Human Settlements, no one protests, or asks for a warrant or identification. Expecting to be shot, the maids close their eyes and shiver.

"What next?" Osong whispers, looking at himself in the mirror beside the nude tribal statue for which, according to guests at the house blessing, Ting Dolor had posed.

"What what?" Benhur scowls.

"Where do we go?"

"You know the layout. Library. Vaults. You decide."

Osong's sneakers squeak, sticking to the marble floor. "Let's go to the bedroom."

"Ask for the secret room. One of us has to stay here or the maids will give alarm. Oh. Whatever. Be quick about it." Benhur looks up the winding staircase. In its stairwell one Christmas, Ting Dolor had a twenty-five-foot Christmas tree against which she shimmered like a flame tree in August against the sunset on Manila Bay. Red gown, red sequins. It sticks to his throat.

Osong slides into the library, remembers to ask for direction. "Is this the library?" The maids have left on the TV a videotape of the Marvelous Hagler and John "The Beast" Mugabi fight, the one Ting Dolor promised to lend. Hurrying, he takes the briefcase on the desk, careful not to leave fingerprints. He is smarter than Benhur gives him credit for. Benhur forgot about gloves. One last look about the library. At the windows the yellow campaniles are large mouths sucking.

Early that evening, the illicit search of the home of a prominent businessman, while he and his wife were away, hits the news. A team of ten or twelve tied up the maids, who took hours to untie themselves. Paintings were taken; rare coins; Ming vases, and, of course, cash and jewels. The list is several paragraphs long, and awaits the return of the businessman from Australia for confirmation of the losses.

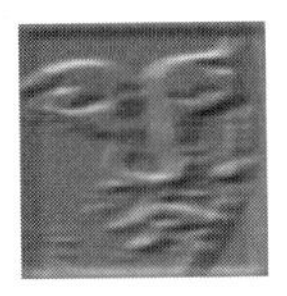

"You're getting too serious again, Brod," Osong throws both arms back on the chairs. "Have another beer and then we'll decide who'll return the briefcase. Let's be clearheaded about it. If you won't keep it, it has to be returned. Then we'll think of a scheme. Foolproof. Until we can get going again. The Customs job does not seem to be open any more, but we could sell fake tickets to the Malacañang tour. P30 per. That's not bad for a peek at Imelda's underwear. Descented. Or we could try another house. This time, really. Did she invite you yet?"

"Who, and to what?"

"I guess not. TD. Her list for the opening night of *Evita,* when she thought she would be Evita, has become her *despedida* list, though she does not know yet where she'll go abroad. Just abroad."

"I feel sorry."

"Don't be. She can't have wanted it badly since she never auditioned. Thought the part would go to her because she wants it. She might not even have the time." Osong lines up the pork cracklings to spell Ting Dolor's name.

"Or the ability to act."

"That, too. She never tried for any of the Repertory Philippine productions. If she really wanted it, she should have gone to the office in the Land Bank Building. Just passing the word that she's interested in the lead role does not get it for her. And she did not want to be just in the cast. You know her."

"So who got the lead?"

"Baby Barredo and Joy Virata alternate at the Rizal Theater until June. Ting Dolor shines in Los Angeles, or New York, or London. She might even join Imelda in Honolulu. Not far-fetched, Brod. Maybe she does not really want the part since *Evita* could not be produced while Imelda reigned."

"Why won't she tell you where she's going, Osong?"

"Now you are getting ridiculous. She does not know where she wants to go. She might even join her husband in Australia and raise sheep. Now, what will we do with the briefcase? We should probably break the lock and see what's inside. All those listed missing! Paintings and jewels and Ming vases!"

"Why is she not telling?"

"You're leading to something, Benhur. What is it you know that I don't?"

"I don't know, Osong. Thanks for the beer."

"We haven't talked this out yet. Let's go to the office. I have a new secretary, a virgin. They're the best healers."

"Not interested, Brod. No aches and pains to heal."

"It's you she's going abroad with, isn't it? The smile on your face, as if it's your picture that will replace Marcos's on the P500 bill."

"You can't be serious, Osong." Benhur stares Osong down. "I'm going abroad, but on my own. Not with anyone. And not right away, Brod." He does not even want to know what office Osong means.

"Benhur, sit down and let's talk."

"Before I go, we'll have a beer. On me."

"Virtue can't keep you alive forever, you know. If you don't listen to your physical needs now, you'll be a dirty old man in twenty years. In ten years! Midlife is your last chance to escape the crisis, and you're three months older than I."

"Thanks." Benhur wishes he could stay, go back to old times, but he no longer wants to feel beheaded, someone talking to his ghost at night, frantic to earn his defection.

As soon as he can put together enough for his fare, and an account from which his mother can draw for the family's needs, he'll be free from Tuesday morning in Constitutional Law, from the services and errands he has had to perform. He can do it. He has been at EDSA. Meanwhile, he knows it is not the consummated but the near occasions of love that will keep him from butting his head against the walls.

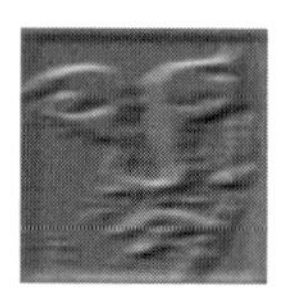

"What is it?"

Aling Patro asks, seeing Loreto look up from the dining table as though to face someone calling.

Everyone else has left the room. Filled with squash flowers cooked with leftover fish, too old to nap in the afternoon, the boys are already outside wandering in and out of yards while waiting for the neighbors to come out from their rest so they can start to play basketball.

"What is it?"

Loreto fills the long pause with her mother's question before replying, "Nothing." In another while, her long fingers folded in front of her, her breasts upon the edge of the table, Loreto says, "I lost the money Sally paid me to sew sequins on her gown."

"How?" Patro asks. Loreto had said nothing when she got home from the market.

"My bag was slashed. I was paying for the little glass deer I want to give Anya, and the money was gone." A pout forms on her lips. "The peddler thought I merely pretended to have lost the money because I had changed my mind. He said there are no bag-slashers anymore since Marcos was thrown out. So I showed him." She leans back while the rest of her thoughts continue: her plan to buy the children potato chips and chocolate milk the way Benhur brought *pasalubong* of pie and cheese and ham when he came to visit, to get her mother a pair of red slippers to replace the straw pair that has become too wide for her feet.

"How much did you lose?"

"Fifty."

"You worked until two in the morning for fifty! Better not let Benhur know. You could get sick working that hard. Another person would devote half the effort and time and charge at least double. And Sally will tell her friends a couturiere made her gown."

"She also promised me a dress but forgot to give it. Anyway, she asks you to cook for her parties and only gives you leftovers." Loreto reaches across the table for the plates, begins stacking them to wash. "By the way, *Nay,* Sally has a security guard who sits just inside the gate with a rifle. Wears a uniform, too. During the afternoons, he falls asleep, the maids say a German watchdog would be better. And did you know Sally is related to Cory? She told me. There's a family wedding and she'll be *ninang* along with Cory. Ten sponsors in all, plus the secondary veil, and candle and rope sponsors. Didn't she also say she is related to President Marcos?"

"Related to a relative of," *Aling* Patro says, picking up each grain of rice on the table. "Pick up those on the floor, Loreto, or the Lord will think we're not grateful. And feed the cat outside. I'll wash. Maybe Sally will be moving out of Gulod." Patro looks at her daughter before leaving the room. Loreto does not very often look so sad, and Patro thinks of lifting her spirits by allowing her to go visit Sally. "After Cory's inauguration, didn't Sally say she has a signed picture of the President? I wonder if she kept the picture of Imelda and herself. Go see."

Loreto has stopped listening; is thinking back to what else happened that morning which had made her forget to tell her mother about losing the money in the market. After she has picked the grains of rice, she looks at them in the palm of her hand, wondering if her mother can tell her thoughts as she goes back over them carefully, back to hurrying home, angry about losing the money, and then meeting Emilio Luna on the trail. They walked past each other, then stopped to look . . . *He* stopped.

As if the sequence of all events is formed by random patterns that do not repeat, she's no longer sure.

Her mother looks at her strangely from the kitchen and Loreto tries to stop her thoughts; but memory rushes through her as if her body is a maze through which her thoughts are trying to find their end or their beginning. The notion is so strange that she smiles, puzzled and yet pleased by the strangeness, as if it is part of meeting Emilio Luna on the trail.

Coming back with the clean plates, Patro is surprised to see Loreto smiling, the angle of her head in a model's splendid pose. If only she can keep Loreto that happy; if only Loreto will have only happy memories to make her smile. Maybe, and even sooner than she hopes for, they will also move out of Gulod, where Loreto was once held at knife-point by a man whose face was covered with a handkerchief . . .

Without being asked, Loreto starts to sweep the floor. Black ants tumble off the soft broom. She begins to feel sleepy. "*Nay,* I'll sleep for an hour. I can't keep awake."

"Go ahead. I won't start sewing. But longer than an hour will give you a headache. I'll see that the boys are not playing near the river. The other day, Ryan had already stripped down to swim when I saw him."

Loreto tries at once to sleep, not wishing to think further of Emilio Luna; afraid he'll live in her thoughts, breathing and acting in her mind, the scene on the trail repeating and repeating for nothing.

Close to tears, she tries to sleep. A kind of absence hangs over her as she fights trying to recall how exactly they met on the trail. Her face quivers. She feels herself trembling the way light shakes as darkness enters; begins. It makes her think of the white *azucenas* in the pots by the door; the flowers opening on the stalk one day and drying up the next; the *kalachuchi* threaded into Hawaiian leis; flowers for caskets.

When she got sick after working six weeks in her *Kuya* Osong's office, she did not cry this way. Those were happy weeks. She wore the mauve uniform, and her bone-colored shoes went so perfectly with the color that the women imitated her. Her *Kuya* Osong would call her to his office to give her a box of candy, or just anything; the way if it had been Benhur, he would have given her gifts. Benhur himself gave her the equivalent of a month's salary so she could buy her uniforms; one to wear while the other was being washed. She filed papers and collected cafeteria receipts from the employees to cover up Osong's discretionary funds. Proud of her for becoming a government *empleada,* her *Lola* Sula gave her a locket and a ring so she would not look disinherited. Then she got sick. For days, she felt flooded inside, filled with odd smells.

Loreto gets up to take out the locket from her *aparador*—a new one without secret panels, so she hides it between the clothes—but changes her mind. Whose picture will she place inside so that, when the halves are closed, his and her face will touch? She never even wore the locket outside her clothes, afraid others would ask to see who's inside and find it empty except for her picture. Besides, women lose their jewelry if they ride in jeepneys. The newspapers are filled with accounts of necklaces being snatched while the jeeps are stopped at the lights, of robberies by fellow passengers. She herself saw the red welt forming around a co-passenger's neck when the gold necklace, sent to her from Saudi by her husband, was pulled off by a passenger on disembarking. It continues, with Marcos gone.

As her thoughts wander, Loreto begins to see Emilio Luna's picture in the locket. She smiles. Why not? Emilio does not look bad, even if he is silent. She prefers silent ones because they are not vulgar.

Sally is vulgar. At her age she still flirts, throwing sticky glances at men along the way. Whenever she goes to Sally, she is asked, "How many girlfriends does your brother have? Why do you suppose he has not gotten married; or *is* he secretly?" Constantly. The same questions. Benhur is forty-six; how could anyone still be interested in him? Who would be desperate enough? though he is still *numero uno* in Gulod, where every male is either married, jobless, or wanted for some crime; or all of those.

Hearing her mother coming, Loreto turns over on her stomach and closes her eyes. Patro comes in to check the jalousies because one afternoon while she slept a man tried to pry loose the wood frame; so Patro asked Benhur for metal bars.

As soon as her mother leaves, Loreto turns away from the wall and thinks of Emilio Luna. Was not Emilio about to turn to say something to her on the trail? As if carrying on a conversation, Loreto asks: Does he even know who I am? Back and forth, questions about Emilio surge through her mind, and she works them the way she sewed sequins, edge to edge, overlapping on the fabric.

Thinking of him fills her with such joyfulness, which sometimes comes over her while thinking of nothing, just staring at the light from the sky, or rain.

Such a lost look he had. Lost. Unhappy. A sadness so mortal, from which one can die. She begins to feel his sadness while she turns the pages of a movie magazine with actors and actresses posing as lovers. She scans, without reading, the columns she has read and knows by heart: whose marriages are being broken up by whom. She used to dream of Christopher de Leon; kept a picture of Gabby Concepcion under her pillow which Anya found and which she tore up to prove it meant nothing. For months she would long for a movie star; then every day a new one; imagining herself tall and lean like Melanie Marquez, who married a rich Arab. Her *Lola* Sula, who at ninety-four still has fine exquisite ears, says, "Marry someone with large ears unless you wish to be widowed early."

She tosses the magazine off to one side and wishes Benhur were there so she could find out directly from him what he thinks of Emilio Luna. When she was about twelve, Emilio Luna might have walked her to church. It was not pre-arranged. More likely they merely happened to enter together, overtook each other on the trail. It was crowded. She stood beside the stone angels at the entrance. Lie and wish compose the thoughts that she defends as fact, part of her body, to do with as she pleases and not needing to conform to external exactions.

Like a flood, the sound of the sewing machine comes from the living room. Her mother has started to work on Sally Moscoso's drapes. The old machine—1910 is worked into the design on the foot pedal across the length of the machine—sounds like a distant train throttling. Patro has been looking for the oil can, last seen being tossed by the boys as if it were a basketball. When she was a little girl, she pretended the fine, long nozzle was a vase for dolls. She used to play house with two small girls who have since moved away. They cut up leaves, stirred them in tiny clay pots over make-believe fire; pretending to cook and then to eat.

Outside her window some children are quarreling in their play. Ryan is saying, "I'm the boss. You're all my deputies. I'm Enrile and I give orders." Atlas is arguing that it is General Ramos who gives orders. Another time, she would have listened to them enacting EDSA, playing General Ver giving orders to attack with General Tadiar and Colonel Balbas refusing to obey. But now she wants silence, to know why she thinks Emilio Luna is in mortal pain, why she concludes this from his looking at her when he must look at everyone he meets on the trail. Motives not attached to the act.

Imagining Emilio Luna, Loreto begins to remember his looking like someone who has started to die and also that her body was burning as they passed each other. A wounding . . . God, I love him; she bites her lips; breathing in and slowly out to hold back the surging she feels going through her. A deep smell. A blinding.

The shouts outside her window and the creaking of the sewing machine merge into the sound of walls marching towards her, and she stares at the ceiling until her body is quiet again. Then she rises.

Outside her room, the cat runs to her, rubs its body against her legs. She picks it up, lets it lick her face, purr in her ear. Full attention returns.

"Your asthma will return. Put it down," Patro looks up, searching Loreto's face. Though it has been months, almost years, the dead look that comes over Loreto's face, bringing her down moaning, is etched in Patro's eyes. "You did not sleep."

Loreto lets the cat leap out of her arms into the fabric piling up in front of the sewing machine. She watches it lie on its side, curled into an open circle. Emilio might have spoken and, distraught with losing the money, she did not hear. She looks away from her mother's hand guiding the panels of fabric past the needle. It feels as if the pins pointed in all directions on the floor are stuck in her head. Inside her eyes swirl blue flames. Deep indigo. She puts her body down against the cat, hears her mother speaking, but not what she says. She watches the flames peak, spark, and slowly die out . . .

Catching her unawares, she asks her mother, "Were the Lunas here before us?" She remembers only that they also had a house in the city and used to own horses. She remembers the name of the one with white fetlocks. Semiramis. Or is that the name of a street, like Misericordia near Soler? On New Year's Eve there were fireworks through the trees in the Luna garden. She remembers being given a sparkler on a thin long wire. Firecrackers came in red lines. Mr. Luna spoiled his children. The girls went to schools run by nuns; married rich. Loreto does not recall being at the weddings.

Now, only Emilio Luna and his mother are left. There is a daughter who might have died, or gone away. She disappeared.

"I met him on my way home today." Loreto places her head on her knees as she sits up on the floor; her voice sounding like her own again.

"Who do you mean?"

Something like grief comes to Loreto that her mother does not know who she means. The Lunas walked past the house every Wednesday to go to Baclaran where Mrs. Luna prayed to the Lady of Perpetual Help. *Aling* Maxima, however, says they go to a doctor; that he has tried to kill himself; this is after his father died; says she has seen the wound and that Emilio Luna should get himself a job to help his mother instead of being served hand and foot by her.

"Get me a glass of water, *hija,*" Patro asks Loreto. "This fabric makes me thirsty and itchy. Tonight I will not be able to sleep from the rashes. That's why I sew while the children are outside, so they will not touch the drapes."

Her mind far away, Loreto pours water from the clay jar that cools their drinking water besides leaching out impurities. The light dancing on the surface throws reflections on the wall. She looks away. Such dizzy movements give her a headache, make her sick in her stomach, and sometimes, though not for a long time now, she falls and does not know what is happening. Vergel gave her medication that she keeps in a white box under her clothes. She knows how to stop herself from falling now, how to contain the flooding that fills her up but sometimes is fire of many colors.

"Who is it you said?" Patro accepts the glass.

"Someone you don't know. No one. They moved away."

"Then why did you bring it up? Something is bothering you, Loreto. Is it the money? *Hija,* you can't get it back. Just be careful next time. Why don't you sleep? Just lie down and rest."

Loreto stands at the window, her eyes closed against the light while she thinks that they have the same hurt probably, only she laughs about hers; uses sounds or silence, whatever stops the hurting. It does not go away. A persistent guest, it comes to catch her unawares; when she is most happy even; when she is thinking of nothing peacefully. She is no longer young. That is worse than being ill. Friends her age talk about their children going to school in another year or so.

The shadow of a branch, refracted by a pane of glass into a wing, startles her. She steps away, looks down at her skirt. It feels as if water over the rim of a glass has spilled. She wipes her dry hand on her skirt, keeps it inside a fold. Her fingers feel as if they have been pricked by pins.

Where is his wound, she wants to know, returning to the floor where she spins the buttons among the pins. Is he now thinking of her? Gathering the pins, she sees again the way he looked at her. It is as if that look is the whole of his life; that look. She wants to dream it away. To destroy it. To save him from ugly dreams.

Now she recalls that an uncle promised him a job with an airline to be set up in competition with the Philippine Airlines. Close to two million was spent and pocketed by officials along the way, but the project had not reached anyone even close to Malacañang by the time the uncle died.

It is like listening to someone else's thoughts and Loreto pricks her finger. She presses out the blood, then sucks it out, deliberately looking the other way from her mother who is watching.

His look is the whole of both their lives and she is prepared to think of happiness for him, to save him from cruelties. This excites her and she rises, thinking of what it will take for his attention to advance to the next step. What if to lead him there, to wish him there, is to risk his dying? She knows the burning in her body from being kissed, but not whether this is what she wants from him. Can she even make him speak? The way he looked—all that his body contains must be sounds, terrifying sounds he dares not let go. Is he also unable to love? What makes him sad?

But are her brothers any better? Vergel became a doctor only to work in a regional provincial hospital, earning practically nothing though he was a college and university scholar through the nine years. He even married a widow. Benhur should be a judge by now, but it will be Osong his friend who will get the appointment from Cory. It can't all be a matter of luck. Are some men afraid to succeed?

Angry at herself over the extreme arching of her thoughts where she exists in memory; angry at Emilio Luna's untamed silence and the wildness of her wish, she gets up.

"Where are you going?" Patro asks, alerted by the frown on Loreto's face. "It's hot outside. Your head will pound from the sun . . . If you're going to your *Lola* Sula, tell Anya to come home. Cover your head or walk in the shade. Can you hear me?"

It feels as if she has several faces and she does not answer. Asleep or awake, either way or both, will Emilio Luna be in her thoughts forever? Not speaking. Eyes dark and sad, like bruises. Making love; looking.

Between the fences and the sounds of neighbors sleeping she walks while her thoughts continue, colliding inside her head like flames firing and surging. Only that morning, on her way out to the market, she was certain she had already met everyone she wanted to meet. Her life is over; nothing good has happened to her. And now she is thinking of placing herself where he can see her. How is that different from Sally chasing Benhur?

Is he lonely? She walks past houses, forgetting to ask permission to go by. May she?

"Lonely?" Her *Lola* Sula asked back when a neighbor's curiosity had offended her. "Why should I be? All the people I care about are with me while I sit here alone. Here is where God will come back for me."

Can she keep Emilio Luna in her thoughts, too? Will that keep him from dying, herself as well; from dying the way flowers decay on the stem in front of everyone?

The sky, a pale sea, falls across the trail. When he looked at her, was he wondering if she has ever been loved, or kissed? There are many reasons not to go on living. Just different. Ready to be faithful, Loreto heads towards her grandmother the long way that passes Emilio Luna's house.

She is almost staggering under the sun. He is crying in her thoughts; his look was something that lived only for a moment because she did not accept it. She could have said something, or smiled. But that might have frightened him. This time will he speak?

The longing about him and herself makes them breathe together while the sun lies in patches across the trail, held by the shadows of leaves which make the light appear torn. She can't understand. It feels like being in love, to think these thoughts that streak the sky like rockets tearing the leaves in their bursting. She closes her eyes, reaches out to hang on to the fence of hibiscus on the way, remembering during the fireworks, once, a boy older than she walking towards her, the sparklers in his hands spraying her with light; and she, afraid of being struck or simply afraid, recoils though he wants only to give her his sadness and the sounds buried in his body.

With more of these thoughts Loreto punishes herself. Was there another time when he came towards her—this time speaking: I want to see what you have—and she also turned away? His words frightening her, making her tremble as if they were parts of his body; his fingers.

Approaching the trees that survived the fireworks of long ago in the Luna yard, Loreto decides she will not look up when she passes the house; she will not be Sally Moscoso but will free herself of the impulse to apologize for not smiling back, for the echoes deep in her of his unsaid words that shake her. She does not want to know what his voice is like. It is herself she must protect.

It is like letting him die, to make this decision; not to look up; not to look for him.

Loreto looks. The old windows, paned in *capiz,* are pushed across the sills like barriers; the space between, narrow and permanent slashes.

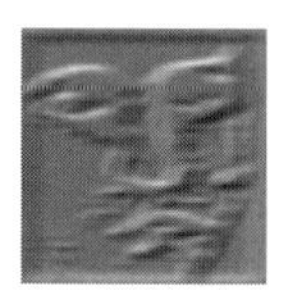

Through the branches of the *seresa,* Patro watches Loreto walking away from the house, head uncovered from the sun and the light rain falling. She wishes she knew Loreto is not looking for a man to sleep with. The Luna house is on the trail she is following. It has to be Emilio Luna about whom Loreto started to ask.

Patro wishes for a devotion to which Loreto can turn the intensity her body feels. But when she acceded to her mother-in-law's demand to convert, she gave up her recourse to the rosary, to litanies and novenas of Masses, to the laws of abstinence and fasting through which she could have taught Loreto to lift her thoughts from herself and her impotent desires.

After the trail descends toward the river, hiding Loreto, Patro continues to watch. It feels as if her eyes are being pushed out while she stands by the window until the sun catches a drop of rain hanging from a leaf of *seresa* and begins, inside its curve, to dance.

When she is asked,
Anya goes to church with neighbors; but she tries on Sunday, before the Chinese Opera comes on TV at nine, to watch the evangelical programs. She turns the sound low so the Hallelujahs will not draw attention. Sometimes she closes her eyes, listening only to the words that hold her upright and remind her of her father when he used to preach in Kapalaran.

Brother Rod in *barong Tagalog* takes over from Reverend Ernest Angley, who warned about disgracing God "in your body." Anya writes his words down on the pad of paper she bought with money from Benhur: *Feed on the works of God, not on the works of the Flesh.* God is crying, "Where are you?"

Now Brother Rod is telling her, "Touch the afflicted part of your body as I pray and you repeat: Thank you, God. Thank you, Jesus. You will feel the Spirit in your hurting part. I want you to get a pen and write to me so we can declare the glory of God."

Next, she listens to Jimmy Swaggart. "I want you to say these words and believe in them. According to your Holy Word, I confess, Jesus Christ. . . . I cry and I am saved. Hallelujah."

Anya cries inside, trying to remember the words that she will add to her letter to her mother. Her whole body aches from missing her brothers and mother, her friends in Kapalaran. She accepts the blows of the words which seem to seek her: "The devil has reached your mind. You want to touch, to feel Satan's works in the world today. Society accepts sinners. Minds are leached by the devil who chisels works of the flesh in the hearts of men. Do you want to go to heaven or to hell? Yield to God. Make sure God's love is the only thing flowing out of you. Leeches are terrible to look at. What if you see them coming out of you? What are you doing in secret?"

Head bowed as instructed, Anya does not see Loreto standing behind her, looking as if she has brushed against fresh thorns.

The mosquito buzzes
inside her mosquito net. Since turning on the light will wake up the three other Sisters—all of them asleep on the floor, their separate mats along the walls but touching corners in the center of the room—Sister Laura waits in the dark for it to alight on her face again. It is quick. Even as she lifts a hand to slap it, it has flown away, taking its time to return.

She's afraid it will not only draw blood, engorge itself from a fine exclamation point to a fat beak, but that it will enter her ear. That bothers her more than how the world will end; and when.

Only those who might have a reason to fear the Lord's second coming would want to know the day and the hour. Others would be happy enough whenever He comes. Sister Clementina, whose gentleness led Sister Laura to enter the order, often says, "Salvation cannot be stolen from us. Honor and possession we can be cheated out of. Not salvation, once deserved by the grace of God." Her own wish is that, through her, someone else will enter that new state of being, freely and lovingly allowing the Lord in. Maybe Loreto Vitaliano . . .

What rests uneasy on her mind is how the world goes on. She worries, hearing through the thin walls children coughing from walking to school in the rain, walking through flooded streets where open sewers, into which they can disappear, lie beneath the water. She worries that they will step onto live wires brought down by the wind; that the coughing weakens their lungs and hearts.

Typhoon Gading left over a hundred dead just in regions one to four. Garbage, left uncollected, floated like waterlilies along the Pasig into Manila Bay. Of the P20 million earmarked for release to flooded areas, only a seventh of the amount has been spent; the rest probably lies deep in some secret pockets.

"It is because we Filipinos are killing our forests faster than anyone else in Southeast Asia," Sister Gertrudis read from the papers. "Deforestation turns farms into deserts. Only private initiative will turn the situation around."

Sister Gertrudis cuts down continuously on what she eats. It is her way of spreading God's love. Less and less of everything but love. Common and ordinary love, not ecstatic. Reliable, not frenzied. Pure. She raises herbs that take forever to dry during the rains. Goats, being raised to send to Saudi, overrun the garden plots. Mothers misplace the packets of seeds.

Even in Gulod, people now trust the pharmaceutical syrups that come in bottles so small they last two days at the most, costing the price of supper for an entire family. Why?—when *makahiya,* the weed, relieves asthma; mango and *chico* leaves are balm for sore throats and fevers; chewed, unripe *calamansi* opens nasal passages. All over Gulod grow weeds that can cure illnesses, yet the people choose chemical drugs that cost all they have, because these are advertised by movie stars whose lives people follow with the interest they used to devote to the lives of saints.

A catalogue of sins in Gulod mocks the vanity that they are spreading knowledge and virtue by living there instead of returning to the convent at night. Close to despair, often, Sister Laura is reminded of Sister Milagros who is old and bent over but continues to go to San Simeon to work with the children of the dissidents. Explaining her vocation, Sister Milagros simply insists that, at the age of eighteen, she eloped with God.

Then she regains humility, returns to the loving silence of God, who knows the time for all things and for each one. And if some in Gulod still refuse to greet them, walking the longer way to avoid passing their door, she remembers the Lord saying: *Offer peace. If the people are peaceful, your peace will rest on them. If they are not, it will return to you.*

Because of EDSA, it is clear the Philippines is the new Jerusalem; and Gulod is part of it, though failures and illness are constant. Psalm 137 tells her to place Jerusalem ahead of her joy.

The mosquito makes a low pass at her; she can almost feel it sting. It will keep her awake until the first cockcrow. She will need all her will to wake up and face the work of the day, knowing it is almost always the same child who falls in and out of illness, the same families who are unable to stop fighting one another; the same people hoarding the love and care they receive, instead of passing it on so everyone can be joined together in love.

She will need several bodies to devote to all the movements needed by the country. The National Greening Movement for Reforestation is just one. Two Columban Sisters from Hong Kong started a Tuberculosis Eradication and Control Program in Zambales with medicine from the American bases. The shelter for unwed mothers and youthful offenders at Marillac Hills is named after the patron saint of social workers. Since they already know how to make a life, they have to be taught how to make a living. Sometimes, she almost wishes God would just give the poor some dignity and good health.

All she has is one body, in one place—Gulod—where the stench and the poverty gave her nightmares when they first started to live there. Leveriza is worse, according to Sister Ana Matilde. "In Gulod there is something to look at. You can see the sky. And a river flows by. It is easier here to look forward to the next day. Easier to share the life of the people for twenty-four hours, day in and day out."

Sister Laura has learned to tuck her mosquito net under her mat to keep the roaches out. Sister Clementina Elena was bitten by a rat and her big toe inflamed immediately. They waited for morning when they could bring her to the clinic, wondering if anti-rabies shots, the same as for dog bites, were what she needed. Injected into the spine, the serum sometimes has paralyzed the patient.

She still dreads passing between the houses, almost touching across the trails; fears the men clustered where trails intersect. She has not forgotten once, with her sisters and cousins during an Independence Day parade at Luneta, being grabbed by men who dared look them in the eye. With no wish to continue remembering, their surprise still makes her recoil. They did not tell their brothers and cousins, who would not have stood a chance had they challenged those men.

Through cardboard walls, Sister Laura hears the Sipalays' nightly coughing spells—first the children, then the father, and then the mother—going on in the other rented room. Five families live in the space of her parents' living room. If it has become difficult for her father to live on his pension and Money Market interest, with rice coming from their farm, how much more for those in Gulod who have no jobs. Her father has been thinking of selling their car, except that the driver and his family would lose their income and the use of the room above the garage.

An infant cries. Another angel for the Feleos, neighbors say. Children bring luck. The nurse who lives in the top room brings home abandoned babies, gives them away in Gulod. Angels get worms, catch pneumonia and meningitis, and grow into urchins who slash handbags for drug money, if they are not swept down into open manholes and *esteros* during floods. If they are not saved.

Rain still comes into their two rooms. The smell of urine leaches through the walls. They are looking forward to getting a sink so they will not have to wash dishes outside the door; but that is not a priority. Nor having an iron to press the altar cloth. Nor a tree in front of the window to shut out the afternoon sun. The *ylang-ylang* tree disappeared. It was taken away whole and chopped up elsewhere.

But in another month the fiesta will be held. Relatives abroad will send money, some of which will be used to buy votes for contestants determined to become fiesta queen. The year before, the winner's carriage was decorated with midribs of coconut through which marshmallows were threaded. *Aling* Maxima complained that many of her wares were "borrowed" because people forgot to pay for them.

Sister Laura is about to fall asleep when she feels a sting on her forehead. Quicker than the mosquito can fly off, she slaps it against herself.

"Are you awake, too?" Sister Ana Matilde asks.

"Yes, Tindeng."

"You remember that little girl who thought I was her grandmother when we first arrived, and who ran away when the other children laughed at her for making the mistake? I saw her on the trail and she went over to me, took my hand and pressed it to her forehead."

"Yes!"

"And I decided, tomorrow, I will go along with the Feleos when they visit their child in the hospital. They don't have P800 for the blood transfusion, so I will give my blood."

"Are you sure? You're not a hundred pounds."

"We can't make miracles wait, Sister Laura. I'll drink a lot of water, then I can weigh more."

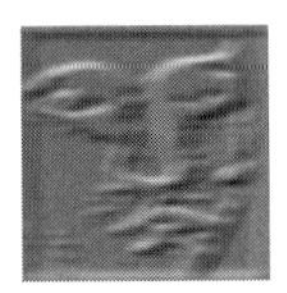

From the week-long vigil
at TV Channel 7 and the barricading of Don Mariano Marcos Avenue; from the rally at Malacañang on the last day in March, when San Juan Mayor Joseph Estrada and the Pampanga delegation called for election, not selection/appointment of local officials; from the two weeks at the barricade in front of the United States Embassy on Roxas Boulevard; from all this, Siso Feleo has developed a sixth sense about when to start running.

On the lookout, he is restive listening to President Aquino. "Purify the ranks of racketeers, kingpins, mini-dictators," she tells the crowd gathered on May First, Labor Day. "Make me prouder, my workers, of this second revolution to make our country free of a tyrant in the Palace, of tyranny everywhere, the tyranny of poverty and underdevelopment, of political power."

Of all the crowds Siso has been in, this is the biggest. For the first time together, five major labor groups have assembled to celebrate *Mayo Uno.* Coming from assembly points all over Metro Manila, by ten in the morning they are all marching toward Luneta from Liwasang Bonifacio, formerly Plaza Lawton. Almost half a million by media count, they pledge support to the government, demand price roll-backs, dismantling of American bases, land reform, genuine industrialization, a pro-Filipino economy.

Siso learns to sing "The Internationale," with Bien Sotero beside him saying: "Two months after EDSA and 500 political prisoners are still in custody."

Among the capitalists on stage, Bastian Canonigo counts Buscayno and Sison. Communist leaders, who appear at ease.

Anti-riot troops watch the color-coded crowd. Yellow marks the Cory crowd; red-white-blue, the Marcos. Gold sickles identify farmers, while gold hammers are on flags carried by industrial workers. Protesting Aquino's speech, some bottles are thrown along with rocks. The troops fan out.

"I won't throw rocks," Siso says. "This is just a living for me. If I can grow two more heads I'll do it, so I can earn a total of three hundred pesos for my children. I have a newborn. Five children, one almost as tall as I." He looks at Bastian Canonigo to confirm what he is saying to those who turn to listen.

"I'm getting only P80," a man says.

"Your contractor must be greedier than ours," Bastian says. "We're not the luckiest, though. Someone said he is getting P200 for today. How much were we paid, Siso, in the march to Batasan? That was the 14th of April when two strikebreakers were killed. Didn't you get sick from sleeping on the ground?"

"I don't remember. No more than today. It was a relative of *Aling* Maxima who brought us there. We were about 6,000 in all." Siso remembers the traffic jams starting from PHILCOA.

The group in yellow shouts them down. "Move away if you want to talk. Go join Marcos in Hawaii."

"We're not loyalists," Siso Feleo says. "We voted for Cory, too. *Peks man.*" He never waved the Marcos posters during the demonstrations. When "Ako'y Pilipino" is sung, instead of "Bayan Ko" in Luneta, he remains silent, watching the *ati-atihan* marchers drumming. That he never harassed motorists or other groups did not prevent his being stoned by groups wearing yellow. One Sunday, hoodlums waited for them in the Chinese Garden of the Park, trying to keep them from going up to the Quirino Grandstand where speakers claimed Marcos was kidnapped by the

American government in order to put Cory in power. A campaign was begun there to get five million signatures to petition for Marcos's return. On April 27 Marcos addressed them from Hawaii on the telephone hook-up.

As far as Siso Feleo can tell, nothing is assured. The last week of April, the Communists ambushed a military convoy. Six were killed and the Reuters photographer was wounded. Still, Cory gives the Communists six months to respond to her offer of negotiations. Before the deadline, thousands could die in ambush. The military has its hands tied in Mindanao, for the Muslims have started fighting for separation. He would not want to be president, even for a day. He might fail, and the country would only suffer greater.

The euphoria over EDSA feels forced now, because fewer and fewer doubt the loyalists' claim that in two months, say in June, Tolentino, Marcos's running mate, will take his oath at the Quirino grandstand in front of two million. Siso Feleo has no feelings either way. But if he were president, he'd do what Vice-President Laurel is urging Cory to do: hold elections and restore constitutional government; convene parliament. The problems are too complex to postpone decisions till the Holy Spirit phones in solutions. One of these days, he tells Nani, we'll wake up and Tolentino will have been proclaimed acting-president. Back to suffering for fifty-four million Filipinos, thirty million voters. Did the one million on EDSA represent the country? He means to ask Benhur.

Benhur will say that EDSA is not supposed to keep anyone alive forever. The Boss contractor said there are about 1,200 of them, all paid to demonstrate against the government. It does not make Siso feel secure. A mayor appointed to the town of Alicia was ambushed and assassinated. Cardinal Sin said that by March 17, the Communists would have defected to Cory. It's already May.

"Let's go," Bastian cracks a joke. "I've already seen Imelda Papin and Elizabeth Oropesa. Meding will say I'm flirting here. She's afraid to be alone in the house during brownouts."

"You won't get paid if you leave now," Siso says.

"That man there is eying us, did you notice? He's closer now than when we arrived. The troops will practice maximum toleration, but that man has devil eyes. Let's go."

Meding, his wife, blames Siso Feleo for taking him to demonstrations. Do only what's good for you, she told Bastian and did not want him to go to the railroad station at Tutuban with Marcelo Andres. Let the three candidates fight, Meding said of Cory's appointee, her brother's appointee, and the Marcos man who fired old-timers to bring in his own men.

It did no good to try to explain that no one else in Gulod knows how to slaughter a pig. What would the supporters of the one from Bicol do with the pig donated to him with sacks of rice so he can barricade himself inside the station at Tutuban?

Two wires were all he needed. Live wires. He ran them to the outlet in the canteen. Wires in hand he faced the pig being held by those employees who had not had a change of clothes for days. It was easy. Coming from behind the animal, he touched the wires to the pig's ears. After it toppled over, he plunged a knife to its heart and the blood spurted, flowed like the eels swimming alongside the bodies Dionisia had found floating in the river. The appointee from Bicol watched from the window . . .

"Bastian," Siso calls Bastian back from talking to those wearing red and blue shirts. "Bastian, when you see me start running, go after me, or you'll never get back to Gulod for Christmas." He had brought Hernan Sipalay once, but Hernan was total worry. All he did was talk about Paradise. One man told Hernan it's all in his head. Like an ailment. And Hernan almost got him in trouble that way, especially when Hernan said the nuns for Marcos were not real nuns. Just fanatics dressed like nuns. Running away, Hernan shouted, "God is not in the head!"

Bastian stands closer to Siso. "If I don't get to Pakil on the fifteenth, we won't have Christmas. Meding's brother gives me a pig on the town fiesta, but if one day there's a ceasefire, and on the next it is just going to be announced, how can I go?"

"One newspaper says it's the fault of the army: if the military stayed inside their barracks, there would be no one for the Communist NPAs to shoot at, and there would be peace and order in the *barrios.*"

What Bastian knows about pigs he learned from Meding's father, who looks for big feet and wide shoulders. Long snouts indicate a quarrelsome animal, noisy and greedy. Meding's father chooses his piglets by pointing and whispers, so the pig will not become noisy. Worse than cats, pigs can keep one awake all night. One year, the pig he was fattening for Christmas was drugged before it was carried away. He heard nothing.

"We might not have Christmas," Bastian repeats.

"Cook one of your roosters," Siso says, watching the man with eyes as deep as bullet holes. He does not know why he would try to help Bastian earn money when he is almost as bad as Hernan Sipalay with his original ideas. Bastian was the one who advised Marcelo Andres to make crowns from his barbed wire fence and hawk them to the lines waiting to tour Malacañang Palace.

"They're not mine, Siso. This morning before we left, I noticed the eyes of the Texas were getting cloudy. If it's the pest, it takes only hours to spread. They could all be dead by the time we get home. I told Meding to send for antibiotics from the Chinese. It's his chickens."

Bastian has lost all interest in the speech. He is thinking of the *lupi,* which ends that Sunday. Meding always brings back souvenirs from the harvest festival—a stub of candle, some rose petals to cure headaches, a small bottle of blessed oil to rub on legs that feel numb. Better, of course, is to dip in the springs of the Nuestra Señora de Dolores, the Lady of Sorrows, before whom cripples and childless couples dance, singing "Torumba la Virgen / La Virgen Torumba." The image looks you in the eye.

Bastian smiles, remembering he used to be part of the world. Now, the river in Pakil is no longer where it used to be, but the *duhat* is ripening fast, fatter than dark beetles.

"Run. Bastian," Siso Feleo calls out, as suddenly the crowd breaks up into fierce head-on collisions. At age forty-five, Siso manages to outrun the anti-riot police and men intent on beating them up. He looks back to see if Bastian is right behind him and is pushed down, slips and hits his face on the broken glass from shop windows and cars. Others stumble over him, preventing him from getting up, out of their way.

Pressing his hands on the wounds starting to bleed, Siso rolls under one of the cars. If it were not for his children, he would not leave Gulod. They would be standing at the doorway waiting to catch him walking down the trail. If only they could have been born in heaven; if only . . .

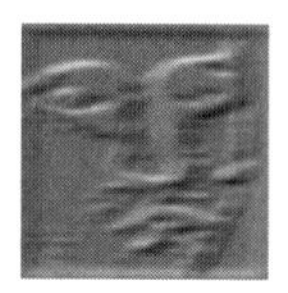

About to go next door
to the surveyor and offer his desk and typewriter for sale, Benhur looks down Orosa and thinks he sees Siso Feleo running down toward Padre Faura, limping. Only a few stragglers are going by when he gets down.

"It happens every rally." Seniong Enriquez is back as security guard. "A few skulls are broken, but the next day there are even more protesting the U.S.–backed Cory dictatorship, as they call it. It's like ping-pong."

"So it is," Benhur says, taking one last look down Orosa. Siso Feleo would have come up to hide, if that was he.

"I was helping my son with his homework and discovered that the first battle for freedom was in 1521. April 27. Lapu-Lapu killed Magellan in Mactan. First freedom fight, Attorney."

"475 years ago Sunday." Benhur uses the new math.

"When President Marcos talked in the open rally via telephone," Seniong says.

The juxtaposition makes it seem to Benhur that they are talking about an imaginary country. 475 years into the future, EDSA might not be in history, its essence diffused like the dust of stars in the population of the earth; indistinct remnants. With this, he further senses that he is leaving the country out of fear, not going abroad towards hope of a new life.

It is a fleeting sense of defeat, for when he knocks at Rafols' door he sees a handwritten quote on an index card pasted to the door frame: *Nothing emboldens the wicked so much as lack of courage on the part of the good.*

He plucks out the word "courage" for his own faltering will and hangs it on himself. Thus armored, he steps in with great confidence to offer the surveyor the option to buy his typewriter, desk, books; whatever in the office might interest him at his price. The Vitalianos are not *comerciantes* intent on profit. He might even give those objects away, except that he is not in a position to be so generous. And if the books are not of any value to Rafols, he will bring them to Gulod, in case one of the boys decides to take up law. He knows that's not likely. He himself can stay only to flunk his last semester, or the Bar. It would be the ultimate. *Did you hear? Benhur Vitaliano flunked. I thought he graduated with us. No wonder.*

"Come in. Come in. Benhur! I knocked at your door a few times but you were not in. Try the darts. I drew the targets myself. Come in. Make yourself at home."

The room is farthest from anyone's idea of an office. Felipe Rafols, in addition to surveying, which has been one long off-season, has sold books on the occult and Eastern philosophies as well as records of mood music to settle the soul's restlessness. In between those ventures, he has run a health shop specializing in imported oils for native ailments. Ginseng cures impotence of the physical kind. Unsold items line shelves pushed to the corners, creating a sense of discord and failure.

"Take your choice of targets, Benhur."

Drawn directly on the wall of composite boards are life-size caricatures of Marcos and his cronies, some of whom are now in Cory's government.

"One day, waiting for clients to interrupt my thoughts, I decided to draw on the walls. I really got the idea from Kakasa Ka Ba, the December fundraising for Cory. This is a new line-up, but also partly old. I'm bothered by all the infighting. *Intrega pa rin.* Competing for the same jobs and favors. How can the Filipino advance? Until I can figure it out, I'm going to throw darts. Won't it be something if there's truth to voodoo and I prick some consciences? Many times, I lift the phone to call Cory. Not that I can get past her *cordon sanitaire.*"

"What will you say?" Benhur holds a dart poised.

"Three sentences: 'Cory, you're not a Girl Scout or a saint. You're our president. Start presiding.' Don't you think I should, before she goes on reigning?"

"She said she will not entertain unsolicited advice." Benhur throws and misses Marcos's heart by an arm's length.

"How then can she learn what the people are thinking? Magsaysay opened Malacañang to everyone who wanted to talk to him. Peasants and workers lined up along with men in crisp *barong.* How else will she hear what hurts the country? A litany of praise is bad for the soul. To have a mind of her own, she should know other minds. Otherwise she's boxed in with her own reflection for company."

"So," Benhur says, his mind on selling.

"You know, that might be how the *politicos* planned it. Let a woman win for them. Install her. Smokescreen for their own agenda. The way we enthrone the Mother of Perpetual Help in our homes, then go our own merry way past heaven, paying no attention to her presence except to make a sign of the cross and give her a nod on our way out of the house. The way we ignore our mothers and sisters and wives, until we have to run to them for protection or consolation; then afterwards, again and again, betray them with our own selfishness."

"Perhaps," Benhur says, with no energy to follow this up with comments of his own. The Cory dolls were already being sold at the second month's anniversary of EDSA in Camp Aguinaldo. Write it down. Benhur aims with the second of the three darts. Mudslinging is easier, like dum-dum bullets.

"You remember reading about the corpses of soldiers unearthed standing upright when the hills outside Capas were cut down for a subdivision or something?"

"Yes?" Benhur anticipates a reference to the memorial to the Japanese on the same highway, always freshly painted, while the Capas memorial stands full of weeds.

"This line-up reminded me. The difference is that those soldiers fought the Japanese invaders, and these monkeys helped Marcos run off with billions from the Japanese in exchange for our future. Maybe not billions, but who can count past a few thousands? Not me. That's why all my business attempts fail, at the outset."

Recalling that 1,200 Americans and 10,000 Filipinos died in the Death March, conservative estimates excluding civilians, Benhur throws the third dart, which bounces off the wall and lands under Imelda's feet.

"Here's three more. You know, I could as easily be in that line-up of crooks except a run of bad luck manages to keep me honest. I can't approach anyone for a favor. I can't make a profit off a gold mine, my mother-in-law says. To her, I'm *non compos mentis.* Nothing in the head. Perhaps in the heart; a little. I agreed to have all the properties in my wife's name—she brought them into the marriage anyway—so I can't misuse the income or so creditors will not take them away. This is my abode. I'm free to survey and sell exotic wares that quickly bore the customers who stumble upstairs. I haven't found my true calling. Which might be just what I am. Placeholder. Saving space for someone else, for something. Frightening if true. I don't mean to tell you my story, Benhur."

Benhur notes that they both look as if they slept in their clothes. "By any chance can you use another typewriter?"

Rafols holds the dart poised to throw. "It works?"

Benhur nods.

"How much?"

"Make an offer."

"Well. They're not making typewriters anymore, and I'm too old to learn the word processor, besides the fact I can't afford one. Let me see. Why don't you look around and pick what you want? Barter. Look. Here are books on divination and psychic phenomena I picked up in the States. I lived there, you know. Instead of hanging out in the bars, I went to bookshops and bought remaindered books. Over here are health items. Ginseng detoxifies. Powders for emotional and physical distress. Oils for incoherence of thought, hallucination. Because these come directly from nature, there are no side effects or hangovers. Just avoid mega doses. Or books. My wife never understood my need for wider and deeper knowledge.

This one is all about homeopathy. Browse. Take what you want."

Benhur scans a book on crystal healing. How does he restate he needs the money, prefers it, without humiliating himself and Rafols?

"When the rains start, there will be a Crystal Conference Seminar in Mt. Banahaw. May 23. Crystals clear the mind by aligning brain waves. They can crack in reaction to patients. We're made of minerals, you know. The processes and knowledge of our planet are inside minerals. Quartz contains the information for our survival. First, you soak the quartz in salt water, to purify it. Dry it in the sun. Then program it by stating your general tasks for it, three times. You receive its energy by meditating. Quartz can remove malignant cysts. Surgery without scalpel or laser. Maybe you will take the bee pollen or royal jelly. Your wife will like them . . . Love is a devotion of the soul . . ."

"I'm moving out. Clearing out. So it has to be money. That gross."

Rafols does not appear to have heard. He leads Benhur deeper into the room, to shelves of classical music, facing a shelf marked Thresholds: *The Absent Years of Jesus Christ, Psychometry, Radionics.* "Scientific black holes. Do you have your bed aligned North to South? This book says: Cry when you feel like it. These are treatises on revolution and revelation. Soft Zen?"

Benhur shakes his head to all that.

Rafols stops at the desk behind the shelves. On the typewriter is a sheet of paper on which is typed: *Politics, the Other Sacrament.* He must have interrupted Rafols.

"It's a letter. To some of Cory's appointees." Rafols sits down, begins to type, as he talks. "Are you the one who acquired a house in Sucat, when in the States you lived in a cold-water flat? If you are, please return the money to the people. Politics is a sacrament. Are you the one who sells naturalization papers to illegal entrants? You are despoiling 54 million Filipinos of their heritage and discriminating against foreigners without the means to bribe officials. Please resign and save the country the cost of an investigation and trial which will only end in a whitewash. Are you the one who, in his hurry to leave the motel before photographers discovered him in a compromising position over a movie starlet, left his suit jacket with his name handsewn into the lining? For the sake of the country, please resign. Immorality is part of the garbage thrown at 54 million of your countrymen by you who are supposed to serve them. Return to your wife when your glands activate . . ."

Benhur watches Rafols typing over his errors without erasing them; so quickly does he type that the two fingers of each hand fly over the keys. From where Benhur stands he can see that the letters *t* and *e* are broken, missing from the keyboard, so the sentences appear to be in code.

"I deliberately don't use religious motifs. I don't talk about crucified land or people. We are oppressed and exploited and should be saved in history, not in some other existence. Internal collapse is what religion deals with. Though maybe the integrity of persons is interconnected with that of ideas. In Negros, children are dying of stage three malnutrition. They cannot be saved by prayers. Forty years ago we were ahead of the countries in Southeast Asia. Now, we're down with Bangladesh . . ."

"I need the money. I can't take books or health supplies." He feels as if he's begging, so Benhur turns around to see himself out.

"I know. But everything is in my wife's name. Her mother insisted. All I have is what I make from surveying. I could survey land for you."

Benhur breaks into a smile. Land! "Shall I leave your door open?"

He closes his own door on entering. There is a hum inside his office, a vibration that comes from nowhere. Sorting the contents of his desk drawers, he finds a photograph of himself and his father which he stands against the phone. What is the connection between that picture and times that refuse to get better?

The picture, from being enlarged, has an oddly faded, indistinct quality. They look like brothers.

Sister Madeleine tells him to be permeable to the Divine Presence; Rafols tells him to be permeable to the country.

A knock breaks into his thoughts. It's Rafols.

"I meant to ask you to join with me and some born-again nationalists. We could use another mind. Jun Enriquez is our president. National Economic Protection Association. Like the pre-war NEPA. If we don't act on our own behalf, no one will; we will end up footnotes in history. The *desparecidos* of the world. Easy to ignore, to stereotype. Will you, at least, consider it? I'm sorry about the typewriter. Even the bank accounts are in my wife's name, until, as my mother-in-law says, I can support her and my family. I can't even see Charles Bronson at the Robinson. Movies are my one weakness. *Death Wish 3* is a blockbuster."

"I would like to, but I'm going abroad." Benhur places an arm about Rafols, then pulls away. It is the same way he posed with his father, before his heart was taken from him and the world died.

His usual self,

trying to be in several places at once. Just as they are leaving, Joel decides instead to attend the third month celebration of EDSA inside Camp Aguinaldo the 25th of May.

"Miggy, this is history continuing. There will be other days to track down those who have disappeared. Besides, Gringo Honasan is going to lead some Reformist colonels in a parachute drop right after Cory's speech. She's expected to name the members of her Constitutional Commission, some Iglesia, some Communists. How can you miss it?"

"I said I'll go to Cavite," Miggy explains, restraining his anger that Joel will make plans, only to change them at the last minute. "Let's just make sure we come home together or Mamá will worry. Let's meet at *Tito* Benhur's office."

"You said to whom? Anita Rolda again. She's using you to get her first by-line as freelance journalist. Imagine hustling for several news agencies. Agence France Press should be enough. It's her being released as a political detainee that gets her the connections." Joel tries one more trick to get Miggy to Camp Aguinaldo.

It makes Miggy even more determined to go to Cavite. Each time suspicious mounds are discovered or bodies are found anywhere—in caves, the seashore or hills—relatives of the disappeared go at once to the place with the media and human-rights workers; and he wants to be there this time.

Miggy waits for the convoy in the parking lot of the Intercontinental in Makati. Joel would have talked him into coffee and sandwiches in the Jeepney Coffeehouse, to waiting in the lobby where he would have tourists and class people instead of drivers and food vendors for an audience. He thinks this, knowing it's not fair. Joel has decided to go to the University of the Philippines, for pre-med. "To work in the slums or some barrio like *Tito* Vergel and earn TYs. Since thank you's will not build me a clinic, I'll start by treating the rich. Together, we can really work much good. We can eventually have a ship that stops at the remote islands, bringing medical attention to those who have never seen a doctor or nurse. We'll call it *Pangarap.* Hope."

He's not proud of the fact that he replied, when Joel asked that they register together, "At EDSA you tried to talk me into becoming a priest. Maybe I'll take the year off and think about becoming a correspondent." No ego-tripping for him.

Because of Anita Rolda? He knows only that she's good; on the verge of tears, tough and bold. Unstoppable. He wants to help her file that breakthrough report. He has checked sources for her, hustled interviews, waited at offices until they closed and before they opened again. For her he trailed potential interviewees and fought to get the policy announcement ahead of the herd of hopefuls. With her eyes, she walks all over him.

He wants to be the one who helps her succeed.

She needs him to flesh out her reports. In her hurry she tends to see only the big movements and gestures: 5,000 wearing Cory souvenirs to the Palace on the International Women's Day, March 9. She got the speeches and the figures on stage correct, the celebrities list that now includes leaders of cause-oriented groups. He inserts the infant, born in prison, resting in the shade of its mother's scarf; the workers in factories owned by foreigners who throw the defective bras at their faces and call them ugly; the Muslim women in their cotton headcovers and deep silence, cautious with smiles.

Sometimes, he suspects she's more into ideology than issues, that what she reports comes from ideas she has read, not from what she's lived or witnessed. He knows it's possible to show compassion without feeling it.

She's into gender issues, as if it's not hard enough for men as well. She has the dramatic sense: *7,000 prostitutes serve American bases.* Her report on mail-order brides she entitled: *Bride Marketeering.* She will not stick to facts, events, and people. "All history is slanted," she says, "I'll slant it the other way so it will stand on its own."

When she calls him "luv" he feels reduced to someone unnamed and without blessings, distorted, about to be eaten alive. Then he thinks of her as a painting by Bacon; skinned flesh, spilled viscera hanging on exhibition: all ferocious pain until something he says makes her smile.

"Are you with us?" A man wearing a jacket with pockets notices him waiting. "Killing fields?"

Miggy nods, follows the man to a van with media people already seated. He is led to a car with room for one more. To save on gasoline, no one has started the motors of the vehicles lined up beside the shrubs.

He's supposed to say Anita Rolda sent him in her place, but he doesn't. Instead of introductions, he shakes the hand of the student beside the driver. In the back seat there are four. Turning around to introduce himself with handshakes, Miggy recognizes Mrs. Luna and her son. Emilio Luna does not look up from his clasped hands.

They start out in silence, until past the highway to the Manila International Airport everyone takes out money for the toll; except for Emilio Luna who looks ahead, not interested in the decision of who would pay the toll going and then coming back. Miggy remembers his mother saying that not even someone who can charm lizards down from the ceiling can hope to turn Emilio Luna's head.

Once into the South Super Highway, Mrs. Luna breaks her own silence. "I have not lighted a candle for my daughter because she is missing, not dead."

"Let me see her picture," the woman behind the driver says. "How old is she in this one?"

"That's three years ago. She was nineteen."

"Over a year, they don't usually surface any more," the student tells Miggy who reads the name on the notebook: Florentino Lazaro. "I was thinking, this is my third trip; if it's the soul that matters, should it be important where the body is buried? If we are sacred because God made us, should not the earth be made holy by each, by any interment?"

Anita Rolda would not be interested in that quote. He worries that she will miss her deadline if he is delayed getting back. The wire agencies have staggered deadlines. Only the *Straits Times* and Singapore have the same dateline as Manila. So far, very little of what she has wired has seen print. Once, she pulled him to herself, took his hand where electrodes had been attached to her body and said, "It's only my body they hurt. In five years I'll be on the cover of *Elle, Times;* name it. And it will not matter I've been through hell. Will it?"

By the time she has become a bureau chief, full-time journalist, he should be on with his life. But not in medicine. Joey might not make it either. He'll get sick over his first cadaver, like a cousin who got up as far as saving the preemies at PGH. "Skin like jellyfish but human . . ."

Parked off the road beyond the exit at Bicutan, a private jeepney, decorated like a passenger vehicle but with a door marked *private* at the back, waits. It is to lead the convoy, from that point on. Farther on they pick up another car, and a Hi-Ace overtakes them. They are now five in all. The driver says sometimes they are about a dozen. Funeral operators meet them with men to dig and carry the bodies back to their chapels.

"You can't identify bodies by their teeth, as the foreign human rights workers thought," the student says. "Usually there are no identifications. Some bodies are without skulls; are partly dressed only." He sounds as if he's describing his life work.

From the back seat, the woman behind the driver offers them sandwiches, then resumes talking with Mrs. Luna. "How good of your son to accompany you. Girls must call him all the time. Nowadays, girls do the advancing, but in our times . . . You know!"

"He's very quiet," Mrs. Luna explains, as if Emilio Luna is not sitting beside her, eyes on the side of the road, which is interspersed with roadside stalls selling fruits, with billboards, tiny chapels and houses or huts through whose windows can be seen wardrobes faced with mirrors, photographs stuck to walls with calendars of Cory now, instead of Imelda and Marcos.

"I can see," the woman says.

"Irene was very different," Mrs. Luna goes on. "She wrote poems, plays, stories in school; helped produce political dramas. She even carried portable equipment to stage those productions in out-of-the way barrios and raise the consciousness of the people. My husband is now dead almost ten years." As if she has been asked, she talks about her other children.

The other woman says this is her first time. Her son Arnulfo Sebastian disappeared just since EDSA. "But the woman in the other car, the one with completely white hair, she has not heard from her son, a seminarian, for six years. She attends all the rallies, carrying his picture."

"Is that so?" Mrs. Luna says.

"My son is not political. He protested the National Service Law—the one obliging all students, women included, to undergo basic military service—because his girlfriend asked him. Thinking of my son, my heart just wants to leap out. I can't breathe and I stiffen and drop. That's why my daughter comes with me." She looks at her daughter, head on her shoulder; asleep. "I fall, biting my lips until they bleed. But the scream, I'm not ashamed to admit, lets out the pain. However, it starts again. My son was wearing a light-blue shirt when he left the house. I ask nuns if they have seen him. I ask priests for prayers. He could be in some barracks, some old house, some field, held against his will. Sometimes he comes back, in my sleep."

"If you think too much about these things, it can drive you crazy," the driver says. "One time the bodies we found were without clothes. The men had their trousers tied about their necks, as if they were carrying someone else piggyback. I was thinking, as they were being dug up, what do their souls think, watching their bodies being uncovered?" Then the driver starts humming "Magkaisa"—which is played during station breaks while videotapes of the People Power Revolution are replayed, slow motion; like waves rising and falling on the sea, sliding—to Virna Lisi's singing.

Florentino offers Miggy and the driver a stick of gum each. *Ginseng.* Red-labeled and wrapped. From China.

"This is supposed to make us *macho,*" the driver says, driving with one hand while he unwraps the gum. "One time we passed the fields three times, circling, and found nothing. Today, we're supposed to stop between Kilometer 33 and 34."

Miggy seizes upon the phrase to start the report: "Between kilometer 33 and 34 . . ." He wonders what Anita Rolda will say. She did not like the beginning of his report on the March 25 rally, when the women of Egypt were extolled for denouncing the orders to kill Jewish infants under the pharaohs. She cut out the paragraph about Andres Bonifacio's statue being decorated with streamers and balloons at Ugarte while "Tie a Yellow Ribbon" was sung to gridlocked traffic in Makati. She did not care about the singing of "American Junk Act" by the APO Hiking Society. She gave him her tickets to the May 10 concert at the Coliseum, saying that a piece on cultural heroes gives no direct focus on the situation.

They were real protest singers, he told her. A six-piece rhythm section and the Hotlegs Dancing Company with Freddie Aguilar.

The driver hits the brakes, seeing a bus almost collide with their lead vehicle. He swears, "There's always a fool trying to get ahead only to cause accidents."

The lead vehicle enters the shoulder of the highway and all the rest follow, since a stop is indicated. They have passed kilometer 33 and 34.

Cogon covers both sides of the road. Mango trees with dark, wet trunks are growing into one another, their leaves very like newly emerged butterflies. The land does not look to Miggy as if it holds anything that deserves a curse.

One passenger from each vehicle gets out for a conference by the side of the highway. Miggy gets out to let Florentino pass. He looks quickly at the back seat. With what face and body does Mrs. Luna expect to see her daughter? How will he stand while the earth is being dug?

Young boys riding bicycles shake their heads when asked for directions.

The driver points out the pathologist to Miggy.

"There are houses about," the driver says, "It can't be around here. We should pass a church first, then start looking. Maybe back where the grass was burned. Sometimes people burn the bodies instead of burying them. They're afraid to go to the police."

One by one, the other passengers come out and confer in a larger circle about how much each is to contribute for the diggers and the burial fees to the funeral parlor. It has been thirty pesos the last few times. Up from twenty-five.

"Hard to believe this is where we are after EDSA." The driver lights a cigarette from the stub of his old one. "I hear the Claim Center for Constitutional Rights is headed by known leftists, and General Tadiar is on house arrest while the Communists are free. They're not even on the hold list of the government."

Another driver comes up to light his cigarette on the same stub. "I heard that in return for amnesty from prosecution, Marcos is offering Cory a $3 million check. And that break-in at the Palace . . . that was to retrieve what was left behind."

Some of the media people from the van are climbing up the rise of the land to check for mounds of earth on the other side.

"Sometimes we find them in gravel pits," the driver recalls. "In one town, every step there was a body. In a poultry farm we dug up a body, the hair stuck to the ground like dried roots. Makes your hair stiffen. How many will God find that way? No. It's not a pretty sight." The driver digs his heel into the ground. "They no longer have eyes."

"In Spain," Miggy says, "they raise markers where people have been killed." He read this in a history book.

"We'd be a land of markers, if we did that," the driver says. "People continue to disappear."

There's not much daylight left, and some decide to return. It will take two hours to reach Manila. Five o'clock commuter traffic will add another hour through the city. At least. The media in the van decide to go on to the next town. Florentino and Miggy go with the van while the others return.

After two more towns, the van passengers head still farther on. Florentino and Miggy decide they will take a bus back. It's almost five.

They wait by the side of the road with commuters. The buses are filled to standing room only, stop only to let out passengers. Occasionally, someone manages to jump on.

Waiting, Miggy thinks of the relief on Mrs. Luna's face that they did not discover the mounds, as if she has been strengthened in her hope that Irene is alive, somewhere. Would she not rather be happy that Irene is dead and safe from being violated?

"I don't know why I'm so anxious to get home when it is simply a bed space. P800 a month for a stinking toilet, a window that does not open, and no water in the pipes until two in the morning. Come on. Grab." Florentino suddenly calls out.

Jumping on a bus that has slowed down to allow a passenger to leap out, Florentino throws a hand out to Miggy. But there is no space left on the steps for Miggy to board.

Every night since Miggy failed to come home, Joel dreams of him. Sometimes he sees his brother floating on a river, attempting to rise, only to slip deeper. Sometimes there is a dog, the color of sand, licking Miggy's eyes.

Awake until the sun is almost up, he goes through his memory; through the things he regrets having done, and not done; while Miggy's bed stands empty against the window.

Could it have been carnappers, who are holding Miggy in some house or mill? He has talked with his *Tito* Benhur who went to Colonel Moscoso for advice, and who asked that Benhur bring him to the house Joel does not remember seeing before. He has talked with the Task Force Detainees, with Anita Rolda, who denied asking Miggy to cover the convoy of human rights workers to Cavite.

He told his mother—"He will walk through the door one morning. You know Miggy"—though that is not like Miggy at all. "Maybe he is with Emilio Luna who goes away for days. Didn't he go to the Trappists in Guimaras once without telling?"

He went to his *Tito* Benhur's mother, sat in the front yard under the trees while she brought him food on little plates, tempting him to eat when he wanted to cry.

He dreams of Miggy and his mother together; as if he himself is the one missing, the body waiting to be found.

Sally decides to buy
the *tubigan.* She came to look at the property and has found it to be prime land, well watered, and she knows that the income from it once supported the saints with ivory faces in her aunt's house. The trip, she hopes, will take her mind off bad dreams.

"Your word is enough," her cousin says. "Just one payment when we pass papers. I also ask that no one be told I've sold the saints."

"Of course, Ester."

"As long as I could, I tried to keep them in the family. I've had replicas made, but I know they're not the same. Painted wood. When I look at them, I think of squatters; but the other day, forgetting, I knelt and prayed before them."

Sally puts her arms about her cousin. She has no words to say, though she wants to let her know that when they were young she was jealous of her: so fair, all the young men asked for her, and she was Elena in the processions, queen at the fiestas because, also, her mother could spend lavishly from their land. "Just have the new ones blessed, Ester."

"Come again. Salud, come again. Soon."

"Come visit. I'll send the driver for you. Just let me know."

"Bring the boys. I have not seen them since they were knee-high. They must be handsome."

"Yes." Sally almost runs out and into a downpour.

Neither of them had noticed it has begun to rain, and the driver is not back from the errand.

Sally would have returned, except as she ran out of the house—her thoughts on Miggy, on her not being able to tell Ester, on Joel's refusing to enroll until he and Miggy can register together, so different has Joel become that she has mistaken him for Miggy—she felt herself being blown away.

She goes as far as she can from the house, away from Ester's windows; venting her anger on the driver and moving on as people come out of the beauty parlor, the bakery; finally stopping at the pharmacy where a young woman sits behind protective grilles among bottles of shampoo, antibiotics, ointments, powders . . . Nothing she needs.

There is a small and weak *ipo-ipo* whirling in the road, lifting a gum wrapper tossed from the car that splashed rain on the sidewalk. Everything else is smeared on the road.

A woman comes out, just out of reach of the rain, carrying a small child in her arms. Sally smiles at them.

"How old?" Sally asks.

"Eight months."

"Such a straight back for eight months."

The woman lifts the baby up, then kisses it on the mouth as she brings it down again. Several times she does this, each time making the child chuckle and smile.

Sally walks the three, four steps to them.

Noticing Sally, the baby reaches out to her.

The woman then swings the baby toward Sally; brings her back; the rocking back and forth movement delighting the child into deeper smiles. *Tsubibo ng tsubibo,* she sings.

Sally reaches out for the small fist, holds it. She is about to ask its name when a man comes out.

"My husband," the woman says kissing the baby under the chin so that it tries to grab her face and rub its cheek against her.

"Step in," he says. "This is a hard rain."

It's only then Sally notices the funeral parlor. Nervous, she gives a little laugh. There is no one being waked in the single chapel.

As if he heard her thoughts, the man says, "There is no one now." He lights a cigarette, blows the smoke at the baby until the mother draws away. "Stop it. He'll grow up hacking in the morning with a cough that does not go away."

"There's one in the back," the man says, swallowing the smoke. "So well-dressed I could tell his family is looking for him, so I embalmed him. I would have put an ad in the papers, except whoever killed him might go after me. So far no one has come."

The woman nods, adding, "Such a handsome face. I washed the clothes he came in and I prayed the rosary. It looks only as if he's sleeping. When he came in, there was a pale band around his wrist where his watch was. I pray for him as if I know him. Do you want to see?"

"No," Sally says. "But I want to share the . . . what you spent for waking him. I'm a mother, too." Even that is hard to say, almost brings her to tears. "I'll pray, too; but please accept this." From what she had brought as down payment, Sally takes some bills to press into the man's hand.

He hesitates. His wife stops dancing with the child on the sidewalk.

"Take it." The rain has started to weaken. She looks up and down the street. The driver has returned, is parked across from Ester's house. Holding her handbag over her head, Sally walks across, then looks back at the woman and her husband who are watching her. The woman is lifting the baby's hand, is waving it after Sally.

The child pulls its hand away, begins to wave both hands up and down.

In quiet steps, Sally crosses back to them, the handbag on her arm. She follows the woman and child, who lead her inside without being asked. "We've had him three weeks. He still looks asleep. See." She switches on the light.

Sally sees the air breathing over Miggy.

Unable to cry, Sally blesses herself. About to run, she goes over to make a small sign of the cross on Miggy's forehead; her hand lingers there, almost staying. Quickly her thoughts become decisions. Osong need not know. This way, he will not bring Ting Dolor or any woman to leave flowers, and light candles on Miggy's grave. This way, Joel can continue to hope his brother will come back; one day just walk into the house and begin telling them where he has been. While she thinks this, she wonders why the income from the *tubigan* cannot be set aside for Miggy.

"Thank you for your donation," the husband comes in now. "I will buy a plot in the church cemetery and place a cross. Thank you. But what name shall I inscribe?"

Sally looks at the man. "What name?"

"Yes. There has to be a name even if we don't know. Can you think of one?"

"Oh, yes. Miguel. Miguel de la Cruz. Name him after the archangel who wrestled the devil and slew him."

"And your name, if I may know?"

"Salud Moscoso," she says, in an almost whisper. "Mrs. Sally Moscoso."

"If you want to stay longer, I will leave the light on," the man says. "My wife is used to it, she can pray in the dark."

Sally thanks the man and his wife. She hurries away but does not feel she is moving; does not feel the pull of her arms; only the weight of something like stone piling up inside her. With no one to help her across she feels she is glass about to shatter; someone the wind has picked up and dropped.

On the trail,

the four men step on their shadows as they carry Sula Vitaliano on a narrow bed up to Patro's house. Alongside, Loreto walks; holding an umbrella over her grandmother while at the same time gripping the old one's hand that tries to pull off the blanket tucked under her body. Loreto cannot see the blind stare of her grandmother's open eyes.

Dionisia had come to the house after breakfast, crying, "She will not take even water, but keeps calling, 'I want to talk to Milang.' Where Milang is, no one knows, for she leaves early and sometimes does not come back at night. But *Impong* Sula keeps asking. Come and see."

Patro, whom the old one chases from her house, asked Loreto to go in her place. Afraid, Anya would not accompany her. "Do whatever you think necessary. Remember, she is your father's mother. Do what Benhur would want done."

Loreto found her partly out of the mosquito net, her skirt pulled up over her body. On her white legs, tiny pricks of red mark where mosquitoes had feasted and fattened during the night. Her nails were dark-rimmed, the way eyes of actresses are lined with black to deepen them. Both feverish and cold, her hair was stiff, blown white. It was hard to recognize, to claim her.

With Dionisia's help, Loreto undressed her grandmother, then covered her with a light blanket. The water boiled while she looked in the *aparador* for a long skirt and a light kimono of the same color, for slippers to wear outside the house; the decision to bring her home was formed by those smaller decisions, to change and dress her, to scrub her legs and arms so neighbors would not detect the grime. Where has Milang been?

Where have they been themselves, that they failed to come the past week. Weeks?

As if she heard Loreto's thoughts, Dionisia offered to get some men to carry Sula out of the house.

"What happened to *Lola?*" a woman stops on the trail to watch them coming out of the yard. "Is she sick?"

Loreto nods, angling the umbrella against the sun and prying eyes. With her free hand she pushes the gate closed and then looks back at the house where they used to play as children. The corrugated roof, which has started to leak and which Benhur promises to have replaced, the work having been started then stopped, is the color of the soil on the other bank.

The sun cuts through the shade of leaves under which they are passing.

How long has her grandmother lain on the wet bed, soaked and unable to move? Perhaps the better thing was to have sent Dionisia back for her mother, Loreto thinks, though she cannot imagine what can be done without bringing her grandmother home. What does her *Lola* Sula think, being carried through Gulod as on a bier? But she did not think of that when she was washing her to bring her out of the house.

Now the men stop, bring down their load. Wiping sweat from their necks and faces, their arms, they tell each other, *"Pagkabigat-bigat nila."* They are surprised at how heavy she is. "How did she become like this? *Napabayaan.*"

The question shames Loreto. She bends over her grandmother, wipes the edge of her mouth where it is pulling down her cheek. If only Vergel were there. And Benhur. If only they do not live apart from each other. Loreto holds the umbrella lower. Her grandmother's hands have not stopped moving: making gestures of digging, tying knots, pulling thread, shredding. Loreto wonders if that is how the mosquito net become stripped into loose threads.

"Don't let them see me." A moan comes from Sula.

"Lola?" Loreto brings her face to her grandmother. She is frightened by the words that keep forming without a sound, that she seems to know without hearing.

"Hindi ko ipagkakait ang buhay ko sa iyo, aking Panginoon." She, who used to be toe-to-toe with God, is ready to die!

"Let's go." The men who have been talking among themselves pick up the bed again. "So Lola can rest." One of the men is Siso Feleo's brother-in-law. Alongside him is the deputy policeman, who is better dressed than the others. The two on the other side of the bed are new to Gulod. They can be offered money without its insulting them. But Patro will decide, what besides a meal can be offered in exchange for the men's help.

On feeling herself moving, Sula thrashes about until her legs are free from the blanket. They are white, like those of store mannikins. Loreto asks Dionisia to tuck the blanket under her grandmother. Her grandmother never wore anything under her skirt. Like the French, Sally used to say, when she visited Sula. "*Lola* Sula is French." Sally tried to endear herself, because of Benhur.

A bee darts under the bed, between the arms of the men who sidestep its flight. The new ones tease each other, "We've been mistaken for flowers."

Looking across, Loreto recognizes the taller one as the one Anya described as having whispered to her, "You don't have to get a boyfriend. I can make you pregnant." Why did not Dionisia choose better?

Two children fall in step behind them, dragging cans tied together with old strings. There is no space in Gulod for children to hit cans as far as they will go, then try to return to base without being caught by the "It". They used to play games that required space to run, all the way down to the river past her *Lola* Sula's house.

Through a window Loreto sees a family altar that reminds her of the large crucifix in her *Lola* Sula's room. Is it still there? She did not notice. Perhaps, Milang has given it away; sold it. It used to frighten her to watch it being washed before, during Holy Week, when it was carried to the chapel. The arms were first removed to allow the velvet clothes to be put on. It looked hacked until it was put together again, looked disinterred until the crown was set over the head of hair, with the wounds still on the corpus.

"I forgot to tell you," Dionisia comes up to Loreto, "that one day, *Impong* Sula called to me across the trail. 'This is not my bed. Someone changed it. Someone moved me to a different house. This is not my house. The furniture is smaller. The house is smaller.' That's exactly what she said to me. I tried to convince her otherwise."

Loreto does not say anything.

"And, you probably noticed when they passed your house, I didn't mention it before so as not to make trouble between your families, that Milang and her children are wearing *Impong* Sula's jewels. The *tambourine.* Then the *diamante.* Earrings, brooch, bracelet, and ring. My mother said, *brilliantes* might cost more, but *diamantes* bring good luck if they are received as gifts. Not if they are taken. Stolen."

Did Milang take the jewels, or was she given them? It does not seem important any more.

Young men throwing coins against a wall to see whose will roll down farthest stop to watch them passing. The man selling vinegar in two *damajuanas* balanced across his shoulders on a pole takes off his hat.

Loreto looks down on the trail to avoid speaking. Is her grandmother dying? A moan like birds flying in and out of the branches of trees floats over them. The last time she recalls she visited, her grandmother asked, "What is that bird doing, Loreto? It seems to be flapping its wings and looking at me. Make it go away. Can't you see it? It's in that tree. The one that stopped bearing. Look, it's getting larger and larger. Now it's all black . . ."

Moving inside her thoughts, Loreto is brought back to the trail when she feels the men's legs brush hers, pressing as she walks into them.

Again, the men bring the bed down.

Loreto holds her grandmother's hand. It used to be, people said, that one cannot die until all the anger and hate have passed out . . .

Bastian Canonigo leaves the pile of rusted cans which he is burning, which flare up into sparks alongside the trail. "Has Benhur been sent for?" His wife, Meding, follows him out of their yard. "I can see where you got your fair skin, Loreto. Your grandmother is still beautiful. I forgot, since I have not seen her in years."

Loreto looks at her grandmother, so white and heavy she looks drowned. The light appears to be fine cracks along her arms, the veins the blood of birds trying to come out of her.

Sister Gertrudis comes upon them looking at Sula Vitaliano, places a hand on her forehead. Rising, Sister places an arm about Loreto. "We will come to the house," she tells Loreto, who thinks she hears Sister whisper to her grandmother, "Don't make the Lord wait. Our Lady will hold heaven open for you."

The light falls like dark feathers.

As the weight of Sister's words falls upon her, Loreto begins trailing the men, the umbrella useless in her hand. But doesn't Sister see her grandmother is breathing, though softly and haltingly as one unused to air?

Farther up, unaware they are passing by, a woman rubs her heels on a piece of hollow block, pouring water on her feet.

Loreto runs ahead. The men are moving too slowly for her. She wants to overtake the morning, before Dionisia came to the house, before she opened her grandmother's room and saw her uncovered on the bed.

Patro is standing by the gate, unsure; as if they are coming towards her in a language she does not understand.

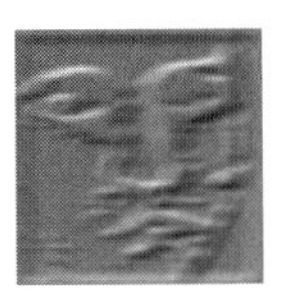

Loreto notices the wind

drifting across the fishpond, carrying with it the sun and pieces of leaves; tiny plants no bigger than pinpricks on which the *bangus* feeds. Just like a river, she thinks, the way the river in back of their house in Gulod is held between its banks.

She watches the sky behind the wind that sweeps around the guava tree, heading back across the land toward the hills. Bending the light, it runs along the dikes that intersect long distances, sectioning off the ponds like rice fields. It makes her think of night, though it is only midafternoon.

By now, she thinks, they are sitting around the table, dishes untouched, wondering if her brother should be notified. Her mother might already have called Benhur on Sally's phone: *Loreto has not come home. With whom? We don't know. Do you think we should wait? By evening. And then? What if. . .?*

When does it become too late? her mother means by those questions. Too late to restore things to the way they were; like the river, like life.

Loreto knows how it is to be worried into silence, then into fear that mobilizes irrationalities of all kinds. They could be thinking her already dead, floating on some *estero,* deep marks of assault upon her body. Her mother might have already sent for the tabloids that run photos of victims on the front pages, exposing wounds and grief.

And Emilio Luna is taking his time trying to reach the guava from the tree a storm has blown over the water. Its roots barely hold it to the edge of the pond; its branches are too slippery even to hold nests in place. He has reached a fruit by leaping. This she holds deep inside her pocket while she waits for him to get another for himself. It is Anya who likes guava. She herself dislikes the tiny seeds that get between the teeth.

She watches him against the sun that has begun its descent hours ago, and she thinks back to this morning when, driving his sister's car, Emilio Luna stopped for her on the highway just past Sally Moscoso's house. He opened the door and she got into the car as if it were Emilio Luna she was waiting for; as if they had gone off together before. She assumed he was offering her a ride to where she was going, was thinking of how to tell her mother that Emilio Luna had given her a ride, when she noticed they were heading north, away. And then, because she did not wish to appear alarmed, or to presume an intention he might not have toward her, she said nothing.

They had stopped for *merienda* at a roadside restaurant. From there, she expected they would head back, so all she asked for was *halo-halo.* Ice had not been delivered, so they waited, watching the traffic go by. He asked if she was going to school.

"Not any more," she said, without explaining. When the glasses of *halo-halo* were served, each glass wrapped with a paper napkin to catch the drip, they stirred the shaved ice into the milk and preserved fruits.

After some silence, he said, "Instead of school, it is better to read books. Everything can be learned from books. One can learn to fly. Aerodynamics. Whatever one wants. That's where teachers get what they teach."

She smiled but not at him. She smiled watching the *pinipig,* newly roasted still-green rice, disappear among the white and red beans. The *ube* jam colored the glass purple. She was not used to looking at him. Nor he to being looked at, for he looked quickly away when she lifted her eyes.

Until they reached the fishponds he did not speak again. On the way, she looked for landmarks so she could find her way back if necessary. She was always afraid of being lost, even in her dreams. They passed a schoolhouse with separate buildings for the Home Economics classes. Then a chapel facing the road, the altar bare, the wrought iron door like stiff cobwebs. A rice mill. Towns with *muncipios* facing statues of Rizal in the plazas. Wild *gumamelas* growing into the road, coloring the sky . . .

Something has distracted Emilio Luna from getting the guava. He is now facing the ponds, sitting on the dike with his elbows on his knees.

She cannot imagine being hurt by him, being hurt in that place.

"This is how Gulod used to be," he says, not turning around. "Remember?"

The single word makes her feel sought, claimed. And a shadow, like a restlessness, shakes her while he sits as fixed as a tree.

He says nothing else and she walks to the hut no bigger than a playhouse. Peeking inside, she discovers she can touch the walls without stretching if she stands in the middle. There is nothing inside. The caretaker who uses it for shelter during the day needs just enough room to rest briefly. The floor is bamboo, split irregularly and spaced apart for air and to allow rain to fall through. There is no door at the entrance, but a kind of awning over the window is made from *nipa* leaves, as is the roof. On reaching the hut, Emilio Luna goes inside immediately to prop open the awning with a stick.

"It's a tree house," she says, but he does not answer. She thinks of walking down to him, of repeating her statement; making him answer. Suddenly piqued, she thinks of throwing the guava in his direction. But what's the use? He is spoiled, willful. She should have looked the other way when he stopped the car. What does he think? That he can have his way with her?

The sun is its own shadow in the sky.

"We used to come when fish were harvested." He stands up to walk to another part of the fishponds. "The men brought up the fish and threw them over there. The fattest they roasted on sticks. No need for salt."

It sounds to her as if he's describing what happened just the day before; as if she was there as well. She waits for what else he will say, wants to say.

From the hut she cannot tell if a fish came up to gulp air or if Emilio Luna dislodged a pebble into the pond, starting ripples that will tear up his reflection on the surface.

"The fish are big," he says. "Come look."

"How do you catch them?" When he fails to answer, she sits down on the last step, her feet on the ground, and watches him walking away on the dike, until in the suffusion of light he appears no wider than a post marking boundaries. The water looks deep enough to drown in, looks dark with patches of green floating slowly across, patches the shape of the sun.

How can she make her words reach him?

At the first intersection of dikes he doubles back. Once more under the guava tree's still upright branch, he stares at the fruit out of reach. Beneath the open collar of his shirt, the skin is white. She is darker than he.

Don't you climb, she warns him silently.

He goes to the hut, pulls out a long stick from an edge of the roof. It is short by an arm's length. He starts to climb. "Catch!" he says, without warning.

The fruit rolls into the pond before either of them can run to where it fell. They just avoid colliding against each other.

"I hate guavas anyway," she says. "I hate fish cooked in guavas; specially guavas cooked in coconut milk and sweetened with *panocha.*"

"I like guavas," he says, returning to the tree. The sky and the intense light give him a partial outline. He appears incomplete, unfinished, someone just happening by, like the shadow of a cloud on the ground. And she is filled with longing.

In all partiality, she wants to yield. She looks over the fishponds toward the sea beyond, miles away, years away from where she stands.

He sits at the edge of the pond again, looking out to where she thinks the rivers flow together into Manila Bay. Her *Lola* Sula said that during the revolution against Spain, the Spaniards from the central plains tried, through the rivers, to reach Manila Bay where the *almirante,* they thought, was waiting for them. They were caught with all the gold they were carrying, with the reliquaries and palms and *cereales* from the churches they had passed.

She wonders how her *Lola* Sula is. She had been heading for the market that morning to buy her fresh bread. Bread and *queso de bola.* Just a slice of the cheese. Just for her. The children do not know the difference between imported and local cheese.

"It's getting late," she says, reminded of time. Her *Lola* Sula will think she has eloped. She is also hungry. They have not eaten since that *merienda.* She gets up, drawn to the hibiscus beside the hut. The buds are half open. Or half closed. She can see the red throat of the flower. It makes her think of the sun flaming when it rises and when it drops into the sea. She thinks of calling this to Emilio Luna's attention but he has dropped his head between his knees.

Suppose she just walks away? Does he expect her to know what's on his mind, to agree to anything simply because that's what he wants?

Thinking over the possibility of simply leaving, she picks up a blade of grass. Sharp-edged, like a knife, it draws blood that fills the long cut. The pain throbs through her body, her little finger. She licks the cut, presses it to the hem of her skirt. It tastes like raw and unripe fruit.

She is glad she did not throw the guava at Emilio Luna. Her *Lola* Sula will like it, will eat it with *bagoong* and rice. She looks up to see if any fruit has escaped Emilio Luna.

"It's getting late." She pulls sighs, deliberately slow, from her body. This is all entirely her fault, of course. She could have looked away when he stopped for her at the highway.

He continues to sit, now watching the light playing on the surface; watching as if his mind is sorting out other things besides her being there alone with him. What does he treasure in silence? Each time he looks away or turns, everything seems to begin again for him. How can he have a memory of her? Any memory? She might not have entered his thoughts at all.

She walks back to the hut. The *gumamela* has opened wider, the color of the pain on her finger. She wonders that bees have not found it, though ants have, are entering its red throat. She leans against the next higher step, wondering where his wounds are that *Aling* Maxima mentioned, how deep.

Benhur has been called by now. Patro will have told him: *Loreto asked permission to go to Sally. It might have merely been an excuse. Sally. Her grandmother blames me for letting her go by herself.*

Sally asked her to go to a movie. *Takaw Tukso* starring Jaclyn Jose and Julio Diaz; but she did not want to see a film with "wet" sex acts; and Sally did not want to see *Napakasakit, Kuya Eddie* about a husband's infidelities.

Looking up, Loreto sees Emilio Luna running towards her, hands cupped and smiling so deeply at her as if she is the only thing his mind contains. "Look." As soon as he opens his hands, a fish drops out. Its wet body catches the dust between their feet.

"It's ugly," she says, drawing away but afraid to move in case she steps on it, or it wriggles against her feet.

He is no longer smiling when she looks at him. A shadow seems to have dropped over him. She has gone out of his thoughts, his mind erasing itself at will. Is the shadow that of an intimidating dream? This thought is an echo of what she thinks he's thinking; a brutal exchange of sorts that makes her wonder if she's the one hurting in her dreams. But it is he who tried to kill himself, or so *Aling* Maxima said.

She's afraid to look at him again, to see the terrifying loneliness in his eyes, in his mouth. Does he respond only to himself?

To bring back his smile, his hurrying toward her, she says, "It's hot. Look, the *gumamela* is open. It took all day. Usually, it's in the morning." She feels like her *Lola* Sula sitting at her doorway, waiting.

He sits below her but says nothing. Only looks over the pond, away from her.

She is close enough to touch him, touch the ear folded like a little child's, the hair darkly soft. But his silence pushes her away. It grows until they are silent together, until—just as if he's reaching out for a dragonfly, he pulls the *gumamela* and crushes it inside his hand.

"Don't!" She wants to tell him to go away.

"It's hot," he says firmly, making the statement final.

She averts her face, thinking of the flower still in his hand, limp like a caught bird squeezed out of life; while the fishponds continue on toward the sky where the sun will go down, red like the thrust of the *gumamela.*

"It's getting late," she says without urgency.

His reply is that they used to go there, and the caretaker roasted the fish on sticks, slicing each side to the bone, close together. He goes on describing the harvest of milkfish, his hand still closed about the flower, talking as if he's completely inside himself; and the flower, a wound that will start bleeding again.

The sun is now still. But something else she cannot see seems to be throbbing, whirling. Her hands are moist as if she held the wet crushed petals. A pain passes through her. After they leave that place, what will have changed? If she walks away, will he bring her back or merely watch her leaving?

Suppose he needs her to be there?

But what will her mother say when she returns? Nothing happened; she will say the truth. Will they believe? Is it the truth?

"You must rest," he tells her, smiling as if remembering her in that place. "It's hot. Go up and rest."

She hesitates, wants to ask if his father was found dead in that part of their fishponds, drifting inside a *banca.* Neighbors said he had come upon a nephew stealing *bangus* fingerlings to export to Taiwan or Jakarta; the nephew who was a pilot and could smuggle out the fingerlings, bringing back appliances from their illegal sale. But she does as he says, lies down on the floor of bamboo that feels like bare knuckles. She turns on her side to face the wall. Can he hurt her while she sleeps? Is he afraid to sleep?

She is tired but she does not rush headlong into rest. She lies there, listening. The wind is picking up. She can smell the sea, the bay. She is wondering if she will remember her dream when she wakes up, who she will meet in it, who she will weep for.

Moving like water under the wind, the dark is spreading when she wakes up. Everything restless has stopped. She walks to the bamboo steps to see where Emilio Luna is.

Close to the guava tree, beside the pond he is bending over a fire, turning a fish on a stick. When the flames rise she can see his eyes almost asleep and she feels an ache and tenderness that wants him, then and forever, safely inside her.

"Are you sure you were interviewed, Siso?" *Aling* Maxima leans over the counter in her store. "I've been buying the newspaper since May, but your picture has not appeared on the front page. It's now August."

The men no longer laugh at Maxima's daily greeting but watch Siso Feleo coming slowly toward the store, this time without his children.

Siso smiles away his embarrassment. "At least I saw what a five-star hotel looks like inside. Manila Hotel is like a palace. The new Malacañang, according to the Marcos loyalists."

There is no room on the two benches in front of the store. It used to be the benches faced each other, but since Elpidio Torres was shot while sitting outside Vilma's store, everyone sits facing the trail in order not to be surprised. They are sure it is NPA, the two young men in short pants who did not hurry even after they had shot Elpidio but walked calmly up the trail. There are more and more accounts of such killings in Metro Manila. Called Sparrows, the young killers supposedly send warnings. Some victims receive condolence cards. One got a black *barong* to wear in his coffin. Some receive no warning, but those could be cases of mistaken identity.

"I wonder what Elpidio Torres's crime was?" Maxima asks, but no one answers.

For four days, a wake was held; until there was enough earned from the gambling tables set in the Torres's yard for the funeral. Dionisia went around Gulod collecting small donations. Next to Patro and the nuns, she is trusted in Gulod.

"I thought there would be a picture of Elpidio in the papers," Maxima says, sitting down. Her rebukes of the men have become mild, as if something has gone out of her. Mostly she worries about her son, who is a strike breaker in Bulacan. One has to earn a living, she says of Robles.

"Everyone has to die of something," Siso Feleo says. The news is all the same. NPAs shooting the military and stripping the bodies of uniforms and weapons. And during the cleaning up operations after an ambush, everybody is finished off. A Vietnam War reporter and photographer died in one ambush. And that young man in a yellow T-shirt who died from kicks and blows of the Marcos mob, right in sight of the news photographers. Siso had wanted to help, but if he did not run as fast as lightning to Padre Faura, stopping for breath in the Solidaridad Bookshop, he might have been waked before Elpidio Torres. Water hoses soaked them.

"How many elevators are there in the Manila Hotel?" Maxima asks Siso. "How come you did not eat? Maybe you're just lying."

"How could I? Order here; order there. Take this to the headquarters. That's up to the fourteenth floor."

"How many floors were there?" Maxima asks.

"I did not count."

"Are you sure you were there, Siso?" Bastian Canonigo asks. He and Siso were at the Marcos rallies, but he asks questions as if he never set foot in Luneta or the Manila Hotel. In fact he was about to enter the lobby when Marcos's vice-president came out on the 6th for his oath-taking as President, with Marcos's blessings. After the short ceremony, the big shots returned to the hotel. He and Siso got separated when truckloads of military in battle gear started jumping off trucks alongside the Quirino Grandstand. They were there on the 27th but did not come together. That was when there was an *ipo-ipo* in the park, a sudden downpour with the wind circling.

Siso looks up. About to say something, he decides to say nothing. Each time he went to the rallies, he thought, at any moment, it might be the very moment his children were being orphaned. Like Steve Salcedo, who fell under the blows of Marcos loyalists, he might have died in Luneta.

"Now we have three presidents," Maxima says, baiting the men who seem not to wish to disagree. "President Cory, President Marcos, President Tolentino. I would not have voted for him. How many wives does he have? Seven?"

"How about if he made you the eighth?" Marcelo Andres asks. Receiving no reply, he turns to Siso. "Did you say the carpets in the hotel are as thick as pillows? And in one restaurant you look over the swimming pool and then the bay?"

"One time we're surrounded; the next, everyone has run away," Siso says to no one. He is lucky to be alive and he will never join another rally. They can offer him any amount, it is not enough. He has to think of his children. He's all they have. He thought of them when he saw in the papers, the general manager from Bicol whom Cory appointed to the Philippine National Railway being led out handcuffed after barricading himself inside the Tutuban station with his supporters. Siso worries what the man's children thought on seeing the newspaper. The last time in Luneta he was pummeled by billboards, sticks, and water cannons. The light could have gone through him.

Maxima looks up the trail. She has been asking Robles to come home, sending word to him when the leader of the strike at Clark Air Base was hit by unknown gunmen.

The men stop asking questions of Siso. They have heard all they want to know about the Marcos loyalists in Manila Hotel, the ministers appointed by Tolentino occupying rooms under fictitious names, the overseas call from Hawaii before and during the coup which fizzled out, with the international news agencies and television crews quartered right inside the hotel. They shrug, learning of the P3 million damage to the hotel, four kilometers from the old Malacañang, twice that distance to the Manila International Airport and right beside Manila Bay. Quick exits. Quick hits.

Their minds circle. Back to Elpidio Torres. They recall the last time he returned to Gulod after weeks of absence. They thought he had emigrated.

"I have not seen the *vaciador,*" Bastian says.

"Maybe he's hiding, too. Maybe he has received the NPA greeting lined in black," Maxima says. She has been thinking, if Elpidio Torres was shot point-blank, did he have time to repent? Anyone can receive death threats. She tells Robles to stay inside the house to avoid trouble, but the boy does not listen.

Hernan Sipalay gets up. Before walking home he says, "It's clear the devil himself is looking for Paradise and he is the one who has found it. No place is safe any more."

The men watch Hernan walking away, his shoulders hunched higher than when he first came, his trouser legs flapping against his bones.

"I have not seen Estong Calero," Bastian Canonigo says, sitting down in the space Hernan left between Siso and Dante Filemon, who never says anything, neither agreeing nor disagreeing, because the men make fun of his accent. Sometimes, though, an unexpected kindness makes him think he is back in his barrio and he lapses into his dialect, excitedly.

"Here comes Ponce Martinez," Bastian gets up. "He was across from Pidiong when the Sparrows fired. He could have warned Pidiong, given him a sign, could he not have?"

"And have the Sparrows hit him, too?" Siso asks.

"I was paying for a stick of cigarette. My back was turned. When I heard the shot . . ." Bastian drops his voice.

"I have not seen Attorney either," Maxima says. "I wanted to ask him about Robles. If that boy does not come home today, I'll go after him myself. If I have to pull him out by the ear."

Siso looks up the trail at the mention of Benhur's name. Nani suggested that he ask Benhur if he might not drive for him, just until he can get a job. He wants to tell Benhur what he cannot tell Nani.

Because he has been joining the rallies, he has not been to see Ramon. He used to go every day to the cemetery. He walked if he had to. The other day, Nani suddenly said, *Go see Ramon today. He must be lonely.* He walked all around but could not find the grave which had an image of the grieving Jesus on a Cross. It was Benhur who paid for that. He walked every inch. He knew it was where the *kamachile* threw its afternoon shadow but the ground was bare there. Just a hole through which he probed with a stick that broke in two.

Stunned, he stood where he remembered it to be and cried. A *sepulturero* came to him. *You are looking for a young child? About five?* The *sepulturero* walked behind a tomb set on top of another, all of them bearing one slab with several names, and returned with a sack loosely tied.

He trembled as the man approached, handing the sack. Inside was Atlas's *barong* Tagalog which Benhur's mother gave them because Ramon had nothing but old shirts.

"I found it on the ground and put it in a sack because I knew someone would come sooner or later to look for it. I have a shovel. I can help you bury it if you get permission from the office. I tell people not to put decorations which only attract thieves. This is not the first time." The man tried to help.

Siso trembles thinking of it. As if a fishbone is stuck deep in his throat, he can't eat or swallow; he can't tell Nani. He just stares at the wall. Nani said: *You have not gone to visit Ramon, that's why.*

Instead of Benhur, it is Maxima's Robles running down the trail as if chased by the devil. Without greeting any of the men on the benches he pushes open the door to the store, comes out again with a large knife. Maxima falls from her chair trying to stand between her son and the door.

Then Robles starts running back up the slope. Three men with long metal tubes are running just as fast after him; and right behind them, a passenger jeep with still more men. It is in front of the store that the men catch up with Robles and, as if there are no witnesses, the men start hitting him, right there, pounding with the rhythm of farmers cleaning *palay* in a pestle. The sun, hungry, sucks his eyes.

It is over before Maxima can cry out a second time. *They're crazy! Help us! Help! Mahabaging Dios!* She tears out her hair, sobbing, watching the men trying to lift Robles up to the roof of the jeep; and it is then Siso sees Benhur coming down, wearing a blue *barong* which makes him look like a senator. Already smiling a greeting, Benhur comes upon the men and Robles's body, no longer moving.

"You can't do that," Benhur tells the men. He looks at those standing in front of the store, turned into stone.

Siso steps forward but no farther when the men start hitting Benhur, too. Siso hears the sun screaming through the trees, as he runs to call *Aling* Patro. In his eyes, the faces of the men are the pigheads stuck to poles at Luneta, the grin of Marcos loyalists carting a dead body to show the press they have a victim, too.

"Is he dead?" Ryan asks, arriving ahead of his brothers up the slope. The sun is a deformed crown on his uncle's head.

Patro sees the beating from the trail as she comes up, fear running ahead of her, winding about her firstborn who emerged with his umbilical cord twisted around and around his neck.

It looks as if the light is feeding upon the bodies when Patro reaches Benhur. The jeepney is backing up on the trail out of Gulod, its hood ornamented with several metal horses bobbing. A border of fluffy white balls beats against the upper windshield, below which is painted, in red and white and blue: *God Saves.*

The light passes over Benhur, stroking him like someone breathing on his body. Then a dark reflection of the sun begins to spread, high above him, and drops until he is wrapped in it.

Though they stand about, watching, no one speaks; as if all they know is a mute language.

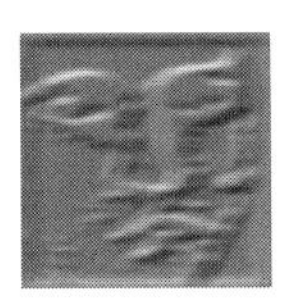

Fixed in Patro's mind,
like a permanent desire, is a picture of the golden shower tree that used to grow directly across the river. Benhur used to swim across, after the petals had fallen, for the long black pods that held the seeds. But they could never grow the tree in their yard.

Though on the other bank there are only makeshift huts scrambling up the slope like hungry goats with dark horns biting off everything that grows, Patro remembers Benhur rising from the water; remembers the flowers clustered like butterflies swinging from one another's wings.

Siso Feleo and Bastian Canonigo have come, asking her permission to avenge Benhur. *We are willing, even if we die. Just give us permission.* Their coming makes her wonder if Benhur had been happy, ever.

"Why did he have to waste his life?" Siso asks. "Robles is not family, or even friend. It's like dying for a stranger. And Benhur never even got to have children."

Patro sits with Benhur's friends to console them. At least Loreto has escaped Gulod. Patro wishes her a good life, somewhere. Maybe Loreto will come to let her know. But she hopes her daughter never realizes . . . Benhur would still be alive if they had not summoned him because they did not know where she had gone . . .

Anya sits beside Patro, the way Loreto used to. "When was *Tito* Benhur born?"

"The year the Japanese bombed Manila."

They fall silent after that and watch the boys playing basketball. Imitating Ricardo Brown, deadliest guard of the season, Atlas jumps as the ball is about to fall into the hoop. To the side, Pitong, hand held to his mouth like a sportscaster's mike, gives a play-by-play account, his mouth moving at the breakneck speed of those reporting for television: "Cage dynasty in the making!" He pulls up his shoulders as if there is a table on which to rest his elbows.

Forgetting her grief for a moment, Patro laughs; she recalls Pitong and Ryan acting in the Teatro Obrero's play just the past year. Atlas mimicked the mimes . . . stretching their bodies to get across in Tagalog, Visayan, Bicolano, Ilocano—all the languages spoken in Gulod—the social and economic issues, nutrition and population control, voters' rights . . . Neighbors called out, applauding him: *Another Christopher de Leon.*

"Three-point shot! Three-point shot!" Pitong insists over protests from the court. "Ask *Lola* Patro. She saw."

Patro looks up, all faces turned to her as if what she will say will make everything right. The question is the sound of the river; and across; crying and dreaming.

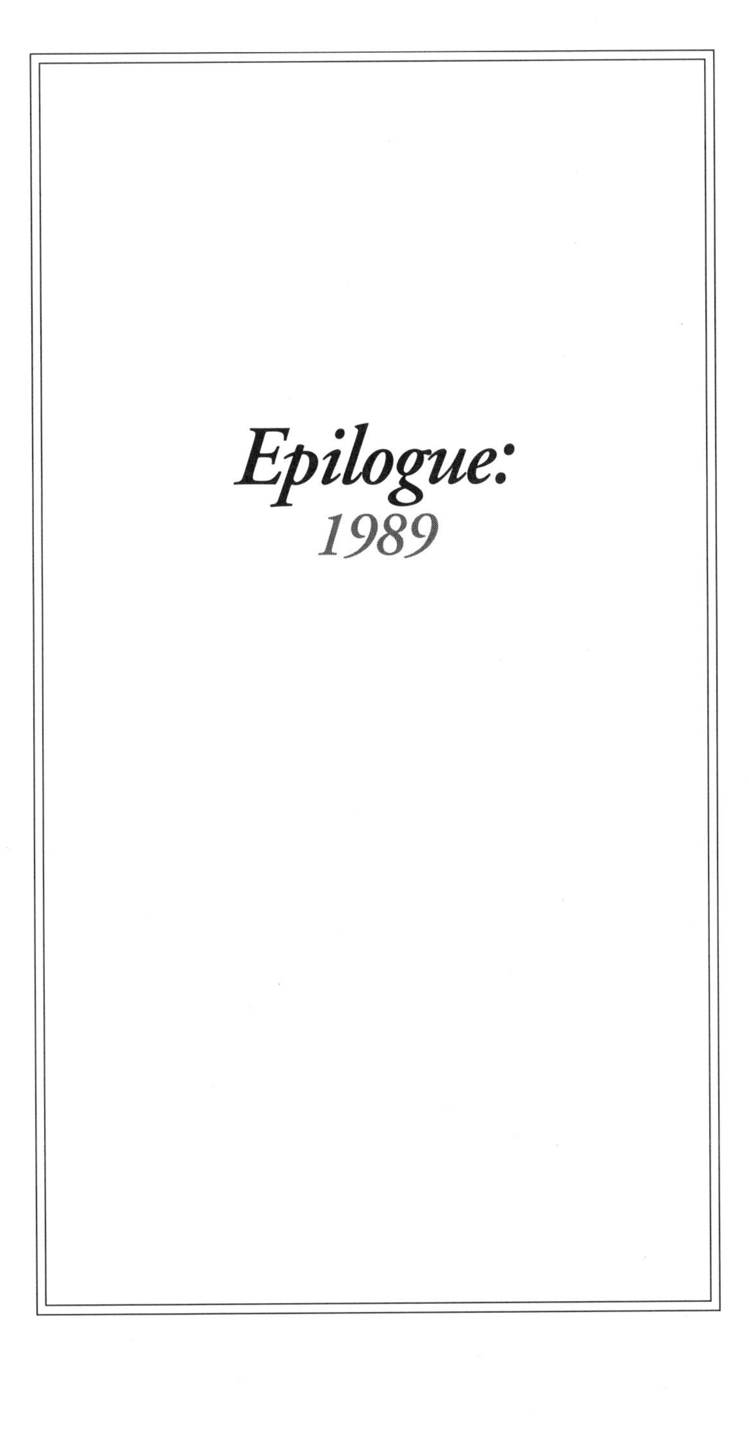

Epilogue:
1989

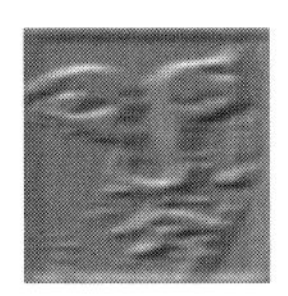

From her bedroom window

Liling Moscoso sees the Colonel closing the gate after Cayetano. Strange that he did not come up to see her, she thinks; and part of her goes out with her son into the street where his car is parked, waiting.

She wonders if another coup is under way, the sixth or seventh since Cory became president. For days there have been rumors. One prediction even set the time: 0300 hours, the morning of Friday, December 1.

0300 hours. Why not 0001? The precision is suspicious; and she understands why the official who gave the government warnings was fired. Under Marcos, rumormongering was a crime, too.

Liling looks at her watch—1800 hours. The Rolex that Osong gave her, which she has not used, would show the date: November 30, Thursday. Nine hours left to find out if they will have a coup, after all.

She goes to the wall calendar. Hand poised to rip the page for November, she decides to wait for the morning to usher in December. Just thirty-one days to 1990. One month and ten years away from A.D. 2000. She never thought she would come this close to the new century.

Liling returns to the window. The car is gone. The sun, about to set, is aimless against the earth.

Whatever it is Cayetano came to say, she knows the Colonel would have said: *I'll tell your mother myself. She's resting.* The Colonel thinks it strains her heart to beat. He tries to save her from life, to make up for the War a lifetime ago. But Liling remembers. With two infant sons and attended only by a lieutenant who could not find a handful of rice if he stumbled on it, she lived away from the towns, crossing by night over dried or swollen fields because if the Japanese caught them, Captain Moscoso, who maintained radio communications with Australia, would, might, be forced to surrender. Afraid to risk arrest, afraid of being hanged or shot, relatives on both sides refused to open their doors to them.

Liling remembers scattering at the slightest sound, like leaves being picked up by the wind and deposited wherever the wind might please. Roots and leaves were all they had to eat. The lieutenant trapped birds but did not know how to cook them. Not recognizing one kind of berry from another, they suffered cramps; grew so thin they could each hide behind a finger. Osong and Cayetano were less than a year apart and were still nursing. The poor babies had sores from sleeping on the ground. The shirts got stuck to their backs. Her fair pale skin became blotched, darker than the wet skin of boiled roots.

Tightly knotted in her memory, those fears of forty-five years ago are merged with earlier frights—the goat-headed devil that appeared in her grandmother's garden under the *alugbati* tree; the burning stakes along the canes of canna; the rain of blood that stained the underside of leaves and the lower walls and fence each time butterflies in droves came out of their cocoons—fears that make her feel she must be the woman who used to walk up and down Horseshoe Drive and Balete, asking for a ride, then disappearing after being let into the car. People said the woman had been in an accident; did not yet know she had died.

As the shadow of those years swings back into Liling's thoughts, she wants fiercely to kneel again in the Church of the Holy Face on R. Hidalgo. She thinks of *Mang* Genio. Before he was hit on Mendiola in 1987, when the guards fired on farmers and workers who were marching to lay their grievances before Cory, he always brought her to the church once a month, on the first Tuesday—her private devotion. The Colonel would wait for her, standing between the stone angels at the entrance, staring into the confessionals or the baptistry and thinking his own thoughts.

Liling returns herself to now—to the time she saw the Colonel closing the gate—by looking out of her window. The light has been turned on by the front door. Once she overheard Cayetano telling his father of an ambush in South Cotobato: *I felt the bullets. Though I was not hit, my boots and legs were smoking from the raking fire. Two sergeants were immediately shot. I could see smoke coming out of the bullet holes when I rolled thirty feet to push Lazar out of the way. He was already dead.* Cayetano used to fall asleep over his plate at the table, so tired out from their maneuvers.

If Choleng had not taken David to stay with her in the province until after Christmas, Liling would ask to be brought downstairs to see him. Sometimes the Colonel carries her down in the afternoon. David, their youngest son, seems less and less to recognize her, so she has taken to watching his face secretly, praying silently all the while. He was only nine when he had the accident. The Colonel was in Korea with the United Nations Forces when David fell out of the *macopa.* Until he began having seizures, he seemed not to have been hurt. Now, when she closes her eyes she can see the way David's eyes turned slowly lifeless. It tears her apart to feel him struggle to be free when she takes his hand.

Perhaps Osong will come, Liling thinks, placing both hands inside the pockets of her flowered housedress. In the mirror, her dress blooms and appears to hold a body whose memories are all happy.

One time, Benhur came with Osong's sons. Briefly in the garden they sat under the trees drinking *calamansi* juice. She would have preferred chocolate with *churros,* but it was so hot. Because of the wedding in Esguerra, the Colonel did not come out. She has tried to make up for the Colonel's stubborn sense of rightness by sending gifts through Benhur. Perhaps the two sons of Osong are in California. She has not heard from them since Benhur died. Priscila, *Mang* Genio's daughter, said the mother called once; but not again. Loreto, Benhur's sister, came up to her room once or twice, sitting at the edge of the bed while they talked. She might be married now. Without Benhur there is no way of finding out. It is not safe to send Priscila to Gulod. *Mang* Genio can no longer drive.

There is her grandfather's sword; her father's gold watch she wants to give Osong's sons because Cayetano's children have received so many gifts already. In addition to clothes and toys, they have bank accounts in which are deposited their share of the harvests. Patty's parents give them even more.

She misses Benhur. Such stories he knew! Osong never talked about the trips they took abroad, but Benhur would tell her about the chapel that used to face the Bay of Barcelona and of Saint Ignatius de Loyola sitting humbly as a beggar on the steps; about Paul Revere's ride to warn of the British coming; about an actual castle in Denmark where Hamlet lived. And when she mentioned having a sword from the revolution, Benhur thought it might be the one captured from the Spaniards when they attacked outside Imus. In their retreat, the Spaniards abandoned the cage in which they had intended to bring back to Manila the Filipino generals.

As Liling turns from the window, light flashes in her left eye. It has happened before each coup, starting with the one protesting Cory's visit to Japan when the people were urged to help "save the queen," as some reporters claimed. Liling walks the steps to her bed carefully. Someone she knew bent over to pick up something and, when she stood up, her sight was gone. There is no point in telling her husband this, in adding to his worries about her.

Nothing more is left of the day. Because there might be another brown-out, she and the Colonel had supper early at five. She hardly tasted the food because every last Thursday of the month her friends, the few friends she still has, come to spend the afternoon with her. The Colonel designed a round table and five black chairs which can be pushed into the corner of the room when not in use. He also brought up the glass cabinet from the dining room to hold the dishes and glassware they received for their wedding anniversaries. From Dao he got a small refrigerator and appliances—coffeemaker, toaster, microwave—so food can be prepared in her room when her friends come.

You're lucky, her friends tell her. *Your husband won't let you lift a finger; never demanded you live wherever he was assigned; never went about with other women hanging on to his arm, women young enough to be his daughters.*

Until they come again, she will think of this afternoon. They talked of long-ago summers, of their schooldays, recalling teachers and suitors; the filigree wrappers of *pastillas* they tore apart carelessly, though hours must have gone into cutting the fragile designs; the cat's-tongue cookies, even smaller and thinner than the actual tongues; the sequins and *abalorios* with which lace overskirts were beaded, the *baros* and sleeves flattened out and starched and ironed after each use and sewn together again. Careful efforts. Wasted, like lives. Useless. Life will never be the same, is gone; the tiny calling cards embossed with flowers and names; the old photographs of themselves, young and wearing crowns to the annual carnivals.

What less sorrowful can they talk about when they no longer feel what Cory says? Just one word after another, like Marcos apologists getting ready to have him reelected. Making claims, disclaiming charges of corruption and incompetency.

For several months before and after EDSA they were caught up in the excitement of forcing out Marcos and Imelda and Ver. Poised to change things, along with their children and grandchildren, her friends went to provincial barrios campaigning for Cory. Liling herself made posters for them to put up in marketplaces, other high-density areas, to make up for the fact that the print and sound media were being monopolized by the government. Cory's Crusaders. Part of a telephone chain, she called strangers to vote for Cory and Doy; to ratify Cory's Constitution so she would not be embarrassed, after she was in office, by a low voter turnout which would have impugned her popularity; to vote in her candidates for Congress. Liling also urged the Colonel to loan their car and the services of *Mang* Genio to those going out to saturate the provinces with Cory's speeches, their tape recorders running on car batteries.

Kept busy, she felt the hours that had been stolen from her during her confinement to her room, were at last being returned to her as she coordinated her friends' sorties into the barrios.

Without violence, at EDSA, a dictator was made to flee. Her friends brought her to the first and second anniversary celebrations, hopeful the government would catch up with the country's expectations—inequities would cease. But they were such tiny forces after all. Nothing changed. The same grievances continued; people started behaving as if Marcos were again president. *Marcos pa rin.* One day, in the same breath, in her room, they said Ninoy would have distributed Hacienda Luisita to the tenants, had he, not the Cojuangcos, owned it.

If it weren't sinful, she could wish the NPAs would hit corrupt officials along with the police and army officers, especially those sitting on the boards of several government corporations—all reporting losses—drawing allowances in the hundreds of thousands. This "reform" government has already killed EDSA as certainly as Marcos killed democracy. This government, whose officials covetously administer sequestered properties, who would convert the American bases into gambling casinos: How can good people do such wrong!

By the third anniversary of EDSA, self-absorbed leaders are again reigning over the country. Disappointed, her friends have begun to help Mother Milagros who, at eighty-seven, still goes out to the children in the barrios. They have begun collecting clothes for the lepers, donating to the children starving in Negros, to the handicapped's *Tahanang Walang Hagdan,* to religious centers for street children. Simple human needs. Instead of worrying about saving the government, they now try to save the nation by helping the helpless, since the dream must be kept alive while the House imports high-powered firearms; and the Senate, luxury cars. New elites, in the Marcos tradition.

She feels she is passing through the same history as the rest of the country; she does not deceive herself that waking up one more day will stop time from dying.

"Are you resting, Liling?" The Colonel comes into her bedroom with a glass of milk, sits down to rub her hands.

"I was about to say my prayers." She waits for him to mention Cayetano. If he suggests going north to Angat, she will know there will probably be another coup.

"The city is so noisy and hot. Perhaps you would like to rest in Angat for a few days; or see David."

"When Cayetano comes this Sunday," Liling says, inviting her husband to admit Cayetano has been there. Awaiting this admission, she takes the glass he extends to her, which she will pour down on the jasmine climbing outside her window as soon as he leaves, for the concoction makes her feel glued together inside. "Who came?" She takes a tiny sip, places the drink down.

"Who?"

"I heard a car."

"That was Pineda looking for Cayetano. I said he might have taken the children out Christmas shopping."

It could have been Pineda, Liling thinks. Even close up, the two could be mistaken for brothers; for twins. "You could have asked him in."

The Colonel kisses her on the forehead. "I'll come in later. Shall I turn off the lights, Liling? Anything else you want? I'll have Priscila come up to stay with you."

Her hand briefly held in his slips through, fumbles for the rosary under her pillow. A decade each, she prays for the unknowing beneficiaries of her petitions. She starts with Cayetano, who has been passed over for promotions again, in favor of someone two class years behind in the Philippine Military Academy.

As her attention dims with the lights outside, unsummoned thoughts about Choleng come to her. Retreating Japanese soldiers pulled Choleng's three sons out of the house and, after shooting them while she watched from the window, pushed them with their bayonets into the air raid shelter along the fence of hibiscus . . .

Including Choleng in her prayers, Liling goes on to say a decade of the beads for Cory. She has been praying for a Nobel prize for Cory since 1987 when, nominated, Cory told reporters she would go to accept the prize, coup or no coup. She prays for the Colonel, for something worthwhile for him, something significant to restore him to the center of life; and also for the Moro whose picture she saw glued to the upper right-hand corner of the green identity card Cayetano showed his father: ID No. 01153. UTARA KUTAWATO STATE REVOLUTIONARY COMMITTEE. MNLF 3/30/87. On the back of the card was a signed pledge to fight for the liberation of the oppressed Bangsamoro. *So help me Allah. Dima Abdul.*

Falling in and out of sleep, Liling wakes up. The rosary has fallen from her hand. Priscila has come in to turn off the lights, leaving only the vigil candles. The flames shake with the burning odor of bones, returning her to the house her father built overlooking the sea. This time she sees it reduced to cornerposts against the sky. It is as if she is drowning in her own womb. She tries to fall asleep so that, with the sun, morning will return to her with the scent of papaya flowers.

Just thinking of the possibility of a coup makes Colonel Moscoso feel that Liling is kneeling inside his body. He has tried everything to protect her and does not know how much harder to try. Every day there seems less of her, and he wants to pick her up and take her somewhere safe.

Pineda said Scout Rangers, Wednesday night, had knocked out the Coast Guard radio repeaters in Tagaytay. 2200 hours. Almost ten o'clock. The parrot is swinging asleep on its perch, head tucked under one wing. Almost Friday. Too long an interval with nothing happening *if* this is indeed prelude to a coup. The coup of all coups, as Colonel Gringo Honasan's interview from hiding seemed to promise ten days ago.

Channel 9 is replaying the wreath-laying at Liwasang Bonifacio, and at the monument that Guillermo Tolentino designed in Caloocan. Before it was designated Bonifacio Day, November 30 used to be National Heroes Day. Men were not as clever as snakes then.

If only the government had faced the problem of coups seriously. Punishment for those involved in the July 1986 coup: push-ups! EDSA put the Philippines on the map, provided a model for nonviolent change in Eastern Europe. Cory's election by popular mandate had to be a factor in the election of Bhutto in Pakistan and Chamorro in Nicaragua. Heads of state. Yet life is back to sudden deaths and disappearances; the rationale for the government has dwindled into *just being better* than Marcos. How much better? Just because Marcos fled does not mean democracy returned.

Before these thoughts can grow horns in his body, Colonel Moscoso goes on arranging safety for Liling. As soon as more definite information comes, he can better plan the contingencies: Angat? Choleng's? Should they wait for morning?

He looks up at the sky. By the sky's quick changes he can tell time. Around 0500 it will be gray, brackish, like the swamp water they drank during maneuvers. It will be darker at the rim. Shadows caught on stiff branches. By 0600 the light will considerably strengthen, will flare pink at the edges. But if they go to Angat, they will need batteries for the radio, candles and the Coleman lamp, blankets and pillows to tuck under Liling's knees, canned meats. The rest house is far from the town. Maybe even too isolated. It may have been broken into by now. They have not been there in two years.

Reduced to living dangerously in his thoughts, the Colonel tries to reach Cayetano again. Still no dial tone. If there were any danger of a coup, Cayetano would have come or sent word. Pineda could be mistaken. A lot of disinformation comes from both sides; the trick of those who, instead of creating trust, manage the media. Manage meaning, until everything becomes subject to interpretation. Inconstant. In flux. They should learn to control their own impulses and thrust; to give the country priority.

Mang Genio no longer drives. Can he himself drive to Angat, if Cayetano does not send a car or a driver?

Cayetano figures in the Colonel's plans; but not Osong who, at his age and with his experience, deserves an ambassadorship, yet is content to run after a married woman whose grown children have scattered abroad while her husband tries to manage a ranch, gentleman-style, in Australia. The woman herself runs from city to city, laying the groundwork for Cory's visits. A government by press release and public relations. If he were young, his own hopes might bring him on the side of the rebels. But a coup is against all his bcst instincts, and hc is glad Cayctano has staycd clcar of coups.

Lives out of order. His anger comes from all the unnecessary helplessness woven into the disappointments in his life. The last time

Benhur was there, Colonel Moscoso almost confided in him. Everything. Without Benhur, Osong has drifted. With how much honor will Osong ever retire? With how little?

It was Osong he had expected would enter the Philippine Military Academy. Osong stands like him, turning heads as he passes. But Osong refused to take the entrance examinations. When the superintendent congratulated him on his son's high marks, the Colonel did not guess it was Cayetano; thought for a moment that Osong had changed his mind, obedience delayed.

Cayetano always knew what he was thinking, could anticipate what he would say. Without being asked, Cayetano named his youngest, born after EDSA, Eliseo Benhur. The Colonel wonders if there is a way of letting Benhur know he has been so honored. If Cayetano had Osong's height and *garbo,* he might have been made an aide. But no one can top Cayetano for courage, as Pineda says. Rolling fifty feet under raking fire to push Lazar out of the way!

The Colonel does not enjoy his bitter thoughts. A Congress of landowners and those aspiring to that status, alert to the privileges and opportunities they can grab but not to the country's needs. The Communist leaders Cory so eagerly released are abroad to raise funds—do they have a better accounting system or more honest genes?—celebrities among the politically naive, locally and in Europe. Money recovered from the Marcos regime's illegal wealth stashed abroad is enough only to pay the fees of international lawyers and the expenses of the investigative commissions. What will the new government leave to the country after six years? Marcos left it debts; and 40 percent of the national income goes to the payment of interest on the loans he malversed. The enemy has acquired impersonal attributes. Corruption. Indecision. Inefficiency. One has no recourse against corruption; only against corrupt men.

Meanwhile the poorest of the poor become even more helpless. The funds allocated to trips abroad could provide homes for not a few of those living in the parks, under the shrubs, in the cracks of the seawalls, on top of garbage. Even he is close to despair. The interests on his Money Market deposits once covered their monthly expenses. Now, he is drawing on the capital. Oil prices increased as of that last day in November. In the morning, the cost of all necessities will rise. A coup will bring a sad Christmas for many; for those waiting to be hired for a few hours' work who spend almost half their wages to get to construction sites. His roof needs repair. The kitchen leaks and they have had to move the table so basins can be placed to catch the drip. The gutters and drainpipes need replacing. It will take everything in the bank to make the house as good as it was. If they have five, ten more years of living left . . .

It is almost twenty years since he was retired by Marcos. Those wives who were aggressive in pressing gifts and favors on the higher-ups are now married to generals. Food of all kinds in crates and baskets arrives at their door. Imported fruits. *Mang* Genio used to feel bad about turning the gifts away, under his strict instructions not to receive any. *Nagpapasalamat po sila, pero hindi po sila tumatanggap.*

As if Liling might overhear his thoughts, the Colonel shuts them off by going to the door. Their street is quiet. If Camp Crame or Camp Aguinaldo is attacked as in the 1987 coup, he will hear it. Sounds of gunfire will reach them through the trees. The TV stations and transmission towers are just a few streets away. Along with the camps, these will be priority targets. He goes to the back door. *Mang* Genio and his wife are asleep. People are lucky if they can still manage to sleep. He himself is kept awake even by his own thoughts.

Since Marcos died in September, this cannot be a coup to return him to power. Satan's or God's angels? Which?

"Colonel. Colonel." The parrot cocks its head towards him. "Colonel."

Colonel Moscoso stares at the bird. He has heard of parrots speaking in the voice of those who have died, or gone away. He waits for it to speak again, in Benhur's voice; but it starts swinging head over tail. Liling will not believe this.

If only he had agreed that Liling visit her sister who has been asking her to come; to visit and see for herself, along the shore road that winds about their hacienda, the sun dancing in the sky and the stars grown heavy enough to fall. When the sister went to Medjugorje—there to pray for David's complete recovery—she heard it predicted that the Virgin is to appear next in Asia.

In any case, Liling cannot stay in that house if there is a coup. The rebels will target Camp Aguinaldo and Camp Crame, and their house is within firing range.

He will have to drive them to Angat, since *Mang* Genio no longer drives and Cayetano has not sent a driver. And they must wait for daylight.

Facing these facts gives Colonel Moscoso a sense of calm, of something inevitable against which there is no point in struggling.

What do they need to bring? This is what runs through Colonel Moscoso's mind. Bottles of water. Liling's medicine. Bread. By morning the groceries will be cleaned out, all the shelves. Coups and typhoons cause a run on supplies. But people will wait till payday. Friday. Will they bring enough rice for a week? Priscila will go with them, but *Mang* Genio and his wife will have to remain behind.

Liling no longer goes anywhere without Priscila. What small pieces of jewelry do not go to Mother Milagros for her projects and charities, Liling gives to *Mang* Genio's daughter, as well as the gifts she is given on her birthdays, although a few she is saving, in case Loreto comes to visit.

Colonel Moscoso wakes up with a start in his chair. The lights are on. The parrot is stretching its neck, its beak open, but no sound comes, just like a person who has lost the power of speech. The Colonel goes to his room.

But sleep has fled. In the dark he rehearses the play of clutch and gas so the car will not lurch forward or the engine kill. The roads through the rice fields are wounded trails. No politicians live nearby. If he remembers right, the better way is past the two *kamachile* trees, through the road beyond the railroad crossing. That cuts the trip by thirty minutes. He must take care not to flood the engine. If he had known, he would have had the brakes checked. Once, visiting Cayetano in the Philippine Military Academy, they had to coast down the mountainous Zigzag without brakes. If it had happened on the way up . . .

Clutch, then brake. Clutch, then gas.

Demanding unreasonable strength from himself, Colonel Moscoso recovers his cunning from the Japanese Occupation, when all he had to trap the enemy were nooses made of grass.

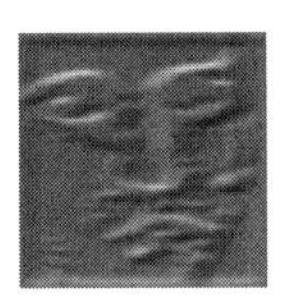

Major Cayetano Moscoso,
a.k.a. Tano the Turk—an interview away from promotion to two suns on his shoulder loops—returns the salute of the guards at Gate One of Camp Aguinaldo. Most of the troops assigned to Manila after the 1987 coup have been sent back to the provinces; now, no more than a hundred secure the camp. That is not enough, with military units in Manila placed on alert and an emergency command conference called at 1730 hours that Thursday evening.

He's glad Patty did not ask why he brought them a day early to Ermita for her father's birthday party. Patty never asks. She might already know from the other wives that the Tagaytay relay station was wrecked before midnight Wednesday; that the captain admitted to drunkenness, to a round of beer with his men. Like earthquake tremors around Taal, rumors of a coup have become daily fare for Manila, especially after the August 1987 coup when rebel troops had to be flushed out of Camp Aguinaldo.

If a coup develops by Friday—it's almost evening and the intelligence reports do not appear to be alarming—and goes into Saturday, he'll have to come up with an excuse why he cannot take the family to Tagaytay for lunch at the lodge overlooking the volcanic lake. Patty suggested he convince his father and mother to come along. "Your Papa and mine think the same conclusions; why can't they be close friends?"

Cayetano decides not to pass by their cottage on Capinpin but to head at once for the intelligence compound. Turning the corner beyond the grandstand, he gives himself just one more thought about his wife. She does not know and will not believe he's faithful. An officer! Provincial commander! What you don't know will not hurt: this is what the wives tell one another, absorb from one another.

He wants to tell her otherwise; but she is almost isolated in her family's wealth, the same way multinationals live away from a country's life. He feels that she drifts, allows herself to be taken along by the flow of life because she is not endangered. Wherever the flow takes her, no questions and no answers necessary. He wants to let her know that she is the one who gives him his moments of laughter, which he attempts to recall when she is away. These moments put in order the wild scatter of his life, the things and thoughts and feelings that form his time and space. Saturday, he will try to tell her this.

Meanwhile he wants to believe his family is safe that Thursday, celebrating National Heroes Day—or is it now Bonifacio Day?—a stone's throw from Manila Bay, the United States Embassy, at home in Ermita, as far as anyone can be from the telecommunication station . . .

Pineda said, "Patty married Cayetano to discover how it is to live in the real world." Is it ever safe in that unreal world? His friends are inclined to think that Patty or he might disappear, suddenly. Might defect like rebels. He wishes he had thought of assuring Pineda that, occasionally at least, he and Patty call each other by name, in secret mostly. How is he to explain to Pineda, who worries like an older brother, that there might not be *any* new defections? Not his. He will always be loyal to the Constitution. RAM no longer speaks for him.

Cayetano turns his thoughts to the conference, already started; to monitoring and analyzing the news for the remaining hours of Thursday.

"Turk!" Titong Valera calls Cayetano's name quietly, pushing a chair toward him as he enters the conference room.

Cayetano takes the chair across from Zeus Imperial. The three of them, with Boy Pineda, survived Fort Magsaysay training and joined the armed forces so as not to be separated. Pineda, however, is off in General Santos, Mindanao. Cayetano wonders how much of the news or rumors might have reached him, since only Manila is under alert.

"Thought you defected," Zeus says, and Titong stares him down. "Just kidding. Tano is as loyal as they come. He knows I'm kidding."

Cayetano catches the red ball of candy Zeus has thrown as a marker across the maps, and with it he stops a yellow ball, thrown almost as an afterthought. He lays them side by side. Not offended by Zeus's question, because he does not expect tact from Zeus, he nevertheless believes in a hierarchy of commitment: oath, vow, and promise in descending order. He has begun to teach his son the absolutes.

"Special Action Forces of the constabulary have been on alert since the Tagaytay incident was uncovered," Titong says. "How did they happen upon the relay station?"

"Captain Junio claims he and his men were drinking," Zeus says. "But I think—either it's truly accidental, or, if not, the coup will be advanced because the sabotage was discovered. SAFs from Fort Magsaysay have been recalled. De Villa counts on the former head of the First Scout Rangers. It sounds as if it's on. Only lacking is Colonel Honasan's name. That's how I see it."

The loyalty of company and field commanders is assessed across the conference table. Chief of Staff de Villa has had a heart-to-heart talk with Brigadier General Blando. Zeus puts one yellow candy in the pile he calls Cory's. Commodore Calajate, logistics chief, has been asked to prepare the defense of Camp Aguinaldo. Zeus rolls another ball of yellow candy toward the pile, then, catching Cayetano's eye, he holds one up: hold-outs?

They were RAM together for the duration of EDSA. Cayetano wonders if that is what Zeus means.

Conference decision: *Red alert. All military units. All major service commanders to return to respective headquarters for conferences with their staff.*

Nodding a dismissal to the two men, Zeus stays a while to count the yellow candies.

"Too bad Boy Pineda is not here instead of Zeus," comments Titong, outside with Cayetano. "Zeus might be the breakaway."

"Zeus?" Cayetano wonders if he should remind Titong that he and Zeus disengaged from RAM during its first coup against Cory.

Patty wanted him to check the vigil lights and tell the boy Noel to take food from the refrigerator. "He will not touch anything unless you tell him, Cayetano."

Approaching their empty cottage, Cayetano feels it strange to keep on living on the same street where he grew up, until after his father moved them to San Juan. His father retired, refusing to follow up his promotions through channels or to seek patrons.

Cayetano recalls the red dragonflies that darted in and out of the zinnias in his mother's garden. She chose bright, odorless blooms to discourage bees inflamed by the nectar of white flowers.

Now restricted to quarters, Cayetano wishes he had passed by his parents' house before returning to camp. It is hard to leave. His mother always says she has his favorite food ready to be served; his father always wants to talk. Lately, and with frequency, his father has been hoping the military can be disencumbered of corrupt officers. The military, he hopes, can once more be at the service of the people, not of politicians and generals.

So sketchy is the information coming in that it may well turn out to be another false alarm. The Scout Rangers may simply have been drinking, as their captain confessed to senior officers in Tagaytay, and out of exuberance accidentally damaged the telecommunications systems.

He wonders how much his father has heard. Patty's father was pleased to have Cayetano's military driver for the weekend; enjoyed hearing the reports coming over the car radio from the headquarters. His father had been careful about using government issue and employees, even when he was in the service. Angat is the only place that gives the Colonel pleasure now. But, too isolated, their hut there is no longer safe.

He might have called his father from Ermita. Was he being indifferent or just careless, selfish, not to try calling? But what can he say? *We might have the coup to end all coups.* Something to get Osong to sit up. His brother thinks of him as someone in whose dreams nothing happens. "How will you become a general?" Osong continually challenges him.

Cayetano cuts across the parade grounds, towards the reviewing stand facing the Chief of Staff headquarters, which was torched by rockets during the coup of 1987, August. And inside that camp, after Marcos was forced out by People Power in 1986, Cory was the star of the show on stage. Gringo Honasan, to whom is attributed every coup against Cory since then, had parachuted down in the midst of nuns and matrons, of vendors offering Cory dolls dressed a la Barbie in yellow dress and eyeglasses, of children dancing and youths on bicycles carrying life-size portraits of the president.

Since then, the earth has turned almost 180 degrees. Democracy is nowhere in sight.

This enduring fact breeds a dilemma—thoughts that argue reasons to defect and reasons to remain; thoughts that might have been struggling for expression in Zeus and even in Titong: thoughts placing them in direct conflict with themselves. To whom precisely is loyalty owed? One can be loyal to the government and disloyal to the people. It feels as if truth is turning upon itself, like a long winding road.

Cayetano once heard Benhur saying, in his father's house, that no thought is harmless, because it is part of what is deepest and most true about ourselves. Therefore?

"Sir!"

The salute comes from junior officers, whose careers are already tainted by the excesses of the vigilantes the government has fielded against Communist insurgents, whose leaders the government so readily pardoned after EDSA. Lately in the news, some of the leaders are reported to be in Europe, luxuriating while their followers starve; one, alleged to have counterfeited Dutch currency, is now fighting extradition.

One of the officers turns slightly to call back: *Ingat, Sir.*

The admonition to take care runs through Cayetano's body like an ache, making him feel as old as his father. Would he want his son in the army, too? From the parade grounds it is too dark to see the statue of General Aguinaldo on horseback, the general who fought the Americans in 1899; like the rest of them now: restricted to quarters.

Entering his cottage, Cayetano feels he has entered a strange house without knocking. It feels vacated, as if, unannounced, Patty and he have withdrawn from each other, retreated. He seeks out an odor to make the rooms his, Patty's. Noel, the houseboy, comes to the front door in shorts.

"Sir, *Mang* Genio called. Colonel and Mrs. Moscoso went to Angat."

Cayetano's mind runs through his earlier thoughts about Angat's isolation. Too late. He should have called. Maybe they were still on their way to pick up his brother David from his Aunt Choleng . . . They will have time to hear the news and turn back.

"Am planting the seedlings, Sir." Noel's speech has the monotony of waves, sound and meaning broken off in his effort to be understood.

Barely, Cayetano recalls the plants his wife ordered from the nurseries alongside the back wall of Camp Aguinaldo. What is it he is supposed to remind Noel, that Patty considered important enough to tell him?

Thinking to change his clothes and then return, as he had told Titong in the hall, Cayetano faces his certificates of attendance in seminars and workshops: Headquarters Philippine Army Special Intelligence and Security, Company Commandant, JUSMAG . . . It adds up to what? Like his father, he will probably choose to retire instead of trading in his honor for another sun on his shoulder loops. It's more than a matter of pride.

Without looking at the wide bed, he thinks of Patty that morning, the soft fragrance of her mouth, the smell of honey buried in the barks of trees, pale as pearl and the sky swinging among dragonflies. Tender thoughts advance upon him like walls closing, part of what might no longer ever happen. He lies down . . .

He is walking back to the Department of National Defense to rejoin Titong and, as he steps on the parade ground, the earth divides in a straight line from the GHQ down to Gate 1, splitting the statue of General Aguinaldo on horseback . . .

Clinging to reason, he wakes up without recalling on which side of the line he stood. He tries to fix what he knows with certainty, beyond details that float back to him at random: his mother's absent smile, Titong's wing-shaped ears much like Benhur's, Zeus' nicotine-yellow fingers, Patty . . . as if that is all there is residing in his life.

The announcement of the coup is flashing on the televisions in the conference room, detailing the Tagaytay incident of almost twenty-four hours before, on Wednesday.

2000 hours.

"Turk," Titong looks up as Cayetano enters. "The reality of the operation . . ."

Friday. December 1. The words come out like print indelibly marked.

"Where's Zeus?" Cayetano asks.

"Red alert now covers Central Luzon, Visayas, Northern Mindanao. Pineda knows by now, Turk. Special Action Force is in charge. Reserve called in. Firearms are secured and the major unit commanders have been informed. Zeus is with the Chief of Staff."

The map on the table appears broken apart by the red and yellow balls of candy Titong is laying down to plot the intelligence reports coming in. Two companies of rebel Marines have crossed over to Villamor Air Base. Backed up by three armored vehicles. APCs. V-150. RAM-SFP painted white on the sides.

"Soldiers of the Filipino People. SFP. What does that make us?" Titong asks.

Verified: 800 soldicrs boarded private fishing vessels anchored off an oil company pier in Bataan. Rebels!

"Headed for Sangley?" Cayetano asks. "The TV announcements must have forced them to advance their attack. It's five minutes to Friday."

Titong aligns his still-unlit cigarette with the naval base at the tip of Cavite where it hooks into Manila Bay, looks at Cayetano, then takes a call.

It is as if suddenly—the way Benhur said of those in Gulod—their lives are not working out. Cayetano thinks of his father and mother in Angat, of Patty and the children waiting for him to take them on a trip to where this coup started. Events have meaning apart from their public effects. Is it, after all, merely power protecting itself? And are they still safe because of affinities that have bound them? What if any one of them dies? Boy Pineda?

Someone asks, "Did no one see the Marines crossing from Fort Bonifacio? Heavily armed Marines on the Super Expressway?"

Cayetano pushes a window open. Too dark to see the palms and mango trees shielding the department building. He looks across camp to the reviewing stand, his cottage, Crame Street, the Ladies Club, St. Ignatius Chapel, the Veterans Hall, the PX, as if those are the permanent parameters of his life, the only things he can be certain of—like the buttons on his shirt, the cigarette in Titong's hand.

Were the Marines headed for Fort Bonifacio through Forbes Park—with streets named Harvard, Cambridge, Magsaysay—where his brother Osong wants to live? He returns to the map on the table, searching the roads that radiate spokelike towards the domestic and international airports, the Manila Polo Club. Until he can save the 1 million peso price of membership, Osong has been borrowing Patty's father's membership card. One square meter in Binondo has been upped by the influx of Hong Kong and Taiwan money to P40,000. Real estate. Also real are the people sifting the waste cans outside Wendy's, Jollibee, and McDonald's for left-overs among the wrappers and disposable cups. And the choir practising in the Evangelical Chapel beside the department building while People Power was converging on EDSA in February '86.

People Power can save the president from this coup.

Cayetano looks across and down the table. How fast the coalition develops and how many defect or stay neutral until there is a winning side will decide the outcome of this coup. One of life's fault lines. What of those who did not break away in '86? Were they more deeply committed to the country than to factions and parties? Or were they merely indifferent? Or timid? During EDSA, through Gate Two from the Logistic Command, Pineda had Enrile and Ramos fixed in his bore sights. One shot, either way, and EDSA would have been over that Sunday; Marcos and Ver, entrenched again. EDSA's heroes had to be those who did not break away but who also did not fire on the people. Yet they were the ones now assigned to commands deep in MNLF and NPA country, where the odds were against coming out alive.

Titong starts placing yellow balls on the map: Camp Aguinaldo and Camp Crame across the highway. Key strongholds for the rebels are marked by red candy: Villamor Air Base; Fort Bonifacio; TV channels 2 and 4; the government channel . . .

"Barracks of the 205th Helicopter Wing burning," a call comes over hand-held radio. "In Agusan del Norte and Surigao del Norte, soldiers in full battle gear have been reported to be headed for Cebu in ferries bringing jeeps, trucks, and armored personnel carriers . . ." Reserves have been summoned to Manila? That provides them with a convenient cover-up, if they're rebels. Cayetano checks to see who are in their seats at the table.

Zeus comes in. "My sister called from Chicago. Cory is on television there, saying: 'They're trying to kill me!' She's asking for People Power. People are willing to die for her, but is she willing to die for the country?" He looks at Cayetano, then at Titong. "This might be Gringo's turn to win."

"The worst is over," Cory announces on Channel 9. "I am safe." She is on her way to meet her Cabinet. 4:30 a.m.

An enlisted man brings in Friday's newspapers. The headlines: *Ship sinks off Jolo. Welga. Marines take over VA Base.*

"There was also a strike the day of the 1987 coup," Cayetano recalls, studying the pictures of Marines alighting from military jeeps.

Four hundred Scout Rangers surround the major buildings in Fort Bonifacio. The Special Intervention Platoon, reserved to counteract coups, has defied the Army Chief of Staff. Reports come in.

Villamor Air Base. Rebel Marines arrive, marching alongside the tanks, fan out around the flight line, disarm unalerted base security units, order the 205th Guards out, take Hangars B and C, two commando vehicles, ammunition and weapons from the base armory, force major units to secure their own perimeters in defensive position. High-tension wires low on the ground. Bursts of mortar shells can be heard over the radio. Heavy automatic fire. M-203 rips through the roof of the 207th THS Building.

Instead of taking prisoners, the rebels tell the defenders to secure their offices, vacate the premises, and depart in civilian clothes.

"Patay kung patay," Zeus says. "I just don't want to be found dead away from my post."

Titong takes the call standing up. Three propeller-driven World War II planes—Tora-Toras—and one helicopter have taken off from Sangley. They could be headed for Camp Aguinaldo since the rebels are targeting military installations.

"They will know where the command posts have been moved," Zeus says. "Marines have transferred to the grandstand."

Over the radio comes news of a firefight around the television compounds. Numbers of dead, but no word on which side. *Red Cross and civilians picking up the wounded. No People Power forming. Just spectators. Street generals in sandos and slippers.*

"Marines from Bataan . . ." Titong moves more red balls in place on the map. Camelot Hotel area. Marines reported in position in Sta. Mesa, Quiapo overpasses, Magsaysay and Quezon bridges, international and domestic airports . . .

"Didn't the electric devices on the fences work?" Zeus asks no one in particular. "If Gringo is doing this for the country, I'm not going to wish him ill. But if it's for Marcos's cronies, or for his own, that's another story. I'm going out for air. I'm not defecting," he says on passing Titong, a grin splitting his face. But he does not leave.

Secretary of National Defense Ramos is in command with Chief of Staff de Villa at his side.

Galido is stripped of command and his brigade commanders have been called in to bring troops to Manila. Their departure is being monitored. For days, it turns out, Scout Rangers have been coming down to Manila in small batches, supposedly to attend army seminars. The Chief of Staff reportedly has had heart-to-heart talks, within the past few days, with the defectors.

Commander Calajate is not returning the calls of the Chief of Operations. The Logistics Command Chief has been ordered to prepare the necessary firearms for the defense of Camp Aguinaldo.

Then news—disinformation?: the Secretary of National Defense and the Chief of Staff are leading the coup.

Zeus crushes his cigarette to a stub in the ashtray. In the other ashtrays, consumed but intact ashes lie side by side like miniature corpses.

It takes fifteen minutes for the Tora-Toras to reach Malacañang Palace and to fire rockets into the grounds secured by troops along its perimeter.

"Rockets," Zeus holds up his radio. "If they mean to kill Cory, they will hit the basement where Imelda's clothes are on exhibit. That's where the president is to be evacuated, according to the last anti-coup briefing. It sounds more like random bombing. Psychological warfare."

In the room they listen to calls to neutralize the rebel planes. Cayetano hears the orders for the F-5 jets at Basa Air Base. Did the rebels forget to secure that base? Then calls are heard between Malacañang and the United States Embassy. Now come the American bases, Cayetano thinks. The coffee is cold, but he drinks.

Hours after the first run over Sangley Air Base, the second one finally drops rockets—along the runway—before the F-5s return to Basa, Pampanga.

Cayetano looks at Titong, who has just received word that General Biazon is having difficulty getting Marines to fight brother Marines.

Government troops are moving. Rebels are still in strongholds. All those in conference since Thursday remain in the room.

On Channel 9, the only channel reporting, Cory Aquino makes her first appearance: "Rebellion will not outlive this day." She asks for People Power, for people to come out not as spectators but as protectors. She has the support of Japan and Bangladesh, she claims.

Strafing sets the air vibrating over Camp Aguinaldo. It beats like the sudden flight of birds. We're the front line now, Cayetano thinks, glad that Patty and the children are safe in Ermita. He begins to smell burning.

Cayetano looks out in the direction of the Chief of Staff's residence, which planes have targeted before moving across to Camp Crame. Helicopters strafe the buildings there with rocket fire. His father's house is close to the Crame area, within the rebel flight lines.

"Don't switch candy balls yet," Zeus says. "Policy meeting in Washington. En route to Malta, Bush can give clearance to persuasion flights. It seems we have requested an aggressive cap. And loyal troops are arriving from thc provinces."

Titong checks: Did Lt. Col. Tecson of the Constabulary Attack Force turn back the 800 troops attempting to dock at Sangley to reinforce the rebels? "Three Hueys arriving from Laoag."

The third air scramble above Sangley comes in over the radio. De Leon of the Philippine Air Force is overheard saying to Major Atienza: "You're the country's last hope . . ." as the major from Basa climbs thousands of feet to prepare for a dive. His every turn is being monitored. It's his third run.

Sharing receivers, Cayetano hears the major saying, "Sir, *malapit na.* My mind is made up . . ." An explosion drowns out the rest of the words.

"Another one died for the country," Zeus says.

"It's first Friday of the month," Titong says. "I think he crashed. In any case, there is no tactical need for the U.S. jets now." He makes a small sign of the cross on his heart.

1430 hours. F-4 Phantoms leave Clark Air Base in Pampanga and one hundred Marines fly from Subic Naval Base, Olongapo, to secure the United States Embassy in Manila. Green Berets on Roxas Boulevard.

The sun has long since started its downward run.

Without their propeller-driven planes, the rebels start coming out full force on the ground. At Villamor Air Base rebels butt-stroke the instrument panels of parked Hueys and hide their weapons in the hangars when the Phantoms scream over the base. No ceasefire.

Both sides are claiming victory. The rebels have named four generals to key positions in the new army: SFP. The Secretary of National Defense announces the surrender of twenty-three rebels. President Aquino declares: *From the U.S. we have gotten American fighters to join us . . . to wipe out the last trace of resistance . . .*

Scattered firing inside Camp Aguinaldo.

Zeus asks, laughing, "If the SFPs burst into the building, do we surrender or fight? Do we surrender to each other?"

"No one ever knows the exact time of defeat or victory," Titong answers. "Go rest, Turk. We'll take turns. This will last longer than '87 by the looks of it." From lack of sleep Titong is blinking rapidly but he will not be talked into having the first rest.

Inside the Moscoso cottage, Noel has fallen asleep on the kitchen table, his head resting on the yellow lined sheets he buys, sheet by sheet, in the store. The houseboy wants so badly to go to school that, at age seventeen, he willingly attends grade four each afternoon. He refuses to be paid, since he considers being allowed to enroll as fair payment for his services.

Noel has scribbled close together to get as many words as he can on each line to his father, who lives in a barrio without radio or newspaper. Cayetano reads part of the letter: *"House to house before daybreak residents asked to evacuate to the Teodora Alonzo Elementary School where I go. Subdivisions included. Green Meadows. Blue Ridge. Gunfire almost all day yesterday. Some fires inside Camp A. Rebels took unfinished chapel on EDSA, television stations. Hard to tell the soldiers apart. Same uniforms and guns. Sometimes by the ribbons on their armsleeves. Listened to Masses and prayers on television. I saw a dead man in one of the yards . . ."*

By the time Cayetano returns, everyone but Zeus is back, freshly uniformed and chairs brought forward. The red and yellow balls of candy have slid past their areas. Strafing can be heard.

"That's either us being strafed, or the government strafing rebel positions outside the walls. Rebel tanks have been spotted outside the health club on Katipunan. Some private homes have opened their doors to the rebels . . ." Titong collates the reports.

Cayetano looks up as if to check whether the noise of the strafing and the tanks also disturb the sky.

". . . rebel pilots who flew the Tora-toras and Hueys have been stopped at checkpoint in Pampanga. One was recognized by his classmate. PMA. Pure luck that they were arrested. Must have crossed from Sangley to

Bataan. Moving out of Fort Bonifacio, rebel Marines tried to win over the Light Armor Brigade. . . . They are believed going to concentrate in the commercial district. Makati. The Blue Diamonds plowed low over the rebels at Villamor, using M-16s and M-60s. They will soon test-flight the Hueys as they are repaired. The rebels hit Huey 213 . . ."

Yellow candy balls standing for the government-recovered areas begin to push out the red.

Walking in as for an ordinary morning conference of the working staff, Zeus stands beside Cayetano. "The strafing is us. We missed target and fired on our troops. Six killed and two wounded. But we're coming up in force from the Mormon shrine end of Katipunan. It will be hand-to-hand when they make contact. Rebels are in Libis, White Plains . . ."

"This is an eyewitness account?" Titong asks.

"I jogged around the back. When bullets started hitting the sides of buildings. . . . There was an emergency landing inside camp. Ours."

Cayetano flips the desk calendar in front of his place at the table. December 2. Saturday.

The newspapers on the chair beside him headline: *U.S. extends aid vs. coup attempt.* On the left-hand side, down the front page, are pictures. One shows flames and smoke billowing from the constabulary headquarters across EDSA. Below it is a photo of Sangley Air Base captioned: *The propeller-driven rebel planes were earlier forced to leave the Metro Manila area by American jet fighters after the Philippine government sought U.S. help.* Another photo shows U.S. Marines landing inside the United States Embassy grounds along Manila Bay. And: *Smash the mutiny, Cory orders.*

Saturday noon, Malacañang press conference. President Cory Aquino announces: *We shall not entertain any effort to negotiate from those who have shamelessly betrayed the solemn oath of a soldier to defend the Constitution. The government will hunt down and bring to justice the treacherous cowards who launched the attack and root out those who have given aid and comfort to those traitors. I reject their proposals. I said they would live to regret their evil acts and so they shall. There shall be no ceasefire. What they started, I will end.*

Ultimate acts.

Cayetano, listening, imagines the houseboy Noel underlining the words for his father to read: *Surrender or die.*

Zeus and two others are called to the battle staff conference. He takes a look at Titong and Cayetano; says nothing. The day's growth of beard on his face is like a birthmark, reminding Cayetano that he and Pineda could grow nothing thicker than fuzz across their faces when they were plebes together.

The hours halt, pass like light flashing. December 3.

Rebels have rammed their way into camp and taken up positions in three small buildings near Gate One. Mortars and cannon fire. From the building can be seen the flicker of lights from tanks. Machine guns and recoilless rifles fire. 0200 hours. Sunday.

Reports come double time. Face-to-face fighting. Cayetano recalls Zeus joking earlier, "What, do I surrender to a brod officer?" If Cayetano and Pineda come face to face, who will fire first?

Cayetano sees on Titong's face the same look as when he told Cayetano that the earliest clear recollection of his life was bringing water to the hospital where his mother had delivered another son. "Every morning before school . . ." It is the look of someone who wakes up just to wait for daylight. The brother's name, Cayetano recalls, was Washington. Washington Valera; shot to death just the past year in ambush by Communist insurgents.

Titong's statement came after years of reunions and rounds of beer which became meetings to discuss the army's isolation, an isolation confirmed increasingly by the raw intelligence reports it was their duty to process, analyze, and interpret.

EDSA, briefly, gave them something to believe in. But the patronage politics of even this administration—the continued decadence of the rich and even of top activists, the lack of professionalism in the military—have rendered the people as powerless as under the last years of the Marcos dictatorship; have reduced their hopes to prayer.

No People Power anywhere.

Government troops jump out of foxholes to confront rebels, led by a priest, who are coming out of the Catholic chapel to surrender. On both sides, men are crying. Cayetano remembers his brother Osong, during EDSA, flashing a newspaper picture of a man in tears, and saying, "It's Benhur. Crying like a baby. Benhur!"

Then he thinks of his mother and her friends, wherever they happen to be at three o'clock in the afternoon, praying that God will take away the blackness spreading inside those of them who are ill. Women praying, soon to become entirely memory.

Mopping up operations take Titong's attention now: negotiations and fighting going on simultaneously; double developments. On TV some rebels' wives appeal for their husbands' surrender.

Cayetano, glancing at the television, freezes. Pineda is on the screen, facing photographers.

"We're here for the country," Pineda is saying, a Galil rifle slung over one shoulder. A beret is on his head. No familiar smile plays on his face. "More effectual leaders should be given a chance. There is no democracy while the people suffer. We want Cory to resign, along with her cabinet. Until elections, the Supreme Court governs. *No relathieves.* No cronies. No amendment of the Constitution to allow Aquino re-election. Then back to soldiering for us."

A reporter asks, "President Cory says, 'Surrender or die.' What is your reply?"

Civilians crowd in, blocking out Pineda. Their faces are reflected on the glass sides of the building, like some kind of countersign for the truth that history becomes what we are.

"He won't save himself even if he can." Titong stands beside Cayetano. "But we didn't join the army to get rid of our conscience. Did we, Turk?"

The television screen shows traffic lights still blinking on Makati's deserted streets. Around a giant Christmas tree some government soldiers stand silent while rebel sharpshooters aim from the roofs of the financial district. Fire trucks parked at right angles to one another. Red Cross ambulances. In the parking lot between Intercontinental Hotel and Rustan, V-150s provide backdrops for souvenir shots. A tourist is seen looking out of a hotel window. Cayetano sees the PCIB building, where Patty's father has invested funds for the children's education, Stateside. Manila Peninsula. Manila Gardens. Landmark.

"Supply line for the rebels," Titong says, tracing the creek that winds through Makati. "Government troops are along EDSA, Senator Gil Puyat Avenue. Defectors occupy hotels, condos, banks. Get a confirmation of the perimeter of areas in their control."

Ayala and Makati Avenues, EDSA, Paseo de Roxas.

Camp Aguinaldo is cleared of rebels by 1400 hours.

Titong and Cayetano run down to the battle-scarred grandstand, where generals and colonels are gathering around Army Chief of Staff Renato de Villa and Secretary of Defense Fidel Ramos. At about the same hour, on the last Sunday of February '86, Enrile crossed EDSA.

"They got within ten meters of the intelligence compound," Titong says. "A corporal fired his recoilless rifle to stop the tank right there." They both turn around to face Gate 1, where General Aguinaldo's statue sits astride his horse, defying the sun.

Titong returns to the staff meeting to monitor negotiations—PMA Superintendent Arturo Enrile has left numbers for the rebels to call—but Cayetano stands awhile beside the statue, trying to work his way through anger and helplessness. Why didn't Pineda stay south in General Santos?

Reaching for some truth for which no one has to die, he recalls Pineda rolling fifty feet to push Lazar out of raking fire; remembers shouting, the light popping out of the holes in Lazar's body, the face already gone, the body becoming a haze of flesh and smoke. It was Pineda.

And in his father's house, the burnished wood incised with his motto: *Courage is finding someone, something to die for.* Caveat. In his mother's garden, a red dragonfly trying to escape, leaving its wings between his fingers; and his brother David, falling from the branches of the *macopa,* looking at him, waiting to be caught. Coarse-grained memories.

Enlisted men draw to a standstill inside the camp where skirmishes have taken place: The 7th Army Division, agreeing to pull out but not to yield arms, will board their trucks to return to Fort Magsaysay in Laur, Nueva Ecija.

Laur. It was there that he and Titong and Zeus and Pineda trained as plebes of the Philippine Military Academy; where Pineda named him Turk, for trying fiercer than anyone to prove himself; imagining as his own the citation his father received for bravery in Korea: *In the face of enormous odds, in utter disregard of his personal safety, he held his position for three hours and led his men across fire-swept fields, against hostile artillery and mortar bombardment.* The strength of those words brings him to Gate One.

It is like finding a tree growing where, once, he had buried a seed.

He passes a crowd taking turns looking inside an armored vehicle from which a dead soldier has been pulled, hit by the recoilless rifle the soldier's own brother had fired, defending Camp Aguinaldo at 0200 hours,

Sunday morning. The torn hatch is the parrot's beak attempting to speak its name, and gagging.

Sir!

Cayetano returns the salute of guards and soldiers with opposing countersigns on their armsleeves and rifles. Do they understand that common loyalties, for the moment, are making them enemies? And also are causing something profound to happen in their lives, something worth the trouble of being alive, and of dying.

Cayetano hurries. Heading for Pineda, he looks up to check coordinates; and direction. The darkening sky feels like steel buried in his body.

Glossary

Abaca — Hemp
Abalorio — Glass beads
Abrazo — Embrace
Accessoria — Townhouse apartment
Almirante — Admiral
Almires — Mortar
Ama Namin — Our Father
Ampalaya — Bitter melon
Andador — Child's walker
Aparador — Wardrobe
Aralin — Moral teachings
Ate — Older sister or cousin
Ati-atihan — Primitive dance
At puno ng carunungan — Full of knowledge
Banca — Narrow, outriggered boat
Bandera española — Canna lilies
Bagoong — Sauce from tiny shrimps
Balat — Wrapper
Balato — Share of winnings
Balikbayan — Emigrant returnee
Balimbing — Turncoat; fruit with many sides
Balisong — Switchblade knife
Balut — Fertilized duck egg
Bangus — Milkfish
Bantay-ng-bayan — Nation's Watch
Barako — Uncastrated male animal
Barangay — Barrio
Barong; Barong Tagalog — National shirt
Bastos — Coarse, rude
"Bayan Ko" — "My Country"; a patriotic Philippine song
Bibingca — Rice pudding
Bilao — Flat, round tray of woven palm
Bilugan ng ulo — Fooling people
Bolero! — Full of bull!
Bulalo — Stew of marrow bones
Buri — Palm
Buro — Fermented fish, vegetables
Buyo — Cud of betel, lime, and pepper leaves
Brazo de la reina — Dessert with a custard core
Bruja — Witch
Buena mano — First customer
Cadangcadang — Disease affecting coconut palm
Caimito — Star apple
Calamansi — Small citrus

Calesa; calesin — Horse-drawn vehicle
Camias — Wild ginger
Camisa — A loose blouse
Camote — Yam; sweet potato
Carburo — Carbide
Cedula — Personal tax certificate
Cereales — Ritual rice sheaves
Champorado — Porridge
Chicos de primera — First class *sapodilla* fruits
Cogonal — Fields of wild grass
Colegiala — Students at colleges run by nuns
Colegios — Colleges run by nuns or religious orders
Comerciantes — Merchants
Compadre — Godparent of one's child
Compañeros — Fellow attorneys
Corchos — Padded slippers
Costurera — Seamstress
Cutsaritas — Bedding plants with tiny red leaves
Dali — Hurry
Datu — Muslim chieftain
"Dahil sa Iyo" — "Because of You"
Dalagang bukid — Fish with reddish scales
Damajuana — Demijohn
Dayap — Lime
De cola — Skirt with long train
Despachadora — Female sales clerk
Despedida — Going-away party
Diamante — Jewel stone without clarity
Diligencias — Extra sources of income
Dinuguan — Blood pudding
Dios; Diyos — God
Dios na walang capantay — God without peer
Dios sa calangitan — God in heaven
Doble vista — Bifocals
Dolorosa — Sorrowing
Domingo de Ramos — Palm Sunday
Elenas — Participants in Holy Cross processions in May
Empleada — Employee
Ensaymada — A type of raised pastry
Escandalong malaki — Great scandal
Escayola — Plaster of paris
Espasol — Pastille of rice flour and coconut cream
Estafa — Swindle
Estero — Creek, canal
Estrellado — Scrambled egg
Estribo — Boarding step on a bus
Flores de Mayo — Flowers of May procession

Frutera — Fruit bowl
Gabi — Root or leaves of a water plant
Galantina — Terrine of chicken
Galapong — Ground-up rice with water
Galyetas — Round biscuits
Garbo — Affectations
Garrote — Machine for execution by strangling
Guardia civiles — Civil guards in Spanish colonial time
Guinatan — Yams and bananas cooked in coconut cream
Gumapang lang si Benhur! — Just so Benhur crawls!
Gumamela — Hibiscus
Gunting kayo diyan? — Have you scissors?
Hakot — Paid demonstrators, trucked to protest sites
Hari nang sang calupaan — Lord of the earth
Hindi ko ipagkakait ang buhay ko sa iyo, aking Panginoon. — Lord, I will not deny You my life.
Huli! — Caught!
Ibon mang may layang lumipad. — Even an uncaged bird
Imprenta — Printing shop
Ingat — Careful
Intriga pa rin. — Intrigues continue.
Ipo-ipo — A whirlwind
Itay; tatay — Father
Kalachuchi — Flowers used in memorial wreaths
Kalsos — Wedges
Kamachile — Beanlike fruits
Kasama sa pulitika yan. — That's part of politics.
Kesong puti — A white cheese made from carabao milk
Kumain ka na? — Have you eaten?
Kung hindi tao, Dios ang sisingil sa atin. — God, if not man, will demand retribution.
Lambanog — Palm wine
Lanzones — Fruit with mark of Virgin's fingerprints
Lavandera — Washerwoman
Lechon de leche — Roast suckling pig
Lola; lolo — Grandmother; grandfather
Lomo — Tenderloin
Longaniza — Sausage
Lugao — Rice gruel
Lumpia; lumpiang ubod — Spring roll; heart of palm
Mababa ang luha — Cries easily
Mababaw ang ligaya — Shallow happiness
Mabait, lubhang maalam — Kind, most wise

Magaling makisama — Relates well to people
Magkaisa! — Unite!
Mahabaging Diyos — Merciful God
Makahiya — Mimosa
Makasuntok lamang — Just to be able to use the fist
Malapit — Imminent
Maleducada — Badly educated
Mamà — Sir
Mang — Mister
Manton — Heavy shawl, usually embroidered
Maong — Jeans
Marcos pa rin. — It's still Marcos.
Mauuna na po ako sa inyo — Expression for asking permission to leave ahead
Mayo Uno — First of May
Mechado — Roast threaded with strips of fat
Mano, hijo — Kiss the hand, son
Merienda — Snack
Mestiza — Of mixed parentage
Milagrosa — Miraculous
Miting de avance — Rally in advance of elections
Molave — Native hardwood tree
Mongo — Green chickpea
Morcon — Meat roll stuffed with cheese, eggs, sausage
Municipio — Town hall
Narra — A native hardwood tree
Napabayaan — Neglected
Naremata — Foreclosed
Nay; nanay — Mother
Nipa — Palm for thatching
Novio — Sweetheart
Okoy — Croquettes of shrimp and vegetables
Pabasa — A Passion reading
Pabirili — Equipment for panning gold
Pakikisama — Relating well to others
Pakikiramay fund — Sharing Fund
Pakwan — Watermelon
Pan Americano — Loaf bread
Panata — Vow; solemn devotion
Panay kabig na lang — Takes but does not give
Pancit — Noodle dish
Pandan — Aromatic grass
Pan de limon — Sweet roll
Pan de sal — Hard roll
Pangarap — Hope
Pare — Form of address for male person
Pasalubong — Gift from one newly arrived
Pata — Leg of pork
Patalim — Sharp cutting instrument
Patay kung patay — Ready to die
Patola — Zucchini

Peks man. — Believe me.
Penoy — Unfertilized duck egg
Pinagbubuti natin. — We're giving it our best.
Pinipig — Green rice, pounded for roasting
Piso; peso — Unit of currency
Plantanillas — A dessert
Po — Word of respect, added at end of utterance
Pochero — Stew of chicken and meats
Polvoron — A dry sweet, made of milk and flour
Pulot — A foundling
Puñeta! Puñeteros! — A Curse
Purihin ang Panginoon. — Praise the lord.
Pusod — The navel
Puta — A whore
Puto — A steamed rice cake
Que ingrato! — How ungrateful!
Querida — A mistress
Queso de bola — A ball of cheese
Ratiles/seresa — A tree with red fruits filled with tiny seeds
Recados — Condiments
Recuerdo — Remembrance
Relleno — Boned chicken stuffed with meat, cheese, olives
Rigodon — Lively dance step with changing partners
Sacate — Fresh grass fodder
Sa kaibuturan — Innermost being
Salo-salo — A get-together meal
Sampaguita — Jasmine, the Philippine national flower
Sando — A sleeveless shirt
Saya — A long skirt
Sepulturero — A cemetery worker
Serpentinas — Long trains on skirts
Sigue na Mamà, makauwi lang ako. — Please, so I may go home.
Simbang gabi — Midnight masses preceding Christmas
Sinangag — Fried rice
Sinubukan — Clam dish
Sipsip — Bootlicker
Suman — Steamed rice or cassava wrapped in banana leaves
Sus! — Exclamation of surprise or dislike
Susmariosep — Contraction of "Jesus, Mary, Joseph"
Tahanang walang hagdan — A house for the disabled, without stairs
Taho — Soybean pudding
Talo na si Marcos. — Marcos has already lost.
Tambourine — An antique necklace of gold beads
Tapayan — Large water jars
Tikbalang — Legendary creature
Tita — Aunt

Tita madre — Aunt Nun
Tocino de cielo — A rich custard
Totoong makapapatay ka ng tao. — One can really kill.
Totoy — Little boy
Tse! — Exclamation of disgust
Tubigan — Irrigated field
Tumbong — Chicken's rectum
Turron — Nougat
Tuta — Traitor; puppy
Ube — Purple yam
Upo — White gourd
Vaciador — Knife sharpener
Viriña — Glass showcase for small statuary
Viuda — A widow
Walang aatras. — No one retreats.
Zona — A neighborhood watch in barrios, barangays